FALLEN CREST PUBLIC

THE 3RD IN THE FALLEN CREST SERIES

NYT & USA Bestselling Author
TIJAN

Edited by Ami Johnson at www.aldjediting.net

Interior Formatting by Elaine York/Allusion Graphics, LLC/ Publishing & Book Formatting
www.allusiongraphics.com

DEDICATION

To the readers, always the readers.
To those that have sent me messages which keep me writing.
Thank you, it means more than you can ever know.

CHAPTER ONE

Samantha

I woke to a hand sliding under my top and cupping my breast.

Mason!

Then I became aware of a very masculine and muscled thigh sliding between my legs and rolling me to my stomach. As he slid my tank's strap down, his lips went to my naked shoulder and nibbled on the back of my neck. Goosebumps broke out as I sucked in a breath. My legs pressed together, and a deep, strong throbbing started. It was pounding in a steady beat. As his lips moved down my spine, I gasped out loud. Arching my back for him, I was pressed against him. He was hard, but Mason didn't grunt, he didn't make a sound. Instead, his hand fell to my hip, and he pulled me even further into him. His hand caressed down my back and my tank top was bunched together into one tiny scrap of fabric. Slowly, so goddamn slowly, he pressed his chest to my back, but he was holding me up now.

I needed him now.

He slid my top up my back, trailing kisses on my spine as he did. When it was lifted over my head, I pushed up from the bed, pushing him upright with me at the same time. Enough. I couldn't handle it anymore. I needed more of him. We were now kneeling together. As the top fell to the floor, I reached behind me for him. I needed to taste him.

My hand slid around his neck to his hair, and I grabbed a fistful of it, taking a firm hold and anchoring him to me. He grunted now, grinding into me as his lips went to my ear. I could feel him smiling as his teeth took hold of it, sucking on it. Still holding me to him, one hand cupped my breast firmly while his other hand went to my underwear. They were pushed out of the way as he slid a finger inside me. Then a second.

"Mason," I wrenched out, turning my head for his lips.

A deep chuckle came from him as he nuzzled along my jawline, so achingly close to where I wanted him. I needed him inside of me. Now.

A shudder went through me.

God. I was already wet. The throbbing was pounding through me. To wake up like this, feeling him slowly rocking against me, I was almost panting.

His fingers pushed further inside of me, building a tempo, going slow. Leaning back into him, my hand fell to his and I urged him to go faster. It was building, but I needed it harder. Faster. His lips curved up as he nuzzled along my cheek. His other hand was rubbing over my breast, teasing me, and I fell against him. He was holding all of me up. I could barely kneel anymore, but I moved my head, searching for his lips. The desire was so blinding, but he wouldn't kiss me, and I growled in frustration. He chuckled as his lips nipped at the corner of my lips.

"More," I rasped out. "Now."

"More?"

A thrill went through me when I heard the thick lust in his voice. I wasn't the only one nearing combustion. He was barely holding back—I could tell—his hips were moving against me harder, faster. Then he started to bend me over. His hand left my breast and it cupped the side of my hip. He whispered against the back of my neck, "Hold onto the headboard."

Shit.

"Mason," I whimpered again. It was too much, but my hands grasped onto the headboard. My fingers curled around it, and I held on. I had no idea how. I was so focused on him, at how he was almost in me now. I could feel him through his boxers. His hand was still between my legs, but he pulled out. Instantly, I ached for him. I was too empty. I groaned in protest. "No…"

Then he was back. He had switched his angle now; he was firmly behind me. Urging my legs further apart, his fingers began pistoning in and out of me faster than before.

I was going crazy.

I needed him, all of him, and I began moving faster, riding his hand at the same time.

"Jeezus," he grunted over me, his mouth next to my ear.

A delicious shiver rushed through me as his breath caressed my skin.

"Now," I cried out, gritting my teeth.

His fingers kept ramming into me, sliding back and forth, going deeper until I wasn't sure they could go any deeper.

"Mason." I was panting now. Goddamn. "Please."

A deep guttural groan was my answer and his hand left me. His boxers were shoved down and in one smooth movement, he thrust deep inside of me.

Finally.

I closed my eyes and welcomed the heat. He was home now. We moved together, knowing each other's bodies so well. Turning my head to the side, his lips were there and they opened for me. I needed him. Sweeping my tongue against his lips, I tasted what was mine. He was mine. All of him was mine.

Bent over me, he held me anchored in place with a hand gripping my hip, but his other reached under me and took a firm hold of my breast. His thumb rubbed against my nipple. Shit. I gasped, pushing back into him so he'd go harder.

"Sam," he whispered against my lips.

I needed him to go faster. I couldn't handle it anymore and began to rock against him faster and faster.

"Shit," he gasped now, but he straightened. Both of his hands held onto my hips and he slammed into me, pushing me into the headboard now. I didn't care. My face was to the side now and I was gasping for breath. Some of my hair had fallen into my face so I couldn't see. The strands dipped into my mouth, but Mason moved them. They were tucked behind my ear and I was gasping for breath. He kept thrusting into me.

I was nearing.

I could feel it.

"Mason." A low groan came from the bottom of my throat.

I was right there.

Then, as his hands dug into my hips one last time, he emptied into me. I was right with him. My body shot over the edge and trembled as the waves rocked over me. He collapsed on my back and chuckled. His hand skimmed past my hip and he pushed off from the headboard. As our skin separated, he grunted.

I couldn't move. I hung onto the headboard, panting for breath. My body was still trembling as the waves kept coming.

"You okay?"

I shook my head. I couldn't even attempt to speak. I'd been weakened by that climax, but then he slid a hand in front of me and I was lifted into the air. Curling into him, my arms wound around his neck and my legs wrapped around his waist. His hands gripped my ass now as he moved from the bed. Mason carried me to the bathroom and tested the water before he stepped underneath. I hung onto him, clinging like a monkey as he washed his hair and then mine. When his fingers started to massage my scalp and he rinsed the shampoo from my hair, I closed my eyes. I enjoyed every last minute of his attention.

I loved him.

A feeling of contentment swept over me, and I could've hung onto him until next week. However, after washing both of us, he moved me back to the counter and I unhooked myself, giving him a rueful grin as he tossed me a towel. When he started to dry himself off, I didn't do a thing. I just watched. My eyes drank in the sight of him.

Broad shoulders. Every muscle defined, all the way down to his abdominals and obliques. Even the muscles in his legs bulged and shifted as he bent low to dry the rest of him. A trim waist. Angular cheekbones. Luscious eyelashes that covered his emerald eyes and lips that a girl would die for. Not me. I just died to touch them and feel them against mine.

I let out a deep breath. I was addicted to him.

He grinned as his eyes darkened. He knew exactly what I was thinking or feeling. He asked, "Are you going to get ready?"

"Sure. When my legs can work again. What *was* that?"

"That," he moved closer, pulling the towel from me, "was the best way to start my last semester."

I flinched as if a cold bucket of water was dumped on me. Those words left me cold. Plucking the towel from him, I hopped off the counter and shoved past him to the bedroom.

"What's wrong?" He followed me.

"That was the best way to start your last semester?" I dried myself off and stopped to glare at him. Seriously? He was an idiot. "Screw you."

The corner of his mouth curved up. "You just did."

"Not funny, Mason."

He frowned and narrowed his eyes at me. "What's wrong?"

"You're leaving."

"Just to college. I'm not going forever."

I rolled my eyes and turned my back. *Says you, you big ass. Just to college. It's not that simple.*

"Wait, are you really mad at me?"

Ignoring him, I grabbed some underwear, jeans, a bra and a shirt. Stopping once, I glanced in the mirror to make sure I looked presentable—I'd do. My dark hair hadn't been cut so it fell below my shoulders. I'd twist it up in a braid later, but the jeans and shirt were snug. Good. I didn't care if every inch of me was on display. The jeans were washed out, but clung to me and my shirt was a simple long-sleeve white shirt. The front dipped low, giving a good view of my cleavage, and my black lace bra showed through the thin material, but I didn't care. *Mason was just going to college, my ass.* Still ignoring him, I grabbed my backpack and purse. Stuffing the purse inside of the bag, I brushed past him and headed downstairs. As I got into the kitchen, Logan was just putting the coffee pot back on the burner. He turned and stopped. Seeing me when I entered, his eyes went wide and a low wolf whistle came next.

"You're smoking, Sam." He gave me a wicked grin. "Mason must've pissed you off, huh?"

"I know I look pissed."

"Nah." He shook his head, his brown locks had been gelled to perfection. "You're smoking hot. I know you're mad because you got that cold as ice look in your eye you always get when you are, but that's not what I meant. You only come out looking hot as hell when my big bro's pissed you off." Checking his watch, he whistled again. "That was fast because I just heard you two going at it like wild animals."

Oh. Jeezus. Flushing, I ignored his comments and gestured to the coffee pot. "Are you going to start that?"

"Nope. It doesn't work."

This morning went from great to crap. "Oh."

Grabbing his keys, Logan dangled them at me. "But if we leave now, we can stop at The Quickie. I need to get gas anyway."

"Sold."

Mason was coming down the stairs as we moved past them. He was pulling his shirt down, and I tried not to watch the movement of his abdominals or how his jeans rode low on his narrow hips. He paused when he saw us. "Where are you guys going?"

My lips were pressed tight together, and Logan smirked from behind me. He shook his head. "Whatever you said must've been good. You pissed your woman off. Not a good move, not on the first day of the semester."

Wincing at how close his words hit the target, I gritted my teeth and shoved out the door.

Mason called after me, "Sam."

"What?"

He looked ready to say something else, glanced at Logan and closed his mouth.

It didn't matter. I didn't want to hear it. "The coffee pot's broken. I'm going with Logan to get some. Did you want some too? I can serve it to you, another thing to add to the 'best way to start your last semester.'" A ball of anger rolled over me.

"Come on…" An apology flashed in those emerald eyes of his.

"You said that?" Logan chuckled. "Dumb move, dipshit."

Moving closer to the door, Mason flashed a warning at his brother. "Give us a minute."

"What if I don't?"

He bared his teeth at him. "Not a request, *dipshit*." Then he shoved him and stepped closer to me. His hand fell to my arm, but he added to Logan, "March. I'll bring her."

Logan smirked at him. "We're going for coffee. Besides," he gestured inside the house, "you've gotta wait for your other girlfriend. His car's still blocked in from the party last night."

"People are still here? Where is he?"

He shrugged. "Nah, they all got rides home, but their cars are still here, and as for your girlfriend, I have no idea. Check his room. I think I heard Parker down there."

"Parker?"

"Yeah. Pretty sure I heard her voice from downstairs. I was headed down to see if he knew how to fix the coffee pot."

Mason cursed under his breath and twisted around. His hand fell from my arm. "He agreed to the exile."

"Guess it starts later today for him."

"Not helping."

"Not trying to," Logan sniped back.

"What is your problem?"

"With you? Nothing. With your other girlfriend, figure it out." Logan's eyes darkened, letting his anger show.

I held my breath. There hadn't been a lot of times when the two bickered, but I could tell that Logan was fed up. Not that I could hold it against him. I was getting fed up as well, but I knew that Mason hadn't let his friendship with his best friend affect our relationship. Not yet. As the two glared at each other, I stepped in between them. Softening my tone, I gestured to Logan's Escalade. "Let's go and get coffee."

Logan turned on his heel, his jaw rigid as he went to his vehicle.

Mason caught my wrist and held me back. "Are we okay?"

"Yeah," I sighed. I had already melted as soon as I saw his regret earlier. "It just sucks, Mason. You're leaving. You. Leaving. As in you're not going to be here on a daily basis anymore. I'm not the only one bothered by that." I jerked my head over my shoulder, where Logan had started the car and was waiting for me.

"That's not Nate's fault."

"No, but it's not the three of us or even the two of you anymore. Nate came back. This is Logan's last semester with you, but..." I gestured inside. "Your best friend gets you for the next four years, you know. You're leaving early for football."

He groaned and his head fell back. "Shit, I didn't even think of it that way."

I shrugged. "Anyway, I really want to get some coffee, and I have to talk to my coach. He said to come by his office this morning."

Mason's head lifted back up and he grinned, his eyes darkening as he tugged me close. "Coach Grath is lucky to have you. He knows that."

I was about say thanks, but then I stopped thinking. He bent closer to me. Closing my eyes, I felt his lips softly touch mine. One damn touch was all it took. A tingle began and the lust for him sparked again. I became heated as he deepened the kiss, and I burrowed closer to him.

BEEEEEP!

Jerking back, I twisted and glared at Logan, who still had his hand on the horn. He flashed me a grin, but hollered out the window, "Let's go! You can screw later."

"Idiot," Mason muttered under his breath.

"He's right. Go see Nate, see what's going on. I'll see you at school."

He nodded, but flipped off his brother. Logan's laugh was heard clearly and I gave Mason a quick wave as I got into the yellow Escalade.

Reversing the vehicle, Logan extended his middle finger in the rearview mirror and gunned the engine. He didn't pause when we got to the road. Clicking my seatbelt in place, I settled back in my seat. Logan liked to drive fast, but he had the reflexes to keep us safe, so I wasn't worried. I did comment, "All you had to do was say something to him, you know. Mason's a good brother to you."

He jerked in his seat. His face grim. "Yeah, well, it's easy for you to say. You're *supposed* to talk to him. You don't come across as bitching and whining."

"I said something."

"No."

"Yes." It was getting ridiculous. "You used to be friends with Nate."

"That was before he turned shady. I know he had Parker over last night."

"You said this morning."

"Last night. This morning. What's the difference? He still violated the exile. Mase won't forget that."

I heard the anger in his voice. It was low and underlining. Frowning, I asked, "Are you mad at Nate about something else? I thought it was just because he came back for his last semester."

Logan jerked a shoulder up, holding the steering wheel with one hand. "What does it matter? He's so far up Mason's ass, I'm surprised my dipshit brother could even hear you."

"Logan."

"It's true." But his voice lost some of the aggression. "Nate's not the same. Mason needs to know that."

"So just tell him."

"Why don't *you* tell him?" he shot back, throwing me a sidelong glance.

"Maybe I will."

Rolling his eyes, he looked back to the street. "Mase won't listen to you."

"Yes, he will."

"No, he won't."

"Mason's always listened to me."

"Things are going to go to shit. I know it."

I frowned, but the knot tightened again in my gut. As Logan turned into The Quickie, I agreed with him. This semester wasn't going to be an easy one.

For anybody.

CHAPTER TWO

When Logan turned into the gas station, I laughed when I saw who was sitting on the bench outside of Quickie's—Jeff. When we got out, a quick grin came over him and he stood up. His hands were pushed deep into his pants pockets and he rolled his shoulders back. His dark hair had been gelled, much the same as Logan's, and as he came closer, I saw the idol worship he had for the younger Kade.

"Hey."

Logan narrowed his eyes at him, but I asked, "What are you doing here?"

He jerked a shoulder up. "My car broke down."

I glanced at his phone. "Who were you going to call for a ride?"

"Not that girl I was telling you about on Friday. She hooked up with this guy Saturday." He gestured to Logan, who had started to reach for the gas nozzle.

"Me?"

"Yeah." Jeff lifted a corner of his mouth up. "No worries. I'm not heartbroken. At least I know what she's like now."

He looked ready to say more, but Logan interrupted after he started the gas, "I'm going in. You want your coffee?"

I nodded. "Thanks."

As he went inside, Jeff laughed to himself. "Man, I forgot how scary—" He stopped suddenly. His eyes darted past my shoulder and widened. I turned to see Mason's black Escalade pulling into the lot. He parked next to us, on the other side of the gas pump, and hopped out. When he came around, Jeff put a few feet between us. "Hey, man. How's it going?" His voice sounded strangled as he jerked a hand up and grabbed a fistful of his hair, making it spike even more.

Mason reached for the nozzle, but turned to me. "Logan's inside?"

I nodded. "Where's Nate?"

The corner of his mouth dipped down into a brief scowl. It was so quick—there and gone in the blink of an eye—but I caught it. No one else would've noticed it. That wasn't good. A knot tightened in my gut. "Did he have company?"

"No, but he did last night." Mason's tone was cold. I knew it wasn't because of me.

"Uh," Jeff's hand tightened on his hair, and he tried to give me a halfhearted grin. His other hand shoved down in his front jean pocket, and his shoulders hunched forward. "Maybe I should get going…"

"Did you call someone for a ride?"

Jeff's eyes darted back to Mason.

Even though he was filling his vehicle with gas and his back was turned to us, I knew he was listening. He was waiting for Jeff to leave.

"Did you?"

"Not yet, but since you're here…" His voice trailed off again. "Oh shit."

Two car doors slammed shut, but it wasn't the sound of them or the alarm that flitted over Jeff's face that sent alarms off in me.

It was Mason.

He wasn't moving. An unnatural stillness had come over him. His hand fell from the nozzle, and he stopped everything for a second. It was a small pause as he took a breath. It lasted only a second. Then his hand reached over and he flipped up the handle so the gas stopped. The nozzle was left in his vehicle as he walked forward.

Then I saw them.

Brett and Budd Broudou. They had gotten out of their car and one yelled inside it, "Hurry up, Shannon. We've only got twenty minutes and you're going to make us late."

She climbed out from the back seat, straightening her skirt so her ass didn't hang out. "Shut up, Brett. I'll take my time if I want to."

"No, you won't," Budd interjected. "Not unless you want to call for your own ride. You better piss here too. We're not stopping."

Her lips clamped shut, but if looks could kill.

Her older brother didn't care. He gave her a look of death right back. "Bitch."

"Screw you." Jerking forward, she tried to hurry inside but stopped and slowed to a casual walk. Her shirt had ridden up, showing a good dose of skin, including the top of her butt crack. Muttering under her breath, she reached up and pulled it back down. As both her brothers started laughing, she turned towards them, but stopped when she caught sight of us.

Mason was in front of his vehicle, a human wall between them and me. I knew he had done it on purpose, but I was surprised when Jeff took two steps and positioned himself in the same manner. He was facing them squarely with me right behind him.

I scooted to see what was going on, but Jeff moved with me. When I went to the right, he went to the right. "Stop. He doesn't want them to see you."

I started to protest, but remembered how Heather had acted when they were at Manny's. She'd been terrified. Heeding all of their warnings, I stayed put. If Budd recognized me from that night, he'd say something and that was still a conversation I needed to have with Mason.

Then Logan came out of the gas station. He had two coffees in hand with his head down, clueless of the Broudou brothers as he crossed the lot. There still hadn't been a word spoken between the brothers and Mason. Yet.

It was coming.

A shiver went down my spine.

Slipping my hand inside my pocket, I made sure my phone was there and pulled it out. If they made one violent move, I was calling 911. I wasn't going to risk them being hurt. Mason's future had already been threatened by Analise. It wasn't going to be threatened again.

Then it happened.

I gulped as I watched it in slow motion. Logan stepped forward, he frowned, and then lifted his head. His eyes found me first. He paused. His foot came down hard in mid-step and he glanced around. He saw Mason before he trailed his head where they were.

It was as if they'd been waiting for him to join.

Everything happened then, at the same time.

Shannon's features scrunched together in an ugly snarl. Her hands found her heavier hips and her arms pinched the sides of her breasts, making them rise from the motion. It was then when her brothers saw us too.

I jerked forward.

Mason shifted in front of his car, and Logan disappeared from my eyesight. I moved to see better, but Jeff moved with me, obscuring my view.

"Stop." I tried to push him aside.

He remained facing them, but his hand went behind him to touch my arm. "Get in the car, Sam."

"No."

He hissed, "Get in the car! Now."

"No."

They weren't going to do anything to them. They couldn't. Terror started to rise up, and the hair on the back of my neck stood up.

They couldn't hurt Mason or Logan.

Then a low baritone spoke up, "Kade."

The other one added, "Shannon, go inside and get your coffee."

"No!" she hissed. "I'm staying, Brett."

"What are you doing here, Budd?" Mason asked. I closed my eyes, falling against Logan's Escalade. He sounded in control, amused even, and a wave of relief went through me at the sound. That meant he was fully in control of the situation. "Quickie's is in Fallen Crest territory. Not Roussou."

"Sam," Jeff twisted around, his cheeks flushed from insistence. "Get inside."

"Who's that over there?"

I held my breath, and Jeff froze.

That was Budd speaking.

"What are you talking about?" Logan tried to sound casual.

One of them, probably Budd, snorted. "You're hiding someone. I heard you have a girlfriend, Mason. That true?"

"Is that her back there?" Brett added.

"You never answered my question." Mason's tone went cold as ice. "What are you doing here?"

A shrill, but cocky laugh came from them. "We don't live far from your butt-buddy's home. Remember? Quickie's is on the way to Roussou."

"That's right." Soft gravel was smashed down. Mason must've taken a step forward. His tone was full of quiet authority. "You have a farm a few miles away."

Logan let loose with a swift curse. "Forget that. This is Fallen Crest. What are you doing coming to this gas station?"

"Fuck off, Kade."

Mason spoke again, a lethal note in his voice, "This is our town. You're not welcome here."

"Last time you came around here, your cars exploded. Are you back for round two?"

I shook my head. That was enough; I had to see. I pushed forward, but Jeff caught me. His arms came around me, and he opened the door before lifting me inside.

"Jeff!"

"Stop." The serious warning in his voice made me pause. I hadn't heard that from him, not in a long time, and my eyes widened. There was a grave note in his usually jovial brown depths. They were as flat as the scowl that hadn't lifted from his face. His hand went and caught his hair, grabbing chunks of it again. "Just stop, Sam. Stay here."

I didn't say a word as he shut the door and then started forward. His hands went into his pockets and his skinny shoulders hunched down. I knew it was his 'I'm serious' walk. It used to excite me during the first year we dated, but it wasn't amusing anymore. My mouth went dry, and I sat back in the seat.

Jeff was serious. Jeff was never serious.

CHAPTER THREE

Through the car, I heard Mason's muffled voice. "Take your sister and leave."

Someone snorted. "Who's in the car?"

"Leave."

"Tsk, tsk, Mason. Your little bro is showing his cards. He must care for her as much as you do." The voice grew louder as if he'd stepped closer. "Come on, just between you and me. Your little bro loves her, too, doesn't he? At least, that's what I've heard."

Then there was silence. I had stopped breathing and clung to the car's upholstery. My fingers dug into the seat, and I couldn't move. It was like a nightmare coming to life. Then I heard a scream. That was it. Flinging open the door, I rushed out. Jeff caught me in the air. "Come on, Sam."

I heard another scream followed by a car's brakes and then a thud. Someone was on the ground. I knew it. "Let me go." I dug my nails into his arm.

"No." He cursed, flinching as I drew blood. "They left me to watch you. Stop it."

I dug harder, hard enough that he cried out in pain, and I was dropped. Scrambling up, I burst around Logan's car. Then I heaved to a stop. Mason and Logan were a united front, but Nate was there, too. All three stood next to each other, another human wall.

Someone was on the ground, and the girl cried out again, "Pick him up, Brett! You're so damn slow."

"Shut up, Shannon. Open the door."

The body was hoisted from the ground, but I couldn't see who it was anymore. A car door was slammed shut, then two more followed it. The car reversed and sped off as dirt kicked up from the tires. There was five seconds of silence before Logan threw his head back and howled in laughter. He clapped Nate on the shoulder. "I can't believe you did that."

Nate's shoulder tensed under his hand, but he shrugged. "Trying to make up. I've recently learned that I've been a dick lately."

"You have." Logan kept chuckling, turning to see me. "You missed it, Sam. Nate clipped Budd Broudou with his car."

Mason's eyes narrowed at Nate. "What were you going to do? You hopped out of your car like you were going to take a bat to him."

Nate shrugged again. A brief glimmer of regret crossed his face, but it was gone instantly. "I needed to make sure he stayed down… and to make sure that I won't get sued."

"He's down now. Don't worry, you just clipped him. Budd's a cockroach. They think a lawsuit is a pansy way to deal with a fight." Logan's hand was still on him, and he used it to push up from the ground in a semi-skip. His eyes sparked from giddiness. Before I knew what he was doing, he had rushed over to me, and I was thrown over his shoulder. "That was awesome, Sam. I can't believe you missed that. Shit. I'm horny."

"On that note." An arm slid underneath my waist and I was lifted from him. Mason slid me down his body and kept his arms around me. I wasn't inclined to leave his shelter. He spoke near my ear, a deep chuckle in his voice, "I'll be taking Sam with me to school."

"Whatever." Logan's grin widened. "I'm off then. Got something to do." He darted to his Escalade, stopping once to punch Jeff in the arm before he climbed in and took off.

"Ow! That hurt. Oh, Sam. Hey…"

I knew what he was going to ask and started to answer, but Mason beat me to it. "We'll give you a ride."

Jeff flashed a bright smile quickly before the stoic mask of coolness slid back into place. I shook my head. This would be interesting. Mason didn't wait around. He got into the front and I climbed into the passenger seat. Jeff got into the back. No one said a word as he turned onto the road leading to Fallen Crest Academy.

The irony didn't escape me—my boyfriend was driving my ex-boyfriend to my old school. A lot had changed in such a short amount of time.

"So, um," Jeff started, leaning forward, "how much does one of these cost, Mason?"

I turned to him. "Don't even start."

He frowned. "Just trying to be friendly."

"Not now."

"Oh." He remained quiet until Mason pulled into the Academy's parking lot. Just like when I went to school here, everyone looked up and saw whose black Escalade was there. They all watched like hungry vultures. It'd been a while since Mason Kade had graced my old school. I remembered their reactions then. The reaction now wasn't a surprise to me. When Jeff got out, everyone's mouths dropped open. When he hid a quick grin, I knew he loved the attention. He lifted a hand in the air. "Thanks, Mason!"

Mason ignored him and pulled away from the curb. "Why is your ex-boyfriend acting all buddy-buddy with me?"

"Because he wants to be cool."

"Is he trying to get you back?"

I snorted. That'd never happen, not even if I developed amnesia, but when he turned onto the road and drove past the front of the school, the comment died in my throat. Standing on the lush green lawn with two gym bags full of equipment at his feet was my father. Or no. David. He stared back at me, but I couldn't see his expression. Reflective sunglasses hid his eyes and his arms moved to cross over his chest. He was wearing a Fallen Crest Academy polo. I had seen him wear the same coach's wardrobe for years, but he looked different. He had bulked up. Gone was the healthy weight he kept while he'd been married to Analise and the twenty pounds he lost when she left him. The weight was back and more so.

Mason saw it, too. "Your dad looks ripped. Not bad for a guy his age."

I slunk down in my seat, ripping my eyes from David. "Whatever. It doesn't matter to me anymore."

It didn't. I wouldn't let it, but I was thankful for Mason's silence all the way to my new school.

When he wheeled into the lot, he headed to the back corner and parked in the slot beside Logan's vehicle. Strauss was rounding the back end of a rusted brown truck that was parked on the other side of Logan's, a book bag over his shoulder, where he met up with another guy. Both went over to the back of Logan's Escalade, where the others were already waiting.

I took in the crowds that were watching them. There were so many cliques. Each looked different, but they all looked the same. They were all students, but those guys were at the top. Cheerleaders. Preppies. Others dressed all in black, even black hair. A few guys lingered around a picnic table in the corner with sleeveless shirts, spiked hair, tattoos and chains.

I kept scanning the back end of the school, and saw a few girls giggling together, whispering and pointing at the books they were holding.

This wasn't Fallen Crest Academy where everyone wore the same uniforms, and the only thing that separated their image was how short the skirts were cropped or how tight the shirts were tied. The top of the food chain had been the Academy Elite, but they wouldn't have made it a day at this school.

Mason glanced over, shut his car off and leaned back. "What is it?"

"Nothing."

"Sam."

"What?"

"Look at me."

"This is my first day here." I hadn't been nervous before. I was now.

"You'll be fine."

"No." I turned to him, but I could see that all the girls had smoothed their hair back and sucked in their stomachs. If that was their response to Logan and the rest, what would it be when Mason stepped outside of his car? Or when they saw me beside him? "I was nothing before."

"Sam."

I looked away. I didn't want to see his green eyes darkened with pity. "Things aren't the same, Mason. People didn't know for the longest time that we were together, and that was only last semester. Analise and I moved in with you guys, and now I've moved out with you and Logan. Even David looks different, like he's a freaking bodybuilder or something. This isn't normal. Is it?"

I'd been a social outcast last semester. I had a feeling I'd be one here too.

I turned now to face him and held my breath. The green was sparkling at me, so clear and warm. One corner of his mouth curved up, and he leaned his head against the headrest. "Everything will be fine. At this school. At home. We're family, whether you like it or not. I thought you'd be used to it by now."

Looking through the window at how everyone was riveted by his friends, I knew I'd never get used to it. I shook my head and reached for my bag. "I'm afraid that when I get used to it, you and Logan will go away."

"We're not going away. You're not going away."

"I can't go back."

It was then a red Mazda parked close to the guys and the door was thrown open. A long tanned leg came out, followed by another. It was like in all the high school movies. The beautiful golden-blonde emerging in slow motion like a goddess from her cliché red sports car, wearing a white shirt that flowed over her, hugging all the right curves, and falling an inch over the top of her grey skirt.

Tate had arrived.

The guys stopped talking. When she turned towards Logan, I sat upright in my seat. He narrowed his eyes and leaned back against his car as he stood in the middle of their friends.

"Did you see that?" I asked Mason.

There hadn't been much of a reaction, but I could sense the power she still had over Logan. I waited for a response, but there was none.

He was gone. His seat was empty, and his door shut just as I glanced over.

Scrambling after him, I headed for the rear of the Escalade. Then I heard the chill in his tone. "I hoped that you would've transferred after my warning."

Wariness came over her, but her eyes sought Logan again. Tate pressed her lips together as her shoulders lifted for a breath. "I'm just walking to class, Mason. I'm not here to cause problems."

He stepped close. His voice lowered as he said something to her, and her entire body went rigid a second later. The blood drained from her face, and her lips parted as her gaze was glued to him, like she couldn't turn away for the life of her. The spell was broken as soon as he stepped away, and she fled.

"Was that necessary?" Logan had come to stand beside me.

Mason turned to his brother. "Yes."

"Come on, Mason. She wasn't even doing anything."

"Why are you defending her?"

"Because you've made her life hell for two years. She's here for one semester."

Mason's green eyes switched to mine, searching if I agreed with him, but I stepped away from Logan. I didn't agree. Tate set off alarms in me. Both of them realized where I stood, and Logan snorted in disgust before he headed back to their friends, brushing past his brother who was standing in his way.

"Not to side with him, but Tate doesn't seem like too much of a threat anymore," Nate murmured lightly, breaking apart from the guys.

"*Now* you decide to be on his side?" Mason narrowed his eyes at him.

"You informed me how much of a dick I've been lately."

"You have been."

Nate grinned. "And I'm trying to make up for it." Then he swiveled to me. "Right, Sam?"

I lifted my hands in the air. The strap of my bag slipped down to my elbow as I shook my head. "Oh no. I'm not getting involved."

"Sam!"

Heather was waving her hands from the door. She yelled again, "Get your ass in here. You're going to be late on your first day. Stay away from her, Mason. I get her for the day."

Grinning, I went up to him and pressed a kiss to his cheek.

His eyes darkened again for a different reason this time. "You alright with what happened this morning?"

"Which thing are you talking about? Your comment? The Broudous at the gas station? Seeing my ex? Or just now, with whatever you said to Logan's ex-girlfriend?" I shook my head at the morning we had. "We are not normal."

"I guess all of it, but I was referring to your dad. I know that bothered you, seeing that he changed."

I shook my head. "Again. Not normal."

Hearing Heather call my name again, I was held back from answering her. Mason hooked a finger through one of my belt loops and pulled me close. "Are you okay?"

I knew he was asking about David, but I couldn't answer. I didn't know myself so I just shrugged. It was all I could do.

He nodded, getting the message and then his lips came down

on mine, and I melted. Home. He was home. Logan was home. No matter all the changes, no matter where he was going, I was home for now.

CHAPTER FOUR

Mason

Sam headed inside with her friend. Watching them, I wasn't sure what to think of Heather Jax. It made more sense after meeting Monroe from Roussou. The girl wasn't a part of this school's hierarchy. That was fine, I just wasn't sure if that would help or hurt Sam. I'd have to wait and see.

"Heads up," one of the guys warned. "Hoe walking."

"Screw you, Ethan," Kate snapped. "You're showing off to get in Mason's good graces, but we both know the shoe was on the other foot last night."

Last night?

I didn't want to turn around. I didn't want to deal with Kate yet. She and her three friends had been the main companions for the guys, but that stopped when I found out about her agenda to destroy Sam. She went after my girlfriend so I went after her. Well, I tried. Sam was adamant about handling this battle on her own so I did what I could. The girls were no longer friends with our group. They were exiled, but I heard the anger from her and I knew she wasn't going to lay down and take it.

I knew about Parker and Nate, but it sounded like there was more. I wondered what else Kate was up to?

Logan laughed. "So desperate, Kate. The look doesn't fit you."

"Keep laughing, Logan. You're going on the list."

He grinned now.

I laughed to myself. She stepped wrong, and judging by the quiet intake of breath, Kate knew it as well. The easygoing air surrounding the group was gone. Knowing that look, I turned now and saw my little brother getting ready to go in for the kill. There was a certain look that came over him. His head would straighten. His eyes would narrow and roam up and down the target. No one knew what he was doing, but I did. Logan was searching for weaknesses. If he couldn't see one, he'd sense for one. It was something we learned over the years after we'd been screwed over by adults too many times. We went with our gut.

I waited for his next move like the rest.

"What list are you talking about, Kate?" Logan's voice grew soft. He was going in for the kill.

Kate seemed frozen, and the rest of her crew had varying reactions. Parker grimaced, her eyes darting to Nate's before looking away. Natalie took a deep breath and Jasmine moved back a step. All of them recognized the tone, they just weren't used to being on the receiving end.

"Come on, Logan," Kate tried to laugh it off. "I was kidding."

A smirk came over me, but then it vanished. As I watched the scene unfold, I saw Logan decide to give her a pass.

No. That wasn't going to happen. "No, you weren't."

All heads jerked in my direction. My gaze caught my brother's in a silent mocking, and a spark flared in Logan's. The message was received: Kate couldn't be let off the hook, no matter what. I wasn't surprised when I heard him add, "What list are you talking about? Come on, Kate. I'd like to know how I rate getting on some list?"

She let out a shaky laugh, glancing between us now. "Seriously, come on, guys. Mason. Logan. I was joking."

"No, you weren't."

She turned to me and her eyes widened. A glimmer of fear showed. "I came over to see if you needed help."

My eyes narrowed to slits now. "With what?"

"With Tate."

"You think we need help with her?"

She peeked at Logan before turning back to me.

Too late. I caught the slight smugness. It mingled with her fear, but I caught it. "What was that?"

"What?" An innocent mask slipped over her.

I shook my head, pointing to her face. "That. That look you gave Logan."

Logan's head straightened. His interest was piqued.

"What are you talking about, Mason?" She was growing cockier now. "I'm trying to be a friend. We used to have your backs. Remember?"

One of the guys muttered, "Oh shit."

Even Nate laughed at that. "Since when? What are you talking about, Kate?"

She turned to the rest of the guys. All of them were looking at her in disbelief. Except Logan, he was grinning widely, leaning back against his Escalade. He shook his head now. "You're digging yourself a hole. Stop talking. It might help."

Jasmine hissed behind her, "Don't you talk to her like that—"

"Like what?" Ethan shot back at her.

That stopped her. All the wind she had ready to let loose fell flat. Her eyes darted to his, and she couldn't look away.

Ethan leaned back against the car beside Logan, and shoved his hands into his front pockets. His shoulders hunched forward, but his gaze never left hers. They were dead-locked as he added, "You're going to tell us what to do? You're going to tell me what to do, Jaz?"

"Stop." Her throat moved as she visibly swallowed. "Ethan—"

"No, Jaz. You picked your side. We're not friends with you guys anymore."

Her shoulders flinched as if he'd punched her.

He nodded in my direction. "And you know why."

She didn't turn and look. She only took another deep breath before her head went down, and she shuffled backwards. Natalie touched her arm softly, and then sidled beside Kate. She whispered something to the other girl, quiet enough so no one else could hear, and Kate's only response was a heavy nod.

All the fight had left her.

I waited, watching the entire thing fold out. I didn't take pleasure in this, but I wasn't going to let Kate get a pass, not when I knew she was just starting. The chances were high that she already had a plan in place, and I wouldn't have been surprised if her next move was to go inside and say something to Sam. She'd pick a public arena, let everyone know that they shouldn't become friends with Sam, or they'd have to suffer the consequences of dealing with her.

As she jerked her head and headed inside, her friends followed behind her. She glanced over her shoulder, and met my gaze for a single heartbeat.

I saw the rage. I even understood it, but when she caught the warning from me to let it go, her rage doubled. The look only lasted a second, but it was long enough. We both knew neither of us would budge.

It was war.

Kate thought she was fighting Sam, but she wasn't. Kate was fighting me. She just didn't know it.

I became aware of Logan next to me. "What was the look she gave me?"

We watched the girls go inside. "She's smug about something. I didn't like it."

"About me?"

"I don't know." I glanced at him. "Any reason she'd be like that about you?"

He frowned and shrugged. "Not that I can think of anything, but I know she thinks she can get you back."

"I know." I didn't care about that. I wanted to know what she was thinking when she looked at my brother like that. Studying Logan, I knew he was telling the truth. He was clueless, but that made me wonder even more. Did she have something planned to hurt him? Hurt Logan. Hurt Sam. Hurt the ones around me?

I didn't know. Yet.

Logan added, "She thinks that if she destroys Sam, you'll go back to her. Doesn't she?"

"Yeah."

Logan started laughing again. "New definition to the phrase 'dumb bitch'."

My gaze lingered on the door, even after it closed behind them. Logan thought this was going to be fun, but he had no idea. It was going to get ugly. I knew it, and I was ready for it.

Samantha

As soon as I was through the doors, Heather linked her arm with mine and pulled me close. Dressed in faded jeans and a loose black shirt, I had to grin when the V-neck dipped low. She didn't mean to, but she oozed sexuality. I had a feeling Heather Jax would look provocative in a grocery bag and she had no idea. Her eyes weren't clueless. They were sharp and focused as she asked, "What was that about?"

"Your ex-bestie."

She froze in mid-step, but was jostled from someone passing by and jerked me to the side for a split second. "Sorry." She patted me, withdrawing her arm at the same time. "Tate was out there?"

"She gave Logan googly-eyes."

Heather grimaced, side stepping a group of freshmen girls before swinging back to my side. "And let me guess, Mason didn't like that, did he?"

"No."

She rolled her eyes. "Tate's a bitch. I side with your boyfriend on this one. If she's already looking at Logan, who knows what she'll be capable of doing later."

"You make her sound like a villain."

"She is." Stopping at a locker, Heather wheeled the lock and opened it. Putting her books inside, she added, "Whatever Tate is saying, don't believe her. We didn't really talk about her before, but there's more to the story then whatever Mason told you."

That didn't sound good. "He told me that she dated Logan and, two years into their relationship she hit on him. There's more than that?"

A hollow laugh came from her. "Oh, a hell of a lot more. Things that Mason and Logan don't even know about."

I narrowed my eyes and moved closer. The hallway was packed. A lot of people were watching us, or me. A sudden wave of nervousness came over me. I had pushed aside the normal first-day-of-school-jitters with seeing Tate in the parking lot, but they were back now. They came back hard, but when I grinned at a few girls, they rolled their eyes and turned their backs to me. If that wasn't subtle, I didn't know what was. I was not welcome here. Glancing at a few others, they stared right back. I tried smiling at a few more, but I got varying responses. None welcoming. A few others continued to stare back as if I hadn't smiled at them, while a couple narrowed their eyes at me. The ones who turned away, bent forward to whisper with their friends. I had a feeling this was my welcome to Fallen Crest Public. I'd have to get used to it.

Heather took out a textbook and a notebook. Shutting her locker, a tired expression came over her as she faced me, but then it was gone in the blink of an eye and replaced with caution. Her eyes locked on something behind me, and I turned, my gut already knowing who it was going to be. Heather was tough and spunky, but only a few things or people could affect her like that.

And I was right. The Tomboy Princesses had arrived.

Kate was leading the pack with the three others close behind.

"I really hate those girls," Heather murmured to me.

Me too, I thought as I locked eyes with Kate. *Me too.*

All four of the Tomboy Princesses stood there. Each wore tight, ripped faded jeans. They weren't designer brands like the girls at Fallen Crest Academy wore, but they clung like a second-skin, and definitely gave off a sexy vibe. Their shirts were a variation of the same. Kate's was plain white that was snug against her tight abdominals, and it was evident she was wearing a pink bra under the sheer material. Her dark hair was swept up into a waterfall braid with the ends curled. They had a healthy glow as they fell past her shoulders. Parker glared at me, her dark eyes were hostile, and her lips were pressed together in a snarl. Unlike their leader, her black hair fell loose. It matched her black sleeveless top that rested an inch above her jeans, showing off a good amount of midriff.

Natalie and Jasmine brought up the last of their group, and they were the two that I was the least familiar with. They had similar black hair. Natalie's was a little lighter with caramel highlights showing through. She was the only one wearing a Fallen Crest Public jersey. It was red with black lettering and had the number eight on the back, the bottom of it tied around her tiny waist. Jasmine was the girliest of the group. Her black hair was pulled into a ponytail that rested high on her head, bouncing back and forth as she followed her friends. Pink lipstick, glitter on her cheeks and pink eye shadow matched her pink sweater that looked like soft cashmere and had a low neckline. Her cleavage was right there, saying hello to anyone who wanted to view the girls.

Heather cursed under her breath when the group stopped before us. She leaned against her locker as I waited. Kate said she'd make our lives hell. First day jitters and surviving my mother's recent attempt at destroying Mason's future had combined together. I was angry. I was ready to fight back. I was more than ready for whatever Kate had in store.

"Last chance, Jax." That was Kate's greeting. "You can back out now and everyone and everything you hold dear will be left alone."

"Shut up, Kate," Heather retorted, shoving off from her locker. She took two steps, sticking her face right up in hers. An inch separated them while her followers surrounded us. As a hush fell over the hallway, I knew all eyes were on us.

Still.

"I don't like when people threaten me or my friends."

"She shouldn't be your friend. She's a liability," Kate hissed back at her, breaking their stare-off to glower at me. She smirked. "What's with you and having bodyguards? Mason. Logan. Now Jax? Don't you have balls of your own?"

I smirked back. Balls? She wanted balls? I opened my mouth, ready to show her some balls when an amused voice broke into the group, "Kate, are you serious? You're still doing the bullying thing?"

Tate stood there, books in hand, as she skimmed the group with a bored expression. She rolled her eyes, flicked some of her hair over her shoulder, and shook her head. "What are you going to do after high school, Kate? You can't bully everyone to do what you want, and why are you even doing it now?" Tate gestured to me with perfectly manicured nails. "Pushing Strattan around isn't going to do a bit of good. You know that you won't get Mason back. He's gone. He was gone the second her mom moved her into his house."

Kate sucked in an angry breath. "Back off, Sullivan. This isn't your business."

"Maybe not, but Heather used to be a good friend and since I'm all about making amends, I can't walk by." She arched an eyebrow. "Wanna hear some advice from someone who has gone against Mason and his girlfriend?"

"Go away, Tate. I mean it."

She shook her head. "Let it go."

"Can't you hear, Tate?" Jasmine stepped right in front of her, much like Heather had done with Kate. The petite black-haired beauty looked even smaller standing in front of Tate, who had model-like long legs and towered over. "Kate said to keep walking."

Tate grinned down at her, like an adult whose child tried to boss them around. "You're like a mosquito that won't die. Back up or I'll swat you down."

Jasmine bristled. "Don't talk to me like that."

Tate lifted her bored eyes again, skimming me and Heather up and down before landing on the leader again. "I've been back a week, been around the last weekend, and I already know you're losing power. You're deluding yourself if you think you can push your way around like this. Let it go, Kate. We used to be friends and this is friendly advice. Stop going down this path, lick your wounds, and find a different guy to latch onto."

Heather shifted back, refusing to meet her ex-best friend's gaze, bumping into me in the process. I sighed and settled back against her locker.

Kate lifted her top lip and bared her teeth. "We weren't friends."

"We were in the beginning."

"When you ditched Jax." Kate threw a smug look to Heather. "Remember that, Jax? When your best friend stabbed you in the back?"

Tate stiffened.

"Or didn't you tell her what you did, Sullivan?"

"Shut up."

"Oh." Kate's triumphant smirk spread over her face. "You didn't tell her? That you slept with her boyfriend at the time?"

"Shut. Up."

"What?" Heather's voice had grown quiet.

"No. You started this. You came over here and interfered. You're on the list now, Tate. I was giving Jax one last chance to get away, but it's too late now. For both of you. You're all going down, right along with Mason's latest screw."

A dry chuckle left me. It acted like a beacon and as one, the rest of the girls turned to face me. I stood from the lockers. I caught movement from the corner of my eye and glanced over. I spotted Logan watching from a distance, frowning. Ethan was with him, and they both seemed unsure of what to do. I gave him a nod and sent him an unspoken message: I would handle this.

His frown deepened.

"You got something to say, slut?" Kate mocked. "Finally?"

"Finally?" I threw back, moving closer, replacing the spot that Heather had been in. Kate was my height, so I could stare her right in the eyes. I did so now, no blinking, no turning away, nothing was going to break our stand-off. "Why break this up? I don't need television. You're entertaining enough. Please, keep going. Threaten Tate some more. I'm not a fan of hers. Or even better, try going after Heather again. Go for it." I bared my teeth. "Fair warning. She bites back."

She frowned.

I rolled my eyes. "Am I supposed to be scared that the four of you ganged up on me? Or that you're willing to threaten my friend? You're making a list? Is that supposed to strike terror in me? Anyone can make a list. I've got one, too. Does it make your knees shake?"

I heard a wolf whistle from down the hallway, followed by, "That is so hot!"

Another guy yelled out, "Girl fight!"

Kate wanted to scare me. She didn't. I'd gone against the best of the beasts: my mother. As Jasmine took another step forward and raised her hand, I shifted so I was facing her head-on. She stopped in her tracks and surprise came over her. Her hand lowered.

"You think physical violence is going to do it?"

Tate started laughing now.

I ignored her. "Go ahead and touch me. I'm not scared to take a hit, but you're only going to hurt yourself. One bruise and I can go to the principal. It's not like there aren't witnesses here."

As those words left me, Kate grabbed Jasmine's arm and shoved her back.

"Kate," she protested.

"Not yet," their leader barked. "Go to class. All of you."

Parker gasped now. "You're letting her win?"

"No." Kate turned her back to me, but I heard the warning in her tone. "It's not time."

"But—"

"Go, Parker. I won't say it again."

All three did nothing to hide their disgust with Kate as they left. Parker glowered at me for a full five seconds before she was dragged away by Natalie, the only one who hadn't said a word. My gaze lingered on her and wondered what she was like. Parker and Jasmine seemed to be the hotheads of the group. They reacted the quickest, but Kate must've been their leader for a reason.

Kate rounded back to me. She took a deep breath and shook her head. "You're not what I expected, Strattan."

Tate snorted behind her. "You haven't even scratched the surface, Kate."

Kate glanced at her. "And you have?"

"I know that Mason Kade wouldn't be in love with her if she were simple."

"Maybe."

Heather burst out then, "Go away. All of you."

"I was trying to help." Tate frowned as Kate followed after her friends.

"You're not."

For a second, the two former best friends stared at each for a second before Tate's shoulders dropped. Her head lowered an inch and she lifted one shoulder in a halfhearted motion. "Fine." She was swallowed up by the crowd that remained behind her. They were all still watching and as I scanned them, a sense of déjà vu came over me. It was like my last semester at my old school, but I didn't know these people. I hadn't gone to school with them since kindergarten. I didn't know the embarrassing stories from middle school or all the cliques.

This wasn't my school. This was foreign territory to me. That should've staggered me, but it didn't. I had endured Analise. I could endure this.

Heather fell back against her locker with a groan. "I didn't expect that."

"I did." I actually expected more.

She eyed me up and down. "I thought maybe they'd steal your clothes during gym class or something. Maybe write the word 'whore' on your locker."

I grinned at her. "And on that note, I need to go to the office to get my combination. When I registered they didn't have that for me."

Heather tried to smile, but the corners of her lips went down instead of up. She glanced in the direction Tate had gone. "Why do you think she did that?"

Because she wants to be friends again. I didn't say that, though. I said instead, "What boyfriend were they talking about?"

Pain flared over her face. "Channing."

"I'm sorry."

She lifted a shoulder and shrugged halfheartedly. She looked away. "Doesn't matter. We've been broken up for a year anyway…"

"It couldn't have been anyone else?"

Heather looked down now. "No. I've only been with him, and we were dating when Tate was my friend. It makes sense now…"

Score one for Kate.

"I'm sorry," I said again, but I knew it wouldn't help.

Kate won this round. She hurt my friend.

CHAPTER FIVE

The first bell went off when I reached the office. The final bell went off when I was given my locker combination. I would officially be late to my first class, on my first day. Wonderful. When I asked where Coach Grath's office was, the secretary informed me that he'd be gone all week. That dilemma was resolved. So with that new information, I headed back out and started my day as a new student.

When I got to my class, the teacher didn't care that I was late. A worksheet was handed to me right away and the rest of the class went fast as I began working on it. There were no Tommy P.'s in there, but there were in the rest of my classes. Jasmine and Natalie were in my second period. Kate was in my third and Parker rounded out the fourth. My mornings were going to be glorious, but the one silver lining was that my locker was still clean when I headed to lunch. No 'whore' or 'slut' decorated it. Yet.

There was no sight of Mason or Logan when I went to the cafeteria, but Heather called me over to her table. There were a few others sitting with her. The guys were friendly or friendlier while the two girls gave me a cold reception. One, dressed in all black clothing, gave me a sneer and turned her back to me.

Subtle.

The other one, wearing a white sweatshirt emblazoned with a large rainbow, gave me a shy grin. She had the softest blue eyes and palest skin I'd ever seen on a person. After we ate, Heather explained on the way to our lockers that the shy one was an albino. I'd never met someone who looked like that, but she warned me not to expect anything nicer than the greeting I got. The shy one didn't talk and Heather said that I was better off not knowing the other one's name. I didn't question it. She added that No Name Chick wasn't a fan of anyone associated with the Kades. Both girls were routine targets by the Tommy Princesses and neither cared that Kate's group was no longer supported by Mason or Logan anymore.

It wasn't until after fifth period when Logan showed up at my locker. "What was going on with those girls this morning?"

It was amazing. Logan Kade appeared at my locker and most everyone stopped to watch us. I sighed as I exchanged one book for the next one. I'd have to get used to the pull he held over everyone.

I shrugged. "It was nothing."

"That didn't look like nothing."

"Stop, Logan," I warned. "I have to take care of them. You can't do this for me."

He rolled his eyes, cursing under his breath at the same time. "We're going to have to step in. It's inevitable. Kate's a bitch."

"Logan."

"You know it, Sam. Stop fighting us and let us help you. You're going to have to at some point." A final warning was in his gaze before he took off.

As he did, all heads turned to follow him. As he went one way, Mason passed him coming towards me. The heads turned and followed him instead.

As I waited, watching him come to me, people parted for Mason. He didn't seem to notice it. His gaze was on me, but I couldn't stop from watching how people reacted to him. Logan too. They knew when Mason or Logan were around. Even if they didn't see them, they still moved out of the way. It was beginning to dawn on me how big their near-celebrity status was at this school. Everything they did, people knew. Everything they said, people heard. This shouldn't have been a surprise anymore, but it was. It was different at their school. It was more than I had experienced before.

As he drew closer, his intensity softened and he gave me a grin. I saw the love in his eyes and it warmed me. Hell, he was becoming like oxygen. I needed him.

"Hey."

"Hey, yourself," he murmured, bending down to give me a soft kiss.

I closed my eyes as the usual ache started in me again.

The whispers started around us. They grew to a low buzz, and I started to turn around, but Mason grabbed my chin. His eyes were once again the only thing I saw—everything else started to melt away. He stepped closer, his hand grew gentle on my face, and his thumb started to rub over my cheek. "What happened with Kate earlier?"

"Nothing." The Kade brothers were consistent. "It's my fight, Mason. Let me fight it."

"Sam, come on."

I felt him now. His arms brushed against me. His stomach flattened and tightened, grazing through my shirt, and his familiar heat started to pull me in. He didn't have his arms around me, but I still felt sheltered by him.

This was what Mason did. His charisma was so intoxicating, and I couldn't blame anyone from wanting what I had. I reached up to his face now, feeling the small dip underneath his lips, before it formed his chin, I couldn't look away from him. Even now, my fingers ached to explore more, to feel his lips, to trace them and then cup the side of his face.

"Hey," he murmured, stepping even closer. He was almost pressed against me. My fingers fell from his face and down his chest. It felt like a cement wall underneath my touch. My hand fell to his jeans. It caught there and I curled my fingers around one of his loops. Then, feeling desire swirling inside of me, I bit my lip and pushed one of my fingers in the waistband of his jeans.

Whatever he was about to say was forgotten.

"Sam," he groaned as he turned us so that my back was against the locker. He was against me now. As my finger tucked further down, I felt him harden. The power I had over him was intoxicating. It wasn't just him. My head fell back against the metal locker, but I didn't feel it. Everything else fell away. It was only him and me. Nothing else mattered.

My desire for him rose, and I fought against letting it take me over.

My eyelids flitted closed and I felt him bend down. His chest rubbed against mine now and then I gasped when his lips found the corner of mine. He stayed there, sucking lightly, as his other hand slid down to my hip and pulled me tighter against him.

"I feel pregnant just watching you two."

Breaking apart, Heather was standing there with her arms crossed over her chest, and the corners of her lips curved down. She looked ready to vomit. "Honestly, come up for air every now and then. The masses look ready to riot."

She jerked her head down the hallway, where Kate and the rest of the Tommy Princesses were.

I sighed, pushing Mason away. "That's her locker?"

Heather leaned against my neighbor's locker. "No, that's Natalie's. She and Jasmine are only juniors. Kate and Parker are seniors. Good riddance too. I'm ready for their entire group to ship out."

Still watching Kate and the glower she was sending our way, I shook my head. "She looks ready to kill me."

"You and me both. I'm not doing what she wanted."

Mason frowned as he deliberately turned his back to Kate, blocking her view. "She wanted you to do something?"

"She told me to stop being friends with Sam." Heather shrugged, but I caught the small look of alarm in her eyes. It flared for only a second. "She gave me the warning this morning and Tate, of all people, tried to help me."

The interest Mason held fell flat now. He straightened from the locker as he ground out, "Don't believe anything she says."

"Well, I'm going to believe Kate." Heather peeked around him, eyeing her warily. "I wonder what she's going to do."

"Nothing." Not if I had anything to do about it. I was getting more and more irritated with Mason's ex-on-and-off-again hook-up. She hadn't even been a full-fledged girlfriend. She'd been used only as a scratcher when he had an itch. "I'm not going to let her."

Mason frowned, twisting around once again.

I held my breath. There was an unspoken message there, and I knew he was delivering it to her. As she made an exasperated sound before slamming Natalie's locker, I guessed she had received it, and whatever she saw, she didn't like. Then he moved again. Kate and her group were coming towards us. I snuck a peek at Mason, whose eyes went flat, but she only hissed as they went past us, "You're going to regret this. All of you."

Her friends smiled at us, following behind her.

Heather shuddered. "Evil. They're all evil."

I agreed with her, but asked Mason, "How'd they take the exile?"

His gaze had lingered on Kate, who paused and glanced back once, but he turned back to me. "What?"

"The exile. How'd they take it?"

"Oh." He lifted a shoulder. "They took it. They didn't have a choice."

"Must be nice," Heather drawled. "You declare it and people have to follow it, whether they want to or not." She snorted, tightening her grip on her bag. "I'd like to declare something. Whoever won the lottery last week will hand their ticket over to me." She rubbed her hands together. "And voila, all my problems—poof!—gone." She eyed Mason up and down. "Must be nice to be rich."

He shot her a dark look. "That's not how it went down." He touched my arm again. "We have basketball practice. What were you going to do after school?"

"Oh." I hadn't driven to school and Coach Grath was gone for the week. I glanced at Heather. I wasn't scheduled for Manny's until Saturday so what else was there? "Running."

"You want to take my car home?"

I held my hand out to Mason. "Yes, please." I didn't care how I got home, I just needed to run.

He grinned as he put his keys in my hand. "Just don't go for hours. Please." He pulled me close and pressed a kiss to my forehead, whispering at the same time, "And be careful. Keep an eye out when you're running."

My throat grew thick at his concern, and I nodded, reaching for him again. My hand clasped onto his shirt's collar and hung there. "I'll be safe."

"Good." He pressed another kiss to my lips before he pulled away.

As he headed down the hall, Heather groaned. "I stand by what I said. You two are disgusting."

CHAPTER SIX

Running was my escape. I escaped all reality and pushed forward. I kept going. It was like a drug to me. It came with its own challenges and obstacles, and as long as I kept going, I broke through every single one of them. Tearing down a wooded trail, the bass was pounding through my earbuds and my adrenalin matched it. My heart pumped as I lifted my knees and pushed off from the ground. Power rippled up through my legs. I ducked my head and raised my hands to keep projecting forward.

I'd never tire of this.

And with that thought, I rounded a turn in the new trail. My eyes widened in surprise as Quickie's came into the clearing. I never knew this path came through here, but it wasn't far from Nate's home. It made sense. There were no cars in the lot so I raced through, but saw the clerk watching me. When our eyes caught for a second, he lifted his hand and I nodded back, but then I was gone again. The path led up a hill behind the gas station and I heaved a deep breath, pushing myself upward now.

There were no thoughts in my head. No concern. No fear. There wasn't even love. When I ran, I was just being. My nostrils flared and I kept going, flying up one hill and then another. I tore past another clearing. The trees parted below me and I braked. My chest heaved up and down, but I couldn't move away.

I was looking down on Fallen Crest.

I hadn't realized how high I must've run, but I couldn't tear my eyes away. It was breathtaking. My old school's campus was on another hill, straight from where I stood. Fallen Crest Public was in the valley below. The massive football field was a patch of green among the rest of the town. Then I looked for the south side, wondering if I could see Manny's. It was surrounded by trees so I wasn't surprised that I couldn't. Then, without thinking about it, I glanced to the neighborhood where David's house was, my old home.

Instead of the old pain, there was nothing. I frowned, but started forward. A chill drifted over me and my blood was pumping. I needed to keep going before the cold settled in. With that last thought, I tucked my head down and pushed forward with a new burst of speed.

After my run, I showered, ate, and then fell asleep watching television in the basement. It was later in the night before the guys got home. A stampede of feet sounded above me, and the door slammed shut as I heard Logan yell, "SAM! WHERE ARE YOU?"

"Logan!"

"What?"

"You don't have to scream your head off."

"Whatever, Nate. You're pissed because you need to work for some pussy now. Can't have Parker running over anymore."

"Shut up."

The door leading to the basement was thrown open and Logan's voice grew clearer as he laughed. "Don't blame me that girls are scared of you. You're a shady, motherfucker." He hurried down the stairs, but stopped before laughing. "Sam? You're down here?"

I scowled at him before rolling back over and pulling my blanket over my head. "You're so loud. Shut up."

He chuckled before yelling upstairs, "SHE'S DOWN HERE, MASON."

I held my breath. I already knew what was coming next, but as he dropped next to me, the couch jerked from his sudden weight, and I went airborne for a second. Oomph. Oh yes. I was fully awake now. I pulled the blanket back to glare at him. "Thank you for being quiet."

He flashed me a grin, pulling the handle to the footrest next to him. "No problem." It came up and he lounged back, getting comfortable. "What are you doing down here? You're never down here."

"Resting. What are you doing down here?"

Grabbing the remote from next to my feet, he switched the channel and pointed at the screen. "Game's on."

Of course. How stupid of me.

I groaned to myself, but sat up and curled my knees to my chest. The sounds of a basketball game came next. It was only the first day of school so I didn't have any homework yet. No shift at Manny's. I already ran. I knew Mason would be heading down soon. I wasn't going anywhere. When Logan reached down and lifted a fast food bag to his lap, I asked, "You guys got food?"

He had pulled his burger out. It was half unwrapped and lifted to his mouth before he stopped and turned to me. "Did you want some?"

My stomach growled. The smell of greasy food hit me like a cement truck. Crap. The little sandwich I had after my run hadn't tided me over.

Logan heard it and one corner of his mouth lifted. He held his burger to me. "You want a bite?"

I shook my head. "No. That's yours. I'll go and find something else." Still. My stomach growled louder.

"Sam." Logan was fighting back a smile. "You can have the entire thing. This was my second one."

"No, then you'll be hungry."

"Nah." The smile won out and he grinned from ear to ear. "I can steal Nate's. He got three of them, and I know he hasn't touched them. He said we should wait till we got home." He snorted. "No fucking idea why."

"Because I was going to ask Sam if she wanted one," Nate spoke up, coming down the stairs. He frowned at Logan, before he sat down on the other couch. He had two bags with him and held one in the air. "There's a chicken sandwich in here. Sam?"

My stomach spoke up with a resounding 'yes.' It groaned, growled, and shuddered all at the same time.

Logan chuckled, but turned to Nate. "Kiss ass."

"Screw you. Mason got the sandwich for her."

"Oh." Logan frowned. "I thought you were going to take the credit."

"What's your problem?" Nate tossed the bag so it landed on the couch next to me. "You've been on my ass all day."

"Because you've *been* an ass lately," he shot back before giving me a wink. He said to Nate, "It's not every day you get knocked down a peg and take it. I have to enjoy this while I can."

Nate's frown deepened to a glower as he rolled his eyes. "Well, it's getting old."

Logan shrugged. "Not my problem. You were the shady motherfucker in the first place."

"Guys," I murmured as I unwrapped the sandwich. My stomach wouldn't stop groaning. I hadn't realized how hungry I was.

Nate glanced back at the stairs. "Your brother's being an asshole."

There was no response, but I knew who it was. I knew who was coming and enjoyed waiting for him. I sunk my teeth into the sandwich. Good gracious, I was in heaven. A chicken sandwich had never tasted so delicious to me. My stomach was doing cartwheels, but then I was being lifted in the air again. I didn't even react. I already knew where he was going. When he moved so he was underneath me, I kept eating as I got comfortable on his lap and rested my head on his chest. One of his hands remained on my leg, his fingers on my inner thigh as I took another bite.

"Did you not eat?"

I nodded, mumbling around the sandwich, "Not enough."

He grinned and leaned back into the couch.

Logan chuckled, turning the volume louder.

"Nice, dickwad."

He only got a shrug in response.

Mason held me on his lap and moved his fingers in a circling motion. It was soothing and sensual at the same time. Part of me was getting excited while the other part wanted to fall asleep. With the chicken sandwich in my stomach, and the warmth from Mason, the sleepy part won out. Then Mason's phone went off. It buzzed from his pocket underneath me, and he shifted me to the side, his arm sliding under me to grab it. Pulling it out, he opened the screen. It was a text from his father: **We would like to invite you over for dinner. When are you moving back?**

"Uh, okay." Logan was reading his phone at the same time. He put it down, his eyebrows bunching together as he said, "I know you talked us into moving back, but no way. I can't do it, Sam."

"What?" I sat forward. "You guys said you would."

Logan shared a look with Mason. I twisted around. "You agree?"

Mason didn't say anything. He didn't have to. I shook my head. "What? Did you guys come to this decision without me?"

"No." Logan shook his head and then nodded. "Yes."

A lead stone dropped to the pit of my stomach. This was my fault. I promised James and now they were changing their minds. "You guys should live with your dad for the last semester. Mason, you only have a few months before you leave."

"Sam."

That big lead stone wasn't moving. I sat up and went to the empty chair.

Nate took the remote from Logan and silenced the game.

Logan snorted. "Why's it so damn important for us to live with our dad? It's not fair to put your daddy issues on us."

Narrowing my eyes, I crossed my arms over my chest. "You can't say that to me. You have no idea—"

"No idea?" Logan scoffed. "Yes, we do. Our dad's an asshole."

"Logan."

He overrode me, "It's not going to happen." Then he stopped, and glanced at Nate.

"What?"

Logan turned to the stairs.

Nate bit out a curse. "Are you serious? You want me to leave?"

"Not to be an ass, but this is family shit."

"What am I then?"

"You're extended family shit. You're one of those long-distance cousins."

Nate looked over. "Mason."

"Just go, Nate." Logan leveled him with a harsh look. "This is family and you've been a douchebag lately."

Nate gritted his teeth at him, but turned to his best friend. "Mason, come on."

Mason sighed. "It doesn't matter what I say. You need to be trusted by all of us and you're not. That's what matters."

He pushed up from the couch and stalked out. No words were shared, and the tension in the room was thick enough to cut with a knife. I didn't dare breathe until he had left. As soon as he was upstairs and the door shut, Mason leaned back and sighed. "I hope you guys know what you just did."

Logan sent him a dark look. "Screw you."

"I already ripped him a new one this morning—"

"Not good enough," Logan interrupted him. He shot forward, his eyes stormy and lips pressed tight in a snarl. "Nate's been so far up your ass, I'm surprised you remember about the rest of us." As Mason glanced at me, Logan added, "Except for Sam. You do need to get your daily screws in, don't you?"

Everything happened so fast after that.

I gasped, but then Mason was off the couch. He had Logan pressed against the wall in the next instant, one hand fisted in his shirt and the other had pinned Logan's arm up. He snarled at him, "Are you fucking with me?"

Logan twisted, jutting his hip out to move Mason aside and then slipped his arm free.

My heart was pounding. It sounded so loud in my eardrums that I struggled to hear the rest. Everything had jumped up in me, and it felt like my pulse was lodged in my throat. It was going nuts.

Mason didn't move against him, but Logan didn't move away. They were almost touching, glaring at each other.

"I'm not screwing with you."

"You sure about that?" Mason lashed back. Every muscle in him was primed. He was ready to fight; his hands had formed into fists and were pressed against his legs. He was holding himself back.

Logan eyed him warily before sending me a furtive look. His shoulders were rigid, but they dropped a fraction of a centimeter. His jaw was still like cement as he clipped out, "I'm not, but I am getting sick of this shit. Nate's up your ass twenty-four-seven. "

"We *are* staying in his house."

"So let's move."

"And go where?" A hollow laugh came from Mason's throat. He turned to me. "Back to Dad's? Sam, there's no way I'm living with your mom again. I meant to tell you earlier, but I forgot."

Rising from the couch, I hugged myself, but spoke up, "It's not right that you guys are here. Nothing against Nate, but you should be with family during this time." My heart kept pounding, thumping against my ribcage. "And yes," I caught the look he sent to Logan, "that means Logan and me, too. I don't have a family anymore."

Mason and Logan had been eyeing each other, but they turned as one now. I was front and center once again.

I gulped. Sometimes their attention was a little much, too much at times. This was one of those times. I felt stripped and raw as I added, "My life went to crap five months ago. My mom left my dad. I found out my dad wasn't my real dad. Then my real dad came into my life, but he's gone. They're both gone and then my mom went psycho. I've got you two, and on the outside, I am so jealous of you. You have a dad. He's still here. He loves you guys—"

Mason started forward. His voice soft, "He's with your mom, Sam."

I flinched at that. It felt as if he'd slapped me.

"I love you and she hurt you. That's the math to me. If we go back there, she's going to keep hurting you." Mason was in front of me now. His hand lifted to touch the side of my face. "There's no way I can watch that and not do anything."

Logan spoke up, "We can't scare your mom anymore. She's too crazy for that, so being there and seeing that happen to you," he gestured to his brother, "I'm with Mason. There's no way I could watch that and not do anything, except this time, we'd really hurt your mom."

"It's best if we just stay away. Our dad knows the deal. As long as he has her in his life, we're out. That's the way it is." Mason's chest lifted as he took a deep breath. His touch was so tender. "He's making that decision. Not us."

A piece of me broke away. It fell to the bottom of my stomach. The sadness that washed over me was overwhelming. "I can't be responsible for you guys losing your dad."

"You're not." Logan frowned, stepping next to his brother. He didn't reach out, but I felt his concern. "It's our dad. He turned into a douchebag, too."

"Logan."

"What?" Logan shrugged, giving his brother a crooked grin. The sudden tension from before was gone. "You know it's true. Well, I guess our dad's always been a douchebag. How many mistresses did he have? Had to be twenty, at least." He whistled in appreciation. "Gotta give it to your mom. She's the one that landed him. Our dad must be really nuts if that's who he chooses to settle down with. He's stuck with her even after all the crap she did to Sam." The other half of his mouth curved up. "Maybe we should have him committed? He can go through one of those brainwashing programs, brainwash him back to being normal." He pondered that for a second. "No, he'd just pick another winner again."

"This isn't funny."

Logan shrugged. His crooked grin didn't lessen. "Has to be. Dad left Mom, cheated on her for years, and Analise is who he ends up with? She's the one that he decides to stick it out with? That's the funniest damn thing I've heard." He clapped his brother on the shoulder. "Come on. You think it's funny too."

When the corner of Mason's mouth curved up, teasing at his own grin, I couldn't believe this. "Stop," I cried out. Shaking my head, I moved away. "I can't believe you guys. You're laughing about this? You can't—"

"We can," Mason stopped me. A tender expression came over him. "Logan's right. It has to be funny. We've lived through all the other stuff. The divorce. Dad's cheating. The only good thing we got from him was you."

"I second that."

I rolled my eyes. They were missing the entire point.

"Sam." Mason reached out and took my hand, pulling me back to him. "We're not laughing to be dicks, but this is our dad. You can't judge us because we're not accepting the crumbs he's giving to us. He's not a great dad."

Logan snorted, "Try he's never been a great dad?"

"We understand what you're saying. Trust me. We do." He tugged me closer to him, but I didn't look up. I couldn't. His finger went underneath my chin, and he tipped my head up. Then I couldn't look away. His green eyes caught mine and the wall he normally had up slid away. He let me see everything—the bitterness, hurt, pain, anger—all of that was there, but it was mixed with love. I saw it. I felt it when he murmured, "I'm grateful to him for you, but because I love you, I can't accept your mother. There's no way. Would you? If you saw someone hurting me, over and over again?"

When he put it like that, I drew in a shuddering breath. "I would kill that person."

Logan started laughing. "We go from scaring to hurting. She jumps right to killing. Hardcore, Sam." He patted me on the shoulder. "It's why you're our Little Kade. On that note, I love you. I'm sorry for my comment before, but I can tell where this is going. Believe it or not, I don't get off on watching the two of you." He pressed a quick kiss to my temple and headed to the stairs. As he got to the top, he called out, "Coast is clear. Fornicate away."

Mason ignored him. "You okay?"

I nodded. My throat was too thick with emotion to speak.

"We can't move back in. We can't watch her hurt you, and he's not going to leave her, so this is how it has to be." He drew me against him and I rested my head on his chest. If the situation had been reversed, there was no way I could do it either. I hadn't been joking. If I saw someone hurting Mason and Logan, over and over again, I would do anything to stop them.

Mason bent down and dropped a soft kiss to the top of my head.

CHAPTER SEVEN

"So you haven't told them yet?" Heather popped her head out from her locker as her mouth fell open. "I can't believe you. That was a week ago. Don't you think they should know?"

"Why? They know that Budd and Brett are trying to find out who I am. They said it to their face."

She slammed her locker shut and handed me her notebook. "Hold this."

I did. "What do you want me to do?"

Heather stopped looking through her book and glared at me. A strand of her hair slipped down, blocking her face, but I could still feel the heat of her stare. "You're not a moron, Samantha. Stop trying to make me think of you are. It's an insult."

"I'm screwed."

"Pretty much." Her eyes lit up as she found her page and folded over the corner. Then she grabbed her notebook from me before shaking her head. "Look, granted, Mason and Logan did their 'run-in' with Budd and Brett. They know Budd's looking for Mason's girlfriend so that's not news to him, but you yourself saw them at Manny's. You work there. They could go there any time. It's something they'd want to know."

An outburst of giggles and yells came from down the hall, and I glanced over. Logan had arrived. He was at his locker, along with Ethan and Strauss. Both guys had smirks on their faces as they enjoyed the cheerleaders next to their lockers. Boobs galore and if their skirts lifted an inch, pussy galore. I snorted, falling back against the locker behind me.

Heather paused, mid-reach into her bag. "What?"

"Nothing."

"What?" And she turned, twisting around to see further down the hallway. I knew when she spotted them. Her back straightened. Her shoulders flattened and she let her bag fall to the floor. "Oh."

Oh, indeed. "I'm starting to get used to this school."

"Uh oh."

"What?"

"No one says they're getting used to this school. Those are the people that get a smack-down." She shook her head, trembling in an exaggerated manner. "I can't let that happen to you."

I laughed. "No, not like that. I meant that I'm starting to understand this school. Instead of the Elite, like at FCA, you guys have cheerleaders."

"And the drill team."

"Drill team?"

"Yeah," Heather nodded towards a group of girls across from Logan's locker. They were dressed in sweaters. Not one of them wore jeans. They all had on dress pants that could've been matched with a business suit. They looked professional, how I would've dressed for a job interview. I glanced over their different hairstyles, all swept down or over the shoulder to look like perfection. I understood what Heather was saying. The Tommy Princesses might've been the girls at the top because of how tough they were, but these girls would've usurped them if given half a chance. They reminded me of Miranda and Cass from the Elite.

"Do they think they're in a walking beauty ad?"

Heather chuckled. As we headed towards them, she added, "Those girls try to get the boyfriends. There's a few that are always trying to land any of the guys in the Kade group, but they'd love to get Mason or Logan the most. Kate and her bitch crew were the main go-to girls for the guys. They weren't into having a boyfriend like the others and each guy kinda had their own. Mason had Kate.

Nate had Parker. Ethan had Jasmine and sometimes Logan would hook-up with Natalie, though we both know he never had a certain go-to girl."

"And speaking of…"

I stopped as Tate came around the corner. She didn't give us a glance as she went straight to Logan and draped herself over him. One arm went around his neck and the other hand rested on his chest. He'd been listening to Ethan, but stopped. As she moved closer to him, his head lowered so it looked as if the two were whispering to each other. A small grin was teasing the corner of his mouth when she started talking.

"Okay." Heather bobbed her head up and down. "I now see what you and Mason are worried about."

My eyes grew wide when he lifted a hand to the side of her hip. That was how Mason touched me. It was intimate and it was his precursor move before he pulled me even closer. Logan didn't pull her closer, but his hand lingered there before moving to the small in her back. Oh yes. He was enjoying every bit of her attention, but then he looked up and caught us staring. Correction. He caught me.

My face got hot. I knew I was probably red, but what was he doing? I narrowed my eyes and tried to ask him that question without saying it.

The other side of his lips curved up and the grin was no longer a tease. He was full-on smiling at me. Another correction. He was smirking at me.

"What?" I bristled next to Heather. Both knew who that question was for.

He lifted one shoulder. It dropped lightly. He said back, "What?"

Tate turned around, a Cheshire Cat grin on her lips as Logan's hand didn't fall away. Instead of being on her back, as she turned to us, it slid around her hip to her stomach and stayed there. She was now almost in his arms.

Heather was frowning at them, but I couldn't hold it in. "Did I miss the announcement? Are you a happy couple now?" There was an edge in my voice, but I couldn't hide it. Tate was bad news. She was slimy. She was sneaky. She hurt Logan. She'd do it again.

"You can't be jealous, Samantha," she taunted me. "You're happy with Mason, aren't you? You can't have both Kades."

I growled, "And you can't hurt him again."

"Uh, guys…" Heather started.

Logan shook his head. "Sam, relax."

"No—" I stopped him.

Tate turned her gaze to Heather and a bitter look came over her. "What's your problem, Heather? I didn't know we were enemies. You don't have to have her back all of the time."

That had me seething, but I glanced around and saw the crowd that was forming. The drill team snobs were mingling with the cheerleaders. Ethan and Strauss had front row seats, leaning against Logan's locker, were grinning from ear to ear. I skimmed the edge of the crowd and saw Kate. She was expressionless, but her eyes narrowed when they met mine. A slight chill went through me. Whatever she was thinking, it wasn't good. I caught Logan's eye and gestured to her. The amusement on his face faded then, and he stepped towards me.

Tate stopped in mid-sentence. "What are you doing?"

Ignoring her, he took Heather's arm and mine, pulling us through the crowd.

"Logan!"

"Your girlfriend is calling," Heather told him.

He grimaced. "Okay, that was a joke. I can't believe you guys got so riled up." He led us into the senior hallway and quieted his voice, leaning in closer to me, "I don't have those feelings for Tate anymore. You don't need to worry. I'd have to care about her to get hurt by her. Those feelings are long gone."

Heather put on the brakes. She went pale as a group broke away from the hall. "Oh, crap."

I recognized two of the girls. "Those are your friends, right?"

"Let's hope." An apology flashed in her eyes as she started for them. "I gotta go. I'm sorry, Sam. Come to Manny's tonight if I don't see you at lunch?"

I nodded as she hurried to catch up with them. When she did, the girl who was dressed all in black refused to look at her. The tiny one gave her a half-grin. It was more like a half-hearted attempt at a grin. It only came out as being sad. As the other one snapped at Heather before stalking away, the tiny one got up and followed. She didn't say a word to Heather either. There were a few guys in their group, and the one with dark hair and a tattoo circling over his jaw slung his arm around Heather's shoulders. He looked to be reassuring her, but she pushed him away and hurried after the two girls. He called after her, "Don't sweat it, Jax."

"Who's that?"

"Uh," Logan tilted his head to the side. "Max Monroe. I don't know him that well. I think Mason might. He's friendly with the Roussou peeps here so don't get close to him."

"There are Roussou peeps here?"

"A few." Logan started to lead me further down the hallway towards Mason's locker. "I think they're cousins or have relatives over there. No worries, Little Kade. They're not going to rise up and mutiny. There's not enough of them here, and they're not really liked by everyone else. Your throne is safe."

"Do you try to be annoying, Logan? Or is this post-coital bliss from whoever you went to see this morning?"

He chuckled, throwing his arm around my shoulder again. "I'm not being annoying. I'm being charming and since when do you want to know who my post-coital bliss is from?"

"I don't. As long as it's not Tate, I don't care."

He squeezed me tight, laughing as we pushed through another crowd. Mason's locker was in the back corner. It was broken off from the main wall with four others besides his. Spotting Nate and some of their guy friends, the other locker owners weren't a big leap. When Mason saw us coming, he straightened up from the wall. Nate glanced over, but he wasn't as welcoming. Shutting his locker, he took off.

"Unlike you, I'm guessing he's not interested in my post-coital bliss either."

"Logan."

"What?" He flashed me a grin, rubbing where I'd hit him. Then he said to Mason, "Nate's still not over our family meeting?"

"Would you if we kicked you out of your own basement?" Mason grimaced as he eyed Logan's arm that was still around my shoulder. "Do you always have to touch my girlfriend?"

"What?" Logan laughed and pulled me tighter against him. He rubbed his hand up and down my arm. "I thought you'd be happy that it's not Tate I'm touching. Sam just saved me from her clutches, you know."

"Your ex is causing more trouble?"

Logan's grin fell flat "I was joking about Tate." His arm fell away and he moved back a step. "You both can let up on Tate. She's not going to be a problem."

"Logan."

He gave me a little wave as he headed off.

"Let him go." Mason opened his locker and grabbed one of his books. Then he skimmed me up and down. "You headed to school early this morning."

"I went running."

He frowned. "When you run that early in the morning that means something's up. What's up?"

I leaned against Nate's locker. Even standing in the back corner, I could feel everyone's attention on us. I still wasn't used to it. "You guys are like gods here."

He grinned. "That's a new deflection."

"No." I shook my head. "It's not meant to be. I just…" I gestured to the hallway. There were students everywhere and most of them kept glancing at us. A couple girls in the far corner huddled together. When they noticed my attention, their heads ducked down and they skirted into another hallway. The last one peeked back. Her entire face was flaming red, even to the back of her neck.

"Sam?"

"It's nothing."

But it wasn't nothing.

"Hey." His tone softened and it did what it always did. It reached inside of me, loosened the knot that had formed in my throat, and pulled me towards him. I had to grin. Mason Kade would always hold this power over me, and as he tugged me against him, all my anxiety and concerns were pushed away. "What's going on with you?"

"Nothing." I corrected, "Nothing that's important. What do you think about Tate and Logan?"

"You mean," he raised an eyebrow, "besides what he just said? We're supposed to let up on her?"

"She draped herself all over him and he seemed to like it."

"Oh."

Nothing. No reaction. Just an 'oh.' Tilting my head to the side, I studied him and narrowed my eyes. "Oh? That's it?"

He flashed a grin before pressing a kiss to my forehead. "I'm not worried about Tate anymore. Not that much anymore."

Bombs exploded. The apocalypse had arrived. I could only stare in shock as he leaned back against the wall and pulled me between his legs. Looping his arms around my back, I was firmly enveloped in his arms, but I couldn't enjoy it. My stomach had started on a loop, rolling over and over again.

He sighed, watching me. "What?"

"Come again?"

"I'm not that worried about her."

"And when did this happen?"

His eyes narrowed, just a fraction, before he caught his reaction. Then it went back to the normal mask he wore in public. I felt like

I'd been kicked in the stomach. It'd been a long time since he used that mask on me and anger started churning inside me. "I think my boyfriend left his body and someone took over. Who are you and what did you do with Mason?"

"You're being funny now?" he shot back, straightening away from the wall.

His arms fell and I stepped back. There was always a chill when I left his shelter, but not this time. I was growing heated as the conversation continued. "I'm sorry. Was that role taken? Only Logan can have his one-liners? Remind me of my role. I wasn't aware that I could never question my boyfriend."

"Sam, come on."

"No, you come on." My voice rose.

He glanced around and reached for my arm. "People are listening."

"I don't care." I stepped further back and his arm fell back to his side. "I want to know when you suddenly decided Tate wasn't something to be worried about."

"It's not like that. I just…" He shook his head. "Can we talk about this later?"

"I want to know what's happened. I know there's a reason why you've decided to let Tate off the hook."

"She does go to school here—"

My voice lifted again. "Not helping."

His shoulders dropped.

I added, "Before we were even together, you hated Tate. You went to parties just to humiliate her. You whispered some mojo to her the first day of school, and I don't think that it was pleasant, and now four days later you don't care? Logan likes her; I can tell. She's going to hurt him again. No one worries you and she worried you. That made me worried too." My chest grew tight and I knew I must've started to look enraged. Mason wasn't even fighting back. "You better tell me what's going on and do it now."

My heart was pounding. I delivered one of my best mini-rants and I stood there, waiting for his response.

My answer?

He shrugged. "I don't know what to say to you. I just don't think he loves her anymore, so I'm not that worried." Then he pushed off from the wall and left.

That—what the hell just happened?

CHAPTER EIGHT

Mason

Walking away from Sam cost me. I was lying to her. She asked me a question, point-blank, and I dodged it, point-blank. She wasn't an idiot, but I couldn't tell her the real reason. Logan said he wanted to play with Tate, fool around with her, use her. So whatever. I wouldn't run interference anymore. It wasn't the best idea. I knew that much, but this was what Logan wanted and a part of me couldn't fault my little brother. She dated him for two years. She'd been the only girl he had fallen in love with, and she hit his older brother up. The need for revenge was too sweet for Logan to walk away from, but Sam wouldn't agree. She wouldn't understand. Sam protected. She loved. She wasn't a vengeance girl.

She was good. Logan and I were not.

Dodging around a group of girls, I headed down the hallway and ignored the two that stuck their hands out. One got a good grope of my stomach and the other tried to hold me back. Her fingers curled into my arm, but I twisted it free, knocking her back into her friends at the same time. As I kept going, one cried out from annoyance and I turned around.

They thought they could grab me, there were things called boundaries. "Try it again and I'll make your life hell."

Their eyes got wide and their heads shot straight up, but the one who tried to hold me back only rolled her eyes. I could tell she was the leader. Skimming over them, I figured they were freshmen—they would be the next Kate and crew—they were tough, popular, and already oozing sex.

"Mase!" Nate called, waving me down.

He was standing at Strauss' locker. The two were lounging back and watching the girls. A group of cheerleaders were next to them. I wasn't surprised. The exile had been broadcasted loud and clear. Kate and her friends weren't on friendly terms with us anymore so there was a vacancy at the top. There was always attention from girls, but it was different since the exile. The girls had become more aggressive with the guys, and more competitive with each other. My eyes fell to the left of Strauss and saw some of the drill team. Two had seductive grins on their faces while their friends were glaring at the cheerleaders.

That was one benefit when Kate reigned. She kept the hierarchy in order.

"Hey." I nodded to Nate and punched Strauss in the shoulder. I pulled it back at the last second so it turned into a friendly nudge.

Strauss gave me a halfhearted grin, his gaze lingering on an ass that walked past us.

"How'd that family pow-wow go? Did you guys get everything straightened out?"

Shit.

Strauss glanced at Nate as well. His hostility hadn't been kept in check, but Strauss didn't comment on it.

"It wasn't like that, Nate."

"Figured I should jet, just in case it was. I wouldn't want it to be awkward." He fixed me with a pointed look.

I lifted a hand and raked it through my hair. This wasn't a scene I wanted to happen here.

"Logan!"

Turning, I saw Logan had a girl pinned up against a locker. He was grinning right in her face, and her cheeks were flushed. She lit up, smiling widely, and took a deep breath. It lifted her breasts, and Logan fixed his gaze on those. He didn't look away, and the girl squirmed again. "Logan, stop."

Strauss grunted.

The girl didn't want him to stop. She was giggling, pressing against him, and pushing her breasts out even further.

"Mr. Kade," a loud voice boomed from the end of the hallway.

Logan stepped back, dropping the girl at the same time. She squealed again, this time not from enjoyment.

"Both Mr. Kades are here. Two for one deal. Lucky me," the voice said again with the same gusto. A hand came down hard on my shoulder at the same time.

Logan glanced up, meeting my gaze with a dark look before we moved as one. I turned around, dislodging the hand as Logan took a few steps to stand beside me.

I spoke first, "Principal Green."

Dressed in a grey suit, green tie, and standing over six feet, he was at eye-level with me. The older man, in his early forties with graying hair, lifted his lip. It was an imitation of a smile, but it didn't match the resignation in his eyes.

Logan snorted.

The principal inclined his head. "Something funny, Mr. Kade?"

He rolled his shoulders back, a cocky smirk coming over him. "Nah, Principal Green, except you look ready to drop on your feet. Busy night with the missus?"

Disapproval replaced the resignation. "I am here to give you both a warning."

"A warning?" Logan locked gazes with me again. "We haven't done anything."

"Yet," someone coughed from behind them.

Nate, Strauss, and some of the others laughed at the comment. A girl added in a groan, "They can do anything to me that they want." Her friends giggled and began whispering together. Someone snapped at them, "Shut it. Stop being so annoying."

Kate.

The girls fell silent.

Principal Green surveyed the crowd in the hallway, shaking his head at the same time. "How is it that you two command so much attention in this school? I've never met another person, much less a pair of brothers that can compete with the level of power you hold over my student population."

Logan shrugged. "We're cool, an inspiration to others."

A smattering of laughter started again.

Principal Green drawled, "I highly doubt that."

"It's true. We're like a walking Hallmark card, full of quotes and bible verses. We make people feel like they've been touched by an angel."

"Oh, shit," someone laughed.

Another commented, "He makes people feel touched all right."

A third snorted, "And not from anything angelic."

I cleared my throat and everyone shut up. "What'd you come here to say?"

"I got an interesting phone call from our local police."

I glanced at Logan. What the fuck? Then I narrowed my eyes at the principal again.

"They're screwed," a guy laughed.

Principal Green twisted around. "Don't you people have classes to go to?"

A few left. Most stayed.

He sighed. "I'd rather not have this conversation with an audience. Mason. Logan. Both of you come to my office?"

It was asked as a request. It wasn't. We followed him to his office. As we were about to turn right into the main office, Sam was coming from the left. Both of us saw her and she stopped mid-stride. The arm that held her books fell to her side and her mouth opened. A questioning look came into her depths, but I also saw the hurt still there. My jaw clenched and I turned away.

Logan wolf-whistled at her.

She didn't reply. I felt her gaze burning into the back of my skull.

My shoulders tensed and I gripped the handle on the office door harder than necessary. I knew Logan caught the exchange and I knew my little brother wouldn't understand.

Fine. He could explain it to her himself. Then Logan would understand.

As we took the two seats across from Principal Green's desk, Logan bumped his knee against mine.

I ignored him.

He hissed, "What was that?"

"Nothing."

"Mase," Logan hissed again.

"Okay, boys," Principal Green started.

I ignored him too. "Remember the thing you talked to me about last night?"

"Oh." Logan fell back against his chair. He let out a long breath. "She knows."

"She picked up on it. You can tell her."

"What? No way—"

"Gentlemen," their principal clapped his hands together and leaned over his desk, "am I interrupting a little spat between the two of you?"

Logan rolled his eyes and slumped down his chair. I leaned forward. Principal Green had never done anything to screw us over, but he was an adult. It was bound to happen. "What do you want? We haven't done a thing so the police stuff has nothing to do with us."

Principal Green smiled to himself, leaning back in his chair. "Always down to business, Mason. I do appreciate that. Like I said before, I received a phone call. I was going to mention it to you at some point, but when I saw both of you in the hallway, I figured I should get it over with." His top lip lifted in an attempt at a smile.

"Congratulations, Principal Green." Logan rolled his eyes. "But here's a tip. Don't give your number out to hookers. They can't call for bail the next day."

"I was called by the police station this morning."

"You know a hooker that got arrested?"

"Logan Kade."

"Or don't even use hookers. If you get a mistress on the side, buy a pre-paid phone. Make sure to use cash. The wife can't catch you and your lady friend can call you all she wants."

"Mr. Kade, you should leave before I put you in detention."

He ignored him. "Don't go on Facebook either. I wouldn't even have an account if you become a pro cheater."

"Leave or I'll give you detention. I am not in the mood."

Logan snorted as he stood up. "Detention? What will the coach say? I'd miss practice."

"Leave, Mr. Kade."

"Leaving, Principal Green." Logan flashed him a grin and lifted two fingers in the peace sign. "Remember my tip: Don't give your number out to hookers and no Facebook. It'll save you a lot of trouble."

As soon as the door closed, I stated, "We didn't do anything."

"I know. They know that, too, but someone else did. Budd and Brett Broudou. They went to Quickie's and beat up a clerk. When the clerk was questioned, he indicated an earlier incident with them this week. He said you almost fought them."

"They beat the guy up?"

"Yes, they did." He cleared his throat. "Everyone is aware of the strained relationship between the two schools. There have been past incidents and this is my warning to you, Mason. Stop it. This rivalry with Budd and Brett Broudou needs to stop. This is between them and you, but both parties have included their schools. Other students will be hurt by this. Have you considered those consequences?"

My tone went cold. "I'm aware of the consequences."

Then I left. Principal Green didn't stop me, but it wouldn't have mattered. I didn't care to listen to any more advice from him. I was more aware of the consequences than anyone else.

Samantha

As the rest of the week passed, I was in an alternate universe. Logan was pissy because I disapproved of Tate, who continued to stop at his locker every chance she got. Nate was pissy…well…that was deserved. We kicked him out of our meeting. I was pissy with Mason because he didn't disapprove of Tate anymore, or because he didn't explain it to me. There must've been more to it than what he said. He didn't have some 'sudden' realization that Logan wasn't going to fall in love with Tate again. There was a reason—this was Mason—there was always a reason, and as the rest of the week wore on, I was starting to realize he wasn't going to tell me.

The conversation was avoided, and when I brought it up, he'd distract me. Of course, most of those places were distracting anyways. In the shower. In bed. In the car. The only place he didn't try was in the kitchen. The one time I raised the question again, he ate quickly and left. Some excuse was thrown over his shoulder as he headed to his car.

I wasn't happy. I wasn't happy at all.

But when Friday came around and I found myself in an empty house, I was ready to admit defeat. I had no idea where anyone was, but I had a shift at Manny's. The evening would go fast, or that was my hope.

When I got there, there was no one. Crickets.

The door shut behind me and sent an echo throughout the place. Brandon stopped wiping the counter and lifted a hand. "All hail, Strattan."

"Are you trying to be funny?"

"Not you, too." His grin vanished.

"Not me what?"

"You're crabby." He gestured inside the kitchen with a glass and towel in hand. "You and my sister. What's in the water at that school? She's been crabby all week."

"Shut up, Brandon!" I heard through the door. "Just be happy you're still getting dates." Her voice became clearer as she stood in the doorway. Her hand was in her hair; it looked stuck there. "You're almost a has-been, tending bar for a living."

"Screw you. I own this side, remember?"

She rolled her eyes, stalking past him and shoved open the screen door. When it banged shut behind her, she plopped down in one of the lawn chairs. The smell of cigarette smoke soon drifted inside.

The usual sibling camaraderie had vanished.

Following her outside, I took one of the other chairs. "What's wrong?"

Flicking the end of her cigarette, she got up and shut the solid oak door. Letting the screen door shut after it, she sat back down and took a long drag before she shook her head. Her voice trembled. "Have the Tommy P.'s done anything to you this week?"

I frowned. "What? No." And I was surprised by that. They'd been so grrr and threatening before, I had expected something. "Why?"

Taking another long drag, she reached inside her pocket and held her phone to me. "They've been sending me texts all week."

"About what?"

She snorted. "Can't you guess?"

I could, but I didn't want to. They were starting with my friend. I knew this was the beginning. The first one read: **First warning, bitch.**

I rolled my eyes at their originality and clicked on the next: **Second warning, cunt.** Again. So original. The third and fourth were the same, more warnings followed by an expletive. Then they started getting interesting. The fifth read: **Ditch the bitch or you'll be sorry.** Something new. The sixth was different: **You used to cut. The word is out. Wanna know who told?**

I paused and glanced over. Heather was on her second cigarette already. I held my tongue and read the next one: **We know about your mom. Want that out too?**

Heather told me her mom left when they were kids. I wondered what more there was to the story, but went to the eighth text: **Fire Strattan. If you don't, we'll destroy your daddy's livelihood.**

I couldn't read the rest. A sick feeling took root in my gut. "I'm sorry."

Heather ground out her second cigarette, and lit a third right away. As she settled back again, she shook her head. "Brad plays ball with Natalie's cousin. Never considered warning my oldest brother not to say a word. I'm guessing that's where she learned all that stuff." Her voice quivered.

"You used to cut yourself?"

She inhaled a long deep drag before shaking her head. "In the seventh grade. That's when my mom took off. I was an idiot. She was a horrible person, but I didn't want a dad that first year. I wanted her back. I blamed him for everything, even though she was the one that cheated, and she was the one that left us. He stayed. She didn't, but I wanted her."

There was more to the story. I heard the pain in her voice. "Your mom cheated?" Something we had in common.

She nodded, looking so bleak and defeated. The wind picked up and blew her hair back. It flattened her shirt against her small frame. She was already slender, but the material was so thin that I could see her ribs. Knowing she couldn't have lost so much weight over just this week, it still made me feel guilty.

"I'm sorry," I told her.

"For what?" She was almost done with the third cigarette. "I don't like being told what to do. That's what she used to do. Kate and the tomboy bitches are just like my mom. I hate being told what to do." She drew in another drag, cursing at the same time. "They want to tell me what to do? Tell me to drop someone who's been a better friend than most of my others? I'm starting to really hate them, Sam. I'm talking really hate them, like I want to cut them how I used to cut myself."

I didn't know what to say. Heather had stood by me, but she'd been distant all week. "You never told me about your friends? They didn't look happy with you the other day."

"Yeah." She drew her knees up into the chair and wrapped her arms around them. They were like twigs. Still holding the cigarette, she drew in a deep breath. I saw how she swallowed, grimacing at the same time. "I can't really blame Cory or Rain."

"Rain?"

"Rainbow."

"Her real name is Rainbow?"

"No." She blew out a puff of smoke. "Her real name is Ginnie, but we call her Rain. She's always wearing something with a rainbow. Always has, now that I think about it, since the sixth grade when she moved here. Rain's short for rainbow."

"You said she's an albino."

"Yeah," her voice softened and her eyebrows set forward. Frowning to herself, she grew thoughtful. "Kate was being the bitch she is, making fun of her. Cory stuck up for her and the two have been close ever since. Helps that Cory understood. Kate's been picking on her since the third grade, I think."

"No wonder they don't like me."

"It's not you." Heather shook her head, lifting the cigarette again. "It's Mason and Logan. It's not even them really, it's just because they were friends with those girls for so long. They're why Kate and the Tommy P.'s got so powerful, you know? They gave them weight or cred or whatever. No one wanted to mess with the girls that were 'friends' with the top guys."

"Hey!" Brandon banged on the door. "Game's going to be over in an hour."

Heather groaned, finished her last cigarette and put it out.

"What game?"

Both frowned at me. "The basketball game."

"Fallen Crest..." A foreboding sense of dread kicked in. "Public?" I didn't need to see their reactions.

"Mason and Logan never said anything?"

"No..."

"Don't sweat it. It's like another day at the job for them. They're more about football games, aren't they?"

"Yeah..." But it still stung. Whatever. Another shitty thing to add on to this week. "So what happens after a game? What are we in for?"

"Before your guys made this the popular hangout? Nothing. We would've gotten a few stragglers in, but now it's going to get packed. Our regulars know not to come in. Even Gus, and you know how much he loves his seat, but they know we'll get swamped. A few girls from school texted and said everyone's planning on heading here. It's going to get nuts."

Forget Mason. Forget Logan. I had a job to do. "You want me in the front or back?"

"I'd say screw it and work the front, but Frank is sick."

"So the back it is."

"That's okay with you?"

It felt like I'd been kicked again when I caught a look of pity in her eyes, but I ignored it. Tried to, but it hurt. No one said a word about the game. I didn't have any friends at school. I couldn't hear it from them, and Heather had been distant on her own. I saw her in the hallways, before and after school, but she had started leaving campus during lunch the last couple of days. I'd been distracted. Mason began waiting for me at my locker during lunch. They had an open-campus policy, so we took advantage of it and left to grab fast food. Most of the time was spent on the drive there, getting our food, and then eating it as soon as possible on the way back. Any free moments were spent in the parking lot with a few stolen kisses and some heavy petting. He made sure his car was always parked away from the school and surrounded by his friends' vehicles, so no one could spy on us.

And thinking about other students, I said, "No one really made a big deal about the game. At Academy, there would've been pep rallies. Posters and banners would've been everywhere. I don't remember seeing any this week."

Heather pulled open the doors as we went inside and answered over her shoulder, "There were flyers, but not that much. Everyone just knows about the game. They go if they want, they don't if they don't want to. Besides, the basketball games aren't like the football games. Those are nuts."

"Are you kidding?" Brandon piped in from behind his counter. "The basketball games are nuts, too."

"I know, but she's asking why it wasn't really talked about at school."

"Oh." He nodded. "It's because everyone just knows about it. That's how it was during my days." A wide grin came over him. "I remember those days fondly. Good days. Good memories."

Heather rolled her eyes as she tied on her server's apron. "You mean, good pussy?"

"Ah." The wide grin stretched in a full smile. "Easy pussy is more like it. I didn't have to search for it. Those girls came to me. I can't imagine how the Kades have it now. Compared to them, I was nothing. They're like gods."

It felt like a knife stabbed me in my chest.

Heather made an exasperated sound. "You're an idiot." She jerked her thumb at me.

"Oh." He sounded sheepish, letting out a weak laugh. "Sorry, Sam. You know what I mean, not that I remember Mason indulging in pussy like Logan does, but—"

"Just shut it, Brandon. You'll be doing us all a favor."

I held a hand up, shaking my head. "No, you guys. Really. I am aware of their near-celebrity status. This is nothing new to me. I live with them, remember? Logan's got a new girl over almost every day." But that wasn't true. He was gone most of the time. During the week we had all settled into a new routine. Logan was usually the first to leave, or he would leave the night before and not come home. He must've kept half his closet in his car because he never wore the same clothes twice, and he was always showered for the new day. Nate was the next to leave. He'd dash out a few minutes before Mason and myself. While I'd be nibbling on a piece of toast in the kitchen, waiting for Mason, Nate would dart through, holler a goodbye, and be on the road before Mason would even come down the stairs.

As for Mason and myself, we began a trade-off. We'd ride together in the mornings, unless I went on a run. I took my own car during those days, but when I would ride with Mason, I drove his Escalade home while he got a ride with Logan or Nate. If he forgot to give the keys to me during lunch, they would be waiting for me in my locker. There wasn't a lot of time for us to talk because he had basketball practice, and I'd usually be itching for a long run, sometimes my second one of the day.

"Game's over," Brandon called out. He was looking down at his phone. "We won: thirty-two—nineteen."

"Here we go." Heather took her place behind the counter. I went to the backroom. It wasn't until hours later that I remembered I had left my phone in my car.

CHAPTER NINE

Mason

I left the gymnasium and pushed through the doors. A lot of the others had already gone. Most were headed to eat and then to Fischer's party, but I needed to go to Manny's first. Sam might not want to go and after the way I'd been dodging her question all week, I needed to make it up to her. Whatever she wanted was whatever she was going to get. My jaw clenched as I remembered the hurt in her eyes when she realized I wasn't going to answer her. Shit. I couldn't. If I did…no way in hell. I couldn't. That was the end of it.

My hand tightened on my bag as I crossed the parking lot. Logan's car was still parked next to mine. What was my brother still doing here? Nate's car was here too. Things were cold between the two, but they could joke around with each other. Still, I didn't see them hanging out together, and I hadn't seen either of them in the locker room. Coach needed to talk to me, and most of the guys were gone when I came out.

"Hey," Logan spoke up, straightening from his Escalade.

I frowned. My little brother looked tired. "You need to stop with this whole sex marathon you've got going on." Unlocking my car, I tossed my bag inside.

Logan rolled his eyes. "Whatever. I hear you and Sam going at it all the time. Don't you guys take a fucking break?"

I grunted. Nice choice of words. "I can have all the sex I want with her. Know why? Because she's my girlfriend, and I love her. I know my dick can be in her, and it's safe. She's safe. We're not going to be having little Kades running around here anytime soon. Can you say the same?"

"You're such a dick."

"A dick that cares about you. Stop all the screwing around. You'll catch something or you're going to end up with a kid."

"What's your problem?" Logan ran a hand through his hair.

"You're my problem. I mean it, Logan. Stop screwing around. Find a girl, get some feelings for her, and be rabbits." He was pissed. We both knew it, but I wasn't going to ask for the motivation of his sudden marathon. "There has to be some girl in this town that you could date who's not Tate."

Logan shot me a dark look. "Get over yourself. I don't love her, and you know it."

I narrowed my eyes, studying him before I relented. "Do whatever you want. Mom'll love being a grandmother."

My brother shot me a different look now, one filled with dark humor. "Can you imagine that? Helen quilting little booties for the kid? She'd flip out."

"If we thought she went nuts after the divorce…" I chuckled. "I've got a feeling we haven't seen nothing yet. She'd go ape-shit."

"I'd feel bad for whoever the chick would be." Logan shuddered, laughing at the same time. Then he stopped and studied me for a moment. "What are you going to do about Sam?"

The amusement was gone.

A cruel glint appeared and Logan added, "Mom's moving back to Fallen Crest. What's Sam going to do when you leave for college?"

I cursed. "That's for me and Sam to deal with. You don't need to worry about it."

"Screw you, Mason. I care about her, too. We both know Mom's going to want me to live with her. I, sure as shit, ain't stepping foot in Dad's place while he's got Psychopath Barbie with him, and I'm not letting Sam go back there. No way in hell."

"No way in hell?" An equally cruel look came over my face as my lips curved in a mocking smirk. "Look at you, already stepping in shoes that aren't yours."

"And they're yours?"

"Yes." My body jerked forward. Logan flinched, instinctually reacting to the sudden threat, but I stopped myself. I was tired of this. "I'll figure something out for Sam. You don't have to worry about her." And I would, even if it meant I'd be commuting to college. Nate would be pissed; he was excited for the whole college experience, but I had football and Sam to worry about.

"Mase." Logan snapped his fingers in front of my face.

"What?"

"Where'd you go just now?"

"Nowhere." All that crap could be dealt with another day. "What's the plan? Why are you still waiting? I thought you'd be long gone by now."

Logan shrugged, shoving his hands into his front pockets as he leaned back against his car again. One of his legs lifted and rested against it. A sudden yawn came over him as he glanced around the emptied lot. "I was. Everyone decided to go for pizza instead of Manny's tonight. I figured you'd go there before the party. Sam's working tonight, right?"

"I was going to see what she wanted to do." And how pissed she was at me.

"You going to eat there?"

"Maybe. You?"

"Thought about it. I'll probably get with someone tonight but we haven't had much family time this week."

"Yeah..." A slight movement from the far end of the parking lot caught my attention. Narrowing my eyes, I moved forward to get a better view. A person was coming around the corner, and that walk...it was Nate.

"What is it?"

I shook my head at Logan. Nate was heading towards us, his hands shoved deep in his sweatshirt's front pocket. His hood was pulled up, and he was hunched forward. I caught the little movement he made in the front. Nate moved to pull up his zipper.

I gestured to Logan, lowering my voice, "Can you take off? Don't let him see."

Logan frowned, but lowered his voice too. "Sure. Why?"

"Nate got laid over there."

"Say no more." And then Logan melted into the darkness, going the other way around his car.

I waited until Nate had almost gotten to our cars before I spoke up, much the same as Logan had done to me earlier. "I thought you'd be gone by now."

Nate's head whipped up and he stumbled in his footing. "Shit, Mason! You just gave me a heart attack, you fucker."

"Relish it."

"You're such an ass." Nate barked out a laugh as he pulled his keys from his pocket. Shaking his head, he asked, "What are you doing here?"

"Coach wanted to talk about the game."

"What about? We killed 'em, like we always do." Unlocking his car, he leaned inside and reached for his bag. Riffling through it, he pulled his phone out and straightened back up as he went through his messages. Then he cursed and took a deep breath. He turned around and I saw it. All the games were done. He handed his phone over. "I just got a text from Kate."

I got video of you and Parker screwing. Do what she told you to do, and it won't go on the internet.

"Is there really a video?" I frowned at the phone as I started looking for more texts from her.

He sighed and leaned back against Logan's vehicle. "I don't know. I've been trying to find out. Parker thinks there is, and I have no idea what to do anymore."

I went cold. "Is this why you've been a shady motherfucker lately?"

Nate nodded. "I've been scared. You and Logan have both been on my ass about not being a good friend. Then I wanted to say something that one night, but you guys closed ranks on me. I was shoved out so I thought, 'Fuck it. I'll fix it myself.'" He gestured to where he came from. "I've been keeping things up with Parker because I need her to find the tape. I have no idea where Kate might've put it, if she even has one."

"She says *do what she told you to do*. What are you supposed to do?"

Nate swore under his breath. "You're going to be pissed."

"Already getting there." And I was.

"They wanted me to drug Sam one night and take pictures of her." Nate didn't hold back the truth. He delivered without missing a beat. "They wanted her naked and put in embarrassing positions."

"Were you supposed to do anything to her?"

Nate hesitated, but answered a second later. "Yes, but you know I wouldn't have done any of it. I've been stalling and trying to fix this on my own."

Kate's fate was sealed. I was going to destroy her. "Push Parker to find out when the tape was created. Maybe we can figure out if there even is a tape before we call her bluff."

Nate flinched. "We're going to call her bluff?"

"We'll search her house first."

"Or you can pretend to be tight with Kate and get the tape from her."

"No."

"That's the only thing she wants—you. Kate's obsessed with you. She'll do anything for you, even hand over a video she used to blackmail your best friend."

"Kate's obsessed with power. She'll go through anyone to get it, even my friends." Nate looked away, and I paused. "Or has she already?"

"What?"

"Don't fuck with me."

He nodded, sighing at the same time. "Yeah, she's come on to me a few times. Parker doesn't know. I haven't told her yet."

If she had with him, she would've with the others. A new plan was forming in my head. "Don't. If Kate does it again, record it on your phone. We can use it against her."

"Hey." Logan came around the car. His eyes darted between us. "What's going on?"

"Nothing."

Logan shot me a questioning look.

"I'll fill you in later." I punched Nate in the shoulder. "Go to your woman. Keep stalling for us."

"Actually," Nate glanced from me to Logan, "I told her I'd meet up with her in the morning. She thinks I'm going for pizza and then Ethan's party."

Logan narrowed his eyes, his jaw locked in place, but he kept quiet.

I kept a wary eye on my brother. He wasn't known for keeping his temper in check. This was one of those moments so I said to Nate, "Then go. We'll see you later."

As Nate went to his car, I knew my brother was a heartbeat away from exploding. I lowered my voice. "Relax, okay? I'll tell you the plan in a second."

"Fine," Logan growled and waited for Nate to reverse.. As he did, Logan said, "He was with Parker just now, but it sounds like you already know—"

A screech of tires silenced him. We darted around my car and heard a thud, followed by metal crashing into metal.

Everything slowed.

Holy shit.

BEEEEEEEEEEEEEEEEEEEEEEEEEEEEEEEEEEEEEEEEEPPPPPPP PPPPPPPPP

"Oh my god," Logan breathed out next to me. We stopped, just for a moment and we stared.

Nate's car was in the middle of the intersection. Another car's front end had barreled into him and both cars were smashed together.

A sudden pause fell over me. I couldn't think, breathe, or hear anything. Then it cleared just as quick. Nate's horn kept blaring as someone screamed. Then I took off, sprinting to the accident. My heart had leapt into my throat and my feet pounded onto the pavement. I couldn't get there fast enough.

Samantha

The place was packed for the rest of the night. Heather popped her head in once to warn me Kate and her Bitch Crew had arrived. When they didn't see me, she said they left right away. A different emotion flared over her face as she passed along the message, but it was gone before I could place it. Maybe fear? But no. Heather seemed to be getting pissed by them. She couldn't be getting scared. A shiver went through me. I hoped she wasn't getting scared. That would mean they were winning. That they were getting to the one female friend I had. No one else had befriended me over the past week, and I wasn't sure if anyone would.

It was later on, a few hours before closing, when I realized she hadn't told me if Logan or Mason had arrived. I was half expecting them to find me in the back themselves. Mason would've helped me, but Heather only came back to ask if I wanted to see any of my Academy friends. I didn't. Adam and Becky both had been trying to remain friends, but there was too much disloyalty and pain that came with them.

When the grill closed, I still hadn't heard a thing. Because I didn't want to make a big deal out of it, or worry Heather, I found her brother during a break. "Brandon?"

He looked up mid-pour. "One second." Finishing, he slid the drink across the counter to his customer and headed over. Wiping his hands on a towel, he raised his eyebrows. "What's up?"

I felt so stupid. "Did any of Mason and Logan's friends come in?"

He frowned. "No, now that you mention it. That's weird. You worried?"

Not helpful. I sighed. "I'm sure things are fine. I'm just surprised, is all."

I was about to go back for the last of the dishes when Brandon tapped my arm. He'd come closer and lowered his voice, "Listen, I know what you're thinking, and that's not the case. I was being a jackass earlier. No way would Mason cheat on you."

Thanks, Brandon. I am now thinking it's a possibility.

Inching even closer, he scanned the room before he continued, "Listen, none of their crew came in." He shook his head, staring at me like I was supposed to know what that meant.

I lifted an eyebrow. "And...?"

"Oh. Yeah," he shuffled closer, "I remember those days. I know what it's like. If none of them showed up, that means something came up."

"Who are you talking about?"

"The popular crowd. You know, the 'in' crowd." He nodded and patted my shoulder. "Something came up. I'm positive."

"Why are you being awkward about this?"

"Oh." He straightened and flashed me a grin. All that awkwardness was gone as he shrugged. "It's called being a nice brother. My sis wasn't a part of the 'in'. She doesn't know what it's like. You and me," lifting an empty glass, he pointed to me and then back to him, "we know what it's like."

Of course. Perfect sense. I shook my head.

"No worries, Sam. If he didn't show, something must've come up."

"What's my brother talking about?" Heather plopped her order pad on the counter and leaned over, stretching her back at the same time.

"Nothing." I needed to know what had 'come up' like Brandon insisted. Patting my pockets, I cursed under my breath.

"What?"

"My phone's in the car."

"Go." Heather waved me off. There was an extra oomph to her grin.

Narrowing my eyes, I paused. "What?"

She went still. "What?"

"What happened to you tonight?"

"Nothing."

She'd said that too fast. My eyebrow went back up. "I call bullshit."

She laughed. "Spoken like a true friend." Then she indicated behind me, and I turned to see Channing at a back table. He'd been watching us.

"Ah." It made sense now. "So the no-boyfriend-not-anymore is here and you two are going to get not-friendly tonight?"

"Something like that." She chuckled before patting my arm again. "Go. I'm serious. I'll have him finish the few dishes that are left. It's not like he hasn't worked back there before."

He had? That was new info. I started for the door after making sure my car keys were in my pocket. As I passed by her, I muttered under my breath, "One of these days you're going to have explain your situation to me."

"Yeah," she sighed. Her tone turned wistful. "Maybe one day I'll know, too."

That was weird. As I headed out, I glanced back over my shoulder. The happiness on Heather's face was unmistakable. She had turned back to Channing and struck a seductive pose. I grinned as I remembered the first time I met her and pushed through the door.

The parking lot was surrounded by trees and on most days it was peaceful. It was beautiful during the day, but at night, it was eerie. It was especially creepy when most of the cars were gone. I had no doubt there was some big party, and drawing closer to my car, I could see that my phone's light was blinking. I had messages—

"You're that waitress from last week."

I screamed at the deep voice, jumping around in one leap. My heart was in my chest, beating loudly and trying to pound its way out. A dark figure appeared at the end of my car, and I couldn't see who it was. A hood was pulled over his face, casting it in a shadow, but he was large and muscular.

I needed mace. Why the hell hadn't I listened to Logan the one time he joked about that? "Who are you?" I demanded, taking deep breaths so my heart could settle.

His hands went in the air, surrendering and he used one to pull his hood down. "I'm sorry. Really. I'm not here to hurt you. I just..." He took a deep breath and I heard his voice shaking.

It was Brett Broudou.

My eyes got even wider and my heart started racing again. His words weren't very reassuring. I started backing away. "What do you want?"

"Nothing." He held his hand out to me. "Stop. Please. I'm really not here to hurt you or scare you."

"I beg to differ. I'm scared shitless right now."

"I'm sorry."

"You're huge."

"I know," he grimaced and slunk back a few steps. His shoulders went down, like he was trying to make himself smaller. "I'm really not here to scare you. That's my brother. He's like that."

I hadn't taken much account of how he looked in Manny's the other week. I'd been too focused on avoiding them and the guys hid me right away at the gas station, but I had a better view now. He had a square face that was a little meaty from his bulky size. His nose was crooked, like he had broken it once and it never healed right. A slight scar ran down from his nose to his top lip. His lips had formed into a tentative grin. Peering closer, I tried to see his eyes better. Mason always told me that you could read a person's intent through their eyes, but I couldn't see his. It was too dark. Again, because we were in an almost emptied parking lot that only had one working light over it. Not the best meeting place to pick.

He didn't look ready to attack me, but looks could be deceiving. My tone went flat. "Tell me what you want or I'm leaving. Next time find me in a crowded place if you want to talk, or better yet, don't." But there had been something in his tone. Regret? Maybe something else, friendliness? I wasn't sure, but my heart slowed a little and my chest wasn't as tight.

"I know." His head went down, and he made a show of taking another large step backwards. "I...um...whoa. This isn't going how I thought it was going to at all."

This? How he wanted it to go? I frowned. What was he talking about?

"Um," he cleared his throat and tried another smile. "So...you're friends with Jax?"

"Jax?"

"Heather." He gestured inside. "Channing, her on-again-off-again whatever they are, goes to my school. He's pretty cool. So's she."

"She threatened you guys."

"Well," he shrugged, shifting on his feet, "I mean, I can understand. My brother can be mean...sometimes..." he trailed off, glancing around.

Was he checking for witnesses?

"Um."

He didn't *sound* like someone getting ready to attack.

"So..."

Yes? My heart began pounding again. Thump. Thump. Thump.

"I was wondering," he stopped, and looked around once more.

Seriously. The guy was going to give me a heart attack. "I'm going to go home."

"No. Wait." His hands fell down and he cupped them together; his head lowered too. "Heather doesn't seem to like us coming to

Manny's, so I've stayed away, but I don't know you. I'm figuring you don't go to our school. I was looking for you this past week." A self-conscious laugh came from him. "I don't even know your name. She might've said it, but I was just paying attention to my brother. Budd can be a jerk sometimes…Shannon too, though she's a girl. There's another name for that."

"I know. It rhymes with ditch."

The corner of his mouth curved up. It started to transform his face, from what I could see in the shadows. "Yeah. So…" His nervousness was now all-too clear.

My heart sank. I was starting to figure out where this was going.

"I was just…um…so, do you… No, that's not right. Uh…" He took a deep breath, pinning me with his gaze now. "Would you like to go out sometime?"

Yep. I saw it coming. I figured it out, but it still didn't curb the shock, and my mouth fell open. He just asked me out. A Broudou brother. Me. It all clicked with me now. He still had no idea who I was. I was just 'that waitress' who works at Manny's. "Um…" I closed my mouth. I had no idea what to say.

"Oh." He drew away from me even further. "I see."

"No," I started, but stopped. What the hell was I going to say? "Um…I have a boyfriend."

"Oh." He straightened, now filled with relief. His voice came out stronger, more confident. "I see. Who?"

"W-w-what?"

"OH!" His head flew up, and he slapped himself in the forehead. "I'm really sorry. It ain't any of my business. I wasn't going to beat him up or anything. Budd does that stuff. I don't. I mean, he gets me in trouble too sometimes, but I wouldn't do that. I think you're really pretty. The guy's lucky, whoever he is, and don't tell me. I don't want to know. I don't want you to be scared. We have a reputation. I understand and all."

He was rambling. I had rejected him, and I was beginning to feel sympathy for this Broudou brother. Hell had frozen over. The world had shifted on its axis.

"I'm going to go now." He started to turn.

"Wait," I stopped him.

He stopped.

Now I wanted to slap myself in the forehead. Why had I done that? I lowered my hand, hadn't realized I even lifted it. "Nothing. Sorry."

"Okay. Well, bye."

"Bye…"

Awkward. The whole thing had been awkward, but lucky me. Brett left in the same manner he had appeared—he just disappeared. I had no idea where he'd gone.

Brett Broudou asked me out. Me, Samantha Strattan. I nodded to myself. There was something funny about that. Then I remembered Mason—my phone. Hurrying inside my car, I grabbed it and hit the screen. The first text stopped everything.

At the hospital. Car accident.

The phone fell from my fingers.

CHAPTER TEN

The drive to the hospital passed in a blur. I was on auto pilot and somehow found myself shoving through the doors to the emergency room without a clue how I got there. Taking two heart-stopping steps, my foot lifted for another when I spotted Logan in the corner. His head was down, his arms folded over his chest, leaning against a wall. His friends were around him—guys and girls I didn't recognize—but no Mason.

My chest lifted and my lungs struggled to take a breath.

Then Logan lifted his head. It happened in slow motion, his eyes scanned the room and then he saw me. Surprise came over him before it clicked. Comprehension flared next. My foot came down hard. It was worse than I thought, but he shook his head and pushed off the wall. His movement drew attention, and everyone watched him cross to me.

"No, no, Sam. It's not like that."

I was too scared to say a word. For one split second, I considered running. If I didn't know, I couldn't lose him, but I had to know. "Is it bad?" *Tell me he's alive.*

"He's fine. The brakes were cut so he got blindsided by an oncoming car. He couldn't stop when he was leaving the lot. I would've driven onto the grass or something, not out into an intersection." Logan rolled his eyes. His arm came around my shoulder and he jerked me against him. I could feel the laughter reverberating through his chest. "He's such an idiot, but it's a good thing he drives like a grandpa sometimes."

My eyes closed and I sagged under his arm. I couldn't believe it. *Mason is going to be fine. Mason is going to be fine. Mason is going to be fine. I could breathe,* I tried telling myself over and over, but my brain and my body weren't working together. My chest was still tight, stretched from fear.

"Sam?" Logan jostled me a little, hugging me tighter into his side. "You okay?"

Mason was going to be fine.

I opened my mouth to fill my lungs. Nothing.

"Sam?"

I heard him and my eyes flew open. Mason was at the end of a hallway, frowning at us, and a rush of relief came over me. My mouth dropped, but then he was heading towards me. As he drew near, he asked, "You okay?"

A buzzing sound was in my head. I shook it so I could hear him, but then his hand was on my arm, and he tugged me from Logan. Oh my god. My arms were numb, but I wrapped them around him and tried to hold tight.

He moved us and somehow we were in a private room. Looking around, I saw a small room with some clothes lying on a cot. There was also a computer and a small TV. It looked like we were in a room where the doctors slept when they were on-call. I closed my eyes when his head bent and I felt his breath on my neck. It felt good. It felt reassuring. I tried to hold him even tighter, but he asked, "What's wrong? Nate's going to be fine."

Wait.

I leaned back. "Nate?" My voice was shaking.

He frowned at me. "Yeah."

"Nate? Nate was in the car accident?"

"Yeah."

He was still looking at me, frowning as his eyes roamed over my face. Then it all hit me and I shoved him away. "I thought it was you! I thought you'd been hurt and that I was going to lose you."

I threw my arm up, gesturing to the lobby. "Logan's talking about what an idiot you are, but I thought someone had crashed into your car!"

"No." He tugged me back into his arms. "You're shouting."

I didn't care. "I thought it was you!"

"It wasn't!" he yelled over me. "Calm down. I'm sorry—"

Shoving my hand into my pocket, I pulled my phone out and checked the number. It was Logan's number. I put it in his face. "Logan texted me. Not you. I thought it was you. Why else would Logan be the one to text me? And he texted! He should've called—no!—you should've called! And why didn't you even tell me about your basketball game? I had no idea. I'm new, remember? I don't know these things, and no one talks to me—"

"I'm sorry." Mason was fighting back a grin as he pulled me against his chest and wrapped both arms around me. He took the phone from my hand and pushed it back into my pocket. The intense anger kept me stiff in his embrace, and I lifted a fist to his stomach. He said, "I knew you had to work tonight. I didn't say anything because I didn't want you to feel bad about missing the game. I'm sorry…again…I'm sorry, Sam. I am. I was the one driving. I told Logan to call you, but we were right behind the ambulance so he texted instead. I'm sorry. Next time I'll be the one to call you."

Oh shit. Next time. There better not be a next time. "Mason…" The anger left me then, and a void took its place. There was a big gaping hole left in me. I thought I had lost him.

"I'm sorry."

Mason…

I couldn't even finish that thought. I was just so relieved it hadn't been him. My knees sagged in relief. "Is Nate okay?"

He nodded, looking down at me, searching inside of me. "Yeah, he's fine."

"Logan said his brakes were cut?"

"Yeah." His jaw went rigid. "My guess is that it was Budd and Brett Broudou."

My eyes got wide. Oh holy shit. "Can you prove that?"

"Who cares about proving? We already know."

Oh. My heart started beating fast. Now would be a good time for that second confession… I took a deep breath and stepped away from him. "Mason?"

"Yeah?"

Three…

Two…

"Yo." The door burst open, and Logan popped his head inside. "The doc wants to see you. He's waiting for you by the nurse's station."

Mason moved around him and took off. He disappeared around the corner. There went one…

"You okay?"

I nodded. "Never better."

"I heard you shouting." He propped his shoulder against the doorframe and kept studying me. "I'm sorry about the mishap. I should've told you we were fine; I just didn't think about it."

"Yeah."

"Sam?"

There was a giant ball of guilt and worry in my stomach. I had to tell them about Budd and Brett. It'd been too long ago, but with Brett asking me out, Mason and Logan needed to know first. "Logan?"

"Yeah?"

"What are you guys going to do?"

He frowned, but moved inside so the door shut behind him. Same room, different Kade. "What do you mean?"

"I mean, you guys are going to do something to get even." It wasn't a question. That was a fact. Everyone knew it. "What are you going to do?"

He lifted one shoulder. "I don't know. Nate will probably make the decision. They did this to him. Of course, I'm guessing they did it because he clipped Budd with his car." His eyes turned feral. "Now I wish he'd gotten hit harder, would've put him in the hospital first."

I sucked in a breath. "Are you guys going to hurt them?" Did I want that? Didn't that mean they'd retaliate? Mason or Logan could get hurt. That couldn't happen. Maybe I could talk to Brett…no. I'd make it worse then. "They'll hurt you guys back."

"Oh." Understanding flashed in his eyes and he lifted a hand. It went to my arm, meant to comfort me, but I bolted into him. Bumping against his chest, I wrapped my arms and hugged tight. Logan was family. Mason was more. I couldn't lose either of them.

I mumbled against him, "Don't hurt them. They'll hurt you back. I can't handle that."

"Oh, Sam."

"Logan, promise me."

He stiffened under my arms and moved me back. "I can't promise you that."

I knew it.

It felt as if a hand reached inside of me and was gripping my heart.

Logan added, "I'm sorry, but they're going to do it anyway. They're looking for you. Why do you think that is?"

"For running lessons?" My voice came out high-pitched and shrill. The panic was full blown. "Why wouldn't they?"

He sighed and shook his head. As he bit down on the corner of his lip, I turned away. I couldn't see the pity there. They were going to do it anyways, no matter the consequences. One of them was already hurt. When would they be next? I knew it was only a matter of time.

I had to try again. "Please, Logan. Go to the police. This is going to end badly."

"They're hoping to hurt you. You're Mason's girlfriend. Everyone knows how protective we are of you. You're our weakness, Sam. We have to finish this before they do something to you."

I gritted my teeth. Mason and Logan would not get hurt, not if I had anything to do with it…

"Logan," Mason called from down the hall.

"Gotta go." Logan cupped the back of my head and pressed a chaste kiss to my forehead. "You okay?"

I nodded. The numbing sensation had left, but it was coming back. As he broke away and headed off, I couldn't shake the uneasy feeling. I was given a glimpse into the future. One where it was one of them, not Nate, in that hospital bed, but it was worse.

"Um," a voice broke through my reverie. I jerked my head sideways and saw a girl standing in the doorway. Her top lip was curled up in a sneer, and she was eyeing me up and down. Dressed in an oversized sweatshirt and jeans that clung to her tiny form, I figured she was cheerleader. The glitter was still on her cheeks. Tucking a strand of her hair behind her ear, she pointed at me with her other hand. "Your leg is ringing."

My leg is ringing… Oh. My phone.

It was James. I closed my eyes for a second and heaved a big sigh. I could only take so much, but I answered as I left the room and headed back outside. "Hello?"

"Sam." His relief was clear. "Thank you for answering. I can't get Mason or Logan on the phone."

"They're busy right now."

"I know. Is Nate okay?"

I frowned. "How do you know?"

"About the accident? His parents were called, but they're in New Zealand so they called me right away."

His parents? Sometimes I forgot he had them. "Uh, I'm not sure. I think he's fine. Mason and Logan are with the doctor right now."

"Yes. His parents told the doctor to release information to them. Are they okay?"

I shrugged. "I don't know. I'm sure they're worried."

He was silent. Then, he added, "No, not Nate's parents. I meant my sons. Are they all right?"

"Oh. Yeah, they're fine."

"Good." I could picture him, nodding with the phone pressed to his ear. "That's good. Do you think I should come down there?"

Oh dear god. "NO! I mean, no." There was no way I could handle Analise right now.

He gentled his voice. "I wouldn't bring her, Sam. Not to this. I know Helen was called as well. I'm sure she's heading there now."

My heart started to race again. I couldn't handle her either. "She is?" My fingers gripped the phone tight.

"Yeah, that's why I'm trying to get ahold of my sons. Could you ask them if they want me to come down? Neither have responded to my earlier text about them moving back in and dinner."

"Um…"

"I'd imagine Helen will want them to stay with her," he commented without waiting, then continued, "and I'm sure they won't want to stay at Nate's house since his parents are coming."

They are? That was not in the conversation. Had I missed that?

"Do you need a place to stay? I couldn't imagine Helen being okay with you being at the hotel with them."

"What?" I squeaked into the phone. Was it possible to have a heart attack at my age? It was pounding in my chest. A rush of heat came over me as chills went down my spine at the same time.

"Sam?"

Hearing Mason's voice, I jumped, and turned in the air. His eyes widened when he saw my face, and he took two steps to reach me. My phone was plucked from my hand and he barked into it, "Who is this?"

The fight left him when he heard his father's voice.

Mason

Glancing at Sam as I drove to Nate's house, I watched as she curled in a ball. The seat belt was restricting her from completing the fetal position, but that wasn't what sent a searing pang through me. It was the look on her face. She was lost. I recognized the look and heard her sniffle, trying to cover up the lone tear at the corner of her eye. I figured it had something to do with our upheaval. Nate's parents were flying in. The last I heard, they were in New Zealand so they'd be here in a day, but we would be booted out when they arrived. James said that Helen was coming as well. That meant she would book a suite in the best hotel, expecting Logan and me to be there.

She had a rude awakening coming. Sam was coming too.

Reaching over, I put a hand on her thigh. She glanced up, her dark eyes made darker by her misery. "Things will work out." I tried to reassure her with a smile.

She closed her eyes. Just like that, I'd been given a window to her soul, and then she took it away. Sam would never know how much that affected me. I needed to feel connected to her. Sometimes it was like air to me—I needed it to breathe. When she would pull away, it staggered me—every time. I tried again, "It will, Sam." They opened again, baring her insides to me. My lungs filled as the connection happened.

"I thought it was you," she whispered.

I frowned.

"When Logan sent that text, I thought it was all over."

Regret washed over me. "I'm sorry. I should've asked what Logan texted. No, I should've called you myself. I'm sorry." I grimaced. If I'd gotten a text like that, I would've gone nuts. My reaction would've been a lot worse than hers had been. Even considering it, the beginning of rage swirled inside of me. I don't know what I would do if she was ever hurt…

Then she sent another pang through me when she said, "I can't go back to my mom's. I thought I could before. I was willing to do it for you and Logan. I think you guys should live with your dad. It's your last semester here," her voice hitched on that last statement, "you should have as many memories with your dad that you can."

"We can't. Sam—"

"I know." She sat up and faced me.

She was now in the shadows, but the streetlights flashed over her, illuminating her for a brief second. As I watched, her eyes never changed. There was always such earnestness mixed with sadness in them. Everything in me sank. There'd always been pain in her, but it had gone away for a little while, but it was back now. It had increased. My eyebrows furrowed together. Was this because of my dad?

She murmured, "You said your mom would get you guys' hotel rooms." She bit her lip. "I can't stay with my mom, not if you guys aren't there. There's no way."

"You won't." My voice grew rough. "You're staying with us."

"But your mom—"

"I don't care about my mom. If she thinks she can push you out…there's no way in hell. You're staying with us."

"But what if she—"

"Sam." My hand gripped her thigh harder, my fingers sinking into her jeans. "I don't care what my mom says. Logan and I both have our own money. We can get our own room. Besides, even if you didn't stay with me, for some unknown reason that I can't imagine, Logan would have you in his room. He'd hide you in his suitcase or something." I grinned at her. "You're covered no matter what."

Her eyes held mine, so stricken and vulnerable.

I tried not to let it slip, but this was killing me. Sam was strong. I knew that. I'd seen it and it was one of the things that drew me to her in the first place, but she was fragile too. I could see her nearing the line of too-much. The fight with her mom had almost defeated her. I couldn't fight for her, not with that battle. It was on the inside. She was still dealing with all the emotional turmoil Analise shoveled at her.

Fuck her, that'd been my theory for Sam's mother from the beginning, but I knew she needed to put Analise behind her on her own. If she didn't, her mother would still hold so much power over Sam and nothing good would ever happen then.

Analise Strattan was toxic. She ruined everything she touched. It was only a matter of time before she'd ruin my father, but James remained with her, his eyes wide open. He knew what he was getting himself into. I would never have sympathy for my dad. He refused to leave Analise, so fuck him. She hurt Sam. I was done with my dad as long as he was with that woman.

Feeling Sam slip her hand underneath mine, I broke out of my thoughts.

She smiled at me. She didn't waver, but the sadness in her eyes would haunt me. I lifted her hand and pressed a kiss to the back of it.

"What was that for?"

I shrugged, putting our hands back in her lap. Then I took a deep breath. I was rattled. I thought my best friend had died. Now his parents were coming back. I knew they would circle the wagons. He'd be banned from seeing me. There was a lot left to handle. Parker. Whatever else Kate was planning. I had a strong feeling when my mom got here, she wouldn't be leaving for a while.

Things were about to get interesting.

It seemed to take forever to get to the house, but when we did, I held the door for her. Sam brushed against my arm, and the need to have her was sudden and overwhelming. I reached for her without thinking, but stopped. More and more waves of intense desire rocked through me. I wanted her. I wanted to be wrapped up in her. I wanted to pin her against the wall right then and there.

Holy shit.

My hand shook as I forced it to return back to my side. She paused in the door, stood on her tiptoes and pressed a kiss to my lips before moving inside.

I let loose a ragged breath. Fuck. Needing Sam had developed into an addiction after my first taste, but she had no idea how she could affect me. If I was being honest with myself, I was scared of letting her know. Marriages could be broken from that. If someone had more power over the other, they could use that love to manipulate the other. It went down the same all the time. Even with Tate and Logan. He adored her, and she didn't care. She had all the power and had used it to walk all over him.

A part of me knew that Sam was different. I could tell her, and she wouldn't use it against me, but I didn't know for certain. I was too scared to find out, so I kept quiet. She knew I loved her. She just didn't know how much.

"You okay?" Her voice carried around the corner.

I needed to clear my head. My dick twitched. I needed to clear that too. Dropping my hand, I adjusted myself before answering back, "I'm fine."

When I entered the kitchen, she had the freezer open and pulled out an ice cream carton. That was good. She was eating. Sam hadn't said a word about it, but I knew she didn't eat enough. "You hungry for anything else?"

"What?" She dug in with a large spoon.

I fell silent, leaning against one of the counters as I watched her put two big-sized portions of ice cream in her bowl before pushing the carton aside. Neither of us had bothered to turn the light on. The moonlight filtered in through the windows enough so we had no problem seeing. I liked it on nights like tonight. It helped with masking emotions at times.

"Nothing," I answered.

"You sure you're okay?" She turned from the counter, bowl in hand, but didn't lift the spoon from it. She wore a small frown and her eyes were filled with concern.

My dick twitched again. And love. Her eyes were filled with love too. I tried to reassure her with a small grin. "I'm good. You want a burger or something?"

"Oh." She glanced down at the bowl. "No, I'm good with ice cream. It's been a long night."

I grunted. That was true enough.

"Are you okay?"

This was the second time she'd asked. "I'm fine."

"Mason."

"Sam?" I grinned at her as fantasies of taking her, pinning her against the nearest counter, and pushing inside of her overwhelmed me. Sam had been through too much tonight for me to be that rough with her. She deserved better.

"You can talk about it, you know?"

"About what?"

"Nate. The car accident. He's your best friend. I'm not stupid. It must have rattled you." As she finished her statement, she sat on a chair at the table and drew her knee against her chest. Wrapping her arms around it, she lifted her bowl and spoon, but propped her chin on top of her knee. Filling her spoon with ice cream, she popped it into her mouth.

I watched how she savored the taste of it. My dick was full force again.

Enough.

Pushing off from the counter, I went to her. I didn't pause, even when her eyes got big and the bowl fell from her hands. I needed her now. I needed her any way I could get her, and I wasn't going to be gentle.

"Mason?" She squealed when I lifted her in my arms.

As she looked in my eyes, she saw the hunger in mine—I wasn't hiding it. That feeling, needing to be enraptured by her, wasn't meant to be hidden or repressed. It was meant to be shared. When her mouth opened, a soft sigh left her, and I knew she felt it too. Her hand lifted to cup the side of my face.

It was one of those touches that I savored.

Carrying her upstairs, I didn't make a sound. Neither did she. I just watched her. When I went inside our room, I lowered her to the floor, but kept her against me before I kicked the door shut.

I savored that feeling, too. Bending down, my hands still on her waist, I breathed her in. She smelled of fresh air and vanilla. She never wore the fancy stuff or the expensive stuff. I'd seen her in the mornings when she would lift her body spray and use one spray. It was enough. The scent of her was embedded in me; I'd never forget it.

I'd never get enough of her.

"Mason?" she murmured again, her voice throaty.

My eyes opened and saw that she was watching me. Her hands were on my chest, but she was clinging to my gaze.

Lifting my hands, I cupped both sides of her face. Without realizing I was going to, I asked, "Do you know how much I love you?"

She shuddered before me, and her mouth fell open another inch. Her eyes got wider and a look of wonderment shone through.

She didn't know the depth of my love for her, but that was part of her magic. It was one of the reasons I loved her. She had no clue what made her special or what made her beautiful. It wasn't her trim body. It wasn't how my hands fit perfectly around her waist or how her breasts fit in the palms of my hands. It wasn't even how her dark eyes would tear up when I'd whisper my love to her, or how her perfect lips would open. Samantha was gorgeous, but she had no idea. She didn't think about looks. I watched her this week at school. She had no idea how people watched her. She thought it was because of me, but it wasn't. People watched her because she was beautiful. She had a look that no one did. It was natural and graceful. She was kind and loving. The guys could see it with one glance. All of them wanted her. I knew it, but she was mine, and the girls, the nicer girls liked her without even talking to her. The others were jealous. She had what they didn't, inside and outside beauty.

She had no idea just how rare she was.

She had no fucking clue, and I didn't have the words to tell her. Even if I did, she'd be uncomfortable at the idea. She'd fidget, look anywhere other than at me, and then convince herself that I was being dramatic. Samantha didn't know how to be loved—her mother made sure of that—so she'd never understand how special she truly was.

With that last thought, my hand fell from her cheek to her thigh. I took a firm grip, my fingers sinking into her leg, and I lifted her into my arms.

She gasped, but she wrapped her arms around my neck. Grinning, she murmured, "What's this about?"

"I'm not going to be gentle." My blood was pumping too much for that to happen. "I'm not going to be quick." God no. I was going to enjoy the feel of her body underneath mine. All of her soft curves, the little gasps she made when I was inside of her, and the feel of her hands skimming over me. I was going to make it last. "And you are going to be thoroughly fucked when I'm through with you."

I lowered her onto the bed. As she kneeled on the mattress before me, her shoulders and chest lifted when she took a deep breath. Her hands were on my chest, and she tipped her head back. Her dark hair fell backwards, and then she grinned. The look of her made my heart skip before pounding back with a renewed vigor.

In a soft husky tone, she murmured, "What's taking you so long?"

That was all the okay I needed.

I took her lips with mine. I claimed her, forcing her to open for me, and swept inside to taste every inch. That was just the beginning. I heard another soft sigh from her. She always did that, right before she surrendered to me. With that sound, she pressed against me so every inch of her was touching me and her hands wrapped around my neck. Then she pulled me down to her, and I knew I could do whatever I wanted.

So I did.

CHAPTER ELEVEN

Samantha

The rest of the weekend passed quickly. Nate had a concussion, three fractured ribs, and a strained back injury. He was kept in the hospital until his parents arrived. When they did, it was with gusto. Their first point of business was banning Mason and Logan from their son's hospital room. They were good enough to be allowed information, but Mason explained later that night that Nate's parents had never approved of their friendship. It was why they moved Nate from Fallen Crest in the beginning. He was only allowed to come back for his last semester because he was eighteen. When I asked how they could even ban them from his room since he was an adult, Mason only shrugged. His reply was, "Guess the hospital has different policies for rich movie producers. I'm sure they're hoping to get a donation out of them."

In the end, he still snuck in to see Nate the next night, but it was after we packed our things and checked into a hotel. He wanted to avoid Nate's parents. Logan overheard him and when the door closed behind him, he commented, "He wants to avoid our mom, too."

That sent panic through me. He wasn't the only one. An hour later, I followed in Mason's trail, except I went to Manny's. When Heather's dad told me it was her night off, I tried their house then. While Mason was seeing his best friend, so was I. I spent most of the night on her couch. We watched movies, and she filled me in on the latest rumors about Nate's car accident. There were two competing theories: The first was that the Broudou brothers cut the wrong brakes; they meant to cut Mason's. The second was that Kate had cut the brakes to hurt Nate, so it would hurt Mason.

There were a few others, but they were ridiculous. Nate's parents owed money to the mob. Nate just wanted attention. Nate was the one that actually caused the accident, and the cops were covering for him.

The first two sent chills down my spine. I stopped asking about any more theories, and we went back to the movie. I thought about asking if she received any more texts from Kate or her friends, but I didn't. A part of me didn't want to know. I didn't want to worry about losing my one female friend.

It was late when I returned to the hotel. Slipping inside the suite, I wasn't surprised to find it empty. Logan texted that Ethan was throwing a party to celebrate that Nate was alive. Mason texted an hour after Logan saying that he was leaving the hospital and was going to the party. He asked if I wanted to go, but I declined. There'd been too much drama for me, so I enjoyed the solitude of the room that night.

My drama free night carried on to the next morning.

Helen had checked into her own room, but she was on a different floor.

When I learned that, my relief was powerful. My knees almost buckled, but I caught the table and plopped down on a chair. I landed harder than normal, but I didn't care. I ignored the smirk Logan gave me and then he gave me even better news. They were going to spend the day with their mother. Neither of them asked if I wanted to go along. They both knew I'd rather hang out with Kate and her princess bullies.

It wasn't long after that when I went for my run, but instead of running from the hotel, I drove to my old neighborhood. There was a trail from a nearby park that connected to the trail that went behind Quickie's. The scenery was too beautiful to miss. Even before I parked, I was already itching to fly up the hills behind the gas station. Maybe it was the anticipation of pushing myself up those hills, but my run went faster than normal. It was invigorating and when I ran back, two hours later, I considered going for another hour, but I didn't. I needed my energy to start on my homework. However, when I drove past my old house, I stopped the car. I don't know why. I wasn't nostalgic about the home. There were a lot of bad memories in it, but I sat in the car and stared at it. Maybe I was more tired from the run than I realized. Maybe I wanted to avoid doing homework. Or maybe I missed the slight semblance of normalcy that the house used to give me, but whatever it was, I stayed for an hour. I didn't move from the car. I just stared at the house. No one was home, but when I saw a car that I thought was my dad's, I started my engine and drove away.

I didn't tell Mason about my run. I didn't know why. There wasn't anything significant about it, but I realized that I didn't want to tell him about my old house. When they came home and he got in bed with me, I asked about their day with their mother. As he filled me in, I kept wondering if that car had been David's. Maybe he'd been home. Maybe he saw me there.

"Sam?"

"Mmm?"

Mason grinned, tipping my head up to meet his eyes. "What's wrong? You spaced there for a second."

"Oh." I shrugged, dipping my head back down. "Nothing."

I could feel his gaze on me and knew his wheels were spinning. "I talked to my mom. She won't come up here. She knows you're staying here and agreed it would be for the best if she stayed away. Is that what's bothering you?"

"Oh." Had that been my dad in that car? Why was I even thinking about him? "That's fine. I'm tired. That's all."

Mason knew I lied to him, but he didn't push. I was thankful.

I was thankful for my social outcast status the next day at school as well. It was peaceful, but when I went to gym class, I should've been prepared. I wasn't. Kate had warned me on the first day, but she spent the rest of the week focusing all her threats on Heather. It was only a matter of time before she turned her attention back to me.

It happened when I was done showering. All of my clothes were gone. It didn't take a genius to figure out where they were.

"Um..."

The locker room emptied as soon as I stepped from the shower. It made sense now, but there was a girl behind me. She wore a baggy sweatshirt and a baggy pair of jeans. Her sneakers might've been white at one point, but they were frayed on the soles and almost black now. She brushed a strand of red hair behind her ear, but it popped back out instantly. It was frizzy, and I knew it would've been beautiful if she would put some hair gel into it. Her eyes held my interest. There was no sympathy or warmth. She jerked her hand over her shoulder and said in a flat tone, "If you need clothes, I might have some for you."

"You wouldn't get in trouble for helping me out?"

She lifted one shoulder, but the blank face remained. "I don't really care. It's not like they'd know who helped you. They aren't my clothes."

"You keep the lost and found in your locker?"

"No." I caught a glimmer of a grin as she went to her locker. When she handed me a boy's jersey, the name on the back made me pause—Kade. "Uh...?"

"Told you." She pulled out a pair of jeans that looked like they'd been on the bottom of her locker for years. They were wrinkly and smelled musky. Then she handed me a swimsuit, which looked new. That was comforting. "The shirt and jeans belonged to a friend of mine. No one's seen them in years since she transferred two years ago, but the suit's mine. It's clean; I was going to go swimming after school, but I can borrow one of my friend's."

They'd do in a pinch. "Did they at least leave my shoes?"

"Yeah." She pointed to my locker. My shoes had been stored underneath a bench. "I don't think they knew which ones were yours." Twenty other pairs of shoes were beside them, lined up and down the row of lockers.

"Small favors, huh?" I gave her a grin, but her facial expression still didn't change. It was still blank and flat. Then she started to go around me. "Wait. Who was your friend?"

"No one you'd know." She didn't stop and continued to the door.

I lifted Mason's jersey. "I'm betting that I might. This was Mason's, wasn't it?"

"Yeah, but like I said, you wouldn't know her. She wasn't his girlfriend or anything." She paused. "And she wasn't a stalker either. They were friends."

Then it clicked. "Marissa."

That finally got a reaction from her. Her eyelid twitched and she frowned. "He's talked about her?"

"A little. I know they were friends."

"Oh."

"And you were friends with her, too?"

"She left those clothes in my locker all the time. Kate and friends did the same thing to her. She liked wearing his jersey because it shut 'em up." She took a small breath. "Anyways, there you go. You don't have to give them back or anything. It's not like Marissa still wants them."

She started to push open the door, but I asked, "Would you tell me about her?"

She let the door close again. "Why?"

I shrugged, clutching the clothes to my chest. I was standing there, dripping wet from my shower and the towel was starting to slip, but I was insistent. "I'd like to know more about her. He doesn't say too much."

She snorted. "I'm not surprised by that." The small opening that had appeared was gone. The wall was back in place. "Good luck with the Princess Bitches. See you."

I didn't move for a while after she left. Mason never talked about his friend except that she'd been bullied by Tate and Kate's group. I never pushed him for information. He'd tell me if I did, but I wanted to hear it from someone else. This girl was Marissa's friend, and in the two minutes that I had talked to her, I could tell she still missed her.

She had been kind to me and I didn't even get her name.

With that depressing thought, I heard voices outside the door and knew the next gym class would be heading inside, so I darted into the bathroom stall and changed. The jersey hung on me and the jeans were a little baggy, but they would do. The swimsuit helped underneath since my bra and underwear had gone missing as well.

When I went into the hallway, the reaction wasn't what they wanted. Mouths dropped and girls bent close to whisper to each other. At the end of the hallway, Kate was at Natalie's locker. She was furious and looked ready to march over, but Mason came up from behind me. He wrapped an arm around my waist and nudged me against my locker. His hand lifted to hold the back of my head so I didn't hit the locker, but he pressed into me.

Dropping his head, he kissed my neck. As his lips caressed me, he asked, "Where did you get this? This was my freshman jersey."

I spotted a few girls beside us, within hearing distance, and shrugged. "Just something I found in the locker room."

One girl made a sound of disgust before shoving from her locker. She stormed down the hallway, past Kate, sneering at her as well before she turned into the senior hallway.

"Who was that?"

"Hmmm?" Mason lifted his head from my neck and glanced around. "Who?"

"No one."

"Hey, nauseating lovebirds." Heather appeared at my locker. She gave Mason a bright smile and placed her hands on her hips like she was going to do a cheer for him. I caught the twinge of tension in her gaze before it slipped away. "I need to steal your gal, Kade. I need her to walk me to my next class."

His hands fell away and he stepped back, but he frowned. "You keep interrupting. When's your boyfriend transferring? I'd like to return all these favors."

"Ha, ha. We both know you're proud of your girl for landing a friend like me." She pointed to her own chest, walking backwards and looping her other elbow through mine. "I'm a hot commodity. There's only one Heather Jax in this town."

"That doesn't make you a hot commodity. That makes you expendable. No one would miss you."

She pretended to hiss, grinning at the same time. "That hurts, Kade. I thought we had something going between the two of us."

"The boyfriend and best friend never like each other."

Her eyes widened and she paused in her footing for a second, but lifted her fingers to her forehead. She saluted him. "You win, Mason Kade. You always do."

But there was no response. Mason had already turned and was walking the other way. Even now, with their little exchange, so many people had been hanging onto every word. As he passed by groups in the hallway, the girls followed him with hungry gazes. A few didn't, but the guys were almost as bad. A lot of them stopped what they were doing and puffed out their chests. Their backs straightened and most struck a cocky pose until he walked past them, without acknowledging them. When he disappeared into the senior hallway, the hallway went back to normal. The girls giggled and whispered. The guys, most of them, went back to their drooped shoulders and lounging stances.

I'd never get used to it. I don't know how he did it.

"I heard what happened," Heather brought me back from my thoughts. Her hand tightened on my arm and she pulled me closer, lowering her voice. "You okay?"

"Yeah." Waves of anger and curiosity mixed together now. One thing at a time. "Do you know a girl that used to be friends with Marissa?"

"Marissa?"

"I don't know her last name. She was friends with Mason and transferred out of here two years ago."

"Oh." Her facial features tightened and her lips pinched together. "Yeah. Red hair? Frizzy? Average weight?"

"Yeah. Who is she?"

"Her name's Paige." She grimaced. "I wouldn't get close to her."

"Why not?"

Stopping at her locker, I leaned against the one beside it and waited as she opened the combination. "Because she will never be your friend. A lot of girls lust after your boys, but there's a few that hate them. Paige is one of them. She blamed Mason for everything that happened to Marissa."

"And by everything that happened to Marissa, you mean…" I gestured to my clothes. "Getting her clothes stolen."

She grabbed her book and shut her locker, but turned to fall against it with her back. "Getting the clothes stolen is the first step. That's why I found you right away."

"How'd you know?"

"My friend Cory's in your gym class."

"The one…" I frowned, trying to remember and then it clicked. "The angry one? She wears black. She hated me on sight."

"Yeah, that one."

"And she's another one of those girls who hates Mason and Logan?"

"No, she doesn't hate them, not like Paige. She hates Kate and her friends. She doesn't like Mason and Logan because they never stopped Kate. She's been okay this semester so far, but everyone can sense she's got things in the works. It's tense around here. Don't you feel it? You're not coming into this school at a good time."

It was because of me. Everyone knew that and it was starting to make sense why the welcome wagon had been missing. It'd been doused in gasoline somewhere, waiting for Kate to strike the match.

I couldn't do anything about it. That was the hard part. "How'd you escape their wrath?"

Heather chuckled. "I don't know, but if I were to guess, it's because of Channing at Roussou. He's still in my life. Everyone knows that and he holds his own over there. If they did anything to me, he'd get even. That," her head bobbed forward, "and because I think one of those four always had a thing for him."

"One of them with someone from Roussou?"

"He's hot. People can still date between the two schools. It's not really encouraged, but it's not forbidden or anything." She laughed again, eyeing me up and down. "But that doesn't matter anymore. We both know I'm on Kate's shit list now."

The first bell rang at that moment, and everyone started to scatter.

I shook my head at the mass chaos. "I feel like we go to school with a pack of wolves. It's everyone for themselves."

Heather grinned. "Only the strong survive here."

"Yeah, well, I don't like to fight back. I will when I can't avoid it, but I'm starting to realize being proactive might be the best solution here."

"Hey." She grabbed my arm before I could go to my class and pulled me back. Her eyes grew hard. "That's why I found you. Stealing your clothes is the first step. Kate and her Bitch Crew don't do cliché pranks. You're not going to find your clothes in a toilet. They did this to Marissa a few times. They'd steal her clothes and put them on a mannequin. Natalie's aunt owns a clothing store and I think that's where they get them. They'll take pictures of it wearing your clothes and then Photoshop it to make it look like you. They'll even have a picture of your face blurred on the thing. It's really creepy how close to being real it is. Then they'll put the pictures on the internet."

"Of a mannequin wearing my clothes? They could use any clothes then."

"They use the person's real clothes. It's the extra kick in their prank. Again, they Photoshop it so it looks just like you. Same hair, same everything. Your name will be attached to it. It's scary."

"But then what? It's just a big doll that looks like me."

She gave me a 'come on' look. "Sam, think about it."

A sick feeling came over me. "What'll they have the mannequin doing?"

"If you're lucky, nothing. If it's what I'm thinking, really bad things. People won't care that it's not you. They did this to Marissa and it was bad. Guys talked about raping the mannequin, but it was like they were saying that they wanted to rape her. With you, can you imagine what all the girls will do? There's a bunch of girls besides Kate and her crew that don't like you. A lot of the drill team. Most of the cheerleaders. They'll be vicious."

The sick feeling spread all over now. "How can I stop that?"

"I know you've wanted to handle Kate on your own, but this is too much. Tell Mason, or at least Logan. They might have an idea of where they're doing this. They could probably stop them."

I shook my head. "I can't. Nate's car accident. I know Mason's going to go see him after basketball practice."

"Then tell Logan."

"He'll tell Mason. I'm scared of what they'd do."

"Are you really trying to protect Kate? She's not sitting back and hoping you'll go away. She texts me every day now, and she's making threats to me, threats to even my dad and my brother. Now this." She stopped and took a deep breath. Her eyes held mine, a plea filled them. "Please, Sam. If not Mason, then tell Logan."

"I'll think about it."

"Don't think about it. Do it."

I frowned. There was an edge to her voice.

She finished, "If you don't, I will."

"Heather."

"No." She shook her head. "Kate's gone too far. She did this to Marissa and she ended up transferring. They didn't stop once they started. I know it's going to be worse for you. I just know it. Everyone else does, too. No one wants to get hit in the crossfire, so they're all leaving you alone. Please, Sam. You've got the two biggest enforcers on your side. Use them. They can stop Kate. I know they can."

As she left, hurrying away for class, I couldn't move. The last bell rang. I was going to be late, but my feet wouldn't budge. Heather's last warning echoed inside of me. It wasn't that they couldn't stop Kate, it was *how* they were going to do it.

They had forced wine down my mother's throat. They did that to prove to her what they could do, but that hadn't stopped Analise in the end. Whatever they did to Kate wouldn't stop her. I knew that in my gut, but I had no idea what to do. A part of me was scared. If I let Mason and Logan loose, I worried they'd cross a line. I couldn't let them do anything that would jeopardize their futures, not after Mason's had been threatened by my own mother. I couldn't go through that terror again, but Heather was right. I had to do something, but I had no idea what.

CHAPTER TWELVE

I couldn't bring myself to say anything, even when Mason caught me after school. He was heading to basketball practice, and I was headed to Coach Grath's office. Heather's warning had stuck with me all day, sending pangs of terror through me, but I was still worried. Being loved and protected by Mason and Logan was like holding a loaded gun. I could pull the trigger at any moment, but the consequences could be disastrous.

When he asked if I was okay, I lied. He knew it, but I wasn't ready to tell him yet. When he pressed a soft kiss to my lips and left, I realized that was my second lie to him. Two lies in two days. What lie would I tell him tomorrow?

Meeting with Coach Grath, he told me to run on my own. There was a select group of girls he wanted me to train with, but he caught wind that I wouldn't be welcomed. I was supposed to train on my own until the time came to 'bite that bullet.' His words, not mine. He wanted me to record my times to check for improvement. That wasn't a hard thing. I was bursting from the inside. Getting to the hotel room and driving to my old park took too long for me. I couldn't hit that trail fast enough and when I soared past Quickie's, I shot past all the cars in the parking lot and hit the hills at a full sprint. Once I got to the top, I skimmed over Fallen Crest below me and kept going to the next hill and the one after. The air temperature had noticeably dipped when I finally stopped.

My heart was racing and my chest was heaving as I gasped for breath.

I'd never felt more alive.

Then it hit me at the same time. It was like a cold wind to the north decided to make an abrupt turn and crash into me. It staggered me.

Kate. My clothes. A mannequin. I gulped. Whatever she was going to do would be on the internet, probably even tonight. Then the lies. I hadn't said a word about my run-in with both Broudous. I had no idea how to tell him Brett Broudou asked me out. He didn't know that I sat outside David's house or that Kate stole my clothes. I knew why I kept quiet about some of those, but not my home. As I thought about it now, my heart began pounding again, louder and louder in my eardrums.

I didn't want to feel any of this. Regret. Confusion. Lost. So I turned around and started my run back home. The adrenalin always pushed everything away, but that didn't happen this time. My body was tired. That was all there was to it. I was tired. For once, running hadn't helped me. It made me feel more defeated than when I had started.

It was later that night when Mason texted me.

Mason: **Nate's at his house now. Going over to hang out.**

Me: **I thought you couldn't.**

Mason: **Banned from hospital, not his place. I need to talk to him about some things. You ok?**

Me: **Yeah. We should talk tonight, too.**

I waited, holding my breath. Then my phone buzzed again: **Ok. Won't stay long. Love you.**

I closed my eyes, let out a deep breath, and replied: **Love you too.**

"Was that Mason?"

I glanced up and tossed my phone to the other side of the bed. My textbooks and computer had taken up most of the bed. Logan was in the doorway to our bedroom. His hair was wet and he had on a Fallen Crest Public athletic jacket. "Did you shower here?"

"Nope. At school. Ran home to get some cash." His eyes fell to my phone. "Where's Mason at?"

"He went to see Nate."

"Oh." Then he turned thoughtful, studying me. "What are you doing?"

"Studying."

I was going to tell him that I was exhausted from the run, but paused. Logan had that look. He was thinking and that meant he was planning something. I kept quiet until he nodded to himself, some decision made. He then said, "I'm meeting the guys for pizza. You want to come?"

"Why do I get the feeling that I don't have a choice?"

He started for me, rolling his shoulders back, a cocky smirk adorning his face. "Because all you do is go to school, study, run, and have coital bliss with my brother. You need to hang out with friends and have fun."

"I do." He was beside the bed now, and I couldn't hold back my grin. "I watched movies with Heather on Saturday."

He snorted, leaning down and taking hold of my ankle. He started to pull me to him. "That wasn't fun. That was hiding from my mother. That's work. Come on." With one abrupt tug, I was jerked to the edge of the bed. He tucked his shoulder down and moved me onto it. As he stood, I was slung over him.

"Logan!"

"You look fine. Always hot, Sam. You never need to worry about that." He patted me on the back and turned for the door.

I was laughing too hard to fight back. He scooped down and handed my shoes to me, along with a coat and my bag. We headed out like that. There were others in the elevator, but Logan commented, patting my butt at the same time, "She forgot how to walk." An elderly couple was confused while someone chuckled. A little kid circled to look up at me, pointed, and said, "You look weird."

I felt Logan's reaction. His body tensed and then shook in silent laughter. When the doors slid open to the bottom floor, everyone let us go first. Logan didn't lower me until he got to his Escalade. I was deposited into the passenger seat, and he jogged over to his side.

When he pulled into Manny's parking lot, I glanced over at him. "I thought you said pizza."

Turning the Escalade off, he shrugged. "They have pizza here."

"And this has nothing to do with my one good friend that's here?"

A shrug was my only response before we went inside. Logan's friends had congregated around two tables in the back section. I recognized some of the girls from the drill team at the second table. I recognized their hostility, too. Brandon lifted his hand in greeting, and Heather glanced up from the counter. Her eyes darted from me to Logan pointedly, and I shook my head. She mouthed back, "When?" I tried to tell her to shut up with an extra oomph in my glare, and I jerked my shoulders up and down. I was going to tell Mason. That was the plan.

As it turned out, it wasn't Heather or myself that brought it up. The first pizza had already been devoured when a few of the girls scooted their chairs to our table. They did what those girls did. The displayed their boobs. They tried to be coy and mysterious. A couple had even pulled their jeans down low so they could show off their thongs. I was certain another girl went to the bathroom and took off her bra. She returned with her boobs bouncing. The shirt she wore did little to cover her nipples. There was one girl that stuck out as the leader. She started talking to Strauss. From what I could overhear, they were discussing a class assignment until I heard the word 'gym' mentioned.

A blast of cold air came over me and I turned, as if in slow motion, towards them.

She was grinning at me and nodded in my direction. Everyone else grew silent and then she asked, her voice rising above the background noise, "Did you ever get your clothes back, Samantha?"

Samantha. That was my first thought. *I don't know her, and she called me by my full name.* Then the rest of her words hit me.

Logan paused and lowered his pizza slice. He frowned at her, then back at me. "What's she talking about?"

Someone muttered in the background, "Shit's about to get reaaal."

I was pretty sure that was Heather, but when I turned she lifted her hand in a rolling motion. I got the message, let's get this going.

"Let's talk outside."

Logan was up from the table before the words left my mouth. His hand was on my arm, and I was hauled behind him. Instead of going through the entire diner, he shoved through the side door. I started for one of the chairs we used when we took our breaks, but he shook his head. His fingers tightened. "Nope. We're doing this over here where no one can listen."

He took me all the way across the alley and towards Heather's house. We were starting up her porch when the door slammed shut behind us. Heather's jaw was set and her top lip curved up, flashing us a warning as she headed towards us. "Oh no. I'm staying. She's my friend too, Kade."

"Fine."

Her arms were crossed over her chest and then both of them moved as one. I was center stage. Lovely. "Okay..."

"Kate, or one of her lackeys, stole Sam's clothes after gym class when she was in the shower," Heather beat me to it. Her eyebrow arched high. "You know what they're going to do. Stop them, Logan."

He threw her a scathing look, but turned and pinned me down. "Is that true, Sam?"

My mouth was still hanging open from my 'okay', but I shut it now. This was it. This was the moment where he went after them and I'd be at home worrying if he was going to be arrested or worse. At least Mason was at Nate's. I doubted Logan would need him for this.

He bit out a curse and hopped off the porch. His phone was pulled out a second later and I heard, "Mase? We have a problem."

That hope exploded.

"Thanks for that," I said. "Note the sarcasm."

She rolled her eyes. "You wouldn't have told them, and you know it. I don't understand why you didn't say something after it happened. It's probably too late now."

"Because I'm scared for them. I don't know what Mason and Logan are going to do."

"Oh please." Another eye-roll. Another swear word. "They're not idiots, and this isn't their first rodeo. This is Mason and Logan Kade. This is what they're known for, this is who they are. I don't know what you're scared about. Stop kidding yourself, Sam."

My head jerked back. "You just bitch-slapped me."

The corner of her mouth lifted in a crooked grin and she shrugged. "Well, that's what real friends do."

"You really think they'll be fine?" No matter what she said, the fear of Mason's future was still in me. My mom had been so close to ruining it.

""Yeah." She softened and reached over to hug me. She whispered in my ear. "I think they'll be fine. I've never seen those two more protective over someone. It's why everyone hates you at school."

I stiffened in her arms. "Quite aware of my popularity."

"Things will be fine." She patted my arm again. "They'll put her back in her place and everyone will relax at school. People will start getting to know you for you. I'm sure of it."

I hoped so. I really did, but Heather was forgetting one thing. Things wouldn't go back to normal. Mason and Logan had been quiet, but I knew they were planning their revenge against the Broudou brothers. Thinking of them… I still needed to tell Mason about Brett. He needed to know sooner than later.

It was then when Brandon stuck his head out the side door. When he spotted us, his face scrunched together. I could imagine a few curse words coming from him until he hollered, "Get your ass in here, Heather! We're swamped."

"Yeah, yeah."

"I mean it!"

Her voice rose another octave. "I said 'yeah, yeah'! I'll be there in a sec!"

His middle finger rose in response before he disappeared back inside.

"Stupid brothers." She glanced at me. "Not step-brothers, but you know what I mean."

"I do."

She jerked her thumb towards Manny's. Another crooked-grin appeared. "Don't suppose you want to work the rest of the night? Lily and Anne both quit last weekend. Lily's dad got a new job so they moved and Anne won't work here if Lily doesn't. That's the excuse she gave me, but Cory saw her working at the Fallen Crest Country Club. The tips are better over there."

"You'd be surprised at how cheap rich people can be."

"You've been there?"

"Unfortunately."

She shrugged, musing at the same time, "That place is too fancy for me. I don't speak hoity-toity."

"That's funny. You named it perfectly right there."

"HEATHER!" Brandon was glaring at us from the door again. "Come on! We're getting killed."

"I'm COMING!" We started down the alley, and she muttered under her breath, "Someone's getting killed tonight. That's for sure."

Mason

The damn mannequin was where I thought it would be—Kate's garage. She was smart, but not that smart. Since it only had a dark wig on it, and Sam's clothing were next to it, I figured they hadn't done anything to it yet.

"Fuck," Logan muttered. "Is that a dildo over there?"

Her dad had an old truck parked on one side. The other side had a yellow-stained refrigerator where Harold stored his beer. He liked to drink while he played around with his truck. He kept the 'good stuff' inside the house. Two worn plaid couches that were torn up, from the cat sharpening its claws, sat next to the refrigerator. A small table with a coffee can full of cigarette butts on top was placed between the couches. There were empty bottles lined up next to the couches Kate's uncles used to spit their chew in.

"Smells like someone died in here."

"Watch it," I warned when Logan hopped off the steps leading from the house. "There might be a dead animal in here. This is where her dad skins his kills."

"You're talking about animals, right?" Logan wrinkled his nose up before covering it with his shirt. "Man, this place really stinks."

This was Kate's world. It was fucked up and I didn't want to be there longer than I needed. I went over and got all of Sam's clothes, making sure the cat hadn't pissed on them. They smelled fine. Sam's vanilla body spray was still on them.

Logan had opened the refrigerator. "Holy shit. Why don't we party here?"

"*Used* to party here?"

"Oh yeah. You know what I meant." The smirk lingered on Logan's face as he grabbed a beer from inside. Twisting it open, he took a good swig before he pointed at the mannequin. "So what's our plan for that thing?"

"No clue, but I know where they get the things."

"Where's that?"

"Sashes and Bows."

"Say again?" Logan had lifted the beer to his mouth, but paused before he took another drink.

"Natalie's aunt. Her clothing store."

"Oh." He bobbed his head up and down. "Makes sense now."

I tried to see if there was anything else we should grab. Once Kate realized we'd been there, the extra key would be moved somewhere else. I didn't know if she would warn her parents about me or not. Her mom worked at the hospital eighty hours a week, and her dad was always gone with his buddies. When Harold was home, he was drunk. If nothing else, I knew where Kate's mom stored her purse at the hospital. Kate told me the combination.

Stupid.

"Let's go," Logan started to say, but broke off at the sound of car doors slamming shut.

Going to the garage door, we saw Kate's and Natalie's cars.

"Come on." I grabbed the mannequin and went to the side door. It led to the outside and I shoved the thing into Logan's arms and pointed to the road. Kate lived in the country. Her house was surrounded by trees, and there was a road that led around to the back of her dad's barns and property. We had parked the Escalade behind one of the barns and crossed through the woods to sneak into the house. I didn't know who was going to be here, so coming in from the north side kept us hidden. It helped Logan now as he nodded and took off with the mannequin.

I stayed behind. I wanted to hear her reaction.

"...isn't that what we're doing? I mean, come on. The girl just can't lay down and take it... Oh, holy gawd!"

The door banged against the wall, and Jasmine's voice stopped abruptly. I grinned to myself.

"OH MY FUCK! FUCK-FUCK!!"

"Calm down, Kate," Natalie drawled. Her voice fell halfway through her statement as if she'd stepped to the side. "You don't have to screech so loud. I just had flashbacks to my mom."

Someone snickered. "From last night, you mean."

"Shut it, Parker," Natalie snapped back. "And speaking of, where were you last night?"

"What are you talking about? I was with Nate. Kate told me to see him." Her voice rose sharply. "Kate, you told me to go see him. I wasn't supposed to?" Her voice was near hysteria.

Everything got quiet.

A door opened and closed. Then the truck's doors were both opened and slammed shut. A thud came next before Parker asked again, quieter now, "Kate?"

"FUUUUUUUUUUUCKKKKK!"

"Kate, why are you flipping out like this? Stop screaming. I didn't give up a shift at Str8t to hear this."

"Shut up, Natalie," Kate shot back.

Something hit the garage door. She was throwing shit. That was good. I didn't think they'd look out the side door, but I tucked my head down in case. It was on the opposite side of the truck, but I didn't know for sure. I tried to blend in with the shadows as much as possible. Then I heard Kate start screeching again. Something else thudded into the garage door.

"Hey," Jasmine spoke up, "where's that whore's clothes?"

Natalie laughed. "You got rats in here, Kate? I'm sure they were attracted to her musk."

"For the last time," Kate's voice turned ominous. "Shut. The. Fuck. Up. You're not worried about her clothes?"

"Well, yeah. We need them for the whole thing. It was pointless to borrow my brother's camcorder, and I won't enjoy doing his chores for the week. Punk kid," Natalie grumbled. A smaller item was thrown against the garage door. "Little does he know that he's going to pay for that."

"You guys are pissing me off."

"Tell us something we don't know," Natalie threw back.

"What are you going to do?"

"I'm going to kill someone," Kate bit out, her voice harsh.

Natalie ignored her. "I sent all his buddies his last video on here."

"Really?" Jasmine sounded curious. "What was it?"

"Him jacking off." She snorted. "Dumb idiot. That's going viral. Douche will be haunted by that for years."

"You're so mean to your little brother. You should be nicer to him."

"And you should be meaner to your sister. She treats you like dirt, Jaz."

"Seriously, guys!" Kate yelled out. "Help me find her clothes or it'll be over for all of us."

"For the last effing time," Natalie barked back. "What are you talking about?"

"Her clothes." I could hear the venom dripping from her voice. I enjoyed it. "They're gone."

"So's the doll thing."

"What?"

"The doll thing."

I shook my head. Parker had no idea what she was pointing out. Kate spat out again, "What the fuck are you talking about?"

"The doll," Parker yelled back. "It was here. So were her clothes."

"I put her clothes on the floor. Where'd you put the mannequin?"

"Here. I just told you. Listen."

"The mannequin was supposed to go DOWNSTAIRS," Kate screamed again. "They took it. They took it all. Oh my god. Oh my god. I'm going to kill someone."

"What are you talking about?" Natalie's voice rose in alarm. "They? You think that cunt came in here?"

"Mason and Logan. Are you a complete idiot? She told them. Shit. Fuck." Kate went through a slew of curse words. "They came in here and took them."

"Oh crap."

"Exactly."

"You think they did anything else?" Parker questioned, a small twinge of fear crept into her tone.

Kate laughed now. "Probably." It came out sounding like she was being strangled. "We're screwed. She told Mason. He's going to screw us."

"Calm down," Natalie clipped out. "Let's calm down and think about this. We're not screwed yet."

"We are. We sooo are. He's going to do something horrible to us. I know it. We're so screwed."

"No, we're not. He has no idea what we were going to do—"

"Yes, he did," Kate continued yell. "It's why he came here in the first place. I can't believe that bitch told him."

"I would, if I was her," Jasmine commented. "I mean, come on. We're mean. You can't blame the girl."

"Whose side are you on?" Kate and Natalie said at the same time.

There was silence before she replied, "Yours. My friends."

"Then act like it."

"So what?" Natalie spoke up again. "We'll be fine. They took her clothes back. Whoop de doo. We can still hurt her. We *do* have other things planned."

"I know." I could imagine Kate now. She was biting the inside of her cheek, thinking over everything that we could've done to her house. She sighed. "Shit. Fine. Come on. Let's go to Tate's and put the camcorder in place and then go to Cake's garage for the other stuff."

"Wait," Parker stopped them, "so we're not putting those pictures on the internet?"

"We can't," Kate snapped at her, her voice heavy with sarcasm. "We don't have the mannequin, and we don't have her clothes. We have nothing else on her."

"Can't we just use someone else's clothes and put her name on it?"

"Not without the fucking doll, and using her clothes is the whole point. It's the added insult that it's her real clothes. Unless one of you guys want to dress up and let us take pictures of you?"

There was silence in the room.

Kate bit out a harsh laugh. "I didn't think so."

"Let's use other pictures and put her face on it?"

"Using her real clothes is the whole point. Did you get anything from Nate's house before they moved out?"

"No. Mason locked their bedroom during the parties, and I couldn't find anything else in the house."

"Of course he does. They have huge parties."

"Whatever. Let's move on. We'll do the thing that we were planning to do next week, this week instead."

"Are you sure that's smart? You just said that we're screwed. Mason knows and now we don't have the pictures."

I pressed my ear closer against the wall. Their voices faded when Kate commented, "It doesn't matter. I'm going to beat her ass one way or another."

Their car doors closed. I turned and headed into the woods to where my Escalade was parked. When I got into my car, Logan put his phone away and looked up. "You learn anything?"

"Nothing we didn't know except that we have to put her down."

Logan nodded and lifted his fist in the air. I met it with mine. As I reversed the car, I asked, "Can you text Sam for me? Tell her we're fine, but we won't get back till late."

"Already did it."

I threw my brother a frown, but Logan wasn't paying attention. He went back to texting on his phone.

CHAPTER THIRTEEN

Samantha

I had no idea what they did, but Mason smelled like smoke when he passed through our room to the bathroom. The shower turned on a second later. Getting out of bed and padding barefoot behind him, he was already under the spray when I got there. His clothes were in a pile on the floor so I put them into the laundry bin. Then I leaned against the counter, and our eyes met through the glass door. He didn't smile or say hello. He stared at me, and I stared back as he continued bathing. Lifting his arms, the water cascaded over his shoulders and down his chest. I could see every inch of him, not that any of it was a surprise anymore, but the hunger was there. Always there.

He smirked, still watching me. I licked my lips.

The wait for him took forever. I was burning up by the time he turned the water off and stepped out. The towels were behind me and he reached past me, leaning into me at the same time. His chest touched mine and he paused. His arm was stretched behind me, but as I turned to meet his gaze, he was looking right at me. Just there. Within reach. I closed my eyes and inhaled when his breath coated my skin. It was a caress of its own. Then a throaty murmur escaped me, "Mason…"

He pulled away and dried himself off.

My eyelids opened, but I was caught and held by his gaze again.

My chest lifted as I inhaled another deep breath. My breasts grew heavy under my thin top. They wanted his touch. Without a bra, he could see their reaction. It took one more second as he finished drying off before he dropped the towel again and stepped close to me.

His hands found my hips.

My eyes closed. My head went down.

Home. Finally.

"Sam," he murmured from an inch away. His lips were there, right there for me to taste.

"What?" I could barely talk.

"She won't hurt you." His hand lifted.

When it touched my neck, my heart jumped into my throat, and my blood began pumping.

He moved it around my neck and cupped the back of my head. I was held, anchored in his hand. It was strong, so sure. My heart was racing now and my chest was heaving up and down. I was struggling to breathe. The knot in me started to loosen. It always did when he made me feel like this. Safe. Then a lump formed in my throat, and I had to bite down on my lip. I would either become a sobbing mess or I'd throw myself at him. I wasn't sure which one I wanted.

He decided for me.

Mason pulled me into his chest. His arms wrapped around me, and I felt his head bend down. He rested his forehead on my shoulder, so I did the same. My hands lifted to his hips, but then with a sob, I wrapped them around his waist.

I'd been so damn worried.

He was safe. They were both safe. My heart kept pounding as the relief washed over me, replacing the desire from moments ago.

Then I peeled myself from him, just enough so I could get answers. "What did you guys do?"

"Nothing bad."

"Mason."

He flashed me a grin, took my hand in his and led me to the bedroom. I checked the door and saw it was locked, but then he bent down and lifted me in his arms. I was upright in his arms as he walked us the remaining few steps to the bed. He placed me onto it so that I remained standing while his hands kept me upright. They gripped my hips, and he tipped his head back. A soft smile gracing his features.

My hand lifted on its own volition and went through his wet hair. He closed his eyes, and I could tell he savored the small caress. My fingers grabbed a fistful of his hair and I pulled with enough force so he'd open them. When he did, I asked again, "What did you guys do?"

A slow grin appeared, and his arms tightened around my legs. That was all the warning I got before he flipped me in the air and caught me again. One hand cradled between my shoulders, and the other gripped my ass. He lowered me to the bed and then climbed on top of me in one fluid movement. It was as if he didn't even move and he was above me, holding himself up with his arms and legs.

His eyes roamed over me as he answered, "We went to Kate's." He dropped a small kiss on my throat. "Everything was still there, so we took it." Another kiss an inch higher. "Then I stuck around and watched the fireworks." The hand on my hip slid around my waist.

My heart started pounding again, and I held my breath.

The hand moved down and pushed underneath my shorts. There was no restriction. They were made of soft fabric and clung to me. As his fingers moved even further down, he slid two fingers deep into me. He moved further up until he was directly above me. His lips were so close to mine again. Watching mine, he murmured, "Kate almost spilled her plans, but her friends were too stupid to let her."

"And then?"

His fingers began moving. Oh god. He pressed another kiss to the underside of my chin.

My heart spiked, and a burst of pleasure rushed over me. I was tempted to say, "To hell with the questioning" and pull him down to me, but I couldn't. This was important. "And then?" I asked again, almost panting now.

"And then." His other hand moved to hold mine. Our fingers slid against each other as he linked our hands together. Then he lowered his body slowly, inch by inch, until he was resting on top of me. He fit between my legs, in just the right spot as his fingers kept thrusting in and out.

I bit my lip, trying to stop myself from moving down. My lips fell open and I gasped, but I kept it silent. I had to. My heart was beating so loud now. "Mason," I groaned, "just tell me."

"Tell you?"

"You like torturing me."

A corner of his mouth curved up. The grin was cruel, but his eyes hadn't moved from my lips. "Maybe." They had already darkened, but they grew black now. "Maybe you torture me, too."

I was ready to start praying for patience. "You're beginning to piss me off."

"Am I?" He moved his hips into me in rhythm with his fingers.

I gasped out loud. Lust and pleasure were rolling through me like a riptide on repeat, over and over again. My hands found their way to his shoulders, and my fingers dug in. Then he moved again. I was pushed further away from consciousness. Desire for him was making me blind. I lifted my heavy eyelids and looked at him. His gaze was transfixed on my lips, and he licked his own, thrusting against me at the same time.

"Mason," I whimpered.

I felt his silent laughter; his chest tightened and jerked before he pulled away, still grinning, but it had softened on the corners. His eyes caught mine and held them. They narrowed, and I caught a spark in them, one that I recognized. He was thinking.

"Mason, tell me."

"They're planning something, said it was supposed to be for next week, but it's going to happen at the end of this week instead."

The heat from my desire lessened. It made room for a chill. "What do you think it is?"

"Honestly?" He pulled his fingers out.

I nodded, a lump was in my throat now.

"I think they're going to hurt you. Physically."

"Oh."

"Oh?" He frowned and lifted his thumb to my mouth. He rubbed it over my lips, tugging the bottom down before his hand fell away. "You're not surprised?"

I shrugged. "Not really. I mean, that's expected. Kate's never struck me as the real smart type."

"Well, she is." The lust in his eyes moved to caution. He warned me, "You have no idea what she can do. Beating you up isn't good, but I'd be a lot less worried if I thought that's all she was going to do."

"She's been texting Heather a bunch."

His body stiffened on top of me. "Saying what?"

"She needs to stop being my friend. Heather said there were threats to her and to her family, too."

"When did this start?"

"The first day of school. She came over and made a big show about warning Heather away. That was when Tate tried to intervene."

"Against you?"

"No, against Kate. She told her that going up against you isn't worth it." I frowned. The sexual intensity was gone, and he seemed deep in thought. I reached for him, curving my hand over his shoulder to his jaw. His gaze had moved past my shoulder, but I touched his jaw. "Hey. What are you thinking?"

"That I'm starting to figure out what else Kate is doing."

"What do you mean?"

"With Tate."

"What?"

He was off the bed in a flash and pulled on his sweatpants. The bed had only settled when he disappeared through the door and hollered, "Logan!"

"What's up?"

Grabbing one of Mason's sweatshirts, I pulled it over my head and ignored how it covered my pajama shorts. It looked like I wasn't wearing anything underneath it.

Logan smirked at me as I came to the doorway. "You cold, Sam?"

"Shut it, Logan."

Mason asked, "Where are you going?"

Logan had showered. He was dressed in jeans and his athletic sweatshirt. Playing with his car keys in his hand, he shrugged. "Was going to head out for a few. What's up?"

"You going to Tate's?"

His question threw both of us. There it was again, the lie Mason never explained to me. Narrowing my eyes at him, I studied Logan at the same time. He seemed cautious now and slid his hands into his front pockets. "Maybe. Why?"

"Kate mentioned a camcorder," Mason said. "And before that Natalie had her brother's camcorder. They were going to use it to take pictures of the mannequin."

"So? They have a camcorder. So do we."

"Kate said they were heading to Tate's at the end. Sam just told me they've been sending threats to Heather. They want her to stop being her friend and Tate tried to warn them off."

Logan nodded. "She told me about that. Said it was a lost cause. Kate's gone off the deep end."

"So," Mason paused and watched him. He was waiting…

"So what?"

"Logan, I spelled it out for you."

"Threats to Heather. Camcorder. Tate thinks Kate's crazy. None of this is really new here, brother."

I sighed. Even I knew what Mason was implying. Logan wasn't dumb. If he wasn't figuring it out that meant something else was going on with him. Moving to the couch, I perched on the end and said, "I think he's saying that Kate might think Tate's on our side."

"She is," Logan snorted. "No way would she go against you. She knows what we'd do to her."

"Logan," Mason groaned.

I lifted a hand to his arm and felt his tension. My hand began to rub. "Do you think Kate would take a camcorder to Tate's out of the goodness of her heart?"

"Wha—oh shit. No. No way. You think?"

"Are you going over there?"

Logan glanced at his brother again. A resigned look came over him. "Yeah, I am. What do you want me to do?"

"Don't say anything or make it obvious, but look to see if there's a camcorder stashed somewhere."

"Wait," Logan shook his head. "You think she's in on it? We do things or we have done things in the living room. They could've put it there—"

"They were going there tonight."

"Oh." His shoulders dropped. "So what do you want me to do? You want me to grab it?"

When Mason didn't reply, Logan looked to me. I shrugged. "Mason's the mastermind. Not me."

"Mase?"

"I don't know. Maybe leave it in place?"

"I'm not going over there anymore. No fucking way, not if they have a camcorder in there. That's messed up."

"I know. I'm not saying that," Mason bit out. "But if we move the camcorder, then they'd have to change tactics again. We know what they're planning right now. Maybe we can wait to see what else she's planning?"

"Should I tell Tate?"

Mason didn't respond.

"Mase, that's not right."

"No," he sighed. "I know. Yeah, tell her, but she needs to act like she doesn't know it's there. We'll figure out the next step later."

"What about her parents?" I asked. "Should they know? They might talk about things that are personal."

Logan shook his head. "Nah. She's not here with them. Her dad lost his job so they shipped her out here to live with her older sister, but she's gone on a modeling trip. Tate said she wouldn't be back for a week or so." Then he jerked his head in a nod and started for the door. "Oh wait," he braked and gestured to me. "Did you tell her about the mannequins?"

"Not yet."

"Mannequins?"

"Yeah." He flashed me a smile as he headed out the door. "We torched 'em, all of 'em. Natalie's aunt's going to get a nice little surprise when she goes to work in the morning. On that note, I'm out." The door shut behind him, but we could hear him whistling as he went down the hall.

"You burned them?"

He nodded.

"All of them?"

He narrowed his eyes, and I got a glimpse of the cruel Mason again. "Every single one of them."

"Was that safe?"

He shrugged, turning to me with a hand on my leg. He nudged it over and stepped between them as he looked down at me. "We were safe. We took all of them to a place where it'd be okay."

"And Natalie's aunt? She won't press charges?"

"We left a note with a few images I kept from when they messed with Marissa. We let her know she could thank her niece for all of it."

I held my breath. It'd been so long since he'd mentioned Marissa, and now that he had, I wanted to ask him more about her. I wanted to understand what had happened to her, but I sensed his unease.

It was like approaching a wild animal. I had to go slow and with caution. My heart started to pound again as I took that first step. My hand raised to touch his arm. The muscles were corded tightly in a bunch. He was so tense, but I had to try. "You still had those pictures?"

His arm began to tremble underneath my touch, just a tiny bit, but it was enough to take my breath away. His voice was rough when he spoke, "Did you know they did the same to her?"

The lump was back in my throat. It was big and wobbly, but I nodded. "Yes."

"Heather told you?"

"Yes." My heart was racing so fast now. He was finally talking about her. I felt the wall coming down. I needed to know so much. She was important to him. I needed to understand. "Will you tell me about her?"

"I thought I had?"

"More. You didn't say much before. She transferred because of Kate and her friends?"

He let out a deep sigh and moved away. I ached, I still needed his touch, but then he surprised me. He came back, a conflicted look on his face, and lifted me from the couch. I was curled against his chest as he sat down on the couch, with me on his lap. Then he tucked his chin over my head and began to talk about her.

"It was Tate, too," he paused for a moment, "towards the end of her relationship with Logan, and before she tried to sleep with me, when Heather had stopped being friends with her. I didn't pay attention. I didn't care about your friend back then, but I remember Logan saying something about it to me. He seemed to care, but then I started noticing that Tate was becoming friendly with Kate and the girls. Made sense. Tate was always around Logan and the girls were always around us. The guys considered them friends, you know?"

"Where'd your friendship with Marissa come in?"

His arms tightened around me, securing me in place. "That was a fluke thing. We sat next to each other in a class and got paired up for a project. My parents were going through a divorce at the time. My dad had been cheating for so many years, and I watched my mom go through that shit storm, then your mom started popping up. Anyways, I had a pretty low opinion of the female gender from Tate and other girls. I didn't even like Kate and the rest of them. Kate must've thought she was my maybe-girlfriend, I don't know what she thought, but I didn't care. I used her so I can kind of see where she got it wrong, but I didn't trust her or any of the others. They were mean."

I hid a smile.

He must've sensed it because he said, "I know. I'm not the nicest person, but that doesn't mean I'm going to choose people like that to trust. I don't trust anyone except you and Logan."

"You began to trust Marissa?"

"Yeah. We'd talk. That's it. We didn't hang out or anything. I think I sat at her table a few times for lunch. That seemed like a big deal to everyone, but whatever. I didn't want to deal with the bullshit from the girls. They're hard to handle sometimes. Logan understood. Just dealing with the divorce and the fights at home, I didn't want to deal with hearing shit at school, too. Marissa was nice. Her friends were quiet, but they didn't seem to mind me when I sat with them. Looking back, I think that's what put a target on her. It was after that when I began hearing things."

My fingers curled into his, interlocking our hands together. "Marissa never told you?"

"No, she never did, but I started noticing things. She lost weight. She looked tired all the time. I don't know. Maybe I wasn't looking hard enough. She wasn't my girlfriend. I didn't care that much; she was just nice to talk to at times. That was it."

I heard the struggle in him. He didn't quite understand. "You trusted her." It was beginning to make sense. "You never trusted those other girls. You tolerated them. They must've seen it." And hated it. The pieces were coming together. They had destroyed

Marissa because he enjoyed her company. If they did that to her, what were they going to do to me? A shudder went through me at the thought. I was much more than a friend. I was beginning to realize he had no idea what they had done to her. Guys weren't told when girls tormented other girls. It was an unspoken rule, one that I had broken. I gulped now. Would it be worse because I brought them in? But no. That wasn't the right thought. They would win if I started to think like that. Heather was right, it was time for me to fight back.

"Yeah, maybe." His chest lifted and lowered as he took in a deep breath. "I'm sure I don't even know half the shit they did to her, but I knew about the mannequins. It wasn't Marissa, but it looked just like her. The pictures were all over. People laughed at them, and it was like they were laughing at her."

"What happened after that?"

He started to lift his shoulder in a shrug, but dropped it. "More," he bit off the end of his word. His hold on me tightened, as if trying to guard me from it, too. "I heard little things they did, like breaking the lock on her locker. She used to ride the bus to school, and I'm sure things must've happened there, too. Towards the end, her parents drove her." His hand had a cement hold on my arm now. "You don't understand. Kate and the girls had a lot of power over all the other girls back then. They don't anymore. When they were exiled from the guys, I knew that would fracture the power they had over the rest. I see it too. The other girls aren't doing what Kate wants. They're starting to go against Kate and her friends."

He was holding me so tightly. When a slight tremor went through him, I knew he wanted to protect me. Turning my head to the side, I looked at him. His eyes were closed and his eyebrows were bunched forward, strained together. Then he said further, "I didn't stop them and I should have. I'm not a bully, Sam. I don't pick on the weak or try to make someone's life hell, but if they come after me or someone I love, then I'll go after them with everything

I've got. I'll use all of their weaknesses to destroy them, but I never start the fight."

He didn't start the fight, but he finished it. I understood what he was saying. "Mason."

His eyelids lifted and the regret in them took my breath away. Then I swallowed over the lump in my throat and spoke, "She didn't tell you what was happening. She wasn't your girlfriend. Your parents were getting a divorce. You can't blame yourself for not stopping Kate. I'm betting that you didn't even know half of what they did."

"That's the problem," he bit out. His eyes growing cold. "I should've. She was my friend. She was a good person, and I didn't fight for her like I should've. What they did to her is on me. I didn't stop them when I could've. No one else could've, so it was my place to do it. I didn't. A part of me checked out, Sam. You're right. All the crap from the divorce. It went on long after Logan dumped Tate, too. She made it worse. Thinking back, it was how Tate hurt me back, through Marissa, but she stopped talking to me at the end. She had the teacher assign her to someone else and she stopped even saying hi to me. It was like we were strangers."

"Did it stop then?"

"No."

That one word came out like an ache. He was haunted by it.

I waited for him to continue, and he did, "I was grateful when she left. It stopped. She was safe."

"You started talking again after she left?"

He nodded. "She emailed me, told me that she didn't blame me for what happened. I was such an ass. I didn't even comment on it. I still have never said a word about it to her."

I didn't know what to say so I moved until I was straddling him. He fell back against the couch. His hands went to my legs, where mine rested on top of them, and he watched me from underneath heavy eyelids. His jaw clenched and some of his old wall came back in place. He was always so guarded.

He shook his head and cursed under his breath. His hands turned to lock with mine. "When she came to Nate's cabin, it's why I wanted him with her at all times. Plus, you were there, and I couldn't stop thinking about you."

"Has she emailed you since then?"

"A few times. I haven't responded. That wasn't intentional, I've just been wrapped up with you and everything going on with your mom."

I saw the struggle in him. He was the unbeatable one, the ruthless one, and that broke me. I would protect him how he protected me. Lifting a hand to his face, I cupped his cheek and leaned forward to press my lips to his. It was a soft graze, but my heart fluttered. The ache started between my legs, and I moved closer, grinding on him. Then I moved back, just enough to whisper, "We'll make it different this time." My lips brushed against his. "We'll change things this time. We'll make it count."

His reaction was instant. His hands caught my face and his lips opened over mine. His hunger had been unleashed, and it was demanding more. He stood with my legs wrapped around his waist and took us to bed. A primal need started in me as I met his ghosts that night, and as he thrust into me, that need took over. The need to protect him was more than before. I had worried before, knowing I could lose him, but now it went beyond that. He hadn't stopped Kate from hurting his friend and it still hurt him, but now I was angry that they had even put him in that spot. It should've never happened in the first place, but that was on Kate. She was going to pay for what she had done.

CHAPTER FOURTEEN

Everyone knew what happened the next day at school. I had no idea how, but the news was out: Mason and Logan torched the mannequins. The truth got stretched to the whole clothing store, and by the end of the day everyone was whispering that they were going to get arrested. Apparently, Natalie's aunt died in the blaze. Poor Natalie. Or that was what I heard a freshman telling her friend as they passed us, heading towards the bus lot.

Heather heard them too and laughed, shaking her head. "They're idiots."

Putting my last book into my locker, I took a few others out and stuffed them inside my bag. "I was an idiot, too. By the time I was a freshman, my boyfriend had already been cheating on me for a year."

She wrinkled her nose. "Were they already sleeping together? Or were they just making out?"

I shrugged. "Who knows? I don't even want to think about it. They were hooking up somehow."

"Speaking of your ex. He came into the diner last night. He was with that other guy. Adam?"

I was surprised. "He's moving up in the Academy social scene if he's buds with Adam now."

"Adam's the top dog at your old school?"

"Yeah."

"He's the guy you avoided the other night?"

We began walking to the senior hallway. Mason wanted me to stop by his locker before he went to practice. As we turned the corner, I grimaced. "Yeah. He said he was okay with friendship, but I can't handle that drama right now." Natalie brushed past me at that moment, glaring the entire time. She took a step into me at the last second to hit her shoulder against mine. I kept going, jerking my thumb in her direction. "I got enough drama like that going on. I can't deal with much more."

Heather watched the Tommy Princess disappear in the direction we had just left. She murmured, "They've been quiet today."

"No texts?"

"Last one was yesterday afternoon. Your clothes were still there after gym?"

"Didn't shower. We only walked during class."

"I see."

By unspoken agreement, we stopped and watched Kate at her locker. She was alone. For once. Then Heather remarked, "I don't like it."

"Me neither."

"Ladies," Logan boomed in our ears before he wedged himself between us, throwing his arms around our shoulders. He squeezed us into his side and made a tsking sound. "Have I not made my wishes clear enough? When you come to greet me, I prefer cupcakes and those skirts that show off half your ass. It's pleasing to the eye and pleasing to my mouth, if you know what I mean."

Heather retorted, "Don't you get tired of hitting on your stepsister?"

"Future stepsister to you." He flashed a dimple at her, his mouth curving up. "Are you jealous, Jax? Do you only want me to hit on you? That could be arranged, you know. Cupcakes and ass-skirts. All I'm asking here."

She elbowed him in the gut, stepping out from his arm. "Whatever, Logan. From what I hear, you've got all your free time spoken for."

All traces of humor left. His arm dropped from my shoulder,

but he didn't move away. He only tensed. "What are you talking about?"

"You and my ex-bestie. I've heard that you two get it on almost every night now."

He narrowed his eyes at her. "Who told you that?"

"Was that supposed to be a secret?"

His jaw tightened as he ground out, "It wasn't supposed to be public knowledge." He cast an accusing look to me.

Heather spoke up, "Nope. No way. She didn't say one word so don't blame her for that gossip. It came straight from Tate's mouth. She was bragging about it in class to Morgan."

"Who's Morgan?"

"Drill team," she informed me.

I nodded. "Enough said."

"She was bragging?"

Heather turned back to him. "Seemed like it. I think Morgan was planning to make her move on you after the basketball game Friday night. Tate was friendly about it, but made it known you've been too occupied to notice other girls."

"We're not dating. We're screwing. There's a difference."

"Then you better handle her because Tate's laying claim to you and no one's going to argue with her. You two were together for two years. It makes sense to people. She's the only girl you've ever loved. That's common knowledge around here too." Heather cast a frown at me, biting her lip and I got the feeling she wanted to add more, but thought better of it.

Logan was like stone beside me. He was standing close enough so his arm grazed mine. I frowned and asked, "Why's this upsetting you so much?"

He swung to me. "What?"

"Tate can't be the only girl who's tried this with you. Just do what you normally do." I paused and when he didn't get what I was implying, I added, "You hook up with someone else. Hook up with someone else Friday night." But he still looked upset and that confused me. Normal Logan would've laughed this off. He wasn't. "Are you developing feelings for her again?"

"Why the hell would you say that?"

"Don't talk to her like that," Heather pulled me from him.

I placed a calming hand on her arm. I could handle Logan just fine. "Because you're not acting normal. Hooking up with someone else shouldn't bother you, but I can tell it does."

"That's not—" But he stopped and left.

Mason was coming towards us with Ethan and Strauss. Logan brushed through them, shouldering the last two out of his way. Both paused, frowning at him until Mason was close enough to ask, "What was that about?"

Heather opened her mouth, but I grabbed her arm. I answered first, "Nothing. Some test that he took."

Mason swung his head so he was only focused on me. When he didn't comment, I felt a swift kick to my gut. It was another lie, but I couldn't take it back. I wasn't even sure why I lied, but I managed a calm smile. "He'll get over it."

"Sure."

"Test, my ass," Ethan griped. His face was scrunched together in a snarl. He raked a hand through his wavy sandy hair before letting it fall to his side. He was shorter than Mason, but just as muscular. He wasn't happy. "Logan doesn't get worked up about tests. I bet it's because of Tate. She could always wind him up like that. Why haven't you stopped that yet?"

"Right," Mason bit out, "because my brother *always* does what I want him to do."

"He has many times," Strauss added. "It's already started. He lost his head over her before. He's doing it again."

"And speak of the devil," Heather murmured, her gaze trained on someone down the hall. The group followed her gaze as one. Tate was standing at a locker, laughing with another guy. He wasn't one of their friends, and I didn't recognize him from any classes. He was built like an athlete. His brown hair was cut short and was spiked. When she flicked her hair over her shoulder, his gaze fell to her shirt. He moved an inch taller and a satisfied grin came over him. I had no doubt he'd gotten a good view of cleavage. Then her hand found his chest and rested there for a moment before she moved it down his stomach. As we watched, she leaned closer, and he sucked in his breath. His chest bulged out, and his stomach flattened as her fingers ran all the way down to grasp the waistband of his jeans.

Ethan grunted. "Whore. Always was, always will be." He left the group, and as he passed the flirting couple, his gaze locked with the guy's. Whatever unspoken message was relayed in his stare worked. The guy straightened away from Tate and moved her back. Before she could say anything, he grabbed his bag and hurried away.

Strauss chuckled. "Well if Tate didn't know she was getting inside Logan's head, she knows now."

And sure enough, Tate was standing in the hallway with her arms crossed over her chest, staring at us. Correction. She was studying us.

Strauss flicked her off before walking after his friend. When he drew abreast Tate, his gaze locked with hers. He smirked and we saw him say something to her before he moved past. There wasn't much of a reaction from her, but she cast condemning eyes back to us.

Mason laughed. "He said the same thing, but to her face."

Heather shook her head. "Tate's always been good at messing with a guy's head."

"You think that's what she's doing?"

"No." I was surprised at Heather's blunt response. Then she added, "For Logan's sake, I hope not." She glanced to Mason, but said to me, "I wouldn't want him to get hurt."

I had an eerie feeling something unspoken passed between the two of them, but then she changed the topic. A bright smile was forced out, and she asked me, "Your shift is this Thursday, but could you pick up a few more? I haven't filled Anne and Lily's positions yet."

"Sure. Yeah. When do you need me?"

"Tonight, tomorrow, and Thursday. We've got the weekend covered so far."

"Uh. Yeah. That's fine."

"It's only the five to nine shift." She rolled her eyes at me. I understood. Five to whenever was what it really was. The nine o'clock person rarely left at nine. I nodded. It was still fine with me.

"I'll go running right after school. See you in a few hours."

"See you." She waved at both of us before she headed to the parking lot.

Growing tired, I went with my gut. "Is there something going on I don't know about?"

Mason's eyes got wide. That was his only reaction before he masked it. "What?"

I knew there was, and I was tired of being in the dark. "Just tell me."

"What are you talking about?"

"I'm getting sick of the looks and the silent vibes. What's going on? My guess is that it has something to do with Logan. What is it?"

"Sam," he sighed, stepping closer to me.

I took a breath. Here it was. He was about to say that Logan had fallen in love with Tate again. I prepared myself for the news, but he said instead, "I have no idea what's going on. I don't. Honestly." When I pinned him with an accusing look, he held his hands in the air as if surrendering. "I mean it."

"Then what the hell is going on?"

He shrugged. One of his hands fell to my hip, and he pulled me against him. "My guess is that Logan's dealing with something. He does that sometimes. When he decides to come clean, he will."

"It's not Tate?"

"I don't know, but he seemed pretty insistent that he doesn't have feelings for her again."

It didn't feel right. None of it did, but I let my forehead drop against his chest. His hand swept up and brushed some of my hair back. I closed my eyes, savoring that little tender touch from him. The slightest touch from him sent me buzzing. I let myself breathe him in, filling my lungs, as I remained in his arms. Then I moved back. Mason gave me a reassuring smile, but it didn't reach his eyes.

I spoke before I thought about it. "So that's what it looks like."

"Like what?" He grew guarded.

"A lie. That's what it looks like from you." And then, even though I loved him so much, I turned and walked away. Mason lied to me. I knew it. He knew it. I had lost count how many there were between us now. We were headed down a bad path, and I had no idea how to stop it.

Mason

It'd been two days since Sam called me out. I still felt gutted, but it wasn't my explanation to give. Logan wanted to screw with Tate, make her fall for him and shatter her to pieces like she'd done to him. I didn't like it, but it was Logan's decision. It was his place to share the details with Sam, and I was taking the brunt of it. I was sick of it. After basketball practice, I headed to the parking lot. Sam worked the past two nights and I knew my little brother would be there. We'd been getting food there every time Sam worked and he was telling her what was going on with Tate, whether he wanted to or not.

When I tossed my bag inside my vehicle, I heard from behind me, "Can I have a minute?"

My blood went cold.

Kate was alone, her hands stuffed in her pockets, and her shoulders hunched forward. It was a meek posture, but she wasn't meek. She was just alone.

"What do you want?" I made a show of looking around. "Your friends going to pop out and jump me?"

She frowned. I knew that look. She was on a fishing expedition. "Why would you say that?"

"That's what you're going to do Sam, aren't you?"

"No."

Her arm twitched. She was lying.

"Look," she cleared her throat and her face twitched. I knew that look, too. She was biting the inside of her cheek. "Seeing you now, I don't even know why I bothered."

She turned to leave.

This was bullshit. She showed up so now it was my turn for some fun. "What do you want to know, Kate?"

She paused and then let out a sigh. "Fine. Listen. I need to know that it's done."

"What's done?"

"You and me."

I smirked at her. "There was never a you and me."

"Yes, there was. I was your girl—"

"That I fucked when I needed someone." I sneered. "You kept yourself clean and you didn't *use* to sleep around. I noticed. That's all there was to it. Nothing more."

She visibly swallowed. "There *was* more—"

"No, Kate." It was the lack of caring in my tone. She heard the truth and jerked to the side, as if she were going to leave, but stopped. Her hands tore out of her pockets and balled into fists. They raised in the air, but not high enough that they could do damage. I waited. Kate was a bitch. I enjoyed that I was hurting her. "Come on. You went after Marissa because I was friends with her. Now my girlfriend? For what? To get me back? You're pathetic, Kate."

"Shut up." She flinched with every word I said, but she swung her heated eyes back to me. "You shut up, Mason. You have no idea, no fucking idea why I'm doing this."

"For power? You lost it. That's long gone." When there was no reaction, I laughed. "Haven't you been watching? No one cares. The girls are turning against you."

"You think they'll follow her?" she sneered back.

"No, but they'll like her. No one liked you. They were scared of you, but no one's scared anymore."

"They should be."

"Why?" There it was. She was starting to show her colors. I could see inside of her now. "Are you going to go after every single girl? You don't have the time, and all you'll do is piss 'em all off again. They haven't turned on you yet, but they will. You go after every person, it'll happen."

"So maybe I'll make an example out of her? Maybe that's what I'm doing because people should be scared. They have no idea what I can do."

It would be so easy to pull everything out from underneath her. I wanted to. I wanted to see that look on her face. She couldn't match me, but I held back. "One word of advice, let it go. You've already lost power. You're not going to get it back."

"What do you know about it?"

"You have three friends right now." I saw the scorn on her face. She was thinking she had more. She was wrong. "If you keep targeting Sam, you won't. I'll take them from you."

Her sneer vanished. "You couldn't."

"I could."

She eyed me, studying to see if I was bluffing. I let her see the truth. "Here's your last chance. Drop it all and you can keep your friends. I won't destroy that for you, but keep doing what I know you're planning on doing, and I will ruin you. You'll have no friends. You'll have no allies. You won't even want to come to this school again."

A strangled laugh ripped from her and she shook her head. "Listen to you, big fucking deal here. You're not God, Mason."

"He wouldn't do these things to you." The cruel mask lifted. I let her see how lethal I could be. She saw it and shrunk back. "If you came here to make sure, one last and final time, that there's a chance of you and me, there never was. There's no chance you'll ever be friends with the guys again. I know how you liked to hang out with them. You liked being at the top of the social chain. Those days are dead."

"You shouldn't talk to me like that."

Really? She had no idea, but I fell silent. She was losing her control and I wanted to hear what else she would say.

"You have no idea, no fucking clue!" she shouted now.

Keep going, Kate. Tell me how I don't have a fucking clue. Lay out the rest of your plan for me.

"No idea," she continued to seethe. "Everyone forgets about you, but I don't. You're slumming when you go to this school. They forget about the rich daddy you've got. No one knows about the moneybags your mom has. No fucking clue, but I do. It's not fair. You've got a scholarship. You're going to college. Your life is set, Mason. Most the people at our school are going to community college. They can't afford your NCAA football school."

"That's where this is coming from? I'm going to a better school than you?"

Her chest began heaving. The fury was bright and burning in her eyes. "Haven't you seen my home? You know my folks. My dad's a drunk. My mom works all the time, but when she's not, she's just as drunk as him. You think they saved up money for me? I'm not going anywhere, Mason, not like your precious princess. I've heard about her running. Track scholarship. Isn't that what you were thinking, to get her here? You're right, too. I know you are. She's going to get a scholarship, probably at the same fucking college you go to, and you wanna know why? Because of you. They'll give her one because you asked, because that's how your life goes. You ask and people do it. I'm so sick of it—"

"You're sick of it?" My eyes narrowed to slits. "Or you're pissed because it isn't you?"

"You're such an asshole."

"Been called worse."

"This is my school. This is my time." She grew quiet, but the hatred still burned. "And you declared that we're out. Just like that and it was done. You have no idea how much worse you made it for her."

"If you're pissed at me, take it out on me. Leave her alone."

"Oh no." She shook her head. "You're unfuckingtouchable. You know it and I know it, but your girl isn't. She's going to hurt by the time I'm done with her. She's going to beg me to stop, but I won't. I'll keep ruining her long after this year, even after you go to college. You'll be gone, Mason. I won't. My life's over after high school. My biggest problem is going to be who I'll marry, if it'll be some jackass, or if I'll win the lottery and get someone who sticks around. That's the life I've got to look forward to, but the one thing that'll give me pleasure is going to be destroying your girl. Just watch it."

"Rethink all of this," I warned. "This is my last offer. Walk away."

"No," she whispered, but her tone was murderous.

"You're not going to destroy Sam."

"Oh really?" She snorted.

"You fuck with who I love, and I fuck with you. You're no exception. I'm going to destroy you, Kate. You're going to have nothing left when I'm finished with you." I didn't wait to hear any more crazy shit from her. I got in my vehicle and left without looking back.

CHAPTER FIFTEEN

Samantha

The weekend passed with little drama. There was a basketball game. I went. They won. There was a party. The only big event there was when Logan took my advice and planned on going home with a new girl, but she had a friend with the same hopes. The two got in a fight. It was full of name-calling. Someone's hair got pulled and the other girl got scratched. Eventful. And Logan? He bypassed the fight and went home with Tate. I had an entire speech ready to deliver over breakfast the next day for why he needed to stop seeing her. I had it all memorized, but the speech died in my throat when Tate showed up at the same restaurant with a different guy.

Logan didn't care. Really. I studied him the whole time to catch the slightest reaction—twitch, twerk, eye-roll—but nothing. Then it dawned on me. He really didn't care if she was with another guy. I was at a loss after that. Later that evening, Helen wanted to have dinner with her sons, but I was spared another run-in with her.

I was also spared another run-in with Kate. Mason told me she had something planned for me, but it never happened. I wondered if she'd been distracted.

When I went to school on Monday, the words 'Roussou Sucks' were spray-painted on a banner. It hung over the archway at the front entrance of the school. Heather explained it was the big rivalry game. Fallen Crest Public's basketball team was going to play Roussou High that Friday night.

Great.

Not.

She further spoiled my day when she told me Fallen Crest Academy didn't have their own basketball game that night so my old friends would be in the stands.

Double great.

Needless to say, I wasn't in a great mood during the next week. Logan noticed and brought me a latte one day during lunch. It didn't work. I still wasn't happy so he told Mason to give me a quickie in their coach's office. That certainly didn't help.

It wasn't until Friday morning when another bomb was dropped.

Helen Malbourne was going to attend their basketball game. From the way Mason worded it and how Logan started laughing behind him, I knew there was a joke somewhere. I didn't care enough to figure it out. Instead, I remarked, "I'm sure she'll have a great time."

"Heather's working." Mason gave me a confused look.

"Yeah. And…"

"And…"

Logan finished for him, "Don't you want to sit with our mum for the game? She gets box seats every time. Thinks she's a goddamn celebrity for a high school basketball game. Jokes on her. She's got to share the box with the announcer, and they won't be farting out popcorn for her."

"Logan."

"What?" He glanced at his brother. "Mom thinks she's a big-time celebrity, and you know it. I love her, but her ego's massive. It's gotten worse in the last few months. Wait." He paused, frowning to himself. "Fuck. Is she dating someone new?" Logan gestured to me. "I'm surprised she hasn't tried with Sam's other dad, David." He asked me, "Is he still dating Mark's mom?"

"Um…" I wasn't expecting the question, but my heart sank. I didn't know. An image flashed in my mind. He looked so different when Mason had dropped Jeff off at Academy. He was heavier, muscled, and looked healthy. He looked good. He looked like he was better. I jerked a shoulder up before I turned away. "I guess so."

As I grabbed my bag and headed for the door, I heard the sound of someone getting whacked behind me. Logan muttered, "Ouch. What was that for?" But I was already in the hallway and headed into the elevator.

I drove myself to school that day.

People were screaming in the hallway. Everyone wanted to murder Roussou that night. I knew Mason and Logan were both itching to do the same. Even Heather seemed excited, and she was going to miss the game. She had me sit with her friends at lunch. Since the clothes incident, her friend Cory had thawed towards me a little. I only got two glares instead of the fifteen. Baby steps. On a normal day, that would've been a big deal to me, but this wasn't a normal day.

Logan's comment about my dad had blindsided me.

Their parents were around. Their mother had come back to town. Where was mine? My mother was unfit. My biological father had disappeared back to Boston and David, there'd been no recent contact from him. I saw him the day I registered for school at Fallen Crest Public, but that conversation had been so slight, it'd been meaningless to me.

He moved on. That was the bottom line.

"Yo!"

Someone snapped their fingers in front of me, jerking me out of my daze. "What?"

"Bitch Crew Walking. Head's up."

I think that came from Channing's half-brother? Max? I wasn't sure. None of them had made overt steps towards friendship. I was tolerated because of Heather.

Kate stopped at our table, and the other three fanned out behind her. Like the rest of the school, she was wearing the school colors. She had on red pants and a black shirt. The pants were more like tights, and the black shirt was transparent, showing off her red bra underneath. Her hands went to her hips and she glared at me.

I was getting used to all the glares. I felt naked without seeing a couple a day now.

I grinned up at her. "I feel like I should be a hot-air machine. For every bad look I get, I could pop out a balloon with a smiley face." I smirked. "Bet the glares would stop then."

Heather snorted.

Some of the guys snickered.

I added, "Like right now. You'd get one in black and red." I gestured to Kate's clothes. "It'd match your outfit."

I caught a faint grin from Cory, but it was masked as soon as she saw me watching. Her eyebrows fixed and her face went blank again. I sighed. So close.

Kate's sneer turned into a snarl. "You think you're funny?"

One of the three added, "Maybe she's taking lessons from Logan?"

Another snorted. "Probably. She needs all the lessons she can get."

My smile had stretched from ear to ear now. It was genuine, too. "Is this another warning from you? I thought you moved past the cliché insults and name calling. Oh wait. You said lessons. Yes, that's referencing that I'm dumb. That's another cliché insult." With my hand in the air, I lifted a finger with each point. "I'm ugly. I'm dumb. I have too much sex. Those are the three main ones most simpletons use to insult others. The clothes and the mannequin gave me hope. I thought you were starting to progress, but then I heard that you've already done that before. It's recycled material. You guys need to find new stuff. You know what they say about comedians?" At their blank faces, I nodded. "What I expected. If they use old material, the act is boring. People move on. If you're going to keep drawing fresh fear from everyone, you need new stuff." I stood and patted Kate's head. "You can do it. I believe in you."

Logan stood by the door and held it open. Mason came in behind him. Both found me immediately. I wondered who had notified them, but then Kate grabbed my arm. She twisted it and got into my face. Her hand tightened on my arm and she lowered her voice, "You have until the end of the day to drop out of school. This is the last warning."

A taunt rose to my tongue, but I swallowed it. The jokes were gone.

Three thoughts happened at the same time. David's image flashed again. "Fuck it," came next. Third, when I knew what I was going to do, I thought, "Let's see how this goes."

Kate's eyes widened as she watched the myriad of expressions before she saw my intent. Her hand let me go, and she started to back away, but it was too late. My hand latched onto hers instead, and I took one second to comment, "Bet you weren't expecting this," before my other hand grabbed the back of her head and used all my body weight to slam her head into the table.

Everything went silent for a moment. The only sound I heard was my heart thumping. It was calm and steady. *Thump.*

"You bitch!" someone shrieked from somewhere, but the voices were so far away. They were a slight buzz to me now.

Thump.

People screamed. I heard a few guys swear. Footsteps pounded on the floor. I kept track of all that was happening in the back of my mind. I got a better grip on her head and held her arm down while I tried to lift her head for another slam. She was yelling. I saw her mouth open and caught the flash of terror in her eyes, but then I was jerked backwards. Someone punched me on the cheek. It hurt, but it didn't penetrate the numb sensation that had taken over me.

Thump.

"You're going to get your ass beat." Someone spit on me, but I wiped it off and twisted around. I lunged for whoever was in front of me. She had black hair, maybe Jasmine? I yanked on it and then punched her face.

"Oh, shit!"

"AHHH!"

"Get her off!"

"GET HER!"

I wound up for another hit when I was lifted off my feet. Two strong arms wrapped around me and carried me away. Kicking at them and trying to squeeze out from their hold, I yelled, "Let me go!"

"It's me. Stop, Sam."

Kate was being held up by a couple of guys. I think it was Jasmine that I had hit. Natalie and Parker stood around her and both were glaring at me. One brushed Jasmine's hair from her forehead and was inspecting her face. I growled. I wanted to get them all. Fuck it. I was out for blood now.

Grabbing onto one of the arms around me, I sunk my nails into it. They protested, so I pushed them deeper. I needed to get free. The need to hurt them back was a frenzy inside of me. So many people had hurt me, I wanted to hurt them all—Analise, David, Garrett, Jeff, Lydia, Jessica, Becky, Adam.

THUMPTHUMPTHUMP

"Let me go," I yelled. My voice broke, but I didn't care. I tried again.

A litany of curses came from behind me and I heard, "Sam, it's Mason. Stop it."

THUMPTHUMPTHUMP

"SAM," he yelled in my ear.

"Get her out of here. No one will say anything."

Mason argued over my head, "Yes they will."

"Not if everyone says they're liars. We'll handle it. Get her gone."

"Fine." His arms tightened around me, and he carried me through a side door. We stepped outside before he let me back on my feet. I knew it was cold, but I didn't feel it. I was heated. Enough logic had filtered back in as they discussed what to do with me, but my blood was still boiling. The need to hurt them was so powerful.

My hands shook, and my head went down. I gasped for air, trying to fill my lungs so I could think straight, but it wasn't working. The need to run back inside was aching. I *had* to go back, and I started to, but Mason caught me around the waist. He pushed me against the wall and positioned himself in front of me as a barrier.

"Stop," he murmured. He kept a hand on my stomach, but it was a light touch.

I drew in more breaths and closed my eyes. *Get it together.*

"Sam?"

I shook my head and lifted a hand. I needed a minute. Enough reason had come back, and I was starting to realize what I had done. I still didn't care. There would be ramifications. There were always ramifications. I was trying to remember why I used to care about them.

Mason's statement came back to me at that moment, *Your dad looks ripped. Not bad for a guy his age.* His statement haunted me. So did mine, *It doesn't matter to me anymore.*

It did. I thought it hadn't, but I was a fool. I was beginning to realize how much it did matter to me.

"Sam?"

I heard the concern in his voice and everything melted inside of me. Just like that. The fight left me, and I wanted to disappear. "Mason," I choked out.

He swept me up. My legs wrapped around his waist, and he turned so his back was against the wall. Sliding down to sit on the ground, he started stroking my hair back and rubbing my back at the same time. I clung to him. A minute earlier I'd been ready to tear someone apart, and now I was trying to hold the tears at bay.

"Are you going to tell me what that was all about?"

I murmured against his shoulder, "Besides Kate being a bitch?"

"Yeah," he laughed. His hand kept rubbing up and down my back in long sweeps. He slowed them down as he continued.

"You mean she didn't deserve that?"

"Sam."

I still had some fight left in me. Grinning at that thought, I pulled away enough so I could meet his gaze. "I'm kidding."

"Hey, man."

"Yo."

"Oh, whoa…"

Three guys came around the corner. They were dressed in black clothing that drowned them. They looked like skinny freshmen. All three braked when they spotted us.

Mason barked out, "Leave."

Two scattered. One lingered.

He added, "Now."

The last one took off after his friends.

"Hey."

We glanced the other way. Logan was standing outside the door. Heather popped her head past him and started to step out. He grabbed her arm and pulled her back in. When she started to push through again, he reached for the door. His arm was a barrier now.

She glared at him, but moved so she could see me better. She gave me a gentle smile. "You okay?"

I nodded. "How's it inside?"

"Okay. No." Logan stepped all the way and pushed the door closed.

"Hey," Heather protested. "Come on. I'm her friend. Let me talk to her."

"Give us a minute." It wasn't a request, and he shut the door in her face. When it started to open again, he leaned against it. "Give us a minute, Jax."

She huffed from inside, her voice muffled, "Fine. One minute, Kade."

He rolled his eyes and said to us, "I'm shaking in my boots here."

I frowned. Mason stood and lowered me to the ground. That was a prime opportunity for one of Logan's smart-ass comments. I asked, "Did it look bad in there?"

"It didn't look like you were holding hands and hugging," he griped at me. His tone was biting. "No, Sam. It didn't look good."

"Relax, Logan."

"There's blood all over the table—" he bit off his statement, clenching his jaw at the same time. "Is she okay? Are you okay, Sam?"

I started to respond, but Mason answered first. His hand tightened on my back and he held me against him, speaking over my head, "She's fine. She took one hit, but she's strong."

Logan cursed under his breath before he replied, "She shouldn't get in trouble. We don't have to worry about them calling Analise in for her."

"What'd you do?"

"They already said something, so I told Principal Green that Kate and Jasmine fought each other. Since they didn't want to get in trouble, of course they're going to blame an easy target. Everyone knows how much they hate Sam anyways."

I asked, "Are people going to back that up? All he has to do is ask a freshman or something."

"He won't." Logan's gaze lingered with Mason's. The two seemed to share an unspoken conversation before he added, "Anyone who rats us out will get hurt. They won't."

"I don't care if I get in trouble." But my stomach was protesting again. They were right. Analise would be called. I'd be forced to move back in. "If someone says anything, I'll tell them about everything Kate's been doing to me: the threats, the text messages, stealing my clothes."

Someone began pounding on the door from the inside. There were a few kicks added in and they stopped when Heather yelled, "Let me out. She's my friend, too. Logan!"

"Let her out."

He nodded and stepped away from the door. As soon as it swung open, she punched him in the gut. He didn't move. He didn't even blink, and Heather seemed taken aback. She rubbed one hand with the other before she hissed at him, "That wasn't nice. I thought I was in the trust circle. That's crap."

He ignored her and said to us, "I'm going. See you later, Sam. That was a helluva hook."

When Mason remained, Heather turned her disapproving eyes to him. His hand tightened on my side in reflex until she said, "You can't miss any classes. If you do, you'll be booted from the game. I, on the other hand, can miss all I want. I won't get in trouble with my dad. Go, Mason. I'll clean her up."

He was reluctant.

"I'll be fine." The pain in my cheek was starting to filter in, and he couldn't help with that. "I mean it. I'll talk to you after school."

He frowned, but nodded. Bending to kiss my lips, he thought better and kissed my forehead instead. When he glanced at Heather, I knew there were words he wanted to share, but didn't. An outsider was present. As he stalked through the door and it shut behind him, Heather frowned at me. Her hands went to her hips. "What the hell was all of that about?"

She meant the fight. I sighed. "I miss my dad."

CHAPTER SIXTEEN

Heather took me to her house after the fight. The bruise on my cheek wasn't too big, and it was easily covered with make-up. When she asked if I'd get in trouble for skipping, I didn't think I would. Most of the teachers didn't take attendance and the ones who did never called my name. Because I was still new, I didn't think my name even got onto the attendance sheets. She seemed okay with that answer. When we first arrived, her dad met us in passing, heading back to Manny's after taking a lunch break. She gestured to me and said, "It was those same girls." That was enough for him. He nodded and replied, "Always stand-up for yourself." Then he left.

I asked her later what he meant, and she explained that she informed her dad about everything. He knew about Kate. He knew they were sending her threats. He knew they'd threatened his and her brother's livelihood. I was surprised that he hadn't gone to the principal, but her dad was realistic. He knew nothing would be done and those girls always got away with their bullying. Heather informed me that he gave her permission to defend herself, in any way she needed, and that he would have her back.

Then she added, "My dad's not stupid. He knows there's only so much a parent can do against these types of bullies. If they get in trouble, they'll only do something worse the next time around. That's why he said I don't have to worry about getting in trouble with him."

I nodded.

I didn't know if that was the right thing to do as a parent. My own weren't stellar, but she talked to her dad. He was here for her.

He would support her if she needed it. Then she distracted me when she asked, "You still going to the game tonight?"

There was no question about what game. It was the game against Roussou.

She suggested, "You could sit by my friends. You remember my friend, Max? Channing's half-brother? Dark spiky hair? Usually wears ripped shirts and has tattoos all over him? He always goes when they play Roussou. He likes to spend time with Channing, but Cory and Rain should be in our stands." I grinned at the thought. Cory was like a feral cat. Her 'warming up to me' was not snarling at me. Then she added, "But you'll have all those Academites there, too. You could see some of your old friends."

Mark would be there. His mother might be there, too and that meant…my father. And hours later when I parked outside of the school, it seemed that everyone had come for the game. There were no spots in the parking lot. There were no spots within a four block radius of the school. I finally found an empty spot near the football field and parked. I jogged over it, heading past the parking lot. When I noticed the line that snaked outside of the gym's entrance, I slipped in a side door. Some of the hallways were blocked off, but not all the way. I could slip past one of the gates, and join the mass chaos once I found one I could fit through. The volume in the building was deafening. People was lined up at the concessions, there were lines for the bathrooms, and people were packed into the entrance hallway. Instead of two people selling admissions, they should've had twenty.

I hadn't gone far when someone touched my arm.

Thinking it was Kate, I swung around with a fist already formed.

Instead, it was Mark. "Hi," he shouted in my ear, but is eyes got wide as he stared at my hand. "Uh… never mind?"

"Sorry. Hi." I gave Mark a grin in response. He was friends with Logan, but since his mother started dating David, things had been awkward between the two of us.

He leaned close again. "You like it here?"

I nodded. I couldn't help myself. I looked around him, but there was no sign of his mother. Spotting Adam in a corner, he had his arm around a girl's waist. Mark must've noticed my gaze. He yelled in my ear again, "Yeah, Adam has a new girlfriend. She transferred in this semester." He let out a little laugh. "Or he's trying to get a new girlfriend. I don't think they're official yet."

She was pretty and petite. Her wavy hair was a wheat-golden blonde color and fell to her shoulders. When Adam saw me, he stiffened. She glanced up, a frown on her face, and followed his gaze. When her eyes caught mine, they were a breathtaking green.

I waved at them. Adam jerked his head in a stiff nod back to me. Her gaze lingered on me, and I could see the confusion there. Lifting a hand to his chest, she tipped her head back, the questions already on her lips. As his jaw clenched, I knew she had asked who I was.

When I turned back to Mark, he lifted a shoulder up. "Her name is Kris. He's crazy about her."

I remarked, "That must drive Cass nuts."

"You have no idea." Amusement sparked in his eyes now. "We miss you over there."

My eyebrows went up at that.

"We do. I do. I know Adam does. Not everyone hates you over there." He skimmed me up and down with a wolf-whistle on his lips. "You look good, Sam. Public school must agree with you."

I shrugged. "Seven hours earlier and you would've *really* though that. You look good, too." And he did. Mark had always looked good, but there'd never been an attraction between us. He was six foot two inches, had muscular shoulders, dark hair and the same almond eyes that his mother had. He wasn't the golden-boy beauty that Adam was, and he didn't have the classic handsome features like their other friend, Peter, but Mark's easygoing personality and contagious smile were like a magnet to girls. Always had been. I had no doubt Mark had his pick of the ladies.

He flashed his dimples. "Logan would be proud. I'm doing that workout he was telling me about last weekend…" He trailed off. "He didn't tell you about that?"

"You saw Logan last weekend?"

"I always see Logan. Same parties, you know? But we haven't been getting invites to the public parties like we used to. A lot of people think it's your fault, like you don't want your old classmates there."

I was public enemy number one at Fallen Crest Academy. Not much had changed. Fond memories. "What'd you talk about?"

"What?"

"You and Logan. What'd you two talk about?" That wasn't what I wanted to ask him, though.

He shrugged. "What we always talk about. Girls and lifting weights. What do you talk about with him?"

My eyelid was beginning to twitch. Screw it. "Is your mom still dating David?"

"Your dad, David?"

I nodded. My heart began pounding.

"Yeah. Why?"

"You told me a couple months ago that you thought they were going to get married."

"I know." He gave me a sheepish look. "I'm sorry. I overreacted. My mom told me that your mom and dad hadn't been divorced at the time, but they are now. Aren't they?"

"Are they here?"

"Your mom and dad?"

"*Your* mom and *my* dad," I shouted in his ear. The crowd had doubled, and we were pressed even closer together. I couldn't see Adam anymore.

"Oh." He laughed at himself. "Yeah, they're here. They're with the adults. Why?"

I shook my head. "No reason."

"Oh." His frown came back. "Was I not supposed to say that? Is that a secret or something? I never know what's going on."

"No, it's fine. You're fine." I patted his arm for extra reassurance while a storm had started inside of me. "I'm going to go and find a seat."

"Wait." He tapped my shoulder again. "We heard there's a party at Fischer's tonight and Academites are invited. Is that true? Are you going to be there?"

"Probably." I waved at him again before moving away. "See you later."

"Oh. Okay." His hand jerked up, and he waved it back and forth. "Yeah. See you."

Before going into the packed gymnasium, I needed to go to the bathroom. The lines hadn't lessened and then I heard a buzz inside of the gym, followed by another deafening roar from the crowd. I'd been to enough basketball games to know the teams just left their locker rooms, which meant I needed to hurry. I didn't want to wait in line so I turned a corner and went down one of the darkened hallways. Slipping past one of the gates, I jogged all the way to the bathrooms at the opposite end of the school. No one should be in them and I wouldn't have to wait in line. I would get back by the time they finished their warm-ups.

Everything was going according to plan.

Pushing through the door, the bathroom was empty. It didn't take me long. I finished and washed my hands. When I turned from the hand dryer, I stopped. Everything stopped. In hindsight, I would realize that the dryer drowned out the sounds of their entrance, but it didn't matter. I couldn't have stopped it from happening.

Kate had come inside the tiny bathroom. Parker stepped around her, Jasmine and Natalie following behind. When the door closed behind them, Natalie reached up and locked the door.

All four of them were dressed in black clothing with hooded sweatshirts. The four reached up and pushed back their hoods as one. Each had their hair tied back in a low ponytail.

My stomach dropped.

This wasn't going to end well, but I couldn't get past them. I couldn't call for help. I tried to grin, failing miserably. "Payback?"

Kate's eyes turned feral. She lifted her top lip in a snarl. "This isn't payback. This is your punishment."

Parker sneered at me, her hands hung loose beside her. They were ready to harm someone.

I gulped.

They were ready to harm me.

Then she added, "This is the first wave."

Kate grunted, taking a step closer. "You should've quit school today. I gave you one last out."

Natalie spoke from the back, "Time's up."

The room plunged into darkness, and I had one second. The sounds dimmed like earlier that afternoon. My breathing was now deafening in my ears. My heart started to race, but the fear threatened to paralyze me.

I pushed from the sink and darted into a stall. Someone reached for me. They grabbed my shirt, but I didn't stop. My sleeve ripped off, and I used that to my advantage. As they fell back with my sleeve, I punched at them. Someone cried out, I assumed it was Kate. The other three were behind her, but I got into the middle stall and locked the door. Before I had time to think, I dropped to the ground and flew underneath to the next stall.

A foot stepped on me. I heard, "She's in this one."

Fuck.

The foot lifted in the air. It was going to kick me, but I thrust a hand out blindly. I caught it, but there was too much force behind it. It crushed two of my fingers, and I clamped my mouth shut. A scream wanted to burst out of me, but I swallowed it. Good god, I swallowed it. No sound. No tears. No cries. They couldn't hear anything from me. I wouldn't give them the satisfaction. Pushing past that blinding pain, I threw my shoulder up and into the person. It was enough. She fell back, and I heard more cries.

"Get off me, Parker."

"It was that bitch."

"Let's turn the lights on. This is stupid."

"No, someone might see. If the door's locked, they won't come in here."

"Shut up and get her," Kate barked at them.

I heard the pain in her voice. I must've hit her harder than I thought, but then I heard someone fall to the ground. They were trying to crawl in like I had. Flipping around, I kicked at them instead.

"Ouch! Bitch!"

I kicked them again, and again, and again. I kept kicking them. It was working, but suddenly two hands grabbed my arm, and I was yanked from underneath the last stall. The exit door was right there. I pushed to my feet and reached for it. My fingers hit it, but then I was pulled back again. I made for one last reach. I grunted from the effort, but I got to it. The lock moved down.

I was thrown back to the floor after that. I couldn't even turn over before fists were coming down on me.

They hit my jaw.

They hit my eyes.

They pulled my hair out.

They ripped my shirt.

They punched my stomach.

And then the kicks started.

To my side. Down on my ribs. On my head. To the side of my head. Then to my hips. They wouldn't stop. I couldn't keep going. My eyes were swollen shut by now. I lifted my hands, but only to ward off their attacks. I couldn't fight anymore. The pain was too much and I couldn't get through them. The door was less than five feet away, but it could've been five miles now.

"HEY!"

Oh, thank god, I thought for a brief second. There was a pause, and they stopped.

The door burst open and someone braked. Their sneakers screeched against the floor from their sudden stop. She choked out, "Oh my god."

"You—" Kate started, her tone menacing.

They took off.

No one moved. The door shut behind whoever it had been. Then Kate screamed, "Stop her!"

Natalie was panting. "She's gone. We should get gone, too."

"We're not done."

"She can't move. Let's go."

"NO."

"Kate, you can't kill her, and that freak saw us. We need to get to her before she tells anyone it was us."

Jasmine spoke up, a tremor in her voice, "You think she's going to tell?"

"Yes," Natalie snapped at her. "Idiot. She's going to get help for this cunt. Let's go."

She stepped over me, but kicked me one last time before shoving through the door. The rest lingered, and she roared from the hallway, "LET'S FUCKING GO!"

Each of them kicked me one last time on their way out. I couldn't fight them. I knew it was coming, but the pain had paralyzed me. This wasn't a pain that I could shut off. It didn't take me away from my reality. I was here the whole time. I could hear, and I could think, but I couldn't do a thing to stop them. When the door shut behind them, and I lay there alone, I finally gasped for breath. Even my mouth hurt. I could taste blood, and I felt its wetness all over me.

Please don't let them get Mason. Or Logan. That was my one prayer. Whoever they were getting, whoever would come through those doors again, I didn't want it to be either of them. They couldn't see me like this. They'd lose control. They'd do something horrific, and I couldn't lose them because of this.

"In there," I heard someone yell from farther down the hallway. Their sneakers were pounding on the floor. I could feel their approach, and then their shapes blocked the light from under the door. They were right there, on the other side.

Please not them, I prayed again to myself.

When they started to open the door, I closed my eye…and then I waited.

A woman choked out, "Oh my god."

That wasn't Mason or Logan. It wasn't someone I knew. My eyelid opened, but I could only see through a small slit. They were too swollen for much more.

Gentle hands touched me as she knelt beside me. "Oh, dear. Samantha?"

The girl remained in the back, but she spoke up, "They were beating her. All four of them."

"Who, sweetheart?" The warmth in that voice washed over me in waves. She touched the side of my face and turned it to the side. More light shined on me, and she sucked in her breath again. "Oh, dear." She glanced up again. "Who did this to her?"

"Some other girls."

Wait—I knew that voice. Images of Heather's friend flooded me. It was Cory.

Then the lady asked, "Can you and your friend go find someone for me?"

"The principal?"

"Yes, dear, but I'd also like you to find someone else."

"Okay."

Gone was the goth girl from earlier, with her constant glares and venom-laced words. Cory reminded me of a little girl in that moment.

"Do you remember the gentleman that was standing next to me?"

"Yes." Her voice dipped again with emotion.

"Go get him."

"Who is he?"

The hand rested on her arm this time. It was strong and healing. I felt this woman's courage through that touch, and I drew in a shuddering breath. I needed it. I needed every bit of strength this woman was giving to me.

"Try to be quiet about this. We don't want to draw a lot of attention."

"Who's that guy?" Cory questioned again.

I drew in another breath. I didn't know why she was insisting, but it felt good. Like she was looking out for me.

Then I heard the answer, "That man is Samantha's father."

The door closed again. I felt the small draft. It was soothing against the burns from everything else. Then the woman moved so I could see her. Dark eyes and brown curls framed her face. Malinda Decraw smiled at me, though I could see the hesitation in her. She nodded, but it was as if she were reassuring herself. She murmured, "We're going to get you some help, Samantha. I promise, honey." Her last word stumbled out and hitched on a sob. "Everything will be fine."

Her hand brushed my hair back. Her fingers trailed through it, and I wondered if it was the only place she could touch me. She repeated again, speaking to herself now, "Everything will be fine..."

CHAPTER SEVENTEEN

My dad was there.

That thought was on repeat in my mind. For some reason it helped block the pain. He came with Principal Green and both of them had been quiet since they came in. I couldn't see them. Malinda kept patting my hand. I wasn't even sure if Cory had returned with them.

When they began discussing plans, and I heard the word ambulance, I tried to tell them not to call for one. My lips cracked open and blood rushed inside my mouth, but I swallowed enough so I could talk. "No." It came out as a whisper.

"David." Malinda stopped their quiet conversation. Her hand patted mine. It was so gentle. "She's trying to say something."

"Hi, honey." He stepped so he was in my line of sight and plastered a fake smile on his face. It was one of the worst I'd seen.

I tried again, "Don't call them."

"What, honey? Sammy, sweetheart." He knelt down and bent closer to my lips.

I repeated, "Don't call them. I can walk."

"Samantha," he stopped and moved out of eyesight. There was a sniffle, followed by a cough before he came back. The light from above reflected off a trail of moisture on his face, but there were no tears. He said again, "You can't move. We have to get an ambulance. There could be internal damages."

I tried to shake my head. Mason and Logan couldn't know. They'd react without thinking or worse. I felt a different pang go through me. They might assume it had been the Roussou people. That would be worse. I whispered out again, "No, please no."

"I'm sorry, honey." He lifted a hand to pat my hand, but held it in the air. There was nowhere to touch.

Malinda moved her hand. "I don't think she's hurt here."

He closed his eyes and took a couple breaths. They came out sounding jerky, but then he reached over and touched my hand in the same spot. He patted it, but it was so light it was more of a gentle graze. "Honey, Samantha, your principal's already gone to call them."

I sucked in air through my cracked lips. I wanted to protest.

"But we'll have them come through the far end door. People at the game won't see then."

The relief was overwhelming. Fresh tears came to me, and they spilled down my face, stinging as they slid over the damage.

He added, "You don't want Mason and Logan to see you right now, do you?"

I stopped trying to talk, but I shook my head. It was the smallest movement I could muster. I was trying so hard.

"We won't let this out, but the paramedics have to come and get you. We're scared of moving you."

I closed my eyes. I could breathe easier, as easily as I could. He understood. Mason and Logan wouldn't find out until later. I hoped to be the one to tell them, if I could, but when the EMTs came in with a stretcher, I was beginning to realize that it would be a long while until I could do anything for myself. When they rolled me onto the stretcher, I couldn't move. My ribs ached. My chest pounded. Sharp pangs stabbed me, shooting up and down, all over me.

As we rolled down the hallway, I saw Cory beside the lockers. She stood there with Rain huddled behind her. Their hands looked as if they were clasped together, but I couldn't be sure. When her gaze caught mine, she lifted one side of her mouth. I tried to relay my thanks. She saved me.

I couldn't see her anymore as they wheeled me the opposite direction and out a back door. I barely felt the cold air. It stung my face, but the rest of me was wrapped in a blanket. I could move my legs, even wiggle my toes, but they hurt. Everything hurt.

"Yo, what's that?"

Principal Green let out an exasperated sound. "If you two are here for the game, you should be on the other side of the school."

"Relax, dude. We don't even go here."

"Then you're trespassing. Get off the school's grounds. Wait," his voice rose, "get away from her."

"Relax…" the voice trailed off, and I saw Brett Broudou standing above me. When he recognized me, his eyes widened, and his mouth opened. The cigarette he had poised at his mouth lowered. "Whoa…"

"Who is it, Brett?"

That must've been Budd.

I wanted to look away, but I didn't. He wouldn't move. He kept staring, so I looked back at him. A storm of emotion flashed in his gaze before he demanded, "Who did this to you?"

"That's enough," my dad stepped forward. He held a hand up and moved him back. "She needs to get to the hospital, son."

"Son," Budd ground out from somewhere. There was a bitter laugh in him. "You hear that, Brett? Geezer called you 'son.' We'll show you 'son'. We'll show you a whole different meaning—"

Brett snapped at him, "Shut up, Budd." He gentled his tone and asked, "Is she going to be okay, sir?"

My dad paused, frowning at him. "Are you friends with her?"

I needed to tell him. I had to stop him.

"Sir, I met her at Manny's."

"Brett, come on." Another menacing growl from Budd. "This is fucking ridiculous. Her pussy's damaged now. Let's focus on the Kades."

That got my dad's attention. His head jerked to wherever Budd was. I could still see Brett, and I saw him flinch, before he sighed and moved out of eyesight.

"Let's go." Principal Green stepped forward. His authority came out full force, and he pounded a hand on the ambulance's door. "David, don't even bother. I recognize these two. They were banned from the game. I'll have security take care of them. You go with your daughter."

"She's your daughter?"

"Who cares? We need to go, Brett. They'll escort us out, and we'll have to sneak back in. Let's tail it now."

Principal Green stood above me now. He was watching them, but he glanced down. He gave me one reassuring look before he murmured quietly to me, "I won't tell, Sam. They won't know."

The relief was overwhelming. Again. Tears burst forth, but I couldn't wipe them away. They had strapped me to the stretcher so I wouldn't shift any bones or my insides. I was in so much pain.

"David," Principal Green said as my stretcher was lifted into the ambulance. The paramedics got me into place. "You can go with her. Malinda already took your car. She's going to meet you there."

"Yeah, okay."

When he climbed inside the ambulance, he sat as close to me as possible. The doors were shut, and it wasn't long until the engine was started. As it turned onto the street, David reached out and took my hand. I'd never seen him this sad. He brushed at a tear, but tried to smile for me. "Don't worry, honey. You'll get looked at and everything will be fine."

No, Dad. Everything wouldn't be fine.

That was the truth. I was just realizing that I still hadn't let him in on it.

Mason

When I left the locker room, only a few were still in the gymnasium. Most were heading to Manny's and then to Fischer's for a big damn party. I knew Logan was riled about it, had been during the whole game and after. When I saw him jumping up and down near the bleachers, and our mom watching him, I rolled my eyes. Logan was ready to tear into someone.

"Honey." Helen stood up from her seat and gave me a gracious smile. If Sam were there, I knew she would've been self-conscious. My mother dressed to impress. I never cared what clothes she wore, but it mattered to her what others thought. She pressed a kiss to my cheek and she patted me on the shoulder before moving to press her hair back in place. "You were fabulous. It was a close game, wasn't it?"

Logan snorted, but kept jumping up and down. He was rubbing his hands together before jabbing them into the air.

"We won by four points. It was close, Mom."

"See. I know a little about basketball."

I didn't care. "Did you see Sam here?"

She stiffened before shaking her head. "No, honey. Was I supposed to look for her? I'm sure she sat with some of her friends."

Logan snorted again, still jumping. "She doesn't have friends at this school."

"Logan."

"What? She doesn't. It's your fault, not hers."

Helen skirted between us. "Are you suggesting Samantha has no friends because of her boyfriend?"

"Yeah, Mom, I am." He stopped jumping and gave her a dead look. "Your son's the cream in a pussy's food dish. The claws come out. Bitches and pussies fight over that shit. You should be proud."

When Helen didn't respond, I chuckled. "Don't worry, Mom. You can be proud Logan's the cat's meow."

Horror flashed first as she twisted around. "Logan? She's with you now?"

Logan glanced at me. We shared a look before he rolled his shoulders back, squared his chin away and threw out his cocksure attitude. "Is this news to you? I'm hurt that you're even surprised by this."

"I... I..." she sputtered, drawing to her tallest height. "I'm not. Of course not, I'm just taken aback by the camaraderie between you two. There's no hard feelings?"

"Why would there be?" Logan asked, throwing an arm around my shoulders. He lifted up on his tiptoes so we were the same height and then he patted me on the arm twice. "She dips in both of our cream dishes."

"Logan!" We waited as she swayed on her feet, a hand to her chest. Then she sputtered again, "This is disgusting. I implore both of you to break up with this girl. If she's doing what you're insinuating, this will go down a bad road. Trust me. You both need to stop seeing her." She paused and an old flare came over her. "Her mother alone is a good enough reason to try for someone better. Horrible breeding. You both need to preserve where your semen goes. Once you've reproduced, there's no going back. That child is in the world for the rest of your life—"

I'd had enough. "Mom." I shrugged Logan's arm off me. "We're joking with you. Sam's still my girlfriend, and it's not her fault she doesn't have friends here. Some of the other girls are jealous."

"Oh."

We waited. One second.

"You two are horrible children. To joke like that? Why would you even think about something like that in the first place?"

"Relax, Mom." Logan threw his arm around her shoulders. When she tried to smooth out her shirt's collar, he said to me, "I already asked around. No one's seen her."

Heather was working. Sam knew her old classmates would be

there. It made sense if she opted out. "She's probably watching a movie at home or something."

"Or she's already at the party and getting drunk."

Sometimes my brother really pissed me off.

"What?" He flashed me a grin. "It'd be awesome if she were. My sis needs to get drunk more. Last time she did, she and Tate got into it. That was hilarious." His smile turned wistful. "I'd pay money to see something like that again."

"Okay." Helen gave us a kiss on our cheeks. "I can tell where this is going so I'm going to be heading out myself."

When she collected her purse from the bleachers, Logan asked, "Are you going back to the hotel?"

She snorted. "Oh no. I'm not eighty years old. I've got plans myself. I'll see you both for dinner tomorrow night? Samantha is always welcome to come. Please extend the invitation to her."

"Wait."

She paused. "Mmm?"

"So what are you doing tonight?"

"Mason, son. I do love you, but just because *your* girlfriend doesn't have girlfriends doesn't mean every female can't have girlfriends. It's a girls' night tonight. I would tell you both not to wait up for me, but you never do. I'll just say my farewell with, 'Don't impregnate anyone tonight.' How's that?" She waved at them as she headed for the doors.

I waited until she was through the door before I commented, "Mom doesn't have friends."

"She has cousins."

"Sisters."

"Sisters-in-law."

"But no friends," I finished. We shared a look before I cursed. "She has a date tonight."

Logan groaned. "There went my pre-buzz. That's like my foreplay before partying."

"I want to get drunk tonight."

"I'm down with that."

We started for the door and as we went through the gym doors, heading for the building's exit doors, I heard my name called. I couldn't see who it came from so I kept going. We hadn't gotten far from the doors before two people stepped from the line of trees near our Escalades. As I recognized the Broudou brothers, five more followed them.

Logan gave me a pointed look. He was down for whatever happened. It was the look we'd been using since childhood. Fuck it. If this was the time, this was the time. The need to bust someone up was with me and I was done waiting to get even with them. "You put my best friend in the hospital. I thought the next step was ours."

Budd shook his head, and the skin on his neck shifted from the movement. He brought a bat out from behind him and tapped it against his leg before leaning his weight onto it. "Well, we were going to do that." He gestured to his brother beside him. "Brett wondered if that was smart. I think he said we should kick the pooch while it's down. I heard he got a few broken ribs and he's being baby-sat by his rich mommy and daddy. It was all over our school. The famous movie folks are back in Fallen Crest."

Logan narrowed his eyes. "You think we're some goddamn pooches?"

"You're a man down." He made a show of looking around. "Looks to me like no one else is around."

"We heard there was a big party," Brett added.

Logan snorted. "Aren't you supposed to be banned from our campus?"

"Yeah." Budd laughed, the sound was menacing. "They caught us twice, but we keep coming back. We'll keep coming back, you know. That's how we operate. No damn Kade is going to beat us."

"That's not what the scoreboard says inside."

The smirk vanished from Budd's face. He brought the bat up and began tapping it against his free hand.

I was done with this. I heard what Budd said, they weren't going away. They would keep coming back. It was the same sentiment from Kate. I had a plan too, but right now I didn't want to wait for it to happen. He brought the bat, but I was going to use it on him and with that in mind, I stepped forward. The movement wasn't to close Logan out, it was to seal our ranks. Our backs would go against each other. It was the same system since our first fight in elementary.

The rest of them registered the movement and they dropped their stance, ready to start fighting.

"Mason!" someone called. It was the same voice from before.

Brett threw his brother a sidelong glance. "There weren't supposed to be any others around."

"Shut up," he snapped back. "I'm aware, you idiot."

Someone darted across the parking lot. It was a girl but not someone I recognized. Dressed all in black, her clothing looked like it was trying to devour her. She stopped before us and held a hand up as she caught her breath. Then she swallowed before she said, "Kate beat Sam up. She's in the hospital."

I went cold.

Sam was hurt.

Sam was in the hospital.

Kate did it. She put Sam in the hospital. My hand jerked at my side. It ached to find her neck, wrap around it, and squeeze.

Logan snapped his head around. "What?"

"Sam?" Brett echoed.

No. I changed my mind. I was going to take her friends away first and then I was going to destroy her for good.

"Was it *just* Kate?"

Everyone went still. The threat of violence had already been in me. That was where it was going with Broudou, but this was different. Everyone sensed it. A dark need rose now. The tension in the atmosphere doubled.

Someone I loved was hurt.

The girl flinched from my savagery, but she caught herself. She didn't cower as she replied, "It was all four of them. I found her and got help. I found the first person I thought was a teacher. They called an ambulance and shipped her out." She gasped again as a sudden wind rocked against her. Some hair slipped to cover her face, but she ignored it. "She was hurt real bad. She wanted me to tell you."

"Wait," Budd ground out. "You mean—"

"Let's go, brother," Brett stopped him. He stepped forward and urged his brother away. "She's not part of this. Let's go."

"Yeah, but—"

"LET'S GO," he barked at him now. "They've got *school* problems. It's not the right time for this." With that last word, he shoved Budd ahead. He was a few inches in front of me now.

Budd opened his mouth to argue, but it only took one punch.

He was right there. I reacted. I didn't want to hear any more from him, so I punched him. I hit him across the face—one hit—and he dropped. He was out cold. I turned to Brett, waiting to see what he was going to do.

The other Broudou stepped back and murmured, "I ain't here to fight any more. You need to go take care of your woman."

It was in the back of my mind to question him. He said we had school problems, but I could see from the other goliath-sized Broudou that he knew better. I didn't care. Not then. I needed to get to Sam. That was my first priority.

I jerked my head towards my car and said to the girl in black, "Get in my car. You're going with us."

Her eyes popped out, but she scrambled around the unconscious Broudou and climbed into the passenger side. Logan was already in his and didn't wait. He peeled out of the parking lot. I sat there and waited, clenching and unclenching my fingers around the steering wheel while they moved Budd from behind my car.

One second.

Two.

They had one more second before I was going to run over him.

Brett dragged his brother clear on the last second, and I reversed, spinning around on the fourth second.

CHAPTER EIGHTEEN

Mark was alone, waiting for us in the lobby at the front of the hospital. He stood as we rushed through the door. Nothing was asked, nothing needed to be asked. He gestured down the hallway. "I was waiting for you. They're in a different waiting room. The doctor's with her right now."

Logan frowned. "What are you doing here?"

He gestured to the girl who had followed behind me. "She got my mom."

Logan and I turned to regard her.

"Uh…" She wavered at our attention. "Um…" Clamping her mouth shut, her cheeks got red, and she began pulling at one hand with the other. "I just found the first adult who looked…" She shrugged. "I don't know why I picked her. I didn't know her."

I didn't care. I turned back to Mark. "Where's Sam?"

She finished, "She looked capable. That's why I picked her."

Logan grunted. "No one cares anymore."

"And she was standing next to the principal," she added. "That was another reason why I picked her."

"Mason."

We whipped around. David Strattan was coming towards us. His hair was sticking up, there were bags under his eyes and his Fallen Crest Academy athletic jacket was wrinkled. Blood was smeared all over it.

I faltered. There was not much that scared me, but I was scared now. I couldn't look away from the blood on Sam's dad's shirt. That was her blood. It had to be. I was gutted at what they had done to her.

"Where is she?" My voice came out hoarse. No way could I be weak. Not now, that's for damn sure. "Where is she?"

"The doctor is with her, but I've been told that it's not as bad as it looks."

I growled. That didn't make it better.

"They think," David moved to stand between us and the hallway. His hand lifted in the air in a calming motion. "They think she'll have a few fractured ribs, but most of the damage is superficial."

"What's that mean?" Logan demanded.

"It means she looks awful, but it's mostly bruising. Her face is swollen. She couldn't open one of her eyes when I was with her, but they're sure it'll heal on its own."

"Where is she?" The need to see her was too powerful. I could barely hold it in, and I looked down the hallway. I'd go from one room to the next to find her. "Where is she?!"

"She's with the doctor, Mason." Mark moved forward.

I jerked my head to him. "Who've you told about this? If that fuckhead Adam walks through here, I'm laying him out. I won't tolerate him coming in here and acting all buddy-buddy with her. Not now."

"Mason—"

"Not now, Mark," I interrupted him.

Mark lifted both hands in the air and took a step back. "I didn't call anyone. I swear. I wouldn't do that to Sam."

"Fuck this," Logan bit out before he shoved past the older Strattan. He started down the hallway and I went right after him. We weren't getting answers, not the ones we wanted. We'd find her ourselves.

"Boys," David called after them. "Mason, I really need to discuss something with you before seeing Sam."

I shoved open a door. "I really need to see Sam first." She wasn't in that one. I moved to the next.

"Mark, maybe you can take the girl to the waiting room?"

"Are you sure?"

"Yes. I'll show them to her room and then I have some things to discuss with them after. Go. I'll send your mother in a moment as well." I heard the exhaustion in David's voice.

Logan was further down the hallway. He'd open a door, poke his head in and leave. A few people came to the hallway and watched as he repeated the process, but I stopped. I twisted around and saw David at the end of the hallway. He was waiting for us and he was too patient about it. I sighed as I went back to him. "She's not in this hallway, is she?"

Logan was at the end of the hallway now. He circled and started opening doors on the side I had stopped.

"As soon as the doctors will let us see her, you'll be the first one in." David frowned as he rubbed a hand over his face. His eyes opened and closed, as if trying to focus on me. Then he began rubbing them with the palm of his hand. "I never thought I'd be here again."

"Again?" I went cold. "Again? You mean without Analise being in the equation."

David hesitated before saying, "Mason, son—"

"I'm not your fucking son. If you're going to throw the father term around, start acting like it with the one person who's still hurting because you left her."

"I didn't..." His face paled.

I watched as the blood drained from Sam's father's face. I didn't care. I was being kept from seeing her. It was driving me nuts. David knew it. Noticing a sign for the emergency room further down an adjourning hallway, I knew where she'd be. "Screw it. She came in on an ambulance. She'd go there first."

"Mason."

I hauled ass down the hallway.

David jogged to keep up. "Mason, I really do need to talk to you before you go in there."

He could talk all he wanted. I wasn't slowing down.

"Because you need to be on board before you go in there."

"Be on board with what?" I got into the emergency room section. This floor was different from the one we were just in. The walls were painted an off-white color. I headed towards the main desk, but began glancing into each room I passed.

"That's what I'm trying to talk to you about." He stopped then, but his voice lifted, "I've already talked to Samantha about it and she agreed. It would be best if you heard about it from me first and not her. She's already worried about how you'll react and this is the best decision for her well-being. You cannot go in there and make her feel guilty about this decision. I won't allow it, not after what she's been through tonight."

I had no choice. The urge to do physical damage had been with me since the Broudous showed up. It had increased since then, and David Strattan wasn't helping. "If you don't start talking, I'm going to start not giving a shit whose father you are. The two things I know right now is that Sam is hurt, and I have to get to her. Logan's still over there. He hasn't figured out that she's not in that part of the hospital. You're doing a lot of talking, but you aren't saying shit. Start talking or I'll let him loose on this department."

David didn't wait another second. "Sam's coming home with me."

"Like hell she is."

"She is, Mason."

"No."

The older man sighed. "It's really not your call. I'm trying to do my 'fatherly' duties as you enjoy throwing in my face. I'm standing here and blocking you because this is the best thing for her."

"Fuck that and fuck you."

"Mason."

"No, she's living with us. We'll take care of her."

"You haven't—"

"Better than you," I threw back. My hands jerked up, but I stopped and stepped back. "I've taken care of her when you let her go with that crazy psycho. We protected her from Analise. Me and Logan. What'd you do? You stood back and let her go with her. You're stepping up now? The crazy bitch isn't here anymore. You're protecting her from me?"

David's jaw tightened. His shoulders lifted as his chest rose. He drew in a deep breath before he bit out, "You are getting on my last nerve, boy."

"Boy?" I chuckled, but I wasn't amused. "Don't stand and puff up your chest to me. We both know where this is going. I should respect you? Because you're Sam's dad? Because you're older than me?" My eyes narrowed to slits. The same lethal intent was there that'd been since I saw Budd Broudou. It was pumping through me and it was growing the longer he kept me from her. "I've been around enough screwed-up adults to know that they don't deserve any respect unless it's earned. I've not seen a damn thing from you except now. I'm the wrong person you need to be protecting from her."

"Right now, you're exactly the person I need to protect her from. She's hurt, Mason." David's jaw was still clamped tight, but he gentled his tone. "She's going to need help all day. Are you going to be there for her? You're going to skip school? Quit the basketball team? Not graduate? I know you have a full scholarship already, but it's contingent on graduating first. You can't be there for her, neither can Logan."

"And you can?"

"Better than you. Malinda doesn't work—"

"You're going to have your girlfriend take care of her?"

"No. I'm going to be there, but I have to work during the day. During that time, Malinda will come to the house and be there. She doesn't work, Mason. Would you rather have someone else?"

"Me."

"You can't," David snapped at me. "Get that through your head. Do you have a better choice? Your mother? I'm not putting Samantha through that. I'm aware of the disdain Helen has for Sam. Analise? Is that a better choice?"

I closed my eyes for a second, pressing my hands against them. A headache was raging in me. Fuck. I was always the cold one. I remained calm when everyone else panicked, but not now. I couldn't get a grasp on that old Mason, but David was right and it was killing me. I relented, I had no choice. "I get to see her at night."

"No deal."

"That's the only deal. I sleep over."

"She's my daughter."

"She's the love of my life." My heart was pumping so damn fast. I needed to see her.

David was searching my eyes.

I let him see the truth. I needed her. That was the only way.

"Fine, but only you. Logan can't start sleeping over, too."

"He'll try."

David groaned. "You two, you just storm your way in—"

"We're family to her. We took her in when you let her go. We protected her from that woman." I was relentless. I knew it was hurting him, but I kept throwing it in his face because it was true. I forced myself to think rationally and I knew what David Strattan was saying was the best thing for Sam. Logan and I couldn't skip school to take care of her, and I didn't want her close to either mothers. I didn't know Mark's mom, but Mark was an okay guy. If Sam wasn't okay around that woman, I would stop everything. I'd hire someone, or hell, I'd take her to Nate's house. She could heal next to Nate. His mom would love Samantha.

David looked away.

I saw it was hard for him to accept. Then he nodded. "Fine. You and Logan can both stay the night—"

"Where is she?"

He lifted his defeated eyes to mine. "Follow me."

Samantha

After being admitted to the hospital, they gave me pain medication that put me to sleep. It was later that night when I woke. No one was there except Mason, who was sleeping in the lounge chair beside my bed. An opened pizza box was on my tray table along with a plastic water pitcher and a bunch of plastic cups. It hurt to talk, but after reaching for his hand, I didn't need to. He woke up and offered me a smile. The worry and love in his gaze made my stomach jump into my chest. I'd never get used to it. Never. When he realized I couldn't talk, he did most of it for me.

Logan had been there earlier and refused to leave, but Mason made him go. He wanted alone time with me when I woke. He said he pulled Boyfriend Rank. It would've been nice to see Logan, but I understood. The pain medication was wonderful, but there was an ache inside of me. I felt hollow, and it had nothing to do with my physical pain. Mason was the only one that could fill that emotional void, and I needed him. I needed him badly. When I patted my bed, he hesitated. I patted it again and scooted as far to the side as possible to make room for him.

"You have two fractured ribs, a dislocated jaw, and you look like a truck ran over you. I can't, Sam." His was gruff and his throat closed off on the last word. After he took a moment, he continued, "I just can't, Sam. I'm so scared I'll hurt you."

I narrowed my eyes and tried to show him my determination. I couldn't do much else, so I patted the bed again with a hard slap.

He still hesitated.

Then I hit his arm before moving onto my back again. I had to go slow, but I couldn't stop the tear that formed and trickled down my cheek. When I lifted my hand to brush it away, my skin felt like it wasn't mine. It was an uncomfortable feeling, an unwanted one, and I needed his support even more to push it away.

The bed dipped under his weight. He paused with one foot before shaking his head and mumbling, "I'm not going to be able to sleep. I'm going to be so damn scared that I'll hurt you."

It didn't matter. None of it mattered. When he shifted to his side and then reached for my hand, I closed my eyes. I could sleep now. Everything would work out. Our hands were tucked between us on the bed. I clung to his, while he seemed scared to hold mine back. That didn't matter either. I just needed to be held, a mere touch from him. It anchored me, and as that feeling of being centered came back, the heaviness of exhaustion folded back over me. It wasn't long until I fell asleep.

The nurse checked on us, but she didn't ask him to leave. When he started to get up, I gripped his hand harder. She caught the movement and only waved for him to stay. "Looks like you don't have a choice." As she headed back out, we heard her mutter to another nurse in the hallway, "They grow them like that nowadays? Sign me up to be a cougar. Holy crapola."

Mason chuckled next to me. He had moved so his mouth rested against my shoulder and his breath teased me. It warmed me even more when he yawned. "They've been coming in every hour to check on you. You wouldn't let me go the first time either."

I couldn't talk, but I tried to smile. I couldn't even do that so I rested my head against his. Sleep overcame me again. The rest of the night was spent like that. I was in and out of it. Mason was always there. I think one of my nurses took pity on Mason. She snuck another hospital bed into my private room and lowered a rail on one side of it and one side of mine, then pushed them together to make almost a full size bed. Mason gifted her with a smile and I thought she was going to pass out in my room. When the other nurses came in, their gazes went immediately to him; it didn't take a genius to figure out that the word had spread. We even heard one comment as she checked my vitals, "They weren't kidding about the hottie."

When she noticed that we had heard, she shrugged. "Nights can be the best shift or the dullest. The girls are in a tizzy about another guy. He likes to streak naked down the halls at night. If he looked like you, I don't think the other girls would mind."

"Can you tell us that?"

As she typed something into a computer, she shrugged again. "He's due for another run soon so you're going to see it with your own eyes if your door is open. Take it as more of a warning. Don't get scared if you see a flash sprinting past your door. He doesn't go into other patients' rooms." Then she patted my other leg as she moved around the bed. "You're looking better, girly. You should get discharged in the morning."

Two minutes after she left, we heard her yell, "Stop right there, four-thirty-two! Do not go into the nursing ward. Four-thirty-two!"

A streak of bare flesh darted past our door.

Mason grinned at me. "It's like we didn't even miss Fischer's party tonight."

My nurse sprinted past our door, followed by another two.

Except there are no nurses at those parties. I tried to say that, but I couldn't. My mouth must've twitched because Mason turned sharply to me. "Are you okay?"

I nodded, sighing at the same time, except I couldn't do that either. Breathing was difficult so I took a small breath, followed by another one. I was closing my eyelids again when he said my name.

"Sam."

My heart began racing as I heard how serious he was. I frowned.

He took a deep breath. "I don't know what I'm supposed to do here. I don't know if I'm supposed to distract you. If I'm supposed to make you laugh, or if I'm supposed to be reassuring you. I have no idea what to do, so all I'm doing is just being here."

Oh goodness. My heart raced faster.

His voice grew rough again, and he added, "You can't talk back to me, and I need to hear your voice. I need to know you're okay."

I tried to squeeze his hand.

He laughed to himself, lifting them, kissing the back of mine. Then he pressed it against his cheek and took another deep breath.

"I'm so fucked up right now. We were going to fight the Broudou brothers when that chick showed up. I don't even know who she is. She took off when we finally got to your room, and I haven't let anyone else in here. Logan was supposed to tell people you're fine." He broke off and cursed under his breath. "I'm so goddamn sorry." He frowned before he shook his head again. "What I'm trying to say is that everything will be okay. Kate won't hurt you again. I'll take care of her, and I'll end this thing with the Broudous. I know it's been bothering you, too. I'll take care of everything. I know you're going to stay at your dad's. That's fine. I want you to know that I'm fine with that. I made him agree to let us stay there, too, so we'll all still be together. What the hell am I saying here?"

I wanted to smile at him. I wanted to pull him into me and have him wrap his arms around me, but I couldn't do either. I couldn't even tell him to shut up because I loved him, too. That's what he was trying to say, but he was never this awkward about it. I lifted my hand to his cheek. I cupped the side of his face the same way he always cups mine, and I pulled him to me.

"Sam?" His eyes grew wide and he hesitated.

I pulled again, this time firmer.

He relented until I had moved his face right to mine. I couldn't feel it, but I pressed his lips to mine. When he pulled away, I saw him brush at something on his face before he settled back into place beside me again.

We remained like that for the rest of the night, but right before I fell back asleep, I felt him kiss my hand.

I was smiling on the inside.

CHAPTER NINETEEN

It sucked being an invalid.

I was released the next day, and it took an entire afternoon before it was decided that I'd stay at Malinda's house for the first week. I couldn't go back to school for a week, and she didn't have a job. It made sense. I would move into David's after the first week since I'd still have four to six weeks to heal. Of course, Mason and Logan followed me where I went. David already agreed, but Malinda hadn't been told of the arrangement. When she was informed, both were adamant. David leaned close to whisper, "I warned you they're protective." A bright smile was plastered on her face, and she waved him off. "Oh no. It's completely fine. The more the merrier."

She didn't know what she was getting herself into. She must've caught my reaction because she broke away from David's side and took the chair beside me. She patted my arm and leaned in close to me. "I mean it. Those two have become your family, and you are David's family so that means *all* of you are welcome in my home, at any time." Her warm chocolate eyes doubled their sparkle as she added, "I grew up with twelve brothers and sisters. You think three more kids are going to scare me?"

She really had no idea what she was getting herself into.

When I was discharged and being wheeled out of the hospital, I felt like I was part of a Brady Bunch sort-of family. All eyes were on us as we left, but most of the nurses waved to Mason and Logan. David was shaking his head when all six of us got to the parking lot. Mason had pulled his Escalade up to the circle, and I was loaded into it. Logan hopped into Mark's car. As everyone followed behind David's Luxury SUV, which I assumed was owned by Malinda, Mason said that Mark and Logan were going to a party that night.

Malinda's house was a massive log home. Logan was shown to his bedroom, which was a guest bedroom in the basement, and we were shown our room. It was tucked into a back section of the house on the main floor, so it felt like we had our own wing. Mason had packed a few bags for me, and as he dropped them on the bed, Malinda chuckled at us. "You two are like a married couple."

Uh… I pointed to my head. "Heavy meds here. Say that again?"

She rolled her eyes. "You heard me just fine. So did you," she threw to Mason. Then she gestured to the door across the hallway. "That's your bathroom. Your father wanted you upstairs in case you needed something during the night." Her gaze lingered on Mason. "But I reminded him that you're not a single package anymore; that you come with a plus-one, whether he likes it or not."

"Thanks for that," Mason murmured, leaning against the far wall. He stuffed his hands into his front pockets, which moved his jeans down an inch. As he hunched his shoulders forward, it gave him a longer and leaner look. The tops of his black boxer briefs were visible now, and I could see a hint of his oblique muscles underneath.

I licked my lips. If only… Desire spread through me. When his jeans moved another inch lower, my body felt engulfed in flames. It was like a drop of gasoline had been added to a fire.

Malinda chuckled behind me. "I recognize that look. You got the good meds, for sure."

I was burning up. "Can we open a window?"

Mason frowned. "What?"

"He says what." She chuckled some more before stepping into the hallway. "When you get an ice pack on those loins, join us downstairs. We got couches, blankets, movies, pop, whatever you need."

Why?

Mason said it for me, looking equally confused.

"Saturday family night." Her eyebrows arched high. "Don't you two know what family night means?"

We were both silent.

She snorted. "It's a night you spend with family. Forget any plans you two might have had for canoodling. You're in my home, and you have to endure the torture. Sorry, Sam. They said you have a mild dislocated jaw, but I got lots of liquids and soft foods for you. Yogurt. Applesauce. The good stuff, but the rest are going to be forced to eat popcorn, pizza, chips, and tacos. You name it, they have to shovel it in. Bahahaha." She left, her laugh eerily close to an evil witch's.

"What just happened?" Crap. I winced from pain. I'd been talking too much.

"Mark's mom is nuts."

I gave him a pointed look. Did he not know who he was talking to?

Mason shrugged. "So's your mom, but this one...she seems nice and...genuine. I don't like it."

That earned a snort from me. A mother who was genuine and nice? It made perfect sense why he wouldn't like it. I'm not sure I liked it either.

He gestured out the window beside him. "Did you know Mark lived down the block from my dad's?"

I had forgotten, but now I wished I hadn't remembered.

"Yo. Mark's mom is hilarious. She just told me she's Queen Royale of Bitch." Logan appeared in the doorway and flashed a grin. Holding onto the doorframe from the top, he leaned forward, laughing at the same time. "You see how close we are to Dad's?"

"I know." Mason gestured to me. "I was just telling Sam that."

"Mom's going to flip when we tell her where we're staying."

"Yeah..." Mason was deep in thought. He leaned forward to look out the window and moved so he could see further up the street. "You know Nate's old house? The one he lived in before his parents moved?"

"The one at the end of the block?" Logan moved next to him. Both were studying a house through the window. "The couple that bought it from them moved, didn't they?"

Mason nodded. "They've been trying to sell it for six months. Want to bet that Mom's going to move in there?"

"No way. She won't buy that."

"Dad's is three houses down. We're in this one, and Nate's old place is three doors the other way. She's going to go nuts when she realizes how close we are to Dad's. She thought she finally got us all to herself."

Logan shook his head. "Man, most of our stuff is at the hotel. She won't think we'll want to drive there to grab anything we forgot... it'd be easier to just leave it at Dad's and grab it when we need it. Or that's what she's going to think."

Mason cracked a grin. "If she doesn't buy that house, she's going to rent it. I bet you money. Somehow, Mom's going to be living somewhere on this block."

A curse slipped from Logan. "And we're not telling her we're only staying here for a week, are we?"

"You want to?"

"No way." A smile stretched across his face. "This'll be way funnier when she learns we've moved to Sam's old neighborhood, the 'poor' community. Mom will shit a brick thinking she'll have to live there. She won't know what to do."

Listening to them and watching from the bed, a pang went through me. David lived in a poor community according to them. I knew neither cared, but their mother thought like that. It was a middle class neighborhood. People weren't poor, but they weren't wealthy. They were normal. I was normal, but I was different from them. It shouldn't have bothered me, but I was reminded of how different I was from them.

It stung more than a little.

"Hey."

Mark stood in the hallway now. He glanced around before stepping inside. As he closed the door, everyone grew quiet. "David and Mom are downstairs, so I thought it was the right time to come up and say this."

The feel of the room changed. It was like a cold blast of wind tore through it, and everyone tensed. Mark said, "I don't know what you guys have planned." He glanced at me, but everyone knew he was talking to Mason. "But I'm in for whatever it is. I know how you are with trust. You don't trust anyone except the three of you in this room. You don't have to tell me the plan; you don't have to explain anything to me. Give me a job to do and I'll do it." His gaze lingered on me before his jaw hardened and he looked away. "No questions asked. That's all I wanted to say."

He started for the door, but Mason stopped him. "One thing."

Mark paused.

"Your friends can't come here this week."

"It's already done. I told them my mom's having guests staying here. My mom never says anything, so if you guys don't say anything, no one will even know you're here. Not like it's a secret or anything." He lifted the corner of his mouth up and shrugged. "Besides, it's usually only Adam that drops by or comes over for dinner. My house is quiet compared to his, but he won't ask any questions. My mom has random visitors all the time. We had a homeless dude stay for a week one time when she volunteered at the shelter last winter."

Logan started laughing. "Your mom can't be any more opposite from ours."

Then we heard from the hallway, "MARK!"

"And she summons…"

"MOVIE'S STARTING IN NEGATIVE FIVE MINUTES."

Mark said to us, "She won't pick a comedy because she doesn't want to make Sam laugh."

That was much appreciated.

"But if we don't get down there and pick the movie first, the scariest damn movie will be starting. My mom never gets scared from horror films. I have no idea why. Her other sisters are like that, too. I wish I had inherited that gene, but she loves watching the rest of us when we're close to pissing our pants." He rolled his eyes. "You're right Logan, but my mom is not like any other mom. She's not normal. For real."

The doorbell rang.

"MARK, GET THE DOOR. THOSE ARE THE PIZZAS."

He grumbled, but left.

"If Mark wasn't a cool guy, and if your dad hadn't got there first, I'd bang Mark's mom."

If I could talk easier, I would've informed Logan my vomit was coming in three...two...one... I couldn't and it would've hurt to throw up. It hurt to do anything, so I gave him the middle finger. That would have to satisfy me for now.

Logan laughed, and for the rest of night, he flirted. Mason didn't care. I did. Mark seemed confused, and David shook his head. As we watched a movie about teen wizards, followed by a documentary about polar bears, Malinda seemed to enjoy herself. Her cheeks were red by the end of the night from her wine.

The first night passed quickly and so did the rest of the week.

Things seemed normal between David and me. There were no awkward silences or uncomfortable moments. In hindsight, I realized it was because of Malinda. She always had a quick retort for Logan, and when there was a lull in conversation, she'd grill Mark on his love life. He was mortified when she suggested getting a vibrator for his girl. "Mom!" he cried out. She shrugged. "You're not a virgin, and I'm promoting her pleasure as well. The girl will enjoy it a lot more. They don't always, you know." She scanned the rest of the table. "I'm sure you two bucks think you're the stud for all those does," she remembered me and amended, "well maybe just you and Logan, but I'm telling you. Girls fake it eighty percent of the time."

That opened a whole new channel of adoration from Logan. He wanted to know it all.

The rest of the conversation was a question and answer forum from Logan while Mark looked ready to throw up. I even caught Mason listening intently to her. He told me later that he'd be stupid to pass up information like that. When I came back from the bathroom, ready for bed, his eyes had darkened in lust. His hand skimmed over my waist, gently rubbing before he moved to cup my breasts. Curling into my side, he kissed the side of my neck and remarked, "Six weeks cannot get here sooner."

I knew what he meant. The ache lingered in me, but it was mixed with pain and stiffness. However, that ache conquered all other aches when he would get ready for school in the morning, or for bed at night, or come back from basketball practice, or being around me in general. By the end of the week, when the pain was starting to lessen even more, the ache for Mason was unbearable at times.

During the time when they were at school, it was easier, but Mason was gone. Malinda didn't hover. Thank god. I had worried she would, but she seemed to pop in at the right moments. She brought me smoothies. At first, my stomach protested at the sight of the green color, but I was reassured it was delicious. I soon craved them, so I spent hours in the kitchen watching her experiment with new recipes.

The rest of the time was spent watching movies and I napped. I napped a lot.

Mason was granted half-day practices. He could leave after an hour into practice, so he was there when I woke from my naps. Principal Green approved of his request so he didn't lose any playing time for their games. Between the two, they got all of my homework assignments for me, every day. It wasn't until the end of the week that I asked, "What's everyone saying at school?" Heather had called a few times, but she hadn't said much either. When she was vague, I let it go, but something was wrong. I wasn't stupid, but I hadn't been ready to tackle this hurdle.

I was now.

Mason, Logan and Mark were all doing homework at the dinner table. An instant hush came over them, and they stopped what they were doing. Malinda was in the kitchen, experimenting on more recipes. She loved sneaking tofu into dinner. We were having chicken enchiladas that night. The tofu was going to be covered in cheese, but she paused as well.

David wasn't there. He had an evening meeting for school.

Everyone looked at Mason. He asked, "You want the truth?"

The truth. That felt like a kick in the gut. The truth was that everyone had been pretending. This week was a haven for me. I was allowed to hide from the rest of the world, but the truth was that I had been attacked. I had two fractured ribs. It still hurt to talk and eat because of my jaw. The truth was that I hadn't been able to bring myself to look in a mirror because I knew I looked like an assault victim, but I was one. It was time I started to deal with it.

I never flinched. "Yes."

Mason narrowed his eyes, searching inside of me. He always did that when he was checking to see if I was being honest. When he saw that I was ready, he nodded. "The truth is that Kate thinks she won."

I held my breath.

He kept going, "She thinks we're friends again."

It hurt to breathe.

"She thinks she's at the top again."

An intense pressure was on my chest now; it felt as if someone was pushing down on it.

"She thinks I'm going to dump you."

I flinched as I felt someone kick me again. I heard the crack in my ribs from that night. I *felt* the crack in my ribs from that night.

He looked like a cold stranger to me as he finished, "And she thinks she's going to be my girlfriend."

I couldn't talk. It hurt to breathe. It hurt to do anything except sit there and let his words sink in. All the pain that my medication had been holding at bay flooded me. It all came back in one wave, all at the same time, and I was paralyzed in my chair. I couldn't fight any of it. "Why would she think that?"

Logan looked away. Mark's head went down, but Mason didn't turn away. He stared right back at me as he said, "Because I'm letting her think that."

CHAPTER TWENTY

I hadn't let myself think about Kate. I couldn't, not the first week. I needed to heal and get through it. Everyone had been so supportive, but now I remembered that I was going back into the lions' den. Fallen Crest Academy had different problems, but no one got assaulted there. I was tired, I was in pain, and I couldn't stop thinking about what Mason said. He was letting Kate think she had won.

It didn't matter what he said after that: he was setting her up; he had a plan; he didn't want me involved because he knew I wouldn't approve; I needed to trust him because he was going to make her pay.

He tried reassuring me over and over that night.

He failed. I wasn't reassured.

I wanted to scream at him. I wanted to pound my fists on his chest. I wanted to throw things. Everyone else had gone to bed by then, but I wanted them awake. No one deserved to sleep. No one deserved to go about their daily routines, not when mine had been destroyed by her, but I couldn't enact my revenge on those in the household. Except Mason. He stayed awake with me during the night. I couldn't sleep. The need to make Kate pay had my heart pumping. I wanted to be the one to set her up, to watch her suffer. I wanted to find her in a bathroom, but there wouldn't be three other friends with me. It would be her and me, and I'd beat her senseless. When she'd crawl to the door, I'd start again.

The rage never simmered. It kept my blood boiling, and my heart pumping the entire night. Mason drifted to sleep around three in the morning, but I was still seething at six. When he woke and glanced over, he saw I was still awake. He leaned over to kiss me, but I moved my head aside. There'd be no kisses. No words were shared as he got ready for school. When Logan came to the door, they had a quiet conversation. Logan was advised to leave me alone, and he did. They both left at the same time. Mark left for his school twenty minutes later. He sprinted through the house, and I heard Malinda yell, "It won't matter that you're late if you're dead. Slow down, Marcus."

He yelled back, "Yeah, okay."

Peeking out my window, I watched as he sprinted for his car and then gunned the engine. I pretended that Kate had been in front of his car. She would be on the street now, laying in her blood and writhing in pain.

"He's going to get in an accident one of these days. Sleeps too late, pushes it so that he's not late for school, and I just know it's a bad recipe in the making," Malinda mused from behind me. The bottom of her white nightgown was underneath her blue robe. She retied the knot in the front before yawning. "You want some pancakes? David told me that Analise never made you breakfast before."

"She didn't, but she had their chef make me sandwiches." I missed Mousteff.

Malinda grunted, a crooked grin on her face. "Some rich folk are like that. They stop doing the little things, think it's beneath them. The only thing beneath them is not doing a damn thing."

She said more, but I wasn't listening to her. I was in my own head.

Analise. David. Jessica. Lydia. Jeff.

A stabbing pain seared through me. Each one of them had betrayed me. Each was someone I once loved. The pain kept coming. It wasn't going to stop.

"Right, Sam?" Malinda laughed.

I turned back to the window. I couldn't face her. She was another one. The same would happen, and she had no idea she'd do it until the day she left me, like the rest of them. "She's going to get away with this."

She grew quiet. "Who?"

I couldn't answer. Kate. All of them. Everyone.

"They followed me into that bathroom." The door opened, but the hand dryer was on. "I remember it now. I knew they were coming. I knew someone was there. There was a small movement from the corner of my eye. It's why I turned to leave, but…" I couldn't go further. That day would haunt me, like so many others.

I turned back now.

Malinda straightened from the doorway. Her hand dropped and slapped against her leg with a soft thud. Her eyes widened an inch, and her mouth fell open.

I didn't know what she saw in me, but she couldn't talk for a second. I could. For once, the words were there, and they were gutting me. "How do I get over this?" How was I supposed to go back to that school? She was there. Mason said they only got in-school suspension. They got a slap on the wrist and were given a holiday from their usual studies.

I couldn't. That was my truth for the morning. I couldn't go back to that school, but I couldn't afford not to. Coach Grath already said that I'd have to bust my ass to catch up to my old times. As soon as I was cleared by the doctor, he wanted to meet for individual training sessions. I needed that scholarship, I had no one to help me now. I needed to go to college. Kate would be there…

I couldn't. I just couldn't.

"What do I do?" My voice hitched on a sob.

"Oh, Samantha." Malinda rushed into the room and folded me against her. She wrapped her arms around me gently and cradled my head to her. "Oh, Samantha, honey."

At the feel of her arms, I was jerked to a different reality. This one felt alien.

This was what a mother did. She comforted. Malinda wasn't my mother. She was dating David, who was rarely at the house. It hit me then that he'd been avoiding me or maybe he'd been avoiding a moment like this. Malinda took his place and because of that I couldn't let her. I wouldn't be reassured by her. There would be a time when she'd leave me too. It was inevitable.

I moved back and tried to give her something that resembled a grin. "It's fine. I'm fine." She grimaced. My smile must not have looked like one. I tried for another and repeated, "I'll be fine. Really."

"Oh, Samantha."

I heard her stricken tone and prepared myself.

She raised a hand and tucked some of my hair behind my ear. Her touch was gentle. "I'm not like the rest."

My eyes jerked to hers.

"I know what it's like to be abandoned and left behind. I do. I know what it's like, and I'm not here to make excuses for your father. That's between you and him, but me—I'm here for you. I won't leave you. I had Mark when I was young. His dad didn't stick around." She chuckled. "His dad didn't even stick around long enough for me to say he didn't stick around. He was out the window the second he saw my pregnancy test. You know what happened to me?"

I was listening to her. There was a pull to her, and I couldn't *not* listen to her, but I didn't answer.

"I got thrown out of my family. I've been out on my own ever since. My family is full of pretentious assholes and bitches that think they're better than everyone else. Pissed my grandfather off. He didn't like not being able to see Mark, so he left me his money." Another dry chuckle. "That changed their tunes. They tried seeing me, apologized out of their asses. They sent over Mark's cousins to be friends. That one I couldn't fight. He's close to a few of them, but I could fight the rest. I was an embarrassment to them, but I became an inspiration when all those dollar signs were connected to me. Pansies. I hated my family. For years I hated them, and now I just want nothing to do with them."

I grinned as an ache started in my chest. "Didn't you hear the phrase that family means everything?"

"Not to you." There was nothing held back from her. "Not to me. Sometimes family hurts you more than they could ever love you. That's a truth a lot of people don't want to hear, but sometimes people get the opposite. They get the families that love you more than they could ever hurt you. Those people are the luckiest in the world. You know what pisses me off? Is that they probably don't even know it. They don't know how lucky they are, but, Sam, you're one of them."

I sucked in a breath. That ache was a stabbing pain now.

She leaned forward. Some of her long hair fell forward, but she ignored it as she grasped my shoulders. Malinda moved so we were eye-level. "Forget the people who've hurt you. You don't have them anymore, but you have two others that'll do anything for you. Mason and Logan would move mountains for you. I see how you are with them. You love them, but you're scared to let yourself be happy. Why? Because that's when they'll leave? Is that what you think? You've got it all wrong. Those two will never leave you." She tapped my chest. Once. Twice. "You. You're the one that's going to hurt them. You have that power, and you don't know it. You could rip those two apart in a second, and they're the ones who are scared of you. Not the other way around. You need to recognize the real situation."

"My situation?"

She moved back. As her hands left my shoulders, I was able to breathe again. My chest was lighter. She went to the far wall and leaned against it. Folding her arms, she shook her head. "You got beat up. Bones and bruises heal. Those girls didn't win because they didn't do what they wanted. They wanted to break you."

I was already broken.

"You're not broken at all."

I held my breath at her words.

She added, "Those two boys have healed you. They took you in. They protected you. They continue to love you because they're your family and both of them know it. They love you for the same reasons they don't love anyone else. You're pure. It might not make sense to you, but you don't use them. You don't want anything from them. You don't want to hurt them. Your love for both of them is pure." Then she cracked a grin. "I might come off as a batty old shithead, but I'm no dumb broad. I know it because I recognize it; it's why I snatched your father up so quick, and I made sure he had no choice but to date me. I'm not saying he's made the best choices, but your father has the same pure love inside of him." She rolled her eyes. "Doesn't mean he knows how to show it. He's dug himself a grave and instead of filling it back up, he ends up digging himself another one. He's been doing that with you all these years, but he's a good man underneath. He's a good man to me. I love your father very much, and I'd like to love you like a daughter." She brushed a tear away, giving me a trembling smile at the same time. "But I'm not here to pressure you or tell you what to do. Believe it or not, I meant to ask you about breakfast, but then I got on my damn soap box. Sorry about that."

You're not broken at all. I couldn't get those words out of my head. "Did you mean that?"

"Mean what?"

"That I'm not broken?"

"Oh, honey. You have so much strength in you. You have no idea how much." She gave me another smile, though it wavered as more tears slipped down her cheeks. "I meant what I said before. I will never leave you. Whether I'm with your father or not, you're friends with Mark or not, know this will always be a home for you. Okay?"

I could feel her love. It was that same alien feeling I felt when I was bleeding on the bathroom floor. I had clung to it then. I was scared of it now, but I nodded. "Okay."

She began laughing. "You're so scared of me right now."

"I'm not."

"You are, but that's okay. Every time you come and I open my door, some of that fear will go away. Being loved and accepting love are two completely different things. It's my job to continue to show it to you. All you have to do is accept it, little by little. That's how I finally convinced your father that I loved him. Between you and me, I still have to convince him sometimes. Being with your mother hurt him, too. That's something both of you have in common." A few more tears had fallen, and she brushed them away. "Look at me. I'm hideous. Alright, I'm off to shower and get ready. You want to go out for breakfast?"

I nodded.

"Good." She gave me a bright smile. "Pound on the wall if you need help getting dressed. I'll hear it all the way upstairs. Oh, and don't tell Mark that. I caught him with a couple girls with that secret. He still has no idea."

When she left, I could her laughter all the way to the second floor. I couldn't move, but I started to hear a scraping sound. That's when I looked down. My hand was shaking. It was hitting the cord for the blinds that was scraping against the window frame.

She said I wasn't broken at all.

Mason

Sam called me before my game. She had an unusual conversation with Malinda that day, but we would talk tomorrow. It was her first night back at her home, her old home. She wanted to spend time with David, which worked for my plan.

"You ready for this?" Logan got into the seat beside me. We were on the team bus, returning from our away game.

I nodded. My phone was out. The last text from Sam said: **I love you. Wake me up when you get here. Key's under the broken step in porch. I want to talk.**

Logan saw the text. He didn't say anything at first, but after a moment asked, "She doesn't know? You didn't tell her last night?"

"Nope."

"And she doesn't know we'll be gone all night?"

"Nope."

"This could backfire, you know."

"I know." I clutched the phone in my hand.

"She might leave you."

"I know."

"You're still sure?"

We were in the back seat, separated from the rest of the team. The guys knew a plan was in motion and I was grateful for the space. I needed to go over all the risks and calculations.

I nodded now. "I am. You?"

Logan flashed me a grin. "I'm down for anything."

"If she leaves, she's leaving you, too."

"I know." His grin vanished. "It'll be worth it."

"Okay." I nodded again as the bus pulled into the parking lot and rolled to a stop. "Let's go to that party then."

Logan got up first, and I followed him. We knew what to do next.

Kate was lying to herself. When I called her Sunday night, I heard the hope in her voice. I said all the right things: I apologized; I wanted a clean slate; I missed our friendship.

She lapped it up. Then I said what I needed to cinch it for her: I'd forgotten that she was my equal in every way. As soon as I said that, she was sobbing on other end. It'd been what she wanted to hear all along. She assured me we could move forward. She would reign in the other girls. They could all be friends again, and it'd be like nothing ever happened.

Stupid girl.

I warned her. She chose to believe my lies. That was her mistake. I didn't change my mind. I never changed my mind.

The plan had been in motion for a while, but tonight was the beginning of the end.

CHAPTER TWENTY-ONE

Logan and I drove to the party. It was spread over a large grassy field surrounded by trees. Trucks were parked so their tailgates could be lowered. People were either leaning, sitting, or standing around them. A few had their own supply of liquor. Pony kegs and coolers were spread out and barrels were in the middle section. Each barrel had been lit so the fire heated the area. This party wasn't like normal Public parties. No Academites were allowed. No one cared about coke and champagne at this party. This was a District party, held on Frisco land. As soon as I got out, people headed over and the divide was immediate. Fallen Crest people stepped toward us, and the rest of Roussou remained on the other side of the barrels with Budd Broudou.

"Mason, my man."

A tall guy came towards us. He was lean and lanky, with a build that resembled a professional basketball player.

"Pailor, how's it going?"

"It's going, man." His mouth curved in an easygoing manner, but his eyes didn't miss a thing. They were clear and alert. As Logan came around his Escalade, he held his hand out. "Logan, my dude."

"Frankie."

"Oh." He drew back and reassessed both of them. "What are you two up to?" His hand ran over his bald head.

I threw Logan a sidelong look. "Nothing. What are you talking about?"

Frankie moved back another step, studying us before he shook his head. "See. This look you both gave me. Intense as hell. With you," he gestured to me, "I expect it, but with this one," he punched Logan in the stomach, "he's never showed up without a cocky smirk. He sure never sticks around long. It takes you five minutes to get a girl—two to pick the girl, one to grab her, and the last two to take her somewhere private. Now you show up and there's no grin, there's no quick wit," he pointed at the crowd behind them, "and you haven't even looked at the girls yet. So that's how I know you two aren't here to party."

Frankie Pailor ran Frisco how we ran Fallen Crest. We played sports against each other, but that was our only rivalry with them. Since Frisco territory touched on both sides of Roussou and Fallen Crest, much like a triangle, we understood Frankie's dilemma. He kept a friendly alliance with the Broudous as well.

"And my night just got weirder," Frankie noted as he watched another person break free from the Roussou side. "Should I run interference already?"

Channing Monroe was headed towards us. His jeans rode low on his hips, the top button loose, and his shirt hung open without another one underneath. As he drew closer, he lifted a hand to run through his hair. His other hand held a beer with four bottles stuck inside his pockets. He fished them out and handed one to me and Logan. "Boys."

Frankie moved back. His eyes skirted from Monroe to me, then Logan before his hands lifted in the air. "I give up. I thought I'd have to come over here and keep the peace. Maybe not."

Channing flashed him a grin before extending a bottle to him. "I don't want you to feel left out, Frankie."

Logan chuckled. He indicated Channing's chest. "Does that work? Showing off the pecs and shit?"

Channing shrugged. His shirt opened another inch as he lifted his arm, taking a long pull from his beer. "Like you need help with the ladies, Kade."

"Okay." Frankie had been studying all of them. "What's going on? You guys are friendly now?" He jerked a thumb towards the Roussou side. "Budd and Brett know this too?"

"We have a few friends in common." Everyone was silent after I said that.

Channing shifted so he stood closer to me and Frankie caught the slight movement. "Let me guess, Budd and Brett have no clue?"

I gestured to Channing. "I suppose that's up to him to answer."

The good-natured glint in his eyes sobered. He glanced somewhere in the crowd before turning back. "They have no clue."

"Good," Logan bit out.

Budd Broudou had been trying to find out who my girlfriend was since he heard about her existence. They asked at Quickie's and had been back one other time. I didn't think Sam's identity had leaked, but I couldn't wait any longer. The situation needed to be dealt with before it was.

There weren't many from my school that were friendly with Roussou. The fact that Samantha had friendly connections through Heather hadn't escaped me. It was ironic, but I was going to use that connection now. Channing Monroe had power over there. He wasn't friendly with Budd and Brett Broudou, but he wasn't their enemy either. If Sam got hurt, that would hurt Heather and I recognized another guy in love. Monroe would do what needed to be done to keep Heather from being hurt, and that meant siding with us.

"Is Jax here tonight?"

Channing hesitated.

Logan cursed a moment later. "She's here, Mase."

"This has nothing to do with her," Channing murmured.

He was mistaken and he knew it. I said, "What do you think they'll do to her if they find out about Sam? Heather knew who she was and she never told them."

"Oh, whoa." Frankie shot his hands between us. "You two aren't friendly? I thought you were. My mind is being blown right now. You guys are enemies? Monroe, I didn't think you had enemies."

"We're not," he snapped at him, but said to me next, "I'm aware of what will happen. Are you aware that *she* knows them?"

He wasn't referring to Heather. Logan and I got the implication. We shared another look.

"Jax?" Frankie asked.

Logan narrowed his eyes. "What are you talking about? She's never met them."

"She has, actually. They went to Manny's one night looking for you. There was a confrontation. Heather had to kick them out."

"Fuck."

Channing glanced at Logan. "Exactly."

"Wait." I shook my head. "They don't know. They were still clueless last week."

"Budd's clueless…" Channing waited.

Brett wasn't. I knew what he was leaving unsaid and I glanced at Frankie. He needed to be gone. With that thought, I nudged Logan and jerked my gaze to Pailor. Logan nodded. He understood and transformed. The cocky smirk came over him. His shoulders rolled back, his head went up, and he threw an arm around Frankie's shoulders.

"Frankie, my man. My appetite came back and I'm thinking you might have some recommendations? I don't think I've tasted too many Frisco girls."

"Oh geez." Frankie shook his head, but he couldn't hold back his smile. As Logan started to lead him away, I heard him continue, "There's too many, Logan, too many. You need to share the love. Anyone from Fallen Crest…" His voice faded as they moved to the Frisco side of the party.

I jerked my head backwards. We had parked near the edge of the party. The grass lot was surrounded by woods, which meant privacy for us. Once we were far enough away, I didn't waste time. "Sam met them?"

Channing nodded. He grimaced, but finished the rest of his beer and tossed the bottle. "At Manny's like I said. They were there hoping to run into you guys. Heather tossed them out. Brett's got a soft spot for her, and he promised they wouldn't come back to start a fight."

"They don't know about Sam?"

"No, but they talked to her. Heather admitted that she didn't make the situation better. She almost let it slip who Sam was, but Sam stopped her. She shoved Budd or something. Brett got him cooled down. It blew over after that. She sent Sam packing and kicked them out, but there's something else."

The idea of them being with her, talking to her, scaring her... My hands curled into fists. A litany of curses flashed through my mind. I wanted to find Budd and Brett. I wanted to finish this entire thing, right now, between them and me. Fuck it. Logan could help if he wanted, but I had enough rage pumping through me. I wanted both of them.

They talked to her. They *scared* her.

I didn't want to know the rest, but dammit, I had to. Sam had lied to me. "What is it?"

"Brett asked her out."

"What?"

"He asked her out." Channing raised his hands in the air, backing away.

I wasn't going to attack him. I had enough control. "Spill the rest, Monroe. Stop wasting my time."

He dropped his hands. "I don't know how it happened or when, but Brett asked Sam on a date. Budd figured it out. He's been teasing Brett all week, asking if he's going to visit her in the hospital or not."

Everything changed then. Brett Broudou liked Sam and knew she was in the hospital. Budd knew she was in the hospital. They knew about Sam. I was going to have to—

"They were waiting by the door where Sam was loaded into the ambulance. Budd keeps calling her Brett's weakling."

I stopped thinking. Everything kicked into slow motion as I heard those words in my head. They were at Manny's. Brett asked her out. He was with her AGAIN when they saw her by the ambulance.

They saw her at her weakest moment.

It was enough. I had to end them.

I started past Channing, but he darted in front of me. "Whoa. Where are you going?"

"Move."

"No way."

"MOVE."

"No," Channing shot back at me. "You need to think, man. I don't know you, but I know your reputation, and you don't react like this. You're cold and calculated."

"They saw her when she was hurting." My tone was like ice, but my blood was pumping. I needed to do damage and I needed to do it now. Brett Broudou would be the first. "Move, Monroe or I will move you."

"We're not buds."

"I know." My tone turned lethal. I didn't want to hurt Jax's on-again-off-again whatever, but I would.

One second.

Two.

Channing's eyes flashed back at me. "I care about Heather and she cares about Sam. You mess with me, and that comes back to you. You know that, and I'm *trying* to help you." Gone was the easygoing voice. Channing straightened and the threat of violence was there. "I understand. I do. I'd feel the same way. We both know the damage Budd can do to someone. He doesn't give a shit who the person is, but you need to hear me when I say that Brett could be an asset to us."

"He went to her."

"I know."

"He was *alone* with her." *He could've hurt her.*

"Everyone at school is teasing Brett about the hospital chick. They've all heard about the girl that got jumped at the basketball game. Half of them think it's because Brett liked her. That psychotic bitch crew at your school jumped her for you. They think it's an entire Roussou/Fallen Crest thing, and they're waiting to see what Budd's going to do now."

"I don't care about any of that."

"I know. I know." Channing pointed to his head. "Think about it. Brett knows who Sam is, he asked Heather if her friend was okay."

The rage in me stalled.

He asked if she was okay… after he knew who she was.

It settled me, enough to slip back into my old skin. I began picking up the pieces. I saw where Channing was leading me. "He covered for her that night. Budd was starting to figure it out, but he stopped him. He said we had school problems."

"Because that makes sense to Budd. Someone got hurt in your school. He knows you'd want to know about it."

I frowned. "We're not that controlling."

"But Budd is, or he tries. Brett covered for you."

"I'm getting that now." It'd been something I had kept in the back of my mind, but I hadn't given it enough time. "Brett's continued to lie for her?"

She lied to me. I flinched at that reminder. It stung.

"He has." The tension left Channing, his shoulders dropped, and he nodded. "Heather was at my place earlier. He wanted to know how Sam was doing. He told her that he'd keep the secret, too. He promised that Budd wouldn't know. In fact," he took a deep breath, "that brings me to the next part of business."

I knew where this was going.

"She said that Kate's back in power. She's acting like your girlfriend and the rest of her friends too, like everything's back to normal. This isn't any of my business, but it's making her lose sleep. I care about Heather and I don't like seeing her suffer. She doesn't know if she should tell Sam you're back with the Bitch Crew or wait till you do. Either way Sam is going to find out." He touched his chest. "And that's where I'm coming in. I'm thinking you're doing that for a reason. Am I right?"

"It's none of your business."

I kept my calm. My voice was cool, but it was the truth. I didn't care what Heather Jax was worried about. She could say all the things she wanted. My relationship with Sam was my relationship with Sam. No one else got in there.

Channing sighed. "I was afraid you would say that."

"MASON!"

Kate had arrived. The bottom of my gut dropped, and I fought against the disgust of being near her. I had two assholes to deal with, Kate and Budd Broudou.

"MASON, WHERE ARE YOUUU?" She hiccupped at the end before shrieking with her friends. All of them began calling my name.

Kate was drunk. Now was the perfect time.

I downed my beer. I emptied the entire bottle before handing it to Channing. Without a word, another beer was handed to me. I cursed before downing that one, too.

"I know what you're going to do," Channing said.

I waited. The judgment would come. I was already preparing myself for Sam's reaction.

"He's going to hurt her."

That was the point. "She hurt Sam."

Channing nodded. He didn't say anything more, but he understood. He'd do something similar if it'd been him and his girl. When I went back, Kate was in the center of the area, dancing around the barrels. Her shirt was off and she was only wearing a bra with her tight jeans. When she swung around, I saw the bottoms were ripped to show the bottom of her underwear.

Giggling some more, she tipped her head back and drank out of a Jack Daniels bottle. Her friends danced with her. Everyone was watching her. Then they saw me. They were waiting now. A group of people moved back for me. A girl lifted her beer to drink from, and as I went past, I swiped the bottle from her.

"Hey. Oh…"

She was ignored, but before Kate saw me, I glanced over my shoulder. Channing had followed me but he headed to the Roussou side of the party. He went to Heather's side. It was then when our gazes collided. Her eyes burned bright with condemnation. Channing hadn't judged me, but she was. Sam's best friend hated me.

Kate gasped, swaying on her feet, "Mason! You're here!"

I hated myself, too.

I smirked at Kate as she came over to me. She was trying to be seductive. She looked like a drunken idiot and reeked of booze. Then she looped her arms around my neck, pressed her breasts against me before sliding them up my chest as she moved into me. Then her fingers curled into my neck and she drew my mouth down. As my lips stopped above hers, she whispered, "Are you going to fuck me tonight?"

I didn't think. I couldn't.

I slammed my lips onto hers.

CHAPTER TWENTY-TWO

Samantha

It wasn't home.

That was my first thought when I walked inside. David unlocked the door, but waved me through first. Nothing felt familiar about my old home anymore. It was cold. It was dark, and there was a musky smell in the room.

"Oh, sorry." David rushed around me, and the door slammed shut in his wake. "I meant to drop by earlier and turn the heat up. I knew you were coming, but things happened at school and…" he trailed off as he stared at me.

"What?"

"Nothing." A quick shake of the head. "It's… you're here. You're staying."

"Yeah?"

"I just thought…" He shook his head again. The corners of his mouth darted up and down as he cleared his throat. "I just never thought you'd be back."

There was so much emotion in his gaze, and they were too visible to me. He hadn't turned the light on, but the moonlight lit the room up. A sudden lump formed in my throat, and I looked away.

"Oh, right." He finished with the heat and flipped the light switch. The room was flooded with new light, and I was struck with the same emotions.

This wasn't home. Not anymore.

The kitchen counter was covered with empty pizza boxes. There must've been thirty of them, and the floor had empty cases of beer scattered around. The kitchen table had mail all over it. Not an inch of the tablecloth could be seen. When I spotted a television in the corner of the room, I gestured to it. "That's new."

"Oh." He sighed, flushing at the same time. "Yes. Before Malinda, I watched a lot of the game tapes here."

"Not in the basement? You used to watch them down there."

"Yeah. I, um, got into a habit of staying up here in case…" His glanced at me, but turned away. Bumping into the pizza boxes, the pile fell to the floor. "Oh no." He dropped down and began picking them up with rushed movements. "I'm sorry. This place is a mess. I haven't cleaned since—" He stopped himself and took a deep breath.

I sensed a change as he straightened. I waited for whatever he was going to say next, and my heart began pounding in my chest.

"I don't know why I'm lying to you. You've been through enough. You deserve me to tell it to you straight."

My stomach tightened.

"I would sit up here," he gestured around the kitchen, "in case you ever came back. It sounds stupid, but I wanted to be here if you ever came back. You never did. Well, you did, but it was the day after you moved."

"Yeah." My voice was hoarse. "She forgot something and asked me to get it. I did…" And he had come home. A stabbing pain pierced me. If only I had realized how final it was going to be. If I had known he wasn't my real father then, but no. It wouldn't have changed anything. She still would have forced me to go with her.

"Like I said before, it became a habit. Sitting here. Eating here. Watching the games here. I did everything here. Even months later when I knew you weren't coming back, I couldn't stop. It made no sense to me."

I nodded, but I didn't know what to say. When I saw the broom in the back, I asked, "Do you want me to clean up?"

"What? No. Oh no, Samantha. This is my mess. I'll clean it up. You can go upstairs if you'd like to get changed or get comfortable.

Maybe email or check your Twitter. Mark's always talking about that with Malinda, but I never understand what they're talking about. I'm not big on technology."

"I know." Neither was I. I thought I had inherited that from him.

"You know what?" With a garbage bag in one hand, he began stuffing the pizza boxes inside. "I bet you're hungry. Malinda asked if she should make us something, but I told her that I'd take you to dinner. Do you want to go out to eat?"

"That's okay. We can eat in."

"Oh." He frowned. "Um…I could go and pick something up. Chinese? You used to like Chinese."

"That's fine."

"Or there's that new noodle place. You want to go there?" His eyes lit up.

I gestured to my face. The bruises had started to fade, but I had another two weeks until they'd be completely gone. "I'm not feeling like going out yet."

"That's right. Your face."

"Nicely put."

"Oh," he sighed again. "I'm nervous, Samantha. I'm your father. I've raised you since you were little, but I'm very, very nervous right now. I can go and get you something from the noodle place."

"You don't have anything in the refrigerator?"

"I don't stay here often." The corners of his mouth lifted again in a quick grin. "Things went fast after my first date with Malinda, and I'm there most of the time. I use this place more for storage. I guess."

Another thing that changed. "It's nice that you've kept the house."

"Yeah, well, I had hoped you might need it someday." He frowned. "But not like this. This was a horrible way to need it."

"I know, Dav—Dad. I know."

A smile formed on his face. It widened as his eyes blinked rapidly. Then he brushed at his eye and jerked his head towards the door. "I'll go and get us something to eat. I'll be back quick. I promise."

Unsure of what to do, I began cleaning up. The rest of the pizza boxes were put in the garbage bags, along with the beer cases. All of that was taken outside to trash bins and then I started organizing the mail. He had bills from the fall. When I found one from August, it was the date we left him. My hand trembled as I stuffed the envelope underneath the rest. The magazines were thrown out— they were Analise's. She never bothered to cancel her subscriptions. The pile I moved to the side were the football ones. All the coaching newsletters went there, too. Then there were the newspapers. Most were still folded together, and I knew he hadn't opened any of them. All of them were tossed. I put what I could into recycling piles. After sweeping the floor and wiping down the counters, I skimmed over the sink. There weren't many dishes, but David never dirtied a lot of dishes. The few he did, he cleaned right away. That was something Analise could never complain about.

I glanced around. He still wasn't back, so I wandered into the living room. I couldn't bring myself to go upstairs yet. I knew too many memories would surface when I went to my old bedroom, but I took one step into the living room, and memories slammed into me anyway.

He hadn't touched a thing.

I couldn't believe it.

The couch hadn't moved. The two blankets were still folded and perched on the ends. I remember putting them there. I was going to grab them when we left, but she told me not to. She said David would need extra blankets, so I left them. He hadn't moved them. A box that I had packed was still in the corner. I hadn't been looking at what I put in there, but she didn't want it. It was filled with pictures albums, but Analise saw the wedding album on top. She wouldn't listen when I explained mine were in there, too. That was another item left behind.

I didn't turn the lights on. For some reason, I couldn't fathom the idea of sitting there with bright light cast over this room.

"Samantha?"

His keys jingled together as he took them from the door and pushed it open, the screen door banging shut behind him. "Are you in here?"

I hadn't heard him open the door. "I'm in here." As I heard him come closer, I brushed the tear from my cheek and stood. I plastered on a bright smile and he paused, frowning at me. He was going to ask if I was okay. I couldn't lie to him, so I pointed to the two pizza boxes tucked under his arm. "Were they closed?"

"What?"

"The pizza. You went for noodles."

"Oh." He glanced down, as if remembering them. "Oh, uh. Yeah. No, I'm sorry. I didn't know what you wanted so I got pizza. You used to like this, so I'm hoping you still do."

My stomach growled at that moment.

His eyebrow lifted up. "I guess you do."

The aroma had filled the room, and I realized I hadn't eaten since breakfast with Malinda. "Pizza sounds great."

"Great."

I nodded.

He stared back at me.

Neither of us moved.

"OH. Um…" He glanced around. "I…we could sit." His gaze lingered on the couch.

"I cleaned the kitchen. We can sit in there."

"Okay." He sounded relieved.

"That's your routine, right? I don't want to break you of any habits you picked up when…" When we left him. I flinched. When I left him.

"It doesn't matter, Samantha. It was something I picked up, waiting if you came back and now," he gestured to me, "we could go downstairs. That's where we used to watch television. We could watch a movie."

"You still have it hooked up downstairs?" A brief spark of hope flared in me. That was our thing. We watched movies together, and Analise stayed upstairs. She didn't like the basement, said it was like a dark dungeon. It was our haven.

He nodded. "Yeah and you didn't have to clean up. Thanks for that. I didn't mean to run out and have you pick up after me."

"It was no problem." Where did I put my hands? I had no idea anymore. I crossed them over my chest, but that didn't feel right. In my pockets? Would that be less awkward?

"Okay." A grin teased at the corner of his mouth. "Why don't you take the pizza down, and I'll grab everything else. There should be pop and water downstairs, too."

"Okay."

"I think I have chips, too. You still like Doritos?"

I nodded and headed for the basement door. Once it swung open and he headed to the kitchen, I stopped at the top of the stairs. I closed my eyes and took a deep breath. I needed one deep breath. Then I felt for the light switch and flicked it on. The stairwell lit up and a glimmer of home came back to me.

It was only a glimmer, but it was something.

Watching a movie with David wasn't so bad after that. The awkwardness or tension had lifted, and it was our spot again. When we started the movie, I closed my eyes halfway through it. I could pretend for a moment. This was before the cheating. Before the divorce. I was transported back to the time before my world fell apart. Then I heard David laugh and turned to him. His eyes were sparkling. His paused with a handful of popcorn going to his mouth as he waited for the punch line in the movie. There it was. I heard the actor say it, and David roared with laughter. His head fell back and his hand waited in the air until he was done. Then he tossed the popcorn like nothing happened and went back to watching the movie.

I felt the tears coming.

This was it. This was the moment I had been craving since Analise took us away. Home. It wasn't my old home. I knew that, but it was a new home. Mason and Logan would join this home and we'd be together. Everything would be fine. I knew it.

"Did you see that?" He laughed and pointed to the screen.

Yes. We put in the same movie we always used to watch. I had it memorized. So did he, but I laughed with him. It felt right to do so. We were still laughing about the same jokes when reality hit me. I remembered everything and stopped laughing. I stopped breathing.

"Samantha?"

"What?"

"Are you okay?"

"Yeah. I'm fine. I just," *remembered that I didn't have a mother,* "realized that Mason never texted me back."

"They have a game tonight? You didn't want to go?"

Pointing to my face again, I grinned. "Look like the walking dead."

"Oh. Right. Sorry."

I shrugged and joked, "What do you do? Life of the Bullied and Attacked, right? I should write a blog about it."

"You should."

I was struck by the serious tone from him. "What?"

"You should."

I laughed again. I must've heard him wrong. "What'd you say?"

"That's how you get your voice out? I say, do it. You have something to say, put it in a blogger. I would be proud if my daughter bloggered."

"It's," blogged and not bloggered, but I kept quiet. He was so proud, and it was because of me. I stopped for the moment. He had no idea what he was saying, but he was trying. More tears threatened to spill, and I turned away again.

I had missed him.

"Samantha?"

"I'm fine." I waved him off.

"Did I say something wrong?" He had grown quiet again.

I wanted to cry, hide, and wrap my arms around him at the same time. There was that hesitation and anxiety in him again. I hadn't heard it in so long, but memories flooded me from their fights. He would respond to a question and Analise would become enraged. I heard it so many times, but it was never him. That's what I wanted to tell him for so long. It was her. She was the problem. She ripped apart our family. Everything was her fault.

"No," I choked out. "You said exactly the right thing."

"Oh. Good."

His obvious relief sent another wave of emotion through me. Malinda had been right. "Does Malinda come over here?"

He froze.

I frowned. What had I said wrong now?

Then he said, "I don't let her."

"Why?"

"I'm ashamed."

So many emotions went through me at that statement. He was ashamed. No one should be ashamed of their home.

"This was," he stopped. When he spoke again, his voice was clearer. "This house is where I failed my family. I failed you. Malinda is a new beginning. Her home is warm and loving."

Like her.

He continued, "I don't want her to see this place. It's mine, but it's still Analise's too."

A shiver went over me. He was right. I'd been feeling her presence since I walked inside.

"I decided that I'd keep this place for you, even if you didn't want me around you. I wanted you to have a home. I can't change the memories of this place, but you can. Even if it means your," he hesitated, "new family comes with you, that's alright with me."

"You're talking like this isn't your home anymore."

"It's not. It hasn't been since she took you. It's been a shelter for me. My home will probably be with Malinda now."

I drew in a sudden breath. It was serious between them. Mark had been right, but I shouldn't have been surprised. The first time I saw them together, I hated it. I hated her. It was more change. She was taking him further away from me, but I could no longer lie to myself. "Malinda's good for you. You're lucky to have her."

His head had been down during our talk. It jerked up now. "You mean that?"

Our father/daughter moment had strayed towards deeper waters, but I couldn't pull away now. I wasn't sure if I wanted to. I hadn't realized how much I had missed him. I couldn't tell him. My throat was filled with tears and emotions, it no longer allowed me to speak. All I could do was nod.

Neither of us talked. We sat in silence. The movie had ended earlier and the credits were done. Every now and then he would wipe a hand over his face. I would do the same.

He broke the silence when he lifted a hand towards me. "Malinda's yours, too, if you want." He stopped and took a deep breath. His voice cracked before he started again, "I'm not going to be like Analise and force you to do things. You've been through too much for me to treat you with kid gloves. You're almost an adult and you're going to be a great one. I can see it already, but you've got a room there, too." His mouth curved up in a rueful grin, and he wiped at his eyes again. "I already know she told Mark that room was yours. It can sit empty for years and it'll be your room. She already loves you, Samantha." His eyes widened. "But I don't mean that to make you feel pressured or anything. It's there if you come or not. You can do whatever you need. I meant it about this place. This can be your home, too. I always meant to tell you, but I was a coward. I was too scared."

He was scared of me.

He opened the door for that talk, but I couldn't. Shaking my head, I got up from the couch. "I—" I couldn't talk. I couldn't be there. "I need to call Mason. I need to check in." Going to the stairs, my hand reached for the rail and my head went down. I couldn't see his pain. I was leaving him now. "And I have to go to the bathroom. I'm sorry."

Then I fled upstairs. I didn't feel my physical pain anymore. The emotional overrode it.

CHAPTER TWENTY-THREE

When morning came, I was pissed. No. I was livid.

Mason hadn't come over, and he hadn't called. He hadn't texted, and a few hours later, there was still no alerts on my phone. It was nearing nine in the morning and I knew he was awake. He didn't sleep late. He wouldn't forget his phone anywhere, so he was avoiding me. That could only mean one thing—it happened last night. Whatever he had planned for Kate had happened and I hadn't known. I'd been left out.

I called Logan. Nothing.

I called Heather. Nothing.

Two hours later. Still nothing. From anyone

I sighed, and changed into real clothes. My face resembled a mix between a panda and raccoon. The little make-up I had on was enough to cover some of the bruising. When I was done, the panda had vanished, but the raccoon remained. I couldn't perform miracles. It would have to be enough.

I wasn't going to get sad. I wasn't going to crumble and ask the 'why me?' questions. Last night had been emotional enough for me, so I skipped over all those crappy emotions and went straight to furious. That felt better. It slipped over me like a second coat. It was keeping me warm and sheltered. That's when I found David.

There was breakfast still on the counter from earlier, but he moved it aside. He was taking out vegetables, dressings, and chicken.

"Let's go to Malinda's for lunch."

His hand jerked and he cursed, whirling around to me.

"Samantha!" He pounded on his chest. "You scared five years off my life."

I didn't care. "Let's go to Malinda's."

"What?" He heard me this time. "Why? I thought this was father/daughter time, though I have no doubt Mason snuck in your room last night. He left already?"

"Let's go to Malinda's."

He paused and then caught on. "Oh."

Exactly.

"Is there something you want to tell me?"

"Nope. I want to go to Malinda's."

"All right... Are you sure everything's okay?"

"Nope. Malin—"

He finished for me, "Malinda's. Got it. You ready to go?"

I was more than ready. As soon as we got there, I said hello to Malinda and bypassed her for Mark's room. It was now nearing noon, but as soon as I pushed open his door, he flew off his bed. "Mom!" He stopped, with one leg already in his jeans and frowned. "Sam?"

"Sam?" a feminine voice squeaked from under his covers. Then a blonde head popped out, and she didn't look too pleased. "What are you doing here?"

"Cassandra?" She'd been obsessed with Adam. I snorted. "Did you give up on Adam finally? Mark told me about the new girl in his life. Must suck. You got booted. Again."

The puzzled look on her face turned to a glare, and she threw the covers back. Wearing only a thin top, half was moved to the side so one breast was exposed. It didn't take a genius to figure out Mark had been getting a handful before my interruption. She snapped back now, "Did you and Mason break up? Are you moving onto your next stepbrother? I'm sorry. Logan must've turned you down. That must suck, too."

A growl came from the back of my throat. I looked like shit. I felt like shit. I wasn't ready to deal with *her* shit. Turning to Mark, I gestured out the doors. "We need to talk."

He nodded, casting a wary glance over his shoulder.

"Are you kidding me?" she seethed at him.

As she sat there with the blankets drowning her thin frame, Cassandra straightened her shirt with one jerk and glowered at me. "Why'd you have to come back? Things were perfect with you gone."

"Cass. Stop it."

"What?" She rolled her eyes. "They were."

She wasn't my problem, but I bared my teeth. "You really want to start a battle with me knowing that I'm probably going to be Mark's new stepsister?"

She cursed at me.

"Right back at you, Cass," I threw over my shoulder as I headed out to the media room.

She yelled back, "Miranda still hates you and Logan. Just wait. Karma's a bitch, Sam. Looks like you got one dose, but you got more comi—" Mark slammed the door shut on her. She paused and then yelled through the wall, "And screw you, too, Mark."

I closed my eyes. The slam was right there. It was on the tip of my tongue.

Mark opened the door and smirked at her. "You already did. Three times. Now get out." The door was shut once again, and he glanced down the hall. "We need to hide. She's going to be a bitch when she comes out of there."

As soon as we got into the room Logan used and shut the door, his opened. We could hear her cursing under her breath as she walked past us towards the stairs. The upstairs door slammed again before either of us said a word.

"You slept with *Cass*?"

He grimaced, raking a hand through his dark hair. It stuck up when his hand fell back down. "I was drunk." He shrugged. "And she's hot."

"Are you going to sleep with her again?"

"If I get the chance." He flashed me a rakish grin. "I'm a guy and she's good in bed."

"I thought you were dating Amelia?"

He snorted. "Hell no. She's crazy and my mom hates her. She's dating a college guy anyways."

"A lot's changed over there."

"Yeah." He shivered and touched his bare chest. "You mind if I grab a shirt? Not that I don't mind showing off the goods, but it's cold down here and you're *taken* taken."

"Yeah, that's fine."

He flashed a grin and hurried off. This time I followed and waited in the media room. Dropping onto one of the couches, I sat where I'd been with Mason a week ago. He held me while we watched movies that night. I'd been in so much pain, but he helped. He pushed the pain away. Being with him always pushed the pain away.

"Sam?"

I jerked back to reality. Mark was standing there, one of his athletic shirts on and his jeans zipped up. He sat on the opposite couch and bent over to pull on his socks. "You okay?"

"No."

He stopped and glanced up.

I wasn't going to lie about it. "I need your help."

"With what?"

"I can't drive and that's where you come in. I need a driver for the day."

"Okay." His shoulders loosened up, and he finished putting his socks on. As he reached for his shoes, he asked, "Where are we going?"

"To find Mason and Logan."

That made him stop and he sat back up. A blank mask came over him. "Huh?"

"They're not answering my calls and I'm not going to sit around and wait. So you're going to help me find them."

"Sam," he started as we both stood up.

"Don't. I don't want to hear it. You offered to help me before. I'm cashing in on it now. Let's go."

I led the way. David and Malinda were at the table, but I veered to the door instead. Mark stopped to talk to them, so I waited at the front entrance. A quiet conversation carried between the two. David didn't join in. I was listening for him, but when he remained silent I wasn't sure if it was a good thing or not. Then Mark came around the corner and tossed his keys in the air. He caught them in a swift hand motion and flashed me a smile. "Where's the first stop?"

"Jail."

"Whoa. What?"

Too late. I was already outside. The door swung closed on him, and I heard, "Ouch," before he followed me out. "We're going to the jail?"

Going to his car, I got inside before answering him. I was on a mission, and I wasn't slowing down for it. My ribs were better after a week of rest, but they weren't a hundred percent better. They were going to be angry with me, and I'd feel their wrath tomorrow, but that was tomorrow. Everything could wait until tomorrow. For today, nothing mattered except finding Mason and Logan. I would not let myself entertain the option that they left me. I couldn't.

Gritting my teeth, Mark had barely slid behind the wheel before I asked, "Can we get going? Please."

He clipped his seat belt on and started his car. "Jail, huh?"

"I need to make sure they weren't arrested last night."

"Jail it is." He wheeled around and took off down the street. As we passed the Kade mansion, I wanted to see if their cars were there, but they weren't. I wasn't surprised. My mom's wasn't either and that did surprise me. She always had her car parked out front. She liked showing off the new car James bought her for an engagement present. What further surprised me? James' car was gone as well.

"You know Mason and Logan went to a District party last night?"

Distracted from those thoughts, I turned back to my mission. "District party?"

He nodded, taking a left out of the neighborhood. "Yeah, you know those parties."

"I don't." This was Mark. He was easygoing Mark, laidback Mark. Right now he was being too much of that, and I needed him to catch on. The urge to snap at him was too much. "Enlighten me."

"Oh, sure." He chuckled to himself. "It's the three town school. You know."

"I don't." My voice rose on the last word. Anger and more anger was roiling together inside of me. "Please. Explain further."

Another chuckle came from him as he moved onto the main freeway. "I think last night's party was at Frisco. Only the public schools can go: Frisco, Roussou, and Fallen Crest. No private schools are allowed. If they catch you there, they trash your car—slash your tires, put scratches in your car, throw eggs on the window. It's not worth it to us so no one's gone for a long time."

My stomach dropped. "Roussou?" The arrested theory was gaining merit.

"Yep, but Frisco's a good town. We play them in football and basketball. They aren't at FCP's standards, which is why we play them, but they're decent."

"Did you hear if anything happened at the party?"

He laughed some more. "Like what? Everything happens at those parties. They find some place in the woods, and the cops are told not to go out there. Anything could've happened. No one talks about it afterwards. If you're caught running your mouth, you get the crap beat out of you. So no one talks."

People talked. The right questions needed to be asked, but people talked. When we got to the police station, I found out that they weren't there. So we went to the hotel next. That was when I found out that they weren't there either. My key card didn't work, and they wouldn't give me a new one. Mason and Logan had checked out last Sunday.

That was news to me, and it was not welcomed news.

As we went back to his car, Mark asked, "You didn't know they left?"

"They joked the first day about their mom moving closer to your house, but they haven't said a word. I assumed it hadn't happened and I haven't thought about it since."

"Their stuff must be somewhere. Both of them didn't keep that much at my house."

He was stating the obvious. *Thank you, Sherlock Holmes.*

Taking a deep breath, I pushed the inner rage away and sighed. "So let's try out that theory."

"What theory?"

"That their mom is living in that house."

"The For Sale sign is still on the lawn."

"Mason said that she would probably rent it."

"Okay." He turned the car back to his home. It wasn't long until we were passing his house and slowing down to see what cars were parked at Nate's old home.

None.

Mark pulled the car over and parked in front. He leaned over, inspecting the house. "There are curtains hung. I don't remember those. Someone's in there."

I hit his shoulder. "You go up there."

"Me? Why?" Cradling his shoulder, he scowled at me. "Stop hurting me. First the door, now your fist. What's next?"

"Your car if you don't go up there."

"No way. I've heard about Helen Malbourne, and she sounds scary as hell. My mom hates her."

Malinda went up a few more notches in my book. "You go. If they're in there, then they're avoiding me. They're not avoiding you and she won't lie to you. She'd *thrive* on lying to me."

He grumbled, but got out of the car. As he rounded to my side, he hissed at me before heading up the sidewalk, "You so owe me for this."

"Yeah, yeah. Go." I waved him off.

He sent me one last glare before the transformation came over him. It was the same with Logan. The head went up. The shoulders rolled back. A confident aura emanated from him, but Mark's strut wasn't as cocky. He was also nicer than Logan. As he knocked on the door, he didn't have to wait long. The door opened, and he went inside.

While he was in there, the knot in my stomach reproduced and birthed triplets. They were like rabbits. Those produced even more and there were too many inside of me. I couldn't handle it. He was gone for a minute, but my hand was reaching for the door handle. Screw it. Helen and I could go another round. I was forcing my way in there and I was going to demand some answers. Even if Mason and Logan weren't there, she'd know where they were. They were nice like that. They tried to keep their mom in the loop. Mason said one time that she hadn't fucked them over. She didn't deserve the freeze-out that James often got.

My hand tightened around the door handle and I pulled on it. It opened. Taking a deep breath, I made the decision. I was going in.

Mark came out.

I wasn't going in.

The door clicked shut and I waited as he jogged to the car, his trademark carefree grin on his face.

As he got inside, I said, "You're perpetually happy."

He paused, but shrugged and got inside. Shutting the door, he started the engine and wiggled his eyebrows at me. "She suggested Manny's. She said they like to eat there since their girlfriend works there."

I wanted to curse. No. I did curse. "Mark."

"What?" He was turning onto the street again.

"They weren't there?"

"Nope."

"What'd you say to her?"

"That I was looking for them." He cast me a sidelong look. "Why? Did I mess up?"

"No," I sighed. I knew they weren't there either.

"What about Nate Monson? He's still recuperating at his house, right? Maybe they're there."

I shook my head. "They wouldn't both be there. Mason said his parents have been pretty strict about who goes over there. They've been allowing him over, but they'd never let Logan and him there at the same time. He explained that they called in some hotshot doctor who said Nate can only handle so much stress." I frowned. "I think it's more about Nate's parents' stress. Logan and Mason together are not parent-friendly."

Mark grunted. "You're telling me." He paused for a beat. "I'm surprised they follow the rules at Nate's house."

"I doubt they do. I doubt Nate even does, but it doesn't matter. Mason and Logan are avoiding me. Even if I go over there, he'll cover for them."

"So we go to Manny's?"

I nodded. It was the 'why not' moment. They hadn't been arrested. They weren't at the hotel. I didn't think they were at Helen's. If they were, they would've called Mark's phone by now to see if something was wrong with me. Nate would never tell me if he knew anything. There was no way they were at James'. I had no more places to try. Plan B: Heather. That meant Manny's.

When we got there, my friend wasn't there, but Mark's were. He headed to their table, and I headed to Heather's house. It was another no-go for me. Brandon answered the door. He and Heather had been banned from the diner and bar for the entire weekend. Their dad didn't want them working as much as they had been so Heather was at Channing's. I asked where his home was, and Brandon laughed. He shook his head. "No way am I giving you those directions. It's too close to the Broudou house. No way, Sam. My sister would skin me alive if you got hurt somehow." He eyed my face. "And you've been hurt enough."

It was official. I had no one now. As I began to turn away, Brandon stopped me. "Hey. Wait." He disappeared inside, and my hope flared for one second. He came back with her phone. "If you see her, here's her phone. She left it and it keeps beeping every damn minute. It's password protected, and I can't get in there to turn off the alerts or the volume."

I had no words. Those alerts were from me. "Okay, thanks, Brandon."

"Yeah. I'm sorry, but I'm sure you'll see her at the street dance tonight."

My heart paused. I'd been heading back down the porch, but stopped in my tracks. "What?"

"The street dance. Aren't you going?"

"No."

Thump.

"What is it?"

My heart began picking up speed. *Thump thump.*

He frowned at me. "It's the District Weekend, right?"

"Yeah…" *Thumpthumpthumpthump.* Whatever he was about to say, I knew they'd be there. All of them would be there. My heart was racing.

He continued to frown at me, scratching his head. "It should be in Roussou tonight. All three towns go. You've never heard about it?"

"No." *Please tell me. Please, please, please.*

"Oh. That's weird. I thought Mason would've told you. He's been going forever."

"It's in Roussou."

His eyes lit up. "Maybe you shouldn't go. That's probably why no one's said anything. Yeah, don't go. Forget I said anything, but if you go, you didn't hear about it from me."

"I know about the party last night in Frisco."

"You do?" A relieved grin came over him. "Oh good. Yeah, all three towns host something over the weekend, but it's always the same thing. The first night, the party's in Frisco. Then Saturday night, the street dance is in Roussou. They shut down one street, and a lot of people from their community go. I think it was originally meant for the town, but the District Festival kind of took over. Then Sunday, Fallen Crest has a huge bonfire in the hills behind Quickie's." He grinned. "It can get crazy there, too."

"You've been there?"

"Once."

"Has Heather?"

"She hasn't in the past, but she and Channing have been tight this weekend, so I'm sure she will. He has to go. Most of his friends go so Channing makes sure no one gets hurt, or gets in a fight with the Broudou brothers."

A party. A street dance. A bonfire. As I waved goodbye and went to get Mark, my heart was pounding against my ribcage. I had a location for the night. I was going to the street dance. There was no way I would stay away. I couldn't think about Mason's or Logan's absence. It was because of their plan. They were doing this to help me. They hadn't left me. There was no way. I wouldn't accept that.

As I pushed through the side door and inside Manny's, I collected Mark. He was laughing with his friends, more people from Fallen Crest Academy that I didn't want to be around. I wasn't laughing. Gritting my teeth, I ignored all their looks. I pretended I didn't notice their stares or the mouths hanging open when they got a better look at my face.

Yes, everyone. I had been attacked and beaten. The bruises were still with me, but I wasn't getting any more. None from them and none from anyone else. It was why I needed answers from Mason. There was a reason for their absence. There had to be.

CHAPTER TWENTY-FOUR

I went to the street dance alone.

I never told Mark about it and when he dropped me off at home, I reassured him that everything was fine. Everything *was* fine. I was going to make sure of it. Getting ready for the street dance was painful in the literal sense, but I chose a white camisole underneath a black sweater and black pants with little black ballet flats. All of it was easy to get into and that had been my main objective. My next goal was make-up. More was applied than I normally wore, and I was proud of myself; almost all of the bruises were hidden by the time I was finished. Then I swept my hair up into a high pony-tail. My hair had grown longer, so it was past my shoulders now. If Heather had been there, she would've told me it looked sleek. I didn't care. I just needed to blend in. I was going into Roussou territory.

I wanted to find Heather first, but as I parked my car and got out, my heart sank. Brandon said one street was blocked off. That was true, but he never said it was the entire main street blocked off. She could be anywhere.

I sighed and started off on my mission.

Going through the first block was easy. It was during the second that people started to look at me. A group of girls jerked together and started whispering. A few pointed at me. My heart sank again. It was already starting, so I veered into the first bathroom I could find. Checking my make-up in the mirror, I didn't see anything wrong. I looked fine. Normal even. The evening had grown dark so my face looked flawless with none of my bruises showing, but when I went back out, they were still there. There were more behind them and they were watching me now.

Frowning at them, I turned to slip away, but came to an abrupt stop.

Budd Broudou was in front of me, a leer on his face as he looked me up and down. I hardened inside. The longer his gaze lingered on me, the dirtier I felt. As they were transfixed below my waist, I shifted on my feet and snapped, "What do you want?"

He grinned and lifted his hand. A forty ounce bottle touched his lips, and he took a long pull from it before wiping his mouth with the back of his hand. Then he licked his lips and tugged at his jeans. They hung low on his waist, already baggy, but the top button was loose so they sagged even more.

I narrowed my eyes.

He chuckled as he caught my reaction. Lifting a hand to his chest, he rubbed it through his white wife-beater. His flannel shirt hung open, the ends of it were frayed and ripped with holes in them. As his hand fell back down to his pants, his finger caught on the end and tore it some more. He seemed unaware that he ripped his shirt, or he just didn't care.

My guess was both. I was getting tired of his silent leering. "What do you want?"

Another deep chuckle came from him, and he pointed his beer at me. "You already said that."

"Then answer the question."

There was a collective gasp behind me, but I couldn't take my words back. I said it. It was done. Now I waited for the consequences.

He started laughing. It was slight at first, but grew. As he kept going, he bent over and slapped at his knee. His beer jostled from the movement and he cursed, but shook his head as more laughter escaped. It took another moment before his chuckles ceased enough so his hand had stopped shaking. As soon as he could, he finished the rest of his beer. When it was empty, he tossed it to the ground. His hand went back out and someone put a new one there. When he went to open it, he kept shaking his head, watching me at the same time. His shoulders jerked up as he started laughing again.

I looked for a quick escape route, but there wasn't one. Everyone around us was watching. They had taken a step towards us and closed ranks. I had to wait.

After another sip from his new beer, he burped. "You got a spine to you. I can see why he likes you."

I stiffened.

His gaze travelled over me again, stopping on my breasts. "You got a nice rack, too. Not too much. You're damn skinny, but you got enough for a good bounce." His tongue darted out and ran over his bottom lip before moving to the top one.

It was in slow motion. I began to feel sick.

"Hmm mmm." He nodded, then took another long swallow. "You're tight." His eyes went to below my waist. "I bet you're real tight there, too. He's a lucky guy."

I frowned. Feeling disgusted aside, he thought Mason was a lucky guy?

"Too bad my brother caught you first."

His brother?

"Budd."

I turned around. Brett Broudou was behind me. He wore the same baggy jeans and ripped flannel shirt, but there was no leering. He was glowering, but not at me. He said again, "Budd. Back off."

Budd snorted. He lifted his beer again, but he stumbled to the side. The beer fell from his hand to the ground, and it sprayed everywhere, most of it on me. I jumped out of the way and slammed into Brett, but I didn't care at that moment. My ribs protested, and a searing pain sliced through me. "Shit," I whispered to myself, but then I bounced off of Brett and began to fall to the side.

The ground was coming at me. My eyes went wide. The pain was going to be paralyzing, so I readied myself for the impact.

It never came.

I had stopped halfway there and looked up. Brett caught me. His one hand held a twin forty ounce beer, but his other hand was wrapped around my arm. Our eyes caught and an apology flashed in his as he lifted me back to my feet.

"Thanks." I had no idea what else to say.

He nodded, his gaze was lidded, but he looked over at his brother. "You remember our talk?"

Budd rolled his eyes and waved him away. "Yeah, yeah."

Brett frowned. "Tink?"

Another goliath-sized guy spoke from behind the counter. "Yeah?"

"Give Budd another beer. He dropped his."

"Already?"

Budd growled. "Fuck you both. I'm fine. I can get my own damn beer." He swung around, but almost clipped a girl in the head as he did. Taking a few extra steps, he regained his balance and shoved through the crowd.

My heart was racing. It wasn't until he left that I gasped for breath.

Brett touched my hand, stopping it from trembling. "Come on."

I followed him through the crowd and concentrated on slowing my heart. It was nearing combustion; it wanted to explode out of my chest. It wasn't until it had slowed a little when I realized that Brett was taking me somewhere away from the street dance. We turned down an alley and ducked into a side door where there was another party. There were people everywhere and most clapped him on the shoulder as he went past. Girls called out hellos, but it was different than when I walked with Mason or Logan. The attention they got from girls was sexual. This was genuine. These people actually liked Brett Broudou.

He went to a back hallway. Only a few others were there, and he moved around them.

"Hey, man."

Another said, "Buddy."

Brett gave each a nod, but pressed forward until he got to the last door.

Where the hell was he taking me?

Then I found out. The last door opened to a back room. Couches were pushed against the walls, lining the whole room. A bar was set-up against the side and a couple small tables were in the middle. A few people were around them, playing a card game. A large pile of money was in the middle, and everyone looked up as we entered.

Brett jerked his hand to the door. "Move the game somewhere else."

I expected protests, but there were none. The room was silent as everyone got up and collected their cards. The dealer took the money and the rest of the chips. They filed past us, taking their chairs with them.

"They literally moved their game somewhere else," I noted. Holy hell. Was I supposed to be scared? Was he going to hurt me?

"Yeah."

"Yeah...?"

There were green couches. There was a blue one. The bar had mosaic tiles on the bottom. The stools were encased in metal—

"You're scared of me, aren't you?"

Oh, dear god. I tore my gaze from the stools to him and gulped. I wasn't expecting that from him. It sounded like raw honesty. "Um..." I stopped beating around the bush. "Can you blame me?"

"I'm not going to hurt you." He went behind the bar and reached for two glasses. "I asked you out, remember?"

As he began filling the two shot glasses with rum, I moved closer. "Do you know who I am?"

He finished pouring and put the bottle to the side, then lifted his hooded eyes back to me. "I know you were dating Mason Kade. That was a nice surprise when I put it together." He paused, frowning at me. "Are you still dating him?"

"I—" had no idea what to say.

He added, "Because he's been having another girl all over him. Did you know about that?"

The air left me, and I sagged forward. My heart dropped to the bottom of my feet and new pain sliced through me. Hearing Mason's plan and knowing Kate would think she was his girlfriend was different from hearing it was happening, and hearing it from Mason's enemy. I couldn't answer him. I felt rubbed raw from the inside out.

His tone didn't soften. It hardened. "I asked around. It's that same bitch that beat you up."

"Yeah."

"And he's letting her crawl all over him? He tossed you aside? For her?" The threat of violence was swimming in his depths. He tossed the shot down his throat and refilled it again. Nudging mine towards me, he waited for me this time.

I took it. I didn't feel a thing.

"More?" He lifted the rum again.

I nodded. I needed all I could get.

We took two more shots before I moved my glass to the side. No more for me, but he still downed two more. Then he leaned against the far wall behind the bar, and I slid onto a stool. The alcohol was beginning to work. I was beginning to feel warm again.

"You never answered my question. Are you still with the guy?"

"I don't know."

Disappointment flared over him, followed by pity. "That's too bad."

"You're not going to tell your brother?"

Pushing away from the wall, he reached for the rum again. He spoke with a savage tone, "Are you kidding me? You know what my brother does? He hurts people."

I frowned. Didn't he?

"I know what you're thinking." He held his glass towards me, the shot ready to go. "I hurt people, too, but I don't hurt girls, and I don't hurt people weaker than me. I don't stop my brother either. I can't. I tried but people only get hurt worse."

"Why are you telling me this?"

"Because my brother *really* wants to hurt you." He downed his shot and filled it again. "No, he wants to hurt whoever Mason Kade cares about. Good thing that bitch has been all over him this weekend. Budd thinks it's her that he cares about, but it's not. Is it? It's you. He almost drove over my brother when he found out you were hurt. I was too stunned. I almost let it happen. Shit."

Mason almost drove over Budd? I couldn't think about that. Grabbing my shot glass, I pushed it to him. "One more."

He grinned, but his eyes were hungry. They were angry.

I didn't care. I was starting to relax. He wasn't going to hurt me. He said it and I was beginning to trust him. "You're not going to tell your brother?"

"No." He set the bottle down. It landed with a thud and he held onto it for a second. His head hung down.

I waited.

The moment grew tense suddenly.

Then he lifted his head again; his eyes were so haunted. "I'm going to let my brother do what he wants to. I know what Kade's doing with that whore that hurt you. It's fucking genius. It's cold, too."

He pinned me down with his gaze. I glanced away. For some reason, I didn't want to see what he was thinking.

"You don't know, do you?" He tone softened. "Or you don't want to know."

I swallowed over a knot. It felt like glue, and it wouldn't go away.

"That's it. You don't want to know."

"Why do you care?" I snapped at him. I was stretched too thin. My need to keep control was beginning to unravel. "Why do you even give a damn?"

"Because of you."

I stopped. There was that raw honesty again, and I felt ashamed. "Why?"

"Because you don't deserve what Budd's going to do to that girl. That's why."

"You're lying to your brother. You're lying about Mason. I'm supposed to believe you're doing it for me? You asked me out once. You don't know me."

He let out a deep breath. His hand gripped the bottle tighter, and he shrugged, but he wouldn't look me in the eyes anymore. His went back down. "I know two things. I can't stop my brother. He's obsessed with hurting Kade's girlfriend, and he won't stop until he does. The other thing I know is that it can't be you. You're a good person. There aren't many around anymore."

Then I damned us both. "Thanks."

He looked up now and our gazes locked.

"But you're wrong," I said. "I'm starting to figure it out."

"Don't," he rushed out. "Stop thinking and go back home. You'll be safer, and the regret won't eat at you then."

I shook my head. "You're too late." It was rising in me, and it was going to eat at my soul. I felt the darkness closing in.

"Brett!" someone called from the hallway. "They're here."

"Yeah."

The door opened. I expected more of his friends, and I waited. They'd come in, or he would tell them to leave. I wasn't expecting to hear my name in a gasp. "Sam!"

I whipped around. Heather was frozen in place. Her mouth hung open, and her eyes were wide, but they darted past my shoulder and grew in size. Channing came around her. He was less surprised and waved at me. Then he nodded to Brett. "Thanks, man."

"Sam," Heather choked out again. She jerked out of her frozen state. "You're okay?"

Brett was behind me so I couldn't see him, but I heard a small growl come from him.

Channing laughed and urged Heather back out the door. "Thanks for letting us know. We'll take it from here."

"Don't let her back here."

"No problem. We won't." Channing pushed Heather the rest of the way into the hallway and came back inside. He held a hand to me. "Sam?"

Glancing at Brett again, I didn't know what to say. I wanted to see Mason. It was why I came.

"Sam?"

Brett jerked his head towards the door. "Go."

I took a deep breath. I was going. There it was. I surrendered to a battle inside of me that I didn't know was going on. There were things at play that I didn't understand. He insinuated the same thing.

Go back home... The regret won't eat at you then. His statement haunted me, even as I took two steps backwards, and Channing grabbed my arm. I was pulled into the hallway and hurried out of there. Heather wrapped an arm around my shoulders. Her hand went to the top of my head and she applied enough pressure to force my head down. I was swept out of there, down a back alley, and away.

"SALUTE!"

I jumped as Budd's voice ripped through the air.

Heather cursed under her breath, and our pace quickened.

He yelled out another cheer, and as we kept going, his voice got quieter. It wasn't until we had covered three more blocks that we slowed down. I knew the second we passed into friendly territory. Heather dropped her hand from my head, and she let out a deep, "Thank God."

My head went up and I saw a lot of Fallen Crest people, but it was the same reaction as before. All eyes rested on me. As Channing led us further down the street, the word had spread. They knew we were coming. One by one, they turned to watch us. I felt their gazes before we went past them, and I continued to feel their gaze on our backs.

"Where are we going?"

Heather's hand tightened on the top of my arm. She pressed into me, and I knew I was supposed to shut up. When we got to a back parking lot, her arm dropped from me and she moved away.

Channing cut across the lot. A group of trucks were in the back. The tailgates had been lowered so people sat on top of them. Lounge chairs were set up in a circle and coolers were spread all over. A guy reached down into one and pulled out a beer.

"What are you doing here?" Heather asked me now in a quiet voice. She moved closer, but her arm didn't reach around me again.

I shrugged. My mind was racing. I didn't have that answer anymore.

She sighed. "We're mostly around Fallen Crest people now, but there's still a few Roussou people here. All of Channing's friends are close by, but you shouldn't have come here."

"Why?" That was the answer. That was why I came. I wanted to know why Mason hadn't called. Why Logan remained silent. Why Heather was with Channing for the weekend. Why I felt like my insides were being ripped out. I wasn't leaving until I found out.

"Holy shit."

Finally.

Logan stood behind me, a beer in hand. I turned all the way around, and when he saw my face, the beer slipped from his hand. It splattered on the ground, spraying everywhere. He didn't move. His eyes never left mine. Then his eyes bulged out before he lunged for me.

His hand grabbed my arm, and he hissed at Heather, "What the hell were you thinking?!"

"We didn't. I didn't. She came by herself."

"What?!" His eyes were fierce. "What are you thinking, Sam? It's dangerous here."

I waited for Heather to tell him the rest. She didn't. As my gaze darted to hers, her head shook from side to side. It was the slightest of movements. She didn't want Logan to know about Brett. I nodded to her, the same slightest of movements. The corners of her mouth lifted up in a faint grin. It vanished as quick as it appeared and then she started to move away.

"Wait." I held her phone out. "Your brother gave it to me. Wanted me to give it to you if I saw you."

"Oh." She ran her thumb across the screen and typed in the password. As she saw the missed calls and text alerts from me, she looked up. An apology was there.

I lifted a shoulder. I was here. It didn't matter anymore.

"Let's go," Logan growled in my ear.

"Be nice to her."

He swung back around to Heather. "Are you kidding me?"

"Be nice to her," she repeated. A different message was sent between them, and she added, "You're not seeing it from her eyes."

He stopped. Whatever she meant, it hit him. More curses slipped out before his hand gentled on my arm. "Come on, Sam. I'll take you home."

"Can you drive?"

"Yes." He looked as if he'd seen his own ghost. "I'm suddenly very sober." Then he turned and I started to go with him. It was then that I saw them.

Everything stopped.

My heart froze.

My lungs shrunk.

Everything shattered.

Knowing about it hadn't prepared me. Hearing about it hadn't prepared me, but seeing it was the worst way for it to become real.

Mason was sitting on the back of a truck. It had been pulled so it was hidden behind the others, but it wasn't the sight of him that had a dagger slicing through my insides. Kate was straddling him.

Her breasts were pushed against his chest, and she had both arms around him. She grabbed a fistful of his hair as she gyrated on top of him, rubbing against him. A smirk came over him as he took hold of the back of her neck and tilted her head to the side. Then his mouth opened over hers, demanding entrance, and she shuddered in his arms.

She shuddered for him and so did I, but for different reasons.

Logan pulled me backwards. "Come on, Sam." His tone softened, and he led me away. He was trying to be gentle with me, all the way to his car and as he took me home, but it didn't matter.

I was numb again.

CHAPTER TWENTY-FIVE

My house was cold when I went inside. Logan flipped the lights on, but I shook my head. I didn't want them on. He didn't see me and went to the counter. A note was there and he lifted it to read, "Samantha, I am at Malinda's. Please call me when you get in and I will come home. Love, David." He lowered it, a slight sneer on his face. "Gee. That's sweet of him."

"Shut up."

He put the note back. "Sorry."

Images of them flashed in my mind. Mason on the truck. Kate on him. His mouth on hers. Her hand twisting in his hair. They kept coming and I couldn't stop them. If I closed my eyes, they were worse. I was there again. When he tilted her head to the side and opened his mouth, I flinched. My eyelids flew up, but it didn't matter. They were still there.

They were all I could see.

"Here."

Feeling something cold being pushed into my hand, I looked down. Logan was holding a glass to me. He held the bottle up in his other hand. "I found your dad's secret stash. He's got good taste."

"What is this?"

"Does it matter?"

I drank it. It was like water, and I held my glass up again. "More." I needed more than more. Tonight I wanted to get drunk. All the pain needed to stop. I wanted to go back to being numb. Life was so much easier then.

We didn't talk. Logan took my glass from my hand and went into the living room. When he went to turn the light on, I cried out, "Don't." He heard me this time and let the dark remain. I sat on one couch, and he took a chair across from me. The large windows were behind him and moonlight shone inside; no curtains restricted it. It felt warming to me. I had no idea why, maybe if the lights were on then I'd have to face reality. If the lights remained off, I could still hide.

If that was the case, I never wanted to turn the lights on again. I wanted to hide from this. I wanted to run, but I couldn't, so I asked for another drink. That'd be my escape for the night.

It wasn't until my fourth drink that I began to feel the alcohol. I drew in a shuddering breath. It needed to work faster. I thrust my glass out and leaned forward. "Again."

Logan raised an eyebrow, but he filled it. Leaning back, he tipped the bottle and drank straight from it. His glass was left forgotten on the table beside him. As he finished and tucked the bottle into the seat beside him, he asked, "You want to talk about it?"

"No." Yes, but not with him. I sighed and gave in. "Did he fuck her?"

"Not that I know."

"What do you know?"

"That he did it all to protect you."

I shook my head. That wasn't good enough. He was with her and not me—he was kissing her, touching her, tasting her—my stomach rolled over, and pain flooded back in. I couldn't get the images out of my head.

"Sam." Logan leaned forward. Resting his arms on his legs, he dipped his head down and waited.

I shook my head again.

He didn't look away.

I waved my hand at him instead.

Still nothing. He gave me a faint grin. "I'm not going anywhere."

"You did," I choked out. "You both did. You left me."

"That was for you—"

"It wasn't." It so wasn't. They did that for them. "You could've texted me or called. You ignored my calls." I was left out of the loop. Didn't they get that? No, Mason wasn't there. Didn't Logan get it? There was complete silence from them and no warning that it was going to happen.

My chest constricted. It was like before. David dropped me. So did Garrett. I had them or I thought I had them and then nothing after that. I drew in a painful breath. I couldn't go through that again, and I thought I had. Mason still wasn't here. He was still with her.

So much damn pain and Logan had no clue how it felt.

"You're lucky, do you know that?"

He frowned, but leaned back in his chair again. The bottle was lifted for another drink. His eyes were lidded, but I knew he was going to let me talk.

"Your parents would do anything for you."

Logan snorted.

My eyes jerked to his. "What's that mean? Your parents would. Your mother moved back here for you guys."

"Yeah and she did that because my dad's choosing his new psycho over his sons." He stared right back at me, without pausing or breaking stride. His tone was cool. "And my dad doesn't love your mom. You have to know that, don't you? She's his pet project. It's like he's trying to make up for all his past fuck-ups by fixing her. It's pathetic. No, Sam. We're not that lucky. We've got a messed-up parents just like you."

I drew in a breath. "Did yours slap you around?"

"Did yours tell you to fuck a colleague's daughter because she was fat and lonely?" Logan laughed to himself. His eyes were hard. "The guy didn't even care that she'd be hurt later. He said the one time would be enough for her to hold onto through college. He said he had no hope for his daughter finding a guy, and one good screw could help her out."

"You know who your parents are."

"So do you," he threw right back. Lifting the bottle again, he drank from it and tucked it back in place. "What are you doing, Sam? Tit for tat? Are you trying to make me feel sorry for you? Mason's not with her because he wants to be. He's with her to protect you."

"How?" It ripped from me. "He gave her what she wants. She won, Logan. Don't you get that? She beat me up, tried to make my friend dump me, and she didn't even get in trouble for it. That's not right."

"She got ISS."

"In-school suspension is not good enough." I shot forward.

So did he. "Stop. Your ribs, Sam."

"I'm too drunk to feel it." But not drunk enough to stop the other pain. Those images kept flooding in. I couldn't get rid of them. "Why didn't she get in more trouble? Why wasn't she arrested? She should've been arrested."

Logan sighed. "You want the truth?"

It was my turn to snort. "It's all I've ever wanted. No one tells the truth anymore."

"Kate's uncle is a cop. That's why she didn't get arrested. When Principal Green was going to expel her, he got a visit from her uncle and some of his buddies. They twisted his arm so she only got in-school suspension, and he can't let the ringleader off and expel the other three, so all four got ISS."

"It's bullshit."

"Yeah." He didn't hide from it. "That's why we don't bother with reporting shit. We learned long ago it doesn't do a thing. We settle things our way now."

Their way? "Screwing the enemy? Is that how you do it?"

"No, Sam." He stood. "Is that all you can think about? Look, Mason didn't want you to know about it. He's protecting you again so that you're not a part of it. I know you've had a rough ride, but what have we done to lose your trust?"

"He's fucking her," I cried out and pushed up from the couch. Then I swayed. The alcohol made me sluggish, but a sudden sharp stabbing had me falling to the side. Grabbing my side, I bent over again.

Logan cursed, but caught me. "Sam, stop. Sit down."

I shook my head and pushed him away. Then I regretted it. He was sturdy. He was strong. I needed his support at that moment. "Logan."

Everything crumbled inside me. A sob escaped me, but then he was there. He sat on the couch beside me and pulled me into him. A hand went to my head, pushing it down to his chest, but then it didn't matter. I was clinging to him as more and more tears racked through me.

The image of Mason with her wouldn't stop. It repeated over and over.

"Logan."

"Shhh." He began running a hand down my back and smoothing down my hair. "You can cry, Sam. You can always cry. You just can't let it stop you from fighting. That's the only thing."

He was touching her. He was kissing her. I couldn't think about it. Shaking my head against Logan's shoulder, I clutched his shirt even tighter and pressed into him.

Logan drew in a breath, and he never released it. He had gone from being comforting to being rigid.

I pressed even more against him. Mason was still touching her in my mind. Her hand gripped his hair, and she was moving over his lap in a seductive rhythm. A growl burst from me. I hated it. I hated her. "Logan." I shuddered against him.

"Sam." His voice broke and he quieted.

I clambered to get closer. Lifting my legs onto the couch, I kneeled beside him, pressing into the couch so I was almost on his lap. His hand swept down and caught one of my legs. He lifted it with me, and I let out a ragged breath. I needed his comfort. That was all I needed. Slipping my arms around him, I hugged him. My cheek went to his shoulder, and my eyes closed.

"Sam," he murmured again. His hand began rubbing on my thigh where he gripped me. "You need to stop. Your ribs can't take this."

He was right. I tried to get closer to him.

"You're going to fracture them again."

I was, but Mason was still touching her. His lips were on hers. He wanted to slip inside of her, and she let him. She savored it. I could tell. That was my place. She had replaced me. "Logan," I whispered now.

His hand smoothed my hair, running down and over my back to circle up and repeat the caress. His other hand was rubbing over my thigh.

I paused.

A small trigger went off. Mason. He was close. I felt his presence how I always felt him, but that wasn't true. It was in my mind. He was with her. Kissing her. Stroking her.

It was like his hand went into my chest and grabbed my heart. He squeezed it with every memory. He was with her. I needed it gone. Now. Anyway I could, and I felt Logan's hand then. It touched the side of my face and I turned back to him. Mason moved to the back of my mind.

"What the fuck?"

But he wasn't. I turned. Mason was standing right there. He wasn't in the back of my mind anymore.

Logan's hand jerked away, like it'd been burned. He lifted me off his lap to the couch and stood up. "It's not what you think."

Mason was there. The timing struck me, and I started laughing. He was there now, and *that* was all he had to say. Neither of them said another word. Both were silent and I couldn't stop laughing. No. I was crying now. The booze wasn't helping. I was still feeling everything, even the pain from my ribs were hurting me again. I tried to stop laughing, but I couldn't. The couch had imprisoned me. I curled to my side and stopped laughing enough so I could draw in a deep breath.

Shit. My ribs were really hurting.

"Is she drunk?" Mason asked now.

That struck me as even more hilarious. High-pitched laughter peeled from me. Then I begin giggling in between, alternating between the two with a sniffle every now and then. Nope. I sobbed now. More laughter, giggle, sobbing. I couldn't stop.

Logan's voice lowered. He was cautious. "She saw you and Kate."

"I know," Mason whipped at him.

The rage was there. He was barely holding it back. I recognized it, but I couldn't say anything. I was able to stop the laughs so only giggles came from me, but then I realized I didn't want to stop. It would hurt again once I did. He'd been touching her.

"Sam."

I held a hand out to stop him and buried my head into the couch. It muffled some of my hysteria.

"What the hell did you do to her?" he growled.

Logan snapped back, "What do you think? She saw you with Kate."

"I told her—"

"She saw you, Mason! You're ready to beat me up because I was *comforting* her. You were *making out* with another girl. Put two and two together."

"I am."

"You're not. She's hurting, like a lot, and not just from seeing you and Kate. She's drunk as hell, but her ribs have gotta be killing her."

Mason cursed.

My laughter had subsided to soft chuckles now, but I still couldn't stop them. So much damn pain was slicing through me. I couldn't move so I stayed there, curled into the couch, my head pressed against the cushion. It hid the tears that I couldn't stop either.

I was a mess.

But they were there. Both of them. This was what I wanted. I needed to know they would come back. Someone sat beside me and the couch shifted underneath me. Another burst of fresh pain went through me. This time it was like a knife had been stuck deep into me. It was pulled back out and back in, over and over.

"I'm sorry, Sam." Mason touched my arm now. It was so gentle, so tender. It brought a new wave of tears. He tugged on me.

"Be gentle with her."

"Can you leave us alone?"

He wanted to talk to me, but I couldn't talk to him now. What had I done? No. What had I been about to do? Another image of Kate straddling him flared again and I stopped crying.

"Sam," he murmured again as a door shut somewhere in the house. His arms slid underneath me on the couch, and I was lifted in the air a moment later.

I froze. He was going to jar everything again, but he didn't. He moved me in the exact position I was in. No new pain went through me. Then I was lifted to his lap instead. It felt wrong. All of this was wrong. Gritting my teeth, I pushed past the pain and stood from him.

"Sam." He stood with me.

"No."

"Yes."

"NO." Everything was muddled in my head, but he touched another girl. That wasn't okay with me. "You shouldn't have done that."

"Sam." He reached for me again.

Slapping his hand down, I seethed, "You shouldn't have. You fucked her."

"I didn't."

"You did." He must have. That was how she was kissing him, as if they had…

"I didn't. I swear." The disgust was clear in his voice. "I only touched her when Roussou people were around. I had to, Sam. I had to do it. It saved you, and it hurt her. It will. I didn't cheat on you."

"You were kissing her."

"Because I had to," he ground out. "I had to. Don't you see that? He had to know about her. He was looking for you the whole time. It was only a matter of time before your name was slipped. I couldn't let him hurt you. I couldn't."

I stopped to breathe. One moment, that was all I needed. My head was pounding. A stabbing pain kept overwhelming me, over and over again. I held a hand out for him to stop. I needed another moment.

"Sam," he choked out.

"Stop."

"I can't."

"Please."

"NO… no."

"Mason," it left me in a whimper. He went away for only one night and day. That was all it took for me to become a mess, for my world to crumble. I swung my gaze to the couch. I'd been there before with—I shook my head. Standing there, I was hurting and all I wanted was to be in his arms. I wanted all of it to go away, but it wouldn't. I shook my head. It wouldn't. I knew too much. "What's he going to do to her?"

"I don't know."

"Couldn't you stop him some other way?"

"Not Budd Broudou. He hates me, Sam. He's going to hurt me the worst way he could, and that's through you. Do you see what I was doing now? He wanted my girlfriend, so I gave him a girlfriend. I spent an entire week with her touching me, but it wasn't until last night that I kissed her. I swear. He had to be there, and he needed to see us tonight, too."

"Is it going to be enough?"

He lifted his hands in a helpless gesture. "I hope. Once Budd sees something for his own eyes, he doesn't go against it. He won't trust what other people tell him. Besides, something tells me that there are people close to him who won't let him know about you."

I felt the extra kick behind his words. He knew. "Brett."

"Yeah," he bit out.

Hopelessness hit me hard then. There was so much distance between us now. Brett had been...what lie? I couldn't remember now. "I meant to tell you about him."

"It would've been nice to know my girlfriend was on a first-name basis with one of them, or when you first ran into them?"

I flinched from the accusation in his tone. "You lied to me, too."

"When?"

"Don't play that game with me."

"When? I told you what I was doing with Kate—"

"With Logan," I cried out. My heart started pounding again. It was racing. "You lied to me about Tate, and why you stopped giving a crap if they hooked up or not. Why, Mason?! Why?"

"Because he wants to screw with her," he threw back. His green eyes were heated, but he was holding back.

That wasn't why. I jerked my head in a nod, but began looking for that bottle again. "You just lied to me. Again."

"What are you talking about?"

It wasn't in the chair. I rounded to the couch and felt under the cushions.

"What are you looking for?"

"Alcohol."

"You don't drink that much."

A harsh laugh ripped from me. "I do tonight. I'm going to keep drinking a whole shitload tonight." My insides were churning, and the hysteria was starting to rise again.

"Sam."

I stopped. His voice broke and I heard his defeat in my name. I turned from the couch, my heart paused and my breath held. He had fallen against the wall and was leaning against it now. His green eyes were stricken as he hunched forward.

Whatever tension that was between us was gone.

I didn't speak. I didn't dare. I felt something coming. It was the old Mason, before the lies got between us. I felt him coming back, and I wanted it so badly. I wanted *him* so badly. *Please...*

He slid down the wall to the floor and sat there. His eyes never left me. They were usually so intense and powerful. They could pierce through all my walls. He had since the beginning, but it was me this time. I pierced through his and he surrendered to me. I took a step towards him. My heart began beating rapidly. I missed him so damn much. "You touched another girl."

"It was the only way, Sam. I know it hurt you, and I'm sorry for that. It was the only way. She hurt you. I can't let that go. No one hurts you and Budd wanted to. I've stopped that too now."

What could I say to that? I had no idea, but I took another step. I saw it then. He was sorry. As I closed the distance and stood above him, his head tipped back. There was agony inside of him, but determination too. He would do it again. That knowledge slammed against me, and I stumbled back a step.

"Sam." He reached for me and caught the back of my leg. His hand cupped me there, and he pulled me back to him. "Please."

"You lied to me."

"Because I see that it's already getting to you. He's going to hurt her. I didn't want you to know. I didn't want that on your conscience."

"But it is now."

"Yeah. It is now."

I drew in a sudden breath. He was right. He was right about everything. He touched her, but it was for me. He lied to me. I lied to him. I was so tired of it all, and I just wanted him again. Mason had been my shelter for so long. The world hurt when I wasn't with him. Folding my knees, I bent, and he caught me. He pulled me onto his lap like I had never left. I was home again. Cradling my head in his hand, he took a deep breath. I felt his relief because it was mine, too. Our old connection was coming back, but I couldn't forget what Brett had warned.

"Go back home... The regret won't eat at you then"

Mason's arm slid around me, and I was moved so my back rested against his chest. "What's Budd going to do to her?" I asked.

She had kissed Mason. She ran her hands over him and pushed her breasts against him. Anger clawed at me. She wanted to take what was mine.

"I don't know." His arms tightened around me. His tone was soothing once again. "But it's not you. That's all I care about. Better her than you."

He knew my lies, but he still held that one truth from me. It took root inside of me, and it was going to grow until it would take over us. I was too weak to fight for it now. He evaded, but he was here. He was mine. That would be enough...for now.

CHAPTER TWENTY-SIX

"Hey." Logan came back from the back porch, the bottle in one hand, his phone in the other, wearing a dark frown. "Not to interrupt, but I just checked my phone."

Mason stiffened underneath me. "Yeah?"

"Yeah." That didn't sound good. "We have a problem."

Of course we did.

"Just say it, Logan. Stop beating around the bush."

"Tate called me. Actually," he lifted the phone as if we could see her calls, "she called me ten times and texted another seven times."

Mason stiffened underneath me. He leaned his head back against the wall. "What about?"

"Uh…"

"Logan."

"Okay." His shoulders lifted when he sucked in a deep breath. "So when you shooed me out of Sam's room when she was in the hospital, I wasn't thinking clear, and I needed to get my mind off things…"

"Spill it."

"Yeah." The hand with his phone went to his hair and he grabbed onto some of his locks, pulling at them so they stuck up. His other hand tightened around the bottle. His shirt rode up, exposing the waistband of his boxers. His jeans slipped down an inch, but Logan wasn't aware. He shook his head. "I forgot all about it."

He stopped again. Seriously.

"Yeah, so I went to Tate's that night, and we were in the living room. No one else was there. There was a time when she went to the bathroom, and I was looking through her magazines."

"Logan, tell us what happened."

His hand dropped from his hair. "They have video tape of Tate giving me a blow job."

"What?"

I began to giggle again. This night couldn't get any worse.

"Like I said," Logan's head went down. His shoulders drooped. "I can't believe this. I wasn't thinking that night. Now Tate's freaking out. She thought I covered the camcorder. She never knew where it was, and I stopped caring. I thought it would've ran out of batteries, but I guess they fixed that somehow."

"How'd they get the camcorder back?"

Logan groaned.

Mason cursed. "Just tell us."

"It's because of you." His hand jerked up and gestured to Mason. "Tate was freaking out because she thought you and Kate were tight again. She said they came over this afternoon to get ready for the street dance together. She let them in. She figured if they were tight with us again, she didn't want to be on Kate's shit-list anymore."

More curses spewed from Mason. He was like cement underneath me. Lifting a hand to his chest, I felt his heartbeat going off like a stampede. His eyes caught and held mine, but I couldn't share in his misery.

They got Tate giving Logan a blow job. That was karma.

He explained the misery. "I have to kiss Kate's ass again and get all those copies from her."

"Yeah." Logan came into the room and collapsed down on the couch. His elbows went to his knees, and he leaned forward. The bottle and phone were left on the cushion beside him, and he covered his face with his hands. They slid into his hair again and he tugged once more on his strands. "This blows."

Literally.

I snorted at the joke, but stopped. Neither of them were amused.

Another curse sounded from Mason, and then he asked, "What do they want from Tate?"

"Huh?" Logan glanced back up. His eyes were glazed over, and I wondered how full that bottle had been in the beginning. There were only a few droplets left inside.

"Tate."

"Oh. Yeah. Uh, she needs to find out where Sam's living now. Guess you weren't too sharing with Kate over the week, huh?"

"Are you kidding me? She's still looking to fuck Sam over?"

"I'm sure Kate thinks she has free reign since you two are hooking back up again. Probably hopes you won't find out until after she finishes whatever she has planned. That's what I'd do." He caught the glare from Mason and corrected, "At least that's what she thinks, that you two are good. Not that you are, not from your side, but whatever. She's a hateful bitch. Let's go blast her. I've had enough dealing with them all week."

Mason groaned as his hand curved on the inside of my thigh. His finger rubbed between my legs in a smooth motion as he started to lift me back to my feet. I gave him a lopsided grin when he stood next to me, and his hands found my waist once again.

I was still drunk. A bit.

He shook his head, but the corners of his mouth curved up. Pressing his lips to my forehead and then to my lips, he whispered at the same time, "I love you. You need to know that."

I did. As they headed off and I stayed back, I continued to know that. Then I grabbed my phone and dialed Mark's number. When he answered, out of breath, I told him, "You need to come pick me up again."

"What? Come on—"

"You said you'd help."

He grew quiet, then groaned. "Fine. Be there in a little bit. I'm in the," he hesitated, "middle of something."

"Again?!" someone screeched in the background.

It was a screech that I recognized, and I couldn't hold back a smirk. "Cass? Really?"

"Yeah," he grumbled. "Hold on. I'm getting clothes on. You're at your dad's?"

"Yeah."

"Alright. See you in a few."

Yes, I knew Mason loved me. Yes, I knew he was doing all of this to protect me, but I wasn't a sucker. I was going to be at that confrontation. Nothing was going to stop me from being there with front row tickets. When Mark pulled into the driveway twenty minutes later, I was glad that I hadn't changed out of my clothes or washed my make-up off. He gave me a quick perusal and nodded in approval. "Can't see the bruises anymore, but you smell like booze."

My day was complete. "Thanks. Just what every girl wants to hear."

He grinned. "Where to, boss?"

Where would Kate and her friends be? Or the better question is, where would they go after sending Tate a blackmail message? I shrugged. "Where's the party tonight?"

"Ethan Fischer's having a big one."

"Isn't there supposed to be a bonfire tonight?"

"That's a no-go. The only way back there is next to Quickie's, and they shut it down. I guess the clerk keeps getting beat up by the Broudou brothers, so they've been banned. I heard police were even going to be there, and if the Broudou's can't go, no one from Roussou's going. Hence," he flashed his dimples at me, "there's a Public party at Fischer's. I was there earlier."

It was perfect. "That's where we're going."

He didn't move. In fact, he turned the engine off.

"Mark?"

"You sure about this?"

"What do you mean?" There was something in his gaze that

made me uncomfortable. As he continued to stare at me, the more I wanted to run. Then it clicked. Pity. He felt sorry for me. "I know."

"You do?"

"About Kate and Mason?"

His eyes widened.

"I know. That's why I'm going."

"They weren't there before."

"Let's go, Mark." They were going to be there. *She* was going to be there, and so was I. I wasn't going to miss this for the world.

Mason

"They're late."

I glanced at Logan as he checked his phone for the fourth time. We were waiting in my car, parked outside of Ethan's house, and I was tempted to punch my little brother. "We've been here five minutes. Relax."

"You relax," Logan shot back. "We need to get in there and get that video back from Kate. If it were Sam in it, you'd go steal the video from Kate's house."

"I wouldn't."

"You would too and we both know it."

"You're not pissed about the damn video and we both know it."

Logan didn't comment on that, not that I expected him to, but I rolled my eyes and sighed as I leaned back in my seat. Twenty people were running around Ethan's front yard in rhythm to the bass from inside. Drunken idiots. The entire night had been fucked up. The hurt in Sam's eyes wasn't something I'd forget any time soon, but I shoved that memory aside, for now.

"Finally." Logan pressed a button and his window went down.

Ethan, Strauss and Derek broke away from the crowd and crossed the street. A few from the front yard watched them, but no one followed.

"Yo." Ethan led the way around to Logan's side. He held onto the Escalade's top and leaned against it. "What's the plan?"

Logan glanced at me.

I leaned forward. "You guys got all your things ready to go?"

Ethan looked to the other two, and they all nodded. "Looks like. That was the plan we hashed out at Nate's. I didn't know it was going down tonight."

"It is."

"Okay. Sounds fine to me." A cruel grin came over him. "I love butchering little shits."

Derek snorted in laughter. Strauss nudged him out of the way, hitting his shoulder into Ethan's harder than necessary.

"Ouch, man."

Strauss ignored him and addressed me, "I thought you were waiting another day."

"This idiot," I pointed at Logan, "got caught getting a blow job on camcorder."

Ethan and Derek burst out in laughter. Strauss grinned, but reached inside and punched Logan's shoulder. "Should I congratulate you or call you a moron?"

Derek snickered. "Depends on who the girl is."

A fresh burst of laughter came from Ethan. "Did she deep throat you?"

"Could she?"

They kept laughing.

Logan cursed and slammed his hand against the car door. "Shut the fuck up."

"Shit." Derek straightened away from the vehicle. "I thought this was a topic we could laugh about. You would be if it happened to one of us."

"You better run, Streeter," Logan threatened, his hand going to his door handle. "I'm going to beat your ass until—"

"Enough." I stepped out and slammed my door. As I rounded to their side, I asked Ethan, "Kate's inside?"

"Not yet. You called her?"

"Yeah. I told her to bring everything."

"You think she will?"

I shrugged, glancing at Logan from the corner of my eye. "She knows I hate Tate."

Derek snorted. "And she thinks the two of you are tight again."

"Yeah."

Strauss slapped his hand to Derek's chest and pushed him back a step. He moved in front of me. "Kate stopped sniffing around us when she thought the two of you were good again. Is that going to be a problem?"

"No. We just need proof she was coming around before that."

"We got that."

Logan got out of the Escalade as I told Strauss, "You and Derek stay up top. We'll do this downstairs."

"I cleared it out when I got your text," Ethan added.

"Good." I glanced at Logan. "Where's Tate?"

He checked his phone. "She's inside. I'll tell her to hide in a room downstairs for now. You know Sam's probably headed here too."

Everything was falling in place, except for that.

As we started for the house, I told Strauss, "Sam will figure out where we're at. She's got too many buddies from FCA here. Don't stop her, just let her through. We'll have Tate play interference when she gets into the basement." I didn't like it, but she was coming no matter what. "And don't let anyone touch her. She's still hurting. A lot."

Strauss asked, "What about the other girls?"

"Kate and Parker can come down with us right away. Hold Natalie and Jasmine back."

"But what about the stuff? They need to hear it, don't they?"

"We'll text you when to let them hear. Ethan, give yours to Streeter. He can play it for Jasmine."

Swapping phones, Ethan smirked at the other guy. "Good luck with that. She's going to go nuts on you."

Derek paled, but jerked around to me. "What do we do then? He's right. They're both going to flip."

"Then let them through."

Logan remarked, "That's the whole plan, dumbass."

When we crossed the street, people stopped what they were doing on the front lawn. A tackling game paused. Conversations halted. People looked up, but no one said a word as we walked past them. It was the same effect inside. The music continued playing, but the partying halted until we were downstairs. As we descended the stairs, I glanced around to find the best room, but Logan tapped my arm and pulled me into a corner. Ethan got the gesture to stay back and he did. Tate came down the stairs a second later, but he pulled her over to him.

Logan waited to make sure she wouldn't head to our corner. He lowered his voice then, "What are you going to do if Kate goes to Broudou? She's going to get mad. She could tell him the truth about who Sam is."

I shook my head. He was right, there was a chance. "There's people in Broudou's camp that are covering for her. He saw Kate and me. We both know he doesn't trust other people's word, just what he sees for himself."

"And when he does whatever he's going to do?"

"Channing said he'd let us know. We'll call the cops."

"She won't go to the cops. Kate hates being the victim."

I flashed him a grin, though my eyes were dead. "We'll make a personal call to her uncle. We both know how protective he's been."

"He's going to hurt her bad. We're okay with that?"

Thinking about what Kate did to Sam and knowing it could happen again, but by Budd Broudou reaffirmed everything for me. I didn't care what he did to her. I was too dead inside to care. "He was going to hurt Sam. All we're doing is giving him a different target. You know that."

Logan nodded with the same darkness coming over him. "Okay."

"Okay?"

"Yeah."

Another look passed between us. An image of Sam in that hospital bed flashed in my mind. It haunted me. All the bruises, dried blood, how frail she looked in that bed would haunt me for the rest of my life. This was what I needed to do to make sure it didn't happen again.

I headed to Ethan's rec room and went to the far wall. Logan filled Tate in on her part of the plan. She disappeared into a separate room. Then he came to stand beside me while Ethan took position next to the pool table in front of us.

The door was left open, but it wasn't long until I heard Kate's voice.

It was go-time.

Samantha

Cars were lined around the block, as well as the next block over. When he pulled into a back alley, there were a few hidden spots open behind Fischer's house. Cutting across the backyard, a lot of people waved at Mark. I recognized a few people from Academy spread out throughout the yard, but when we went up the back porch, the Elite had taken their spots. From how they were sitting, with everyone beneath them, it looked like they were perched on their thrones, reigning over the lower class. All of them were there: Miranda was on Peter's lap; Amelia; Emily; even Adam was sitting with them. When I turned to go inside and make my way to the kitchen, Cassandra was pushing her way out. Both of her hands held cups of beer. A sneer came over her when she saw me. "You really need to get over this stepbrother thing. It makes you look like trash, but then again, you are trash."

"Does Adam know that you finally gave up your obsession with him? Or is it not public knowledge you're stalking Mark now?"

Mark laughed from behind me.

Cassandra sucked in her breath, and her hand raised. I was waiting for it. It wouldn't be the first beer thrown at a party.

Adam swooped in. His hand covered Cass's and he took the cup from her. "Thanks, Cass. I owe you."

"Yeah," she said, raking me up and down. "You sure do." Storming past me, she would've rammed her shoulder into mine, but Mark stepped right next to me. She would've ran right into him, but growled as she was forced to go around him instead. I waited. She rammed her shoulder into his. Mark's laugh was cut off, but then he started chuckling again.

Turning to us, he rubbed at his shoulder. "The girl can hit. If she can do that with her shoulder, I'm excited to find out what else she can do in bed when she's angry."

Adam frowned, but shook his head. "I said it before, and I'll say it again. Are you sure you know what you're doing?"

"Screwing Cass?"

"Dating Cass."

"Oh, come on. It's not like that."

"You will be. Before you know it, you will be."

I was still wondering what happened with Amelia, but I caught a glimpse of Logan. He was walking past the kitchen door. "I have to go."

"Sam," Adam started.

His hand caught mine, but I shook him off. "I'm fine."

"Sam."

"I am," I reassured both of them before turning and following Logan.

Kate walked past the kitchen door, too. The rest of the Tommy Princesses followed behind like ducklings, but there were too many people between us. I couldn't get to the living room fast enough. When I did, it was full of Fallen Crest Public people, but no Mason. All the people I wanted to see were nowhere to be seen.

"Sam?" Jeff stood up from a couch. His arm had been around a girl, and he grabbed her hand, pulling her with him as he crossed to my corner. "What are you doing here?"

A light bulb was flickering as I stared at his girl. She looked familiar—wait. Adam. Basketball game. "Your name is Kris. I saw you at the basketball game last week."

"Oh." A faint smile came over her small lips. Her hand was pulled from Jeff's, and she wrapped her arms around her petite frame. "I didn't see you there."

Jeff threw an arm around her shoulder and pulled her against his side. He announced to me, "She's friends with Jessica and Lydia, but I'm trying to make her see the error of her ways." He sent her a pointed glance. "Sam would know. They were best friends with her and…" he flailed, closing his mouth. "Never mind. So you've met Kris, huh? Quinn's trying to court her, too."

She gasped, and her head jerked down.

I gestured to the girl. "You embarrassed her."

Her shoulders stiffened, but she didn't correct me.

Jeff's smile was blinding as he squeezed her again. "It's like you 2.0, except I have a clean slate and I'm hoping without the Kade part. I can't hold up against your…" He cringed. "I need to stop talking tonight."

"Yeah, you do." Kris nudged him with her elbow.

He laughed, squeezing her again.

I sighed. "Young love. Too bad you're going to get screwed over. It's inevitable."

Jeff dropped his arm from her shoulders and they watched me with pity. I could detect that look from a mile away now. He asked, "You okay, Sam? I tried getting my 'friends' to help you, but they all said you were handling yourself fine."

"Uh. Yeah." I pointed to my face. "It's not porcelain skin underneath all this make-up."

"I know." His mouth dipped down. "I meant that I tried, you know. I told you at Nate's party that I'd try to get them to help."

This conversation was going to a bad direction. He was talking like I had died, and I still had fight in me. I needed to find Kate. I had a whole lot more fight in me. "Where'd they go?"

"Who?"

I snorted. "You're a bad actor, Jeff. You might've been able to lie to me before, but I'm smarter now and I hang out with liars who are in the professional league. Tell me where they went."

"Sam, don't do this." He reached for me.

My arm swung away from him. "Don't."

"It's not going to end well. We heard about it."

"Where are they?"

"She's been all over him this week. Even if it's not over between you two, it's," he hesitated, "it's over, Sam. He's back with her."

I was getting really sick and tired of hearing this. "You tell me where they are, or I'm going to give a character reference to your new girlfriend." I bared my teeth at him. "And it won't be a good one, if you know what I mean."

"They went downstairs. That door right there." He pointed at a door behind me. It was closed with Jasmine and Natalie guarding it. Strauss and another guy stood with them, but I marched over anyway.

"No. No way—" Jasmine started to say, raising her hand at the same time.

Strauss caught it and twisted it behind her back. The other guy opened the door for me and stepped so he was blocking Natalie from me. I sailed behind both of them without breaking stride. As the door closed behind me, I heard Jasmine cry out, "What?"

As soon as the door clicked shut, I stopped on the other side of it. The stairs were in front of me, but I grabbed the railing and held onto it. I couldn't move. Everything in me was trembling. I felt them kicking me. Hitting me. *Shut up and get her.* Kate's voice came back to me. Images flashed in my head, and I flinched with each one. I felt every hit and every kick all over again. I was back in that bathroom. It was dark, like it is now. They were coming for me.

"Hey."

I cried out, shooting my hand out. They wouldn't hurt me. Not again.

"Bitch," someone hissed at me.

My eyelids flew open—when had they closed? My hands jerked up, ready for an attack. It never came and I was staring at Tate. She was pressed against the far wall, rubbing at her throat. She cursed at me. "You hit me. That hurt."

"Oh."

We stared at each other, and no one said a word. She snorted then. "Of course you're not going to apologize."

Waves of anxiety were still crashing over me, but I wouldn't have even if I was fine. She knew it. I knew it. Why lie about it?

"I'm in this mess because of you, you know."

"How?"

"Because I backed you in the hallway."

"You backed Heather, not me."

"It doesn't matter to Kate. Once someone crosses her, she doesn't let it go. So thanks for this."

"You blew Logan when you knew a camcorder was there."

"I thought he covered it up. We don't make noises when we do things like that."

"Why in there then?"

She shrugged. "I don't know. He looked stressed. I was giving him a treat."

A bitter laugh came from me. "I don't get you two. You guys just hook up now? There's no feelings anymore?"

She smirked. "Wouldn't you like to know?"

My smile matched my tone. Brittle. "Just don't screw him over again."

"Hard to hurt someone who doesn't give a flying fuck about you anymore."

I paused.

As she started down the stairs, she added, "And he doesn't, you know."

"What? Give a flying fuck about you?"

"Care about me like that. We're friends, only friends."

I followed her to the bottom, but no one was around. "You didn't come back to be friends with him."

"No." She jerked her head to the right. "They're down there. Logan said you'd be coming, so I came to get you. They need to get the tape first."

"You didn't come back to be friends with him," I pressed.

"I didn't. You're right. My parents shipped me out here so I thought it was my second chance." She skimmed me up and down. Her top lip curved up in a sneer. "It didn't take me long to catch on that I was wasting my time."

Pausing outside a door, she reached for the door handle, but stopped. "You ready for this? Logan told me a little of what they've been planning. It's going to be brutal."

"Besides setting her up for Budd Broudou?"

"What?"

"Nothing."

"Okay. Showtime." She flashed me a grin and opened the door.

I held back. Mason had more planned? Then I heard Kate's shrill voice. "What is that whore doing here?"

CHAPTER TWENTY-SEVEN

Mason

Kate had dressed for me.

Her jeans were ripped in the crotch area. She'd worn them before, always with a skimpy thong underneath. Kate thought they turned me on, but they didn't. They never had. Those jeans were her signal that she was down for anything. I knew I could have her anyway I wanted and some of those times, I'd take her up on the offer. That was all Kate had been to me. I had an itch, and I used her to scratch it.

I regretted it now.

She came in with no question, no regret, no doubt and she came straight for me. I didn't do a thing. Someone normal would've reacted. She was coming into a trap for slaughter, but I wasn't normal. She was going to touch me and I wanted to shove her away. I didn't do that either. She ran her fingers over my chest. The tips of them trailed down to the front of my pants, and she rubbed there.

I turned it off. This was Sam touching me. This was Sam in front of me, pressing against me. I did what I had done all week. I pretended. "You have a present for me?"

"I do." Excitement lit up her face and she held up the camcorder.

I took it from her and saw she had the video ready for me to watch.

There was no sound, just an image of Logan on the couch and Tate kneeling before him. His eyes were closed as he leaned back on the couch. His hand was tangled in her hair as her head moved, sucking on him.

I passed the camcorder to Logan.

"Hey—" Kate stopped herself.

There it was—doubt. I caught it and it was the first time it showed all week. Then she stopped and it was shoved aside. Desperation flared for a moment before blind trust came back over her. She gave it so readily to me.

I told her, "He doesn't care. He just wanted to see the evidence before it goes viral."

"Oh." Relief flashed over her face.

"You have other copies?"

"Just what's on there."

"And this." Parker held up a USB drive. "We'll keep it safe."

Ethan snatched it from her hands. "I don't think so."

"Hey!"

"We'll keep it safe," I said.

Parker cast Ethan a sidelong look, but quieted.

Kate's hand grew bolder as she continued to rub on me. She was more insistent. "So what's next?"

"Did you email this to anybody?"

"Just Tate. I'm sure she's freaking out."

I glanced at Logan, who nodded. His thumb hit a button. The video was gone. With that done, I texted Nate and then nodded to Ethan. Without hesitation, Ethan took off the case, pulled the chip out and tossed the case to Logan. Then he left the room.

"Hey!" Parker cried out again. "What the hell?"

Kate frowned. "What's going on?"

I waited a minute. They needed a head start. "That was Ethan destroying your USB drive."

"What—"

"I knew we shouldn't have trusted these guys. You're an idiot, Kate," Parker snapped as she started for the door.

"It's already gone," I stopped her. "It's pointless to go after him."

"You're such an asshole."

She had no idea. "There's more to come, some of it you'll want to see."

Kate grabbed the camcorder from Logan and started searching through it. We waited, and her eyes widened the more she searched.

Logan grinned. "It's gone."

"You wiped everything."

"You're the dumb bitch who handed it over."

"Not to you," she seethed. "To Mason. I trusted him."

He rolled his eyes and laughed. "I don't even feel bad for you. You're so stupid."

She jerked back. "Mase?"

There it was again. She still didn't believe it. "I agree with my brother."

It was at that moment that she started to get it. I watched as each piece of the puzzle began to fit into place and she stumbled back a step. When she ran into the pool table behind her, she choked out, "It's on my computer. It's in my email. You're going to regret this."

I lifted my phone. "Both of those are gone. Say goodbye to your email."

My phone beeped.

"What's that?"

Parker whispered from behind her, "Oh no."

Logan began laughing. "You guys are so screwed. Getting it, Park? Did you get a text, too?"

Kate whipped around. Parker had gone pale, and she showed her phone to Kate. "It's Nate."

"Nate?"

"Yeah, Nate, you fuckheads." Logan shook his head. "He might be injured, but he's not out of action. He hasn't been the whole time. We knew about your plans for Sam. You wanted to drug her, have him make a sex tape with her?"

"Oh my god." Kate lifted stricken eyes to me. "You knew?"

Logan started to say it, but I shook my head. I needed to do this. Everything was cold inside of me. I'd been hiding it for the past week. They should've known better. Smarter people would've, but Kate wasn't sane. She was desperate so I used that to pull her back in. She saw what she wanted, but she couldn't mistake it this time. I let her see my loathing. I let her see the cold calculation and when she did, she began shaking. The blood drained from her face, and I knew she was going over everything in her head. I waited and when she gasped, I knew she remembered.

"You should've listened to me that day."

"No." She shook her head. "No. You dumped her for me."

"Did I?"

"You—"

"She hasn't been in school since we attacked her," Parker said.

Kate's mouth clamped shut and she began to turn away. "No, no, no, no... No. It can't be."

Parker growled. "It is. Get with the program. They played us. They all played us. Nate just sent me a text. It's done between me and him."

"What did you do?" Kate turned back to me. She cried out, "What did you do?!"

"Nate sent me a text just now, too." I would spell it all out for her. "He went to your home, Kate. I told him how to get in. Your dad's at the VFW, and your mom's working a double shift tonight."

She paled even more, stumbling back another step.

I continued, "That's what you told me earlier. Your mom won't be back to the house until seven tomorrow morning. You had a gift for me, and we'd have your house to ourselves for the entire night. Your dad would go to some whore's house after closing. Those were your words."

"So? I mean..." She looked to Parker, who rolled her eyes and moved away. Kate shook her head. "This can't be happening. Nate can't do anything. He—all of you guys are here. I mean..."

Logan snorted. "You're too slow to deal with us. You never should've tried."

"Nate was at your house. That was him texting me. I gave him your password, sexcontrolsthemall. You never changed it. You told me it last summer. You laughed about it. Did you forget that? You should've remembered telling me. You should've changed it when I brought Sam around."

"Sam," Kate spewed out. "Her. This is all about her, isn't it?"

"Yes." Logan hit his palm against his forehead. "Are you seriously only now getting that? He worked you, Kate. You went after the woman he loves. He TOLD you he was going to fuck you over. You didn't listen. Listen now!" He laughed to himself. "You might pick up a few pointers for the next time a guy screws you over, and it'll happen. You're dumb enough to think you're smart, but you're not. You need to be smarter to realize how stupid you are."

"Hey," Parker started, but stopped.

Logan cut his gaze to her. When she couldn't say anything, he nodded. "Exactly."

"Stay out of this Logan," Kate cursed at him. "This has nothing to do with you."

An exasperated laugh ripped from him. "You took a video of me getting a blow job? AND you beat up my stepsister. Sam's not loved by only Mason, you know. I care about her too. Any of this filtering in that thick head of yours? I can't believe how you're not shitting your pants right now. He hasn't even gotten to the good part. Parker, grab a bucket. Stick it between her legs. Shit's going to fall any second now."

"ENOUGH." Parker jerked forward a step and pulled Kate back to her. She glared at him. "She's getting it. The guy she loved just stabbed her in the back. Let her figure it out without all the insults."

"No."

Logan opened his mouth, but stopped. All three turned back to me.

I said it again, "No. You don't get to think like that. I'm not the guy she loved who turned out to be an asshole. I've always been an asshole, and I've never cared about her. I used her for sex. That was it. You don't get to spin it how you're doing it. I've been honest about that with her. I told her it was just sex with us. No girlfriend/boyfriend status. No lovers title on us. Sex. That was it."

Parker glared at him. "We were your friends."

"The group of you hung out with us, but you were never considered friends on my part. You kept the other girls away. That's the only use I enjoyed from you. You were deterrents. That was all."

"You're such an asshole." Parker wrapped her arms tighter around Kate. "It'll be okay."

"No, it won't."

"Would you stop?" Her eyes were heated now. "We got it. Nate broke into her email—"

"And put a virus on her computer," Logan added. He began chuckling again. "You guys have nothing now."

"We're getting that, too."

I nodded to Logan. It was time the rest joined the party. He sent another round of text messages to the guys, and I said, "Kate." I knew each guy would share their own recording with her friends.

She lifted her head from Parker's shoulder. It was tear-streaked, but I saw the resolve there. She was hurt. I knew that, but she would come back. She would garner the strength and support she needed from her friends and she'd launch another attack. I couldn't have that.

I shook my head "Now's not the time to act like a victim. Everyone in this room knows what you can do."

Her chest lifted as she took a deep breath, but the acknowledgement was in her depths. I baited her just now. I called her weak and Kate wasn't weak.

I was right. Everyone in the room knew it too.

She stepped away from her friend's shelter.

I smirked at her. Good. It'd be the last time that shelter would be offered. As the door opened, I asked, "You remember what I said to you at my car?"

Tate led the way. She came in first.

Kate saw a new target. "What is that whore doing here?"

"Kate," I brought her attention back to me, "do you remember?"

I felt Sam's presence and gestured for her to come to me, and she did. Kate sucked in her breath when my hand reached for Sam's, and she took it. I pulled her behind me now and Logan moved closer to shield her from the other side.

"Do you remember, Kate? You have three friends. I told you that I'd take them away." I paused for a beat. "Hey, Parker."

"What?"

She wanted to murder me, but I was going to change her mind in the next second. "Right before Nate told me what you guys wanted to do with Sam, he told me something else."

She froze. Her chest stopped moving as she stopped breathing.

Kate started under her breath, "Nononononon—"

My voice lifted over Kate's protests as I told her friend, "There's a reason why Nate wanted to be the one to go to Kate's house. He told me about the video Kate said she had. That video of you two. That bluff started this whole thing."

Kate's voice rose in volume. "Nononononon."

"Oh my god," Parker was connecting those dots too. Her eyes were glued to Kate as she started trembling. Then her phone beeped again. Her attention was torn away as she checked it once more. When she hit a button and noises came over the room, this was it. It was a matter of moments before the rest exploded into the room.

"What is this?" Parker asked as her eyes got even bigger. They were bulging out of her face as she thrust the phone at Kate. "What the HELL IS THIS?"

She pressed a button, and the volume rose so everyone could hear.

"Come on, Nate, Parker doesn't have to know. Come on. I'll make you feel good."

"Get away from me, Kate. I know you've been going to the other guys, too."

"Only you. You help me. I'll help you."

"You can help me by telling me where the video is."

A seductive laugh came next. "There's no video, but there could be. Of you and me. If you'd like."

"There's no video?"

Her voice grew louder, as if she had taken a step closer to him. "You're hurting. I know Parker hasn't come to see you since the accident. I'll make you feel good."

"There's no video?"

"No—"

The recording stopped after that, and Parker remained holding it in the air. Her hand gripped it tightly as her chest lifted up and down. She was seething as she stared at her friend. A strangled laugh came from her next. "Were you with him? Nate's mine. MINE. You went to him and—" she choked off again.

Kate jumped back, as if expecting to be attacked. She hissed first, "I needed help. I had to find it from somewhere. I had to *create* it. We had nothing. I didn't think beating her up was going to be good enough. We needed something to make sure she stayed away. I did it for us. I needed him to help us get something on her. We needed to destroy her." As she said the last word and her lip curved in a snarl, she looked at Sam. Everyone knew who she meant. "She took him away from me. She took all of them away from us. I had to do something. We were nobodies in school again. I did that for you, too."

"You bitch—"

"He didn't believe you about the tape. He wasn't going to help, but I needed help from somewhere. It's the only reason I went to Nate. I promise. That was it. You would do the same thing…"

A door banged shut in the hallway.

They were coming, but I said first, "You did it for power, Kate. Don't delude yourself. You wanted to make Sam's friends turn on her so I did it to you first. I just used what you were already doing.

I didn't blackmail you. I didn't have to threaten you, drug you, or video you. I didn't have to do any of that. You handed it to me on a silver platter."

"What else did you do?"

She snarled at me. She shouldn't waste the energy. She would need it to run from her friends. "You went to each of the guys: Nate, Ethan, Strauss, even Derek. You tried it with each of them."

"I didn't do anything with them."

"But you tried, even after they reminded you about your friends. Nate hooked up with Parker. Ethan and Jasmine used to do the same. I know Natalie's fond of Strauss. You went after their guys."

"They weren't exclusive."

I grinned at her. "I doubt they feel the same."

Then the door flung open and Jasmine stood there. She locked gazes with Parker, who said heatedly, "She hit on Nate. She hit on Ethan too?"

"Yeah," Jasmine clipped out.

Ethan stood behind her, a Cheshire Cat grin on his face. "It was a nice little recording."

"Guys." Kate began to back up.

The two joined forces and started after her.

Kate continued to back up. Her hands lifted in the air. "Come on, you guys. I needed their help."

"NO," Parker barked out. "It's just like Mason said. You wanted power and you went crazy for it. Fuck you, Kate. You lied about the video and then you hit on him? Did you suck him? You made sure to tell me to do that. You said it'd make him do whatever I wanted. That he'd be wrapped around my little finger. It didn't work, did it?"

Her voice rose on the last statement, but it didn't matter. Kate shoved past them, past Ethan and up the stairs. The two took off after her.

The room remained in silence for a beat. Then Tate started laughing. She stood next to Logan and hung on him, bending over as more laughter spilled from her. Shaking her head, she tried to calm down, but couldn't. More and more kept coming until Logan was holding her up. She clung to him and then took a deep breath, tears rolling down her cheeks from the laughter. "Oh my god. I can't believe that happened. You just ruined her life, Mason. Holy shit."

Yes. I had.

Sam's hand tightened around mine and she moved closer to me.

Glancing down into Sam's eyes, I'd do it again.

CHAPTER TWENTY-EIGHT

Samantha

Mason took me home that night. He parked in my dad's driveway, but there were no other cars. I knew there wouldn't be. I texted David to stay at Malinda's and that I'd be with Mason. We were there, and it was time to go in, but I couldn't bring myself to open the door. So many emotions and thoughts were swirling through my head.

"What is it?"

There were no back lights on so we were in complete darkness. The moon shone down, casting a soft glow over us. It matched his soft tone, but I couldn't get what he'd done out of my head. He'd been ruthless and knowing what more was coming to Kate, I didn't know what to think anymore.

I glanced at him. He was watching me. He was always watching me. I was coming to realize it would never be the problem if he wasn't going to be there for me, but what wouldn't he do for me. I said, "I'm very lucky."

A grin appeared over his face. "What makes you say that?"

"You're willing to ruin someone for me."

The grin vanished. "That's not it, Sam."

"Can you explain it to me?" I didn't get it. I really didn't. "You took away her friends, and you made Budd believe that she's your girlfriend. She has no power. She has no support, and he's going to do something horrible to her. It's like you gutted her and threw her into the ocean for a hungry shark to devour."

"The choice was you or her. I lined things up so that it wasn't you. I'll never let it be you. That's what I did."

I drew in a breath until my lungs hurt. A tear slipped from my eye, and I brushed it away. Jeezus. What was I doing? He was right. Budd Broudou was a serious problem. He saved me from him.

"You're not remembering what she did to you."

"What?" I looked at him again.

He was so beautiful—tall with broad shoulders, a trim waist, and emerald eyes—but it was his angelic face that held me spellbound right now. Mason wasn't an angel. That was obvious, had always been obvious, but when he loved, he truly loved. It was beautiful, and it was something that I'd forgotten the past couple days.

He leaned back, but he watched me. I caught the wariness in his eyes.

He was always so cautious and on-guard. He was scared of me right now. This man that could render so much power was fearful of me. The irony was not lost on me. "I'm not remembering her the right way?"

"She wanted Nate to drug you, Sam."

I sucked in my breath. "I didn't know that."

"He was supposed to get you naked and then he was supposed to take pictures of you. He was supposed to do worse things, too."

Nate. My ribs were in flames now. Everything was screaming from pain inside of me. Nate... I couldn't believe it.

Mason added, "Heather and Tate."

My mind was reeling from Nate, what they wanted him to do. I frowned. "What about Heather and Tate?"

"Heather stood against them. Tate did it once, but it was enough." He paused a moment. "Kate wanted to take your friend away and I think she wanted to make Tate your enemy again."

He was right. He was so right. I sucked in another breath. Why did it hurt so much to breathe? I shook my head and pulled my shirt away. I needed to breathe, but I couldn't forget. "She sent Heather text messages threatening her."

"They were going to go to Manny's tomorrow night."

An invisible hand went to my chest. It began pushing down on it, pushing down on me. He was saying…

"They were going to break in and destroy as much as they could before anyone woke up in the house. You said they sleep with loud fans because they're all light sleepers. Think about how much damage they could have done before someone woke up."

I turned away. I didn't want to hear any more, but his voice had a soft beckoning to it. I couldn't look away. His eyes darkened, but I couldn't tell if it was from pity or regret. I didn't want to know. They were going to hurt my friend.

He continued, "She wanted to take your friends away and Tate would've turned against you too. I know what kind of person she is. She would've blamed you for that. Heather would've eventually grown leery. She wouldn't have turned on you like Tate would've, but she would've distanced herself. She would've done it to keep her family safe unless she knew a way to handle Kate, but there's no way to handle Kate. It's why I had to gut her. It's the only way to take care of Kate. I removed any power or support she might've gotten."

"I took everybody on at the Academy. I didn't have any friends there."

"You can't do it alone at our school. This is a school where you can get jumped in a bathroom."

I flinched as I was transported back to that room. The door closed, but they were already there. All four of them. They chased me into the stalls. They crawled underneath to grab me. I'd been so close to the door, but they pulled me back in.

Mason was right. Kate had to be destroyed. He had done it for me. He had done all of this for me. "Thank you." The words wrung from me.

"Sam?"

"Mmm?"

He had turned away, and his hand gripped the steering wheel tightly. "Next time you're pissed at me, can you do me a favor?"

"Yeah?"

"Don't go to Logan." His eyes moved to mine and held them captive. My mouth dropped open as he stole my breath away. That hand went back into my chest and squeezed, but it was a different pain this time. It was from the pain I caused him.

I nodded. "I'm sorry."

"He's my brother. You're my other half. I can't…"

When he struggled for words, I reached for his hand. I started to go to him, but my ribs protested, so I gripped his hand as tight as I could. "I won't ever do that again. I promise."

He nodded, but I saw that he couldn't say anything.

"Mason," I whispered.

"What?"

"I'm sorry for that."

He nodded again, exhaling a deep breath at the same time.

"That must've looked," *horrible* "not good."

A harsh laugh came from him. "Probably the same as you seeing me with Kate."

The anger began to flood back in, but I didn't want to think about it. I felt bad for her, but he was right. Kate got what she had coming to her, and whatever else was going to happen, it wasn't me. Mason took care of me again. The magnitude of everything that had happened over the last few weeks rushed in, and I grew overwhelmed. "Let's go to bed."

As we went inside, the lights were left off, and I took his hand, leading him to my room.

I hadn't taken full inventory of my room my first night back, but taking Mason to it made me look at it through new eyes. My desk was covered in old pictures: Jeff. Lydia. Jessica. All four of us at various events and Jeff's football games. Jessica and Lydia were both on the cheerleading squad our freshman year. I was the only one not in a uniform. I hadn't cared then, but now it struck me. Had I always been the odd one out?

Mason went to sit on my bed, and I held my breath.

My quilt was patched together with different patterns and colors. My grandmother made it before she died, and it was an item I was surprised Analise let me keep. As she handed it over to me, her jealousy had me clutching it close. I had come home every day for a year wondering when she was going to ruin it. She never did, but as Mason stretched over it, it looked too old-fashioned for him. My entire room was too old-fashioned.

"What's wrong?" He followed my gaze as I studied my old books. "*Babysitters Club?*"

"I used to read a lot." I used to do a lot of other things, but that seemed so long ago. I sat beside him and felt him take my hand. "I'm seeing everything through your eyes. It must seem so…"

"This was your home, Sam."

I ended with, "Childish."

"Why do you think that?"

Gesturing to my desk with my old books, my old CDs, the pictures, even my old backpacks. "Analise told me not to bring a lot of my stuff. She said it was pointless. That none of my stuff would fit in at the Kade house. Your place was too modern and wealthy. My stuff would remind everyone of how poor we were."

He laughed, tipping my head up to his. "I never thought you were poor."

"You didn't? You could've. I forget sometimes that you come from money."

"Why does that matter?"

"It doesn't." But it did.

"Then why'd you look away just now? Sam," he brought me back to face him, "money is just padding. It can be used to shelter you from some things, but there's no sheltering from other things like love and kindness. Money has no effect on the real stuff."

"Is Helen going to buy that house? Nate's old house?"

"Wait. Where'd that come from?"

Money was important to her. Helen Malbourne would never approve of me; she didn't think I was good enough for Mason. "I know she's there. It's another thing you didn't tell me this past week."

"Oh." His hand fell away from my face. "You don't trust me now?"

After all he had done, that was the last thing I should be feeling. "No. I'm sorry."

"Sam."

I sighed on the inside. Would I ever be secure enough?

"Sam."

"What?"

"Look at me."

I refused, glancing at my hands. Twisting them in my lap, I looked again after he gently nudged me with his shoulder. He smiled at me. Seeing the tenderness in his gaze, I melted inside. Then he murmured as he drew closer to me, "You have baggage. I understand. Your mom betrayed you. Both of your dads left you. Your two best friends and your ex screwed you over. I start keeping secrets, and you see me kissing another girl. I get it. I'm sorry for making you doubt me."

"This week sucked."

He laughed, capturing my hand again and bringing it onto his lap. He held it with both of his. "The past couple weeks have sucked."

"Is it done?"

"Who knows?"

I cracked a grin. "That's not very reassuring."

"Whatever else happens, we'll deal. We always do." Turning to me, he lifted me onto his lap and scooted back until he was resting against my headboard. For some reason, sheltered in his arms in my old room gave me a peaceful feeling. My old and new had combined and somehow that was all I'd needed. He pressed a kiss to the side of my head. "You don't believe me?"

I did, but words weren't coming to me right then and there. My throat swelled and a big knot lodged in my chest, but it was the good kind. For once.

"Sam," he whispered, his breath caressing my skin, "I love you."

I clasped my other hand over his and squeezed with as much force as I could. I loved him. I just couldn't say it. The knot had doubled, so I tried to turn around so he could see it. I needed him to see my love. Tears and all, they were shining within me, and I wanted him see it all. He always saw everything.

Then he groaned, "Do you know how hard I am right now?"

A laugh broke free. My ribs hated me, but I kept laughing. It wasn't until later that night when the lights were off and we were in my bed that I was able to speak over the pain, "So your mom really is buying that house?"

His arms tightened around me. "Yeah, I think so and especially after last night."

"What else happened?"

He stiffened underneath me. "I got a call last night from my dad, and I didn't even think about it until now, but you should know something. Your mom had another freak out. My dad had to call the cops on her."

I didn't know what hit me first: fear or hope.

He added, "She was admitted to the hospital and she's under a seventy-two-hour psychiatric hold. My dad says that your mom has a disorder or something. She's going to some treatment center."

"For how long?"

"He's hoping for as long as it takes."

"Takes? For what?"

"I don't know. For her to get better, I guess. Maybe just for her to deal with things before bringing her back. The bottom line is that they're going to be gone for a long time. My mom hasn't said anything, but I'd be surprised if that doesn't seal the deal. She'll buy that house or another one in the same neighborhood."

"To be close to your dad's house?"

"Because of you."

I lifted my head from his chest. "What?"

"Because of Malinda Decraw. It's where she lives."

"What are you talking about?" I sat up and leaned against the wall, gazing down at him.

He grinned at me, reaching for my shirt and pulling down on the top so he could graze against my breasts. He captured one in his hand. "Your dad's going to marry that woman, and you'll be there from now on."

"We could go back to the old house, your dad's."

"Nah." His thumb rubbed back and forth over my nipple, and I sucked in my breath. A burning sensation was going through me, the kind that I couldn't do anything about. "I'm not dumb, Sam. You moved back in with your dad. You can't leave him, not when you just got him back, and that's his woman, so I'm guessing we'll be spending a lot of time going between Malinda and my mom's houses."

"What about this house?" I just got it back, too.

"You really want to stay here? We can if you want."

But he was right. This home was cold now. David was right. This was Analise's home. There were too many bad memories here. Malinda's was warm. Loving. Caring. She was the future for my dad. I sighed out loud and laid back into his side. "Well, that'll be interesting."

"What will?"

"Going between Helen and Malinda's houses all the time."

"Yeah." His voice dipped and he shifted to his side. His arm tightened around me and he slid his hand down the length of my side. When he stopped and began to rub my thigh, he said, "I know you can't do much, but maybe I can make you feel better."

His hand inched down and began to rub between my legs. I closed my eyes and laid there as his fingers dipped inside of me.

Later, as he moved down between my legs, and I felt his lips on me, I opened my eyes and gazed at him. His lips were sending me over the edge, but it was the sight of him that sent a burst of desire through me. His back was sculpted. All the power was there, but he held himself so he wouldn't hurt me. Even now, he protected me. Then his tongue swept inside and I was gone.

CHAPTER TWENTY-NINE

Kate dropped out of school. Heather told me the rumor was she was going to get her GED, but I didn't care. I was happy she was gone, although in her absence Natalie became the new leader. She appealed to Mason and promised they learned from Kate's mistakes, but it didn't matter. The guys were done with them. The bathroom beat down finalized the decision for each of the guys, which I was thankful for. School was easier when I returned. People were friendlier.

Once I healed enough, Coach Grath had me running with a select group of girls in the mornings before school. There were five of us, but there was only one that was competition for me, or she was the closest thing I had to competition. When real practices started, I was still leery about running with so many others, but I went at my own pace. I shut it all out. The guys. The girls. The people who were talking with each other, the girls who gossiped, the ones who complained about practice. All of it. Half way through the season, after a few scouts started coming around, my status changed again.

I was one of the best.

I was also becoming popular. Slightly.

Heather snorted when a few of the drill team girls hurried to open a door for me one day. She said I was now the prime target—get close to Samantha Strattan meant getting close to Mason and Logan Kade. They didn't care that I was Mason's girlfriend, they were lining up to be his next one or Logan's go-to girl since Tate had stopped his all-access to her.

When I asked Heather if it was because they felt sorry for me, she started laughing. "Are you kidding me? People don't give two shits if someone gets hurt or not unless you're their friend. You weren't friends with anyone. They're being nice for two reasons: you got Kate out of here and they want to use you to get in with the Kades. It's a good thing I don't give a damn about either Kade."

My eyebrow arched up at that. "You going to finally talk about Channing?"

Heather kept her lips sealed tight about that relationship, but I wasn't blind. Channing was at Manny's more often than not. He now had his own stool right next to Gus and they kept Brandon entertained during the slow nights. Logan and Mason joined them after their basketball practices, and all five of them had become friendly. Logan mentioned going running with Gus since the guy had a beer gut that was bordering on becoming a bear gut.

He even invited Gus to family dinner at Helen's. That didn't go well.

Nothing went over well with Helen.

Mason had been right and wrong. She didn't buy Nate's old home. She bought land at the end of the block. She was going to build her ultimate dream home. Since James and Analise were gone, she moved into their house until it was done. I moved into Malinda's home, and that seemed to be the official move in day for David as well. He reassured me he wouldn't sell the old house. It would be there for me if I ever wanted it. Mason spent the nights with me while he 'lived' with Helen in the old house. Logan came over for almost every breakfast and they were around most of the time during the weekends.

This was another arrangement Helen didn't like, neither did David, but neither of them could say anything—it was going to happen whether they wanted it or not. We'd already fought one parental unit about our relationship. They knew we would've done it again, but it didn't mean Helen didn't make things uncomfortable at times.

Today was one of those days.

It was a Saturday, and Mason had spent the night, but so had Logan. Helen didn't like that. He and Mark came back to the house after a party and played video games all night. He fell asleep on the couch, and Helen started calling at eight that morning. She called both of their phones, and then she began calling the house phone. When she asked for her son, Malinda knocked on our door and gave the phone to Mason. Wrong son. When he sat up and I heard her yelling on the other end, I rolled out of bed and grabbed my running clothes.

Helen was a saner version of Analise.

It was time to run.

I headed towards my favorite path. Instead of driving to my old neighborhood and jumping on it from the park, I found another trail that connected to it from behind Malinda's house. When she learned where I ran the most, she pulled out a map of walking trails and showed me new trails, but I kept with the one that ran past Quickie's and into the hills behind it. I could get lost back there and today was a day I needed that. It was when I came back that I noticed something was wrong.

The clerk was pacing back and forth outside the side door. He would stop, wring his hands together, shake them out, and return to pacing. After a few moments, he stopped again, took a deep breath and peeked around the back corner. Jerking back, he shook his head and started twisting his hands together again.

I made my way down to him. My heart was pounding so I pulled my earbuds out and silenced the noise. As I got to the bottom of the hill, I took a few breaths so I could talk and not pant through a conversation. He was turning around again in another sharp circle when he saw me, and his eyes bulged out. I recognized the same clerk from all the other times I'd been around here. I saw him through the window the first morning when the Broudous showed up for a pit stop and a few times when I've run past here.

"Hey," I murmured, "are you okay?"

He jerked his head in an abrupt movement. "No."

"Okay." I frowned at him. When he didn't say anything more, I leaned my leg against the building and started to stretch it out. "Can you tell me what's wrong?"

"Ahh-hmmmggbbb—"

"What the hell?" I whipped around. It sounded like someone was being strangled. I started to step towards the back, but the clerk grabbed my arm.

He held me back. "Don't." His voice was trembling, as was his hand. The longer he held me, I realized all of him was shaking.

A foreboding sensation started in me. "What's your name?"

"Ben."

I nodded. This guy was about to piss his pants and I glanced down. He hadn't, but he was close. Reaching up, I started to remove his hand from my arm, but his fingers tightened. He hurried out, "No. You can't go over there."

"Okay." I let his hand stay in place. "Where?"

"They're on the other side of the gas station, by the back."

I nodded. He looked ready to bolt. "Why?"

"AHHHHHHHHHH! No..." The last ended on a whimper. A girl's whimper.

I started to turn again. The girl was in trouble, and it wasn't because she was crying to cry. She was crying in fear, the kind that comes from deep inside a person.

"No." Ben pulled me back, firmer this time. He had stopped shaking so much. "You can't go back there."

"Okay, but why?"

His mouth closed and his lips pressed tight.

"Ben, you have to tell me or I'm going to kick you in the balls so I can go and see who that is."

He winced and tried to cover himself with one hand. I snorted. *That wasn't going to help.*

"Ben," I started again.

The girl cried out again, but it was hushed by someone else. A male someone. The foreboding sense kicked into full gear. Disgust was next. I had to go. Whether this clerk was going to let me go or not, I was going. "I mean it. Let go or you're never going to have children."

"You can't."

"Why?"

"You just," he faltered. "You can't."

Slap!

I started around the corner, dragging Ben with me. My blood was still pumping from adrenalin. I hadn't gone numb like I usually did when I run. I was going to help whoever was back there. I'd been hurt. Someone came to help me. I was going to do the same.

"You can't," Ben grunted as he held me back. He was scrawny, but he was stronger than me. I was hauled back and then shoved towards the front of the gas station. "Budd Broudou is back there."

I stopped. Ice cold water filled my veins, and I couldn't move.

That was Budd.

So that was Kate. This was it, this was what he would've done to me if Mason hadn't manipulated everything.

"Nnoo… AH! Wha—"

"Shut up," he hissed at her.

I flinched. I could imagine him slapping his hand over her mouth. Then he continued doing whatever he was doing.

"Oh my god."

"See." Ben yanked me the rest of the way. "You can't go back there. He'll hurt you. She told him that you were Mason's girlfriend and not her, but he didn't believe her. You can't go back there. He might not care and hurt both of you."

"Call the cops."

He stopped, and I ran into him. Shaking his head, he started trembling again. "Yeah, right."

"You have to."

"No."

"Ben."

"NO. No."

"He is hurting her." It didn't matter. None of it mattered. If she hurt me, if she hadn't. What he was doing—I didn't even want to know, though I had a good idea—was wrong. Revulsion swept through me, but I shoved it down.

I'd been hurting. Someone helped me. That kept running through my head. I had to help her, no matter who she was.

"We can't call the cops."

"We have to. Do you have cameras? Anything? Her uncle is a cop."

"He is?"

I nodded.

"Okay." He still looked ready to piss his pants. "We have two cameras, no—three. We have three cameras."

He stopped. Nothing.

I asked, "Where are they?"

"Oh. One is pointing towards the front. One is where they are and the other is inside."

My heart sank. "So none on him?"

He shook his head and pushed up his glasses. They began sliding down right away, but he didn't notice. His eyes were glued to me and his hand went back to his hip, his very tiny, scrawny hip. I sighed. What the hell was I doing?

"His truck is over there."

"What?"

He pointed down the road where his truck was hidden in a copse of trees. It was far enough away from the gas station and surrounded by healthy trees. If…a plan began to form, but as I went over it in my head, I couldn't. There was no way.

"HELP—"

He slapped her again. It was followed by a thud.

I closed my eyes. He hurt her again.

That sealed it. Looking at Ben, there was uncertainty, but panic mixed with trust. He was trusting me, but I had no idea what I was doing. I did, but I held no promise it was going to work. It had to. I pushed all the fear down, and I remembered everything that had made me angry.

Analise.

David leaving me.

Jeff cheating on me.

Jessica and Lydia stabbing me in the back.

Adam lying about me.

Becky believing him.

Kate and her friends. She wanted Mason back. All of them hurting me.

And now Helen. I knew she didn't want me to be with Mason. Everyone knew it. It was another obstacle in our relationship. I felt it coming, so did Mason, but neither of us knew how to stop it before it began.

By the time I remembered everything, all that old anger had mixed with the adrenalin from my run. I was heated. I was sick and tired of being hurt, being shoved down, being pushed around, being punched, stabbed, and being replaced.

"Ben." My voice was firm.

He settled down and nodded.

"Turn your cameras off in the front. There can't be any evidence of me."

"There won't, but," he hesitated, "what are you going to do?"

"I'm going to distract him."

"Okay." Another beat of hesitation. "What do you want me to do?"

"Wait until I light it before you call the fire station."

"Okay." He rushed back inside.

I waited a second.

He rushed back out. "Light what?"

I took a deep breath. "I need some gasoline."

His eyes popped out, but he went inside and brought back two full red containers and handed them over without a word. This was the time when I was making the decision to help someone else. This could cost me my life. I had no idea, but he was hurting another girl, and I couldn't let that happen. There was no way I could walk away from it without losing a piece of my soul, so I took the two containers of gasoline Ben gave me, and I carried them to Budd's truck. It was hidden, and I had no doubt that he was going to use the running trail to slip past the cameras and drive away.

That pissed me off even more. I had no idea why, but he wanted to get away with it, using *my* trails. Everyone got away with screwing people over.

Not this time.

I didn't touch the truck, but I doused the entire thing with gasoline. When I was done, I heard Kate cry out again. He was still doing whatever it was he was doing. I closed my eyes and pulled my sleeves over my hands. I wiped down the containers. Ben told me to do that. He said they could maybe get my finger prints off of them. I had no idea what he was going to say when the police would come. He said he would turn the cameras off. He was an accomplice, but he told me not to worry about it. He had my back. Apparently, he had my back the entire time. Budd kept coming back to the gas station and questioned Ben about Mason's girlfriend. He never told him, not once. I could only imagine what Budd must've put him through.

I'd never come to Quickie's again without being thankful.

"Oh…God…" Kate moaned, but not the good kind. It was the kind that reached inside a person's darkest parts and took root.

I moved far enough away before I flipped the lighter and bent down. Grabbing some old branches, I put the flame to them and waited. My heart was pounding in my chest and everything went to slow motion then.

I was going to do this.

I kept hearing her cries.

You should've quit school today. I gave you your last out.

My thumb slipped off the lighter, but I couldn't move. I remained crouched down, the lighter to the tree branch and my hand never trembled.

This isn't payback. This is your punishment.

She wanted to destroy me, but she had only hurt me. I fought back. When I was down, I got back up. She hadn't destroyed me.

Shut up and get her.

I dropped the lighter. My hand jerked as I felt their first hit, their first punch, their first kick, and when I dropped to the ground. I felt them again. They were closing in on me. I'd been so close to escaping.

You can't kill her. Let's go.

When would she have stopped? She had wanted to do more damage that night. Her friends stopped her and he was hurting her now, but it didn't matter. He was killing her on the inside. I heard her cries and I knew that agony. It had been me, but at her hands.

I reached for the lighter again. This time there was no wavering and I waited until the branch was burning before I tossed it towards the truck. Then I ran.

When he saw the fire, Ben was supposed to call the fire station and the cops. I wasn't going to wait and see the fireworks. I needed to leave. As I sprinted across the road and over to the next running trail that would take me back to Malinda's, I froze for a second.

Kate saw me. Even from this distance, I could see the pain in her eyes.

They were right there, pressed against the side of the wall. He had taken her near the dumpster, but I could see them. A passing car wouldn't be able to, and I knew that was why he chose that spot. Only someone walking or running by would see them.

He had a hand to her throat and another hand between their bodies. I didn't know what he was doing, and I didn't want to know.

BOOM!

The explosion had enough force to it to push me back, but I didn't look away.

Budd let her go, and he ran around the side of the gas station. "What the hell?!"

Kate pushed herself up, but she didn't look away from me. Her hair was matted, and she had scrapes over her face. It was red from where he had slapped her. Her throat was already bruising, but she mouthed, "Thank you."

She knew.

I jerked my head in a nod. She had hurt me and I had saved her. The irony was not lost on me, but I didn't wait to see what else happened next. I took off. As I pushed up another hill, just nearing the trail to Malinda's, I heard sirens in the distance. I couldn't help myself so I stopped and looked down. There was a tiny opening between some trees so I could see Quickie's. The flames had lifted high in the air, but that wasn't what I cared about. Budd was pacing back and forth.

I laughed to myself.

He tried to get inside the gas station, but he couldn't. The doors were locked. Ben and Kate stood inside and watched him. He kept trying, but when he heard the sirens, he started running.

He wouldn't get far enough. I heard him yell, "FUCK!"

I turned and started walking now. The need to run had left me. I wanted to savor this. He'd gone after Mason. He'd gone after Logan, put Nate in the hospital, and terrorized way too many others. Budd Broudou was going to jail. I knew it, and he knew it. It was a day that I would enjoy for a long time. Maybe Mason was right. Maybe taking control into your own hands was the best way to serve justice?

I remembered Kate's whimpers and my conscience was clear. I did more for her than she had done for me. It was good enough for me.

CHAPTER THIRTY

Three Months Later...

Budd had been arrested for trying to rape Kate. Her uncle was first on scene, and they arrested him right away. He hadn't gotten far down the road, and there was enough evidence to send him to prison. As for Kate, she moved in with her uncle. Heather heard through the rumor mill that he hadn't been happy with her parents for years, and with so many problems happening at the same time, he had her move in with him and his wife. Her mom and dad never fought the decision so as everyone else was finishing up their spring semester, Kate was working on getting her GED through the alternative school.

I was just happy that I never saw her again. I was also happy that no one knew who set Budd's truck on fire. Ben and Kate kept quiet. I was relieved, and I wasn't going to start questioning her motives. If she talked, I'd set her truck on fire, too. I was done dealing with her.

"You got a visitor."

I glanced up from the register. Heather had a tense smile on her face. She was standing with her back to where the guys were. Mason, Logan, Channing, and Gus were all lined up on barstools in front of Brandon. A baseball game was on the television, and Logan was goading Gus into betting against his favorite team.

"Who?"

"Ssh." She leaned closer and rolled her eyes to the back of her head. "You have a visitor."

There was a message in there somewhere, but I couldn't decipher it. Mason was leaving in a few months, and I was already dreading his graduation in a week. All emotional energy was spent towards that, not figuring out cryptic messages from my friend.

"Spell the name," I said instead of guessing. I wasn't going to go and see. It could be Kate, or worse, one of her friends trying to apologize again. I wasn't having any of it.

"Just go," she hissed before expelling a frustrated sound and grabbing my hand. She pulled me through the side door, and announced as she passed the bar, "Smoke break. No boys allowed." No one moved, but then we were through the doors before anyone had the chance. Before the screen door could slam shut, she caught it and reached inside for the main door. Both were pulled shut.

I glanced around the alley, but no one was there.

Heather dropped down in a chair and pulled out her cigarettes. I started to sit as well, but she waved me away. "No. Go."

"Where?"

"Oh." She glanced around and frowned. "Where'd he go?" Then her eyes lit up, and she pointed to the back end of Manny's, right next to her house. "There. I see him."

Uh… I was putting my trust in my friend as I started to the back. When I got there, I relaxed. Slightly. "Brett."

He was leaning against a tree with his hands stuffed inside his front pockets. As he stood, his goliath-sized body unfolded and grew again in front of me. If he hadn't asked me out and if he hadn't protected me from Budd, I would've been pissing my pants. All I did was wipe my hands off on my pants and give him a relieved grin.

He grinned back, but grimaced. "I'm sorry for not doing this earlier."

Oh whoa. That wasn't what I expected to hear. "Do what?"

"Come to apologize."

"Apologize? For what?"

"For my brother and what he must've put you through. For me too." He glanced down as his shoulders lifted when he took in a deep breath. "I should've stopped him a long time ago, but I didn't. I never had incentive to, and I guess it was easier to let Shannon get in his ear. This all started because my sister told us Mason Kade used her for sex. I know what she did wasn't right."

"Shannon?"

"She lied all those years ago."

Oh, whoa again. "You knew?"

"Not then, but I found out the truth a few months ago. I never told Budd." He shrugged, reaching up to scratch his face. As he did, his arm doubled in size, and I gulped again. It was the size of a tree trunk. Then he added, "My brother doesn't work like that. Once he hears something, it's it in his mind. Your man knows that, too."

I flushed at the memory. The image of Kate writhing on top of Mason had my stomach churning, but I shrugged it off. It was over and done. He had his revenge. She got her due. I helped her out in the end. My conscience was clear when it came to Kate.

I cleared my throat. "What do you want, Brett?"

"Just to extend an olive branch, I suppose." His jaw hardened, and he glanced to the side. Lifting his arms, he folded them across his chest. If it was possible, it made him look even bigger. "And to let you know that the beef is over between my town and this one. As far as I'm concerned, we got no problem with Fallen Crest folk anymore."

"Oh."

"Is that right?"

I stiffened, but I couldn't deny the relief that went through me. Mason came up behind me and stood next to me. He didn't touch me or pull me against him. For some reason, I was thankful.

Brett stiffened too, but he jerked his head in a nod. "I was telling your woman that I consider the rivalry done. Budd's in jail. Whoever set his truck on fire made that possible."

"You make it sound like you wanted him in jail?"

He frowned at Mason, and the two engaged in some unspoken message between them before Brett slowly lifted his head up and down. "My brother was hurting a girl. He needs to take the punishment for it. That's all I'm saying."

Mason didn't respond. The two continued to stare at each other.

I shifted next to him, unsure of what to do. The air had filled with tension when Mason spoke up, but I didn't feel that it was nearing any violence. I hoped not. "So," I gave each a forced smile, "Brett came to say that Budd's in jail, and Shannon lied all those years ago. We've made progress, I think."

Faint grins came over both of them, but disappeared instantly.

Mason spoke, "You know Shannon lied? That I never slept with your sister and used her?"

Brett jerked his head in a nod. "I do. Her best friend told me the truth. She came onto you and you rejected her." His gaze lingered on me. "I know you could have your choice of women so it never felt right, my sister's story, but she's kin, so we did what we did."

"If someone rejected my brother, I wouldn't force her to date him." Mason's jaw had hardened. "It's an extreme response."

Brett lifted his head, and his shoulders rolled back. As his arms fell back to his side, my eyes widened. His hands turned back as if they were going to form into fists, but they didn't. I let out a small puff of air, and then he replied, "We're old fashioned. Big brothers look out for their little sisters."

"Your sister's a bitch."

I closed my eyes in frustration. Logan had the worst timing. Ever.

He strolled to the group, his eyes narrowed and lethal as he added, "And she's a viper. There's no way in hell you have to look out for her."

Brett's head lifted even further, and I saw the storm brewing.

"Okay." I stood between them and shooed Logan away. "Get out of here. You're not helping."

"Not going, Sam."

"Go. I mean it."

He ignored me. His gaze trailed past me to Brett, and he asked further, "What are you here for?"

I lifted my voice, "He came to make peace, so get out of here before you blow it."

Logan's narrowed eyes turned to me in disbelief.

My eyebrow arched high, and my hands found my hips. "I mean it. Go," but I stopped as Mason's hand curved around my waist, and he pulled me against him. His fingers slid under my shirt and pressed against me. I got the message. I shut up.

Logan stepped next to me now so that all three of us stood in a line. As he did, I understood Mason's message. The three of us were together, no matter what. I'd forgotten the rule, and it felt good. It felt like home once again.

Brett skimmed over us and nodded to himself. It was a faint nod, but I caught it. He gave me a small grin before he moved back a step. "I came to see how Sam was doing, but to say what I already said. Budd's in jail, and he ain't getting out any time soon, so I run Roussou now. As far as I'm concerned, there's no beef between us anymore." He paused a beat. "And Fallen Crest is closer to our farm than Roussou, so I'm also warning you that I might be grabbing a bite to eat every now and then at Manny's."

Mason narrowed his eyes.

Logan raised his chin. "You put our buddy in the hospital. We never got even for that."

"You had a hand in putting my brother in jail. I think that evens the field."

Oh boy. That can did not need to be opened. I nodded. "That's fine with me."

The two glanced down at me as I stood between them. I ignored them. Heather would be fine with it. She'd be happy even. If Brett stopped by for a bite that meant the rest of Roussou could come, too, and that meant Channing's friends. They had stayed away because of the rivalry. He'd been the only one to come around, and had started an odd friendship with Mason at the same time.

"Okay." Brett nodded to himself, and then gestured to me. "It's nice seeing that you're better."

I told Mason what Brett had done for me at the street dance, and I felt him relax beside me. I gave Brett a small grin. "Thanks for coming."

He lifted a finger to his forehead in a slight salute to me, but it was his farewell. Turning, he headed back around Manny's. It wasn't long before we heard his truck leaving the parking lot.

"Well, shit. Who do we prank now?"

Mason grinned. "What do you mean? I think we owe Principal Green a few times."

Logan flashed a smile. "You're right. We never got him back for not expelling Kate in the first place." He asked Mason, "Where's Nate? I thought he was supposed to be here by now?"

"He's got a new girlfriend. Relax," Mason chided, but pulled me close and pressed a soft kiss to my forehead.

As he moved back, his eyes caught mine and held them for a second. A shiver went through me at the heated promise, but I caught the underlying message, too. Brett was in the past. So was a lot of other stuff. I caught his shirt and pulled him back for a real kiss. As his lips covered mine, the need for him began inside of me. Logan groaned. "Come on, guys. You've been going at it like rabbits since she got all healthy." His phone beeped. "Thank god. That's Nate. He's done with the girlfriend, so let's go."

Mason pulled away, but not before giving me a tender kiss.

I shook my head. Every part of me was trembling. No matter the distance and no matter the obstacles, he'd always have this hold over me. As he stepped back, his eyes never left mine. I caught another message. I was his. I sent one of my own to him. He was mine, too. When the corner of his lip curved up, I knew he read it loud and clear.

"You guys were going to prank Roussou tonight?" I asked hoarsely. They had never told me.

"We need to do something. Graduation's in a week." Logan threw an arm around his brother and pulled his head down. He tussled his hair before Mason shoved him off. "We got two more months with this guy. We need to make memories, and that means we gotta do some damage." He let out a loud whoop. "Let's go, Mase. I'm in the mood to get in trouble tonight."

He pressed a quick kiss to my forehead. "If we don't come home tonight, check the jail first, Sam."

As he disappeared around the corner, I asked Mason, "Is he serious? You're going to get arrested tonight?"

"Nah," he paused, "I don't think so."

"Come on, Mase!"

He grimaced. "Maybe."

"Mason."

He shrugged before giving me another kiss on the lips, then he whispered against them, "We'll be fine. We always are."

He started to pull away, but I grabbed him one more time. He caught the need in my eyes and took over. I was lifted in the air and pushed against the wall. He pressed into me, and it was a long time before he pulled away. When he did, both of us were panting. The rest of the night was going to be uncomfortable. I knew I'd be walking with this ache between my legs, and it wouldn't go away until he got home. He flashed me a rueful grin and smoothed a tender hand down the side of my face. As he tucked some hair strands behind my ear, he asked, "Are you okay?"

"I'm hot and bothered."

"No," he chuckled, but stepped close again. His hips pressed against mine, and I felt his own need as he ground it into me. "I meant if you're okay after seeing Brett Broudou again?"

"Oh." Some of the desire lessened, but he moved into me in a rhythmic motion, and it came back again. I struggled to think over what he was doing to me. "Uh…yeah. I guess." My head went against the wall, and I gasped as he moved even closer. "Are you okay?"

"I will be," he murmured under his breath. His gaze was on my lips. "I will be." Then his hand went to my pants, and I felt him grab for my zipper.

"No." I caught his hand. Shit. Then I shoved him back. Logan had been right. Since I was given a clean bill of health, we'd been insatiable. Another second longer, he would've slipped inside of me, and I would've let him. "Tonight."

He nodded and stepped closer once more.

"Mason," I warned softly.

A grin appeared as he kept his hips away, but rested his forehead on mine.

I sighed a breath of relief mixed with bitter longing. He was leaving. I knew that was the reason for this need that had become so overwhelming, and I didn't want to control it anymore. He was leaving. I couldn't get enough of him until he left for college. Logan had been right. Two more months was all we had with Mason.

I closed my eyes as my hands went to his jeans. My fingers caught a loop on the waistband, and I struggled. I wanted to pull him back to me. I wanted to forget where we were and forget where we were going. I wanted all of it to go away, but I couldn't.

"MASON."

He chuckled softly against my skin and pressed another kiss there.

How many had there been? I needed so many more.

Then he stepped back. "I'll see you tonight."

"Do not get arrested."

He flashed me a grin. "I won't. Promise."

Then he was gone, and I was left to collapse and pick up the pieces. I had a feeling this was my future. I'd be picking up the pieces every time he left. Tonight. We had tonight, and we had over sixty more of them before he left early for football practice.

It'd be fine. I'd make sure it'd be fine.

When I was able to go back, I stopped again as I went around the corner.

Tate was in one of the chairs Heather and I sat in when we took our breaks. As I came closer, she readjusted her legs, throwing one over the opposite knee and doing it again before she realized I was there. Her fingers had been tapping on the chair in an impatient motion, but she stopped all of it and threw me a forced smile. "I should've figured you were there. Your two men took off a second ago."

"Yeah." I frowned at her. "What are you doing here?"

Since she got the blow job video back, Tate had melted into the background. I rarely saw her at school. She called everything off with Logan, no longer hooking up with him when he wanted. If she was here, it was because of Heather and that had me worried.

She sighed, rolling her eyes. "Don't worry. I'm not here to mess up your holy trinity with the two gods. I'm here to see Heather."

"Like I said," I clipped out, "what are you doing here?"

Mason had told me what he thought would've happened with Tate and Heather if Kate had done everything she wanted. I agreed with him about Tate. She would've turned against me, but I didn't agree with him about Heather. He thought Heather would've distanced herself from me, but she wouldn't have done that. If they destroyed Manny's like they were planning to, Heather would've torched Kate's house like I torched Budd's truck.

I knew she would've reacted like that. I told her Kate's plans, and she exploded. Natalie and Jasmine had been at their lockers at the time, and she tried to head over to them. I held her back, but the two caught the commotion and scurried away.

They were smart. I'd been touched by Heather's loyalty. She wouldn't have pulled away from me. Because of that, my protective side was coming out. Tate had hurt Heather too much in the past. I wasn't going to let her do it again.

When Tate flicked her hair over her shoulder and ignored my question, I yanked her chair towards me. She was trapped by me now, and I repeated my question. "What are you doing here?"

She rolled her eyes. "Seriously. You're mama bear now?"

"Violence doesn't scare me. You should remember that."

She started to roll her eyes again, but stopped at my words. Her shoulders dropped in surrender. "Fine. I finished all my classes. I'm out of here tonight, and I have no wish to stick around for graduation. This school has been nothing but a pain in my ass." She gestured inside, but the movement was halfhearted and it fell in her lap. "I came here for two reasons. Heather and Logan. I can see now that both reasons were stupid. I'm an idiot."

My eyebrows went up, and I moved back as she stood up. "Does Heather even know that you're out here?"

"No, and it doesn't matter. I'm wasting my time. I'm going to go."

That was odd, but I wasn't going to stop her. I agreed. She should go. Heather wasn't going to forgive her. Ever.

She went a few steps, but stopped and swung back. "You know what? Fuck it. I don't give a shit. He can't hurt me anymore."

What the hell?

She gave me a bright smile. The renewed zeal behind it had me holding my breath. That wasn't a good look, not on Tate. Then she said, "My dad lost his job, and when he said I could move back with my sister, I had no problem with it. I was an idiot before and because of it I lost two great people in my life: Logan and Heather. I thought I could come back, grovel for a while, and both would let me back in." She gestured to Manny's. "You can see that's not happening. Heather will never forgive me, and I know it. I just haven't wanted to accept it, but not with Logan. I got it through my thick skull a month after I moved back."

She grew serious and a knot formed in my stomach. This wasn't going to be good.

"Logan was never going to love me again, but dumb me. I still tried. It was useless, and I know why."

It loosened a little, but I knew she wasn't done.

Tate took a breath, shook her head at me and a bitter smile flared for a second. "Mason hated me. I thought it was going to be the same as last time. I thought he was going to humiliate me at every chance he could, but he didn't. That threw me for a loop. For a while."

"Why are you telling me this?"

She shrugged. "I have no idea. Maybe to piss him off one last time? Maybe because I'm the only one who'll actually say it to your face? I don't know. I don't care. I'm done with high school. I'm off to college, and Mason Kade can no longer fuck with my life."

That sounded worse than the first part. The knot doubled, and I was starting to struggle with breathing.

"Has he told you that Marissa's going to Cain University too? That's where he's going, right? He and Nate. They're roommates."

He hadn't. A part of me sank inside.

Then she laughed some more, the same bitter sound from earlier. "I started to suspect a while back, but it's beyond me why no one else has. I was at Fischer's party earlier, you know. The one where Mason relished ruining Kate's life. Guess who I ran into there? Miranda Stewart. I heard that she dated Logan for a little bit, but I never thought about it. Who would? He goes through girls like beer. He chugs one down and throws the can away."

This wasn't going where I wanted it to go. I knew where it was going, but I didn't want to know. I didn't want to hear the words and I began to shake my head. Things were good. Things were better than good. The three of us were united again. Mason and I were together. I needed him...

She kept laughing. "Miranda has no idea what happened. From what I heard, she got all judgment on whoever slept with Logan, then he turned the tides on her and seduced her. She dumped her long-time boyfriend for him, only to get dumped by Logan a month later." She nodded. "She told me about that night at the party. She told me that she had words with Mason and Logan and that was when he seduced her. It was that night. It was because of Mason, wasn't it?"

Dread began to form in me. It went deep, all the way down, and I couldn't answer her. I started to turn away.

Tate kept going, as if she was enjoying this. "You see, Logan rarely does something without a reason. Not a lot of people know that about him, but you and I do. So does Mason. I was curious, so I kept asking her more questions. She explained everything, how she was a hypocrite to her friends." Tate paused and drew in a ragged breath. She bit out, "She has no idea. That's the beauty of everything. She has no fucking clue."

"No, no, no." I shook my head. I knew what was coming, and I didn't want to hear it.

"And she didn't even say anything. It was all in her look. She told me how she was so confused. She thought you were dating Logan, but then Mason stepped up and set her straight. She couldn't believe it, but that was all that was needed. Mason saw it. Didn't he?"

This couldn't be said. It would make it real.

"She saw what he already knows." Tate kept going. Her voice was so goddamn cheerful. "And I love it because it sent him into a tailspin. It wasn't that he couldn't lose his brother, it was you. He couldn't lose you. I don't know what he did, but I'm not stupid. I know how Mason works. He was behind Logan dating her and dumping her, wasn't he? I love this. I love that I'm the one that's going to spill it."

I held my breath. My hands were in fists now, and I pressed them into my legs.

"He wanted to silence the one other person that caught on, and she might've said something. Too bad she never figured it out, but she is dumb. Quite dumb, though she acts like a princess." A hollow laugh came from her. "She saw the same thing. She saw why Mason stopped giving a damn about me this year. That's what she saw and why she was so confused that you were with Mason."

I continued to hold in my breath and kept my eyes closed. *No, no, no, no…*

"Mason didn't get that video of me sucking off Logan out of the goodness of his heart. He didn't even get it to help Logan. This is Logan. He doesn't give a shit if someone watches him getting a blow job. Oh no. Mason got that video because he was hoping it'd keep my mouth shut because he knows I figured it out." She snorted to herself. "He didn't want me to tell you what I know. And like I said before, I no longer give a shit. You want to know what Miranda saw all those months ago, even though she never connected the dots?"

I shook my head. I couldn't lose them.

Tate continued to laugh as she started to back away. "Logan couldn't love me because he's in love with you. It's finally out there now." She paused and an abrupt laugh came from her. "Logan's in love with you."

She kept laughing all the way to her car, but I couldn't move.

Logan was in love with me.

Fuck.

http://www.tijansbooks.com

CPSIA information can be obtained
at www.ICGtesting.com
Printed in the USA
BVHW042003291018
531536BV00031BA/1398/P